Sidequest for Love

L.H. COSWAY

Copyright © 2021 L.H. Cosway.

All rights reserved.

This is a work of fiction. Any resemblance to persons living or dead is purely coincidental. No part of this book may be used or reproduced in any manner whatsoever without written permission from the author, except for the use of brief quotations in a book review.

Cover design by L.H. Cosway.

Editing by Olivia Kalb.

www.lhcoswayauthor.com

The quest for love changes us. There is no seeker among those who search for love who has not matured on the way. The moment you start looking for love, you start to change within and without.

– The 40 Rules of Love, Shams Tabrizi.

1.
Afric

"Okay, so let me get this straight," I said as I eyeballed the instructions on my computer screen while my gaming buddies, Yellowshoes and TheBigSix, waited for me to finish reading. "First, I have to disguise myself as a fair maiden in need."

"Might be tricky," TheBigSix pointed out.

I arched an eyebrow. "How so?"

"Have you taken a look at your avatar lately?" he asked, and I took in the sight of the little gargoyle with more hair sticking out of his nose than he had on his head.

"Afric doesn't subscribe to the mainstream standard of beauty," Yellowshoes argued, her tone fixing for a fight.

"Well, there's the mainstream standard of beauty, and then there's plain hideousness," TheBigSix griped. "Afric's goblin is hideous."

"Hey! He's not a goblin. He's a gargoyle. He's also considered quite handsome where he comes from," I stated.

"And where would that be, exactly? Some rat-infested hovel that stinks of piss?"

"You're cruising for a bruising," I warned.

"Can you two focus? I have an early shift in four hours, and I'd like to get this sidequest completed before then."

I sighed and brought my attention back to the instructions on the screen. "So, after I disguise myself as a maiden, I then have to ride out to Redcrop Manor, gain entry, seduce Lord Varady, and shag him to sexual exhaustion. When he's finally fallen asleep, I have to sneak into his study, steal the Ruby of the Forgotten, bring it back to Laurel Garden, place it upon the Giving Fountain, and then all the mermaids trapped in Seacroft Cove will be freed?"

"That's about the size of it," TheBigSix replied through my headset, a rumble of amusement in his thick Scottish accent.

I blew out a breath. "Talk about a sidequest. My poor gargoyle is going to be exhausted by the time he's completed all that."

"But you love sidequests," Yellowshoes said. "They're your catnip."

"You're right. I do love a sidequest for my sins. I'm just wondering how I'm going to manage this disguise."

"You could pay a visit to the Field of Bargains," TheBigSix suggested. "Someone might barter with you and grant you the magic to glamour yourself as the maiden."

I chewed my lip. "That seems like an awful lot of work."

"It'll be worth it to free the mermaids," Yellowshoes urged.

"Yes," TheBigSix agreed. "Just think about how grateful all those gorgeous mermaids will be after you've freed them."

"My gargoyle isn't interested in sexual favours. He's like Varys from *Game of Thrones*, all political intrigue and whispers. The mechanics of power is what turns him on."

"Well, then think about how grateful they'll be to *me*," TheBigSix replied. His avatar was a tall, silver-haired warrior with a scarred face and golden armour.

"I'm not here to facilitate your sexual exploits."

"How does a person even have sex with a mermaid?" Yellowshoes mused, her multi-coloured unicorn avatar kicking back its hind legs. "Their entire bottom half is a fish tail."

"They still have mouths," TheBigSix muttered under his breath, and I chuckled while Yellowshoes made a grossed-out noise.

"You're disgusting," she complained.

"You love how disgusting I am," he shot back.

"I do not!"

"Are you both going to accompany me to the Field of Bargains so that I can barter for this magical glamour then?" I interrupted because the two of them would argue for hours if left unchecked.

"Yes," they replied in unison.

I grinned. "All right then, let's get this show on the road."

Several hours later, we'd successfully completed the sidequest and TheBigSix was off enjoying himself with all those freed mermaids. Yellowshoes and I decided to call it a day since she had to work and I had to meet my best friend, Michaela, for lunch. Glancing at the clock, I decided that I'd better get a move on if I didn't want to be late. I stared longingly at my computer as I powered everything down. The addicted part of my brain just wanted to stay in all day and game.

When I was a teenager, I discovered *Greenforest*, an online game set in a high fantasy, medieval-style world filled with magical creatures, political corruption, power grabs, and adventures galore. After a few years of obsessively playing the game, on a whim, I created a stream for other people to watch me play. I never expected it to turn into an actual job, but over time, I accumulated an audience.

Now I was twenty-five years old, and my streams regularly attracted thousands of viewers. Sometimes I played alone, and other times, like today, TheBigSix and

Yellowshoes joined me. TheBigSix was from Edinburgh, while Yellowshoes hailed from Miami, and though I currently lived in London, I was originally from Dublin, Ireland.

There were a lot of heavy accents going on when we streamed together.

But that was one of the things I loved about the internet. You could have friends from all over, instantly connecting with them from the comfort of your bedroom. At least, my bedroom was where I typically streamed since my flatmate, Sarita, didn't enjoy being caught coming out of the shower while I went live to thousands of strangers on the internet.

That really happened once. She still hasn't forgiven me.

As I rifled through my wardrobe searching for clean clothes to wear to lunch, I caught sight of a red hoodie, and my stomach lurched. Dev broke up with me months ago, and I thought I'd purged my room of all his things, but I'd clearly missed this old hoodie. I pushed the offending item deeper under a pile of other clothes and tried not to let our break-up conversation intrude into my thoughts, but it was useless.

I don't want to go out with you anymore, Afric.

But why not?

Because you spend far too much time gaming. It isn't healthy.

You game, too. You game almost as much as I do. It's also my job if you hadn't noticed.

That's just it. I want to be in a relationship where gaming is my hobby and my girlfriend does, you know, normal stuff.

So, I'm not normal enough for you?

Look, I'm sure you'll find someone who's really into you one day, but that someone isn't me.

I finally managed to mute the memory. I was completely over Dev, but his rejection still smarted a little, mainly because in all my past relationships, I was always the one being broken up with, never the other way around. It was such a recurring theme that I'd now come to believe there was something about me that simply turned men off after a while. It could be a broad range of things, from my obsession with computer games to my quirky fashion sense to my lack of a verbal filter. Hell, maybe I had a really bad body odour, and no one was brave enough to tell me.

Anyway, I'd decided to quit dating for the foreseeable future. What was the point if they were only going to reject me in the end?

Not wanting to inadvertently stumble upon any more of Dev's things, I barely looked at the clothes I grabbed as my phone buzzed with a message.

Michaela: I'm about to head to the restaurant. Do you mind if my co-worker Neil joins us?

I vaguely remembered that Neil was a personal assistant, the same as Michaela, and that he was supposed to be a really nice bloke. My friend had spoken highly of him at least. I typed a quick response.

Afric: Sure! The more the merrier!
Michaela: Great. See you soon. x.

Neil

At work, my duties ranged from the ordinary to the downright odd. The ordinary would be picking up dry-cleaning, while what I was doing right now would certainly be considered odd. I was logged on to my boss, Callum Davidson's, social media accounts and responding to messages while pretending to be him.

Jocelyn561: Last week's episode was incredible! I can't believe you managed that jump!

Callum: Thanks so much! I'm glad you enjoyed the ep.

I was a personal assistant to the cast of *Running on Air*, a reality TV show about a group of freerunners from London. I carried out duties for all six cast members, but lately, I'd been dealing with a heavy workload for Callum in particular. He was the stud of the show, the one female, and even some male, viewers obsessed over, which meant he tended to get a lot of attention online. And since Callum had no interest in maintaining a social media presence, that task fell to me.

It was also awkward because I'd once had a thing for Leanne, the only female member of the cast and Callum's current girlfriend. Add to that the fact that I'd confessed my feelings to her, and she'd promptly informed me those feelings weren't reciprocated. So, now I had to spend hours at a time pretending to be the bloke she chose instead. Fun, right? Callum was my complete and total opposite, too. He was handsome, athletic, and muscular, with tattoos covering almost every inch of his skin. I was the plain guy in the background who was so unremarkable that people rarely even noticed I was there.

Yes, while my bosses completed death-defying stunts such as jumping between the roofs of ten storey buildings or scaling down the side of football arenas, I was normally somewhere close by with my tablet, making hotel arrangements and answering emails. But to be honest, that was much more my speed anyway. I also had a fantastic co-assistant in Michaela, who was sweet and kind and just as much of an organisation enthusiast as I was.

"Are you going for lunch?" I asked her when we finished up for the morning. I was desperate for a break from pretending to be Callum. It was a constant reminder of how I was screwing my life up from the comfort of my very own smartphone.

Michaela glanced at her watch. "I'm meeting my friend Afric for sushi. You're welcome to join us."

"Great, I love sushi," I replied, jumping up from my seat eagerly.

"Just to warn you, Afric is ... a little unusual," Michaela said as we made our way out of the gym.

"Do I even want to know what that means?" I questioned, raising one eyebrow.

Michaela fussed with the strap of her handbag. "It just means that she's not everyone's cup of tea."

I nodded warily, still not entirely sure what Michaela was getting at until we arrived at the restaurant and my attention was immediately drawn to a young woman standing outside, her eyes on her phone. She had blue hair and wore green leggings, pink Balenciaga's, and an oversized black jumper that appeared to feature a person being abducted by an alien spaceship.

It was accompanied by the text, *Get in, loser. We're doing butt stuff.*

Both my eyebrows shot up as I asked, "Is that your friend?"

Michaela nodded, and my eyebrows rose higher. I wasn't judging. I just hadn't expected she'd be friends with someone with outrageously blue hair who wore tops displaying obscenities.

"Does her top say what I think it says?" I went on.

Michaela didn't answer, but she looked like she was trying to contain her amusement as we approached her friend.

"You're late," Afric commented before her eyes landed on me. "Who's this?" She had an Irish accent, and though her appearance was somewhat unusual, I appreciated the musical lilt of her voice.

"This is my co-assistant, Neil. Don't act like I didn't text you he was coming," Michaela chided primly before turning to me. "Neil, this is Afric."

"Nice to meet you, Afric," I said and held out my hand to her.

She glanced at it, a wide, dimpled smile spreading across her face as she chuckled. "Oooh, a handshake, aren't you posh!"

A feeling of awkwardness settled in as I quickly withdrew my hand, rubbing it on the side of my pants as though I'd just been stung. So, this was what I got for having manners? Michaela sent me a look of apology while Afric gave a hoot of laughter. I bristled as we stepped inside the restaurant, not very keen on eating lunch with this woman. Admittedly, I just met her, but I couldn't imagine us having very much in common.

A waiter seated us at a table, and my attention went to Afric's top again. Okay, so I could admit it was a little bit funny, but how did she keep a straight face while walking around wearing a top displaying the phrase "butt stuff"?

"Michaela, why is your friend staring at my boobs?" Afric questioned, and I immediately averted my gaze.

"I'm not staring at your ..." I paused, lost for words. Had she really just asked that? She seriously didn't have a filter. And I wasn't looking where she said I was. Not that you could see anything under her baggy top anyway. "I was looking at your jumper."

Afric glanced down then slapped her head like she was an idiot. Had she forgotten what she was wearing?

"Oh, right. Are you into UFOs?" she asked with a curious light in her eyes.

Don't tell me Michaela's friend was one of those conspiracy nuts.

"Not particularly," I answered dismissively since this wasn't a topic I was interested in discussing.

"Why not?" Afric asked, tilting her head as she studied me.

"The California rolls look good," Michaela said, a welcome change of subject.

"You're right. They do," I agreed, glancing at the menu.

"So, you don't believe in aliens?" Afric pushed, not letting the subject drop.

I brought my attention back to her, hoping to dispel the topic once and for all with a simple, "No, I don't."

A small smile shaped her lips. "Interesting."

There was something about the sparkle in her eyes as she took me in that bothered me. "Why is it interesting?"

"Well, there are typically three types of people when it comes to this sort of thing: believers, non-believers, and agnostics."

"Okay," I said, turning to Michaela. "Shall we order?"

She nodded. "The waiter should be back over soon."

"You seem to be a non-believer, and that's the worst kind," Afric went on.

If there weren't only three of us at the table, it might've been easier to ignore her, but since she was staring right at me and the restaurant was relatively quiet, it was impossible.

"Pardon me?" I asked.

"You're a non-believer. You shut down the possibility completely even though the existence of aliens has yet to be proven or disproven. It's very close-minded."

"I am not close-minded," I blurted, and she smiled, seeming pleased that she'd gotten a reaction out of me.

"Well, then why don't you give aliens a chance? They could exist, but you're just completely writing them off."

I couldn't believe I was actually having this conversation. Why were we even talking about this? The annoying part was there was something about Afric's attitude that riled me up, and while I'd attempted not to argue with her, I couldn't help it.

"Okay, so how about this," I said, and her blue eyes lit when she saw I'd become worked up. "If they do exist, then why haven't they made contact? And why are the people who claim to see them always hicks who live out in the middle of nowhere with too much time on their hands?"

Afric sat back, folding her arms as she smirked at me. Her smirk was entirely too aggravating, especially because it caused two ridiculously mischievous dimples to appear in her cheeks. "That's not true. There are plenty of eyewitness accounts from pilots and respected military personnel. It's not all hicks, as you call them," she responded. "And besides, how do you know they haven't made contact? Perhaps they have, and the government is keeping it all under wraps."

"I might actually get the sashimi. It sounds delicious," Michaela went on, her shoulders tense. She was clearly worried about us getting into a full-blown argument, and we'd only just met. I couldn't help it, though. This woman irritated me, and that was saying something because I barely knew anything about her.

"Yes, and I'm sure all those respected individuals are getting lucrative book deals and television interviews to talk about what they saw," I shot back.

"Just because a person is getting paid doesn't mean they're lying," she countered.

"Do you know what? I might even get a glass of plum wine," Michaela commented, but I barely paid her any attention. This woman, Afric, aggravated me, and I was suddenly determined to win our little debate.

"Okay, let's say they're telling the truth," I said. "Why haven't the aliens come out and shown themselves to everyone? Why only a select few?"

She threw her hands up in the air, her tone sarcastic, "Oh, I don't know. Because humanity has always been so kind and accepting to those who are different. Besides, have you ever considered that beings from another planet might be so far advanced that there would be no point trying to talk to us? It'd be like a human going into a field and trying to have a conversation with a cow. It just wouldn't work. Cows can't speak. Maybe the difference between humans and aliens is that vast. Maybe they're here to observe us, the same way we observe animals in the wild, but they aren't going to get involved in our daily lives because that's not what they're about."

Michaela's phone buzzed, and she busied herself responding to a text while I continued eyeing Afric. She wore a triumphant smile, and I couldn't believe I'd allowed her to get under my skin discussing a subject I had little-to-no interest in. What was wrong with me today? Perhaps running Callum's social media was stressing me more than it normally did.

I glanced at Afric one last time, realising that arguing with her wasn't going to get me anywhere. And that was why I didn't respond to her counterpoint. Instead, I glanced down and frowned intently at my menu.

A moment later, the waiter arrived, and we made our orders. Afric must've sensed my disinterest in talking to her further because she focused on chatting with Michaela about how things were going for her at work.

"Well, this was great," Michaela said with a forced smile as we finished up lunch. My co-worker was clearly too polite to mention the awkwardness that had ensued after my and Afric's argument.

Afric pulled Michaela into a hug. "Yeah, see you later," she said, casting me a small, curious glance before she turned to wave down an approaching taxi. The taxi stopped by the kerb, and Afric climbed in.

"Well," Michaela said, folding her arms. "I guess you won't be coming to lunch with Afric and me again any time soon."

I shot her an arch look. "You've guessed correctly."

Michaela chuckled. "I warned you she wasn't everybody's cup of tea."

"Seems appropriate that I've always preferred coffee," I replied, and we made our way back to the gym.

Hours later, I was still irritable when I arrived at my grandma's house for dinner. My younger sister, Rosie, still lived with her since she'd raised us after our parents passed away. I had my own place in the city, but I preferred to eat here rather than prepare a meal for one and eat alone in my sad little flat. Besides, nothing could beat Grandma's cooking.

I smelled the shepherd's pie as soon as I stepped in the door, and my mood improved substantially. As expected, my lunch hadn't gone down very well. I liked sushi, but it'd probably be a while before I could stomach it again. What a horribly rude, argumentative woman. And what kind of name was "Afric" anyway?

I rarely said this about people, but I'd be happy if our paths never crossed again.

"You look like a brewing storm," Grandma commented when I entered the kitchen. She stood by the cooker, removing a dish from the oven.

I sighed and took a seat by the table, rubbing the tension lines on my forehead.

"Is everything all right?" Rosie asked. She was already at the table, a worn paperback in front of her. My sister was never without a book. She'd graduated from university last year and managed to snag her dream job as a trainee librarian.

"Everything's fine. I just met a particularly unpleasant person today, but with a bit of luck, I'll never see her again, so every cloud and all that."

"Oh?" Rosie said curiously as she pushed her glasses up her nose. Neither of us had managed to escape the short-sighted gene that seemed to run in our family. "Who was she?"

"Just a friend of Michaela's," I answered, hoping to change the subject. "Anyway, how was your day?"

Rosie smiled. "I convinced someone to give *Neverwhere* a try, so that's another literary good deed completed."

"She never gets tired of recommending books to people," Grandma said fondly, her perceptive gaze coming to me. "Are you sure you're okay? How are things with Leanne?"

I frowned at the mention of my boss/ex-crush. It had been over a year since I'd confessed my feelings for her, and aside from my current predicament managing Callum's social media, I was completely over her. Unfortunately, Grandma still liked to check-in with me about the whole thing since I hadn't had a girlfriend in the interim. She thought I was still pining, but I wasn't. I'd moved on to an entirely new crush, but that was something I'd yet to discuss with my grandmother for various reasons.

"Things are fine with Leanne," I replied. "I told you, it's all in the past now. We've moved on from it."

"Hmm, well, if you ask me, you're a much better catch than that Callum. All those tattoos won't age well. You mark my words."

"I'm not sure the vast majority of the female British public would agree with you, Grandma, but I appreciate the sentiment."

If you looked up "sexy, tattooed bad boy" in the dictionary, you'd find a picture of Cal.

"The vast majority must be blind if they can't see what a fine gentleman you are. You'll make some young lady very happy one day."

I shifted, uncomfortable by all the fine gentleman talk. If my grandma knew the thoughts I'd had about Leanne, she might want to reconsider her words. Rosie grinned at me, enjoying my embarrassment, so I decided to turn the tables on her.

"What about Rosie? Do you think she'll make some man very happy one day, too?"

"Oh, yes," Grandma exclaimed. "Rosie is a smart, beautiful woman." A pause as she studied my sister. "She could have men knocking down her door if she'd only put herself out there."

"Grandma!" Rosie exclaimed, cheeks reddening.

"What?" Grandma retorted with a twinkle in her eye. "You know I'm right. You'd rather stick your head in a book on a Friday night than go out dancing. You might encounter some dashing heroes in the pages of a fantasy novel, but you'll never meet a real one."

"Real heroes are few and far between these days," Rosie shot back. "If you ever tried those dating apps, you'd agree with me."

"Have *you* ever tried them?" I questioned.

Rosie stiffened. "Well, no, but from what I've heard, I'm better off steering clear."

At this, my phone buzzed in my pocket. I pulled it out and saw I had a new message from Annabelle. Remember the new crush I mentioned? Well, Annabelle was the lady I was currently pining after. Sadly, the entire situation had become far more complicated than I'd ever intended. Let's just say my decision-making skills had been lacking when it came to Annabelle.

I was thinking about you a lot today.

I couldn't help it. Her message piqued my curiosity. I typed a quick reply.

Oh?

It's probably because I had a dream about you last night.

Now my curiosity was at optimum pique-age.

What was the dream about?

We were camping and there was only one sleeping bag...

I swallowed tightly. My cheeks heated against my will.

Did we share it?

We did.

I hope I kept you warm. x

Grandma cleared her throat as she placed my dinner down in front of me, and I quickly shoved my phone in my pocket. It was rude to text at the dinner table, even if the conversation was as interesting as the one Annabelle had started. Man, I really needed to come clean to her.

I just had to figure out how to do it without completely destroying our relationship *and* rendering myself unemployed.

2.
Afric

Okay, so ... one thing you should know about me: if I'm rude or argumentative with you, it probably means that somewhere deep down in my psyche, I actually like you.

I'm not saying it's a good thing. It just is what it is. Most people don't understand that teasing is my special brand of affection, and you know what, that's my fault. How can I expect virtual strangers to interpret the deep-seated issues in my head and translate *Fuck off* as *Let's be friends*?

Being the second youngest of eight siblings meant I grew up fast. Winning arguments while also making my brothers and sisters laugh was big currency. And making them laugh often meant insulting one of them.

Maybe the fact that I'd spent most of my life not taking insults personally meant I was ill-equipped to understand people who did.

Neil Durant was one such person.

Yes, after our first meeting, I discovered his surname easily enough by surreptitiously quizzing Michaela. I then proceeded to look him up online. *What?* There was just something about him that rubbed me the wrong way enough to want to torture myself. For some reason, I needed to know what he was about. It was an itch that I couldn't resist scratching, and I didn't know how to explain it.

Sadly, though, when it came to social media, Neil went bare-bones, which only made me more curious.

Neil was my opposite; neatly dressed, professional, and reserved. And yet, behind all that, he had a look in his eyes that spoke to me. It drew me in. It was the look of a person who'd lost in life enough times to know that things didn't always go your way. There was nothing I disliked more than people who always got what they wanted, having no idea that it wasn't normal. I hated trying to explain a bad experience to someone who'd never had it happen to them. I felt like they were judging me, thinking that whatever happened, I'd somehow brought it upon myself and that it wasn't the way of the world to lose far more often than you won.

So, yeah, going by first impressions, Neil and I didn't get along, but despite that, I was intrigued. I sensed a lot more going on behind the conservative facade, and I wanted to get to the bottom of it.

Don't get me wrong; my interest wasn't romantic. I'd learned my lesson the hard way not to go searching for love after being abandoned by one too many boyfriends. You might as well walk outside with your chest cavity wide open, waiting for the nearest careless fuckboy to tear your heart out.

No, thank you. Not for me. Not anymore.

If I wanted companionship, I made a friend. I endeavoured to be interested in people on an intellectual level only, a little like my gargoyle in *Greenforest*. Except, unlike him, I did enjoy sex from time to time. And if I wanted sex, I found someone to do it with then went on my merry way. Simple as.

Anyway, I didn't think I'd run into Neil again, but several weeks after our ill-fated sushi lunch, Michaela asked me to do her a favour by covering for her at work for a few hours. She was in a tight squeeze, and I couldn't say no. Besides, it might be fun to ruffle Neil's feathers.

I took the Tube to Notting Hill, where Michaela and Neil's bosses were hosting a screening of a special episode of *Running on Air*. When I arrived at the small boutique cinema, the place was still locked up. I pressed on the buzzer, and a few moments later, Neil's voice came through.

"Hello?"

"Hey! It's Afric. Remember me? Michaela asked me to cover for her for a few hours," I replied, pulling the collar of my coat up to stave off the chill.

There was a noticeable pause on Neil's end, and my lips began to curve in a grin. He definitely wasn't pleased about me showing up, and the part of me that enjoyed riling him was amused by that.

I heard him clear his throat. "Why can't Michaela be here?"

"Women's issues. She'll stop by later."

Another pause. Oh, this was going to be *fun*. "Are you going to buzz me in or leave me standing out here all day?"

"I should be able to handle things on my own. You can go," he replied stiffly.

"I'm not going anywhere. Now buzz me in before I freeze to death."

"Listen, I'm very grateful to you for coming, but I really don't need the help."

Huh. So, he was going to be stubborn, eh? I exhaled heavily. "Is this about how things went at lunch last time? Because if it is, I'm sorry, okay? I don't always mean to be a bitch. It just happens sometimes."

Neil

"I don't always mean to be a bitch. It just happens sometimes."

She could say that again. It felt like the world was continually trying to test me, and Michaela's friend Afric was one of the most aggravating people I'd ever met. The woman was a walking, talking annoyance, and I definitely didn't have time to entertain her today. She struck me as the sort of person who made tasks take twice as long as they needed to, and there was nothing I hated more than time-wasters.

"Thank you for the apology, but as I said, I really don't need any help."

"Okay, well, could I use the bathroom before I go? I've come all the way from Brixton, and I'm busting for a pee. It's also cold as balls out here."

She looked up into the security camera, her big blue eyes pleading, and I had a brief pang of conscience. Even if she did annoy me, it wasn't pleasant to make a journey only to be told to go home as soon as you got there. Grandma raised me to be a gentleman, and the least I could do was allow Afric to use the facilities before she made the journey back.

"Okay, then, I'll buzz you in."

I pressed the button to release the door then headed out to show her where the bathroom was.

"This place is fancy!" Afric exclaimed as she entered through the lobby. "Is this where posh people go when they want to see a movie? How the other half live, eh?"

"The ladies' bathrooms are just through there," I said, gesturing down the hall.

"Oh, yeah, I don't need to go," she waved me off. "I just said that so you'd let me in. Now, pull that stick out of your arse and let me help you. I know you can't handle everything on your own."

My lips formed a straight line as I levelled her with a hard stare. So, this was where being chivalrous got me. Tricked. I didn't want her here, but she was right. Preparing for tonight's event would be difficult to do solo. Perhaps I could just give her tasks and interact with her as little as possible.

I ran a hand down my face. "Okay, well, if you insist on being here, then come with me."

I led her to the office at the back of the building and handed her the bundle of programs. "Place one of these on each seat inside the theatre."

"And after I'm finished doing that?"

"Come find me, and I'll give you something else to do."

She saluted me. "Righteo."

Afric left, and I was surprised by how easy that was. Maybe this would be okay. About twenty minutes later, I was taking a quick break to check the messages on my phone when someone crept up behind me.

"Who's Annabelle?"

I bristled, stomach churning as I turned and found Afric standing behind me. How much had she seen? "Don't you know it's rude to read people's messages like that?"

She shrugged her shoulders. "I'm nosy. Can't help it. So, what's next?"

I glanced at the clock. "The caterers should be here any minute. Go wait out front and let them in when they arrive."

She nodded but hesitated to leave, eyeing me with what appeared to be curiosity. "Is she your girlfriend?"

I frowned. "Who?"

She rolled her eyes like I was being dim. "Annabelle, who else."

My lips firmed, and I shifted from foot to foot under her scrutiny. "No. She's just a friend."

Afric started to smile. "But you'd like her to be your girlfriend?"

"That's none of your business. Now, will you please go and wait for the caterers?"

She placed a hand on her hip and cocked her head. My attention wandered to the bottom half of her hair, which was still dyed bright blue. The top half had grown out a little, displaying her natural blonde roots. The blue ends matched her eyes, and they were ... Okay, so I could admit her eyes were kind of spectacular. So bright they almost sparkled. I shook myself from the thought.

"Has anyone ever told you that you're a bit rude?" Afric questioned.

"*I'm* rude?" I scoffed. She was one of the rudest people I'd ever met, and I worked as a PA for reality TV stars, so that was saying something.

"Yes, you are. I think you're a bit of a snoot, too, to be honest," she went on, a light behind her eyes like she enjoyed giving it to me straight.

I gaped at her. "I am not a snoot."

Afric chuckled. "Oh, really? You've been looking down your nose at me since the day we met. If that's not a snoot, then I don't know what is."

"I have not—" The loud noise of the buzzer for the front door went off, interrupting what I'd been about to say.

Afric smirked. "I better go answer that." She turned and left the room, then reappeared a second later, her head peeking around the doorframe. "Did you know you've got this little blood vessel in your forehead that pops up when you talk to me? I wonder what that's about."

Then, with a chuckle, she disappeared again, not allowing me a chance to respond. I rubbed at my forehead and wished I'd never fallen for her trick and allowed her into the building in the first place.

Michaela seriously owed me big time for this.

Afric

Once the caterers were gone, I took my time checking out the food for the night's event. Glancing over my shoulder, I stole a stuffed grape leaf and shoved it in my mouth. Mmm, free food was always so much more delicious. They'd splashed out for the good stuff, too.

"What the hell do you think you're doing?" a familiar voice demanded.

Damn, caught in the act.

I plastered on a carefree expression and turned to face Neil. "I'm hungry. Are you a slave driver as well as a snoot? Do you expect me to work my fingers to the bone without a single crumb of sustenance?"

"You haven't come close to working your fingers to the bone," Neil replied derisively as he re-covered the plate. He was standing close, and I caught a faint whiff of soap. "What is it you do for work anyway?"

"I'm a gamer," I answered proudly, and Neil looked at me like I was talking a foreign language. "You know, like computer games? I do live streaming, mostly, but I also take part in tournaments sometimes."

"Ah, well, that explains a lot," Neil said, and I raised an eyebrow.

"What explains a lot?"

"Gaming isn't exactly a real job now, is it? You sit around playing computer games and get paid for it. Sounds like a holiday to me."

"It's not as easy as it sounds, especially to be as good as I am. And you can quit giving me that look, Sir Snootsalot. I've worked plenty of 'real' jobs in my time, too."

Neil scoffed. "Sure, you have."

Something about his tone got my back up. Yes, I enjoyed arguing with him, and I could take a slagging as well as the next person, but this was different. He'd made it a little too personal. People thinking I had an easy life because of my job really bothered me, especially since it had been far from easy to get where I was.

"Yes, actually, I have. I've worked some of the toughest minimum wage jobs out there, from fast-food kitchens to cleaning toilets, so I know all about hard graft. A lot more than some pampered celebrity's assistant, that's for sure." I reached out and grabbed both his hands, turning them palm up.

"What are you doing?" Neil questioned, bristling at my touch.

"Just as I expected. Soft as a baby's bottom," I declared. "You haven't done a day of manual labour in your life."

Neil yanked his hands from my hold, something hardening behind his eyes. "Do you know what? I think I can handle things from here. You should go."

"I'm not going anywhere. You offended me, and clearly, I just offended you, so now we're even. How about a truce?"

I held out my hand, and his lips formed that straight line again. I was learning this meant he was aggravated.

Then, after a few more seconds of consideration, something in his expression softened, and he emitted a heavy sigh.

"Fine. Let's just stay out of each other's way." He shook my hand, and I was briefly aware of his warm palm on mine before he let go and started to lay out the food. I quietly helped. For the next two hours, we worked mostly in silence. He only talked to me when he needed to tell me what to do, and before long, the place was all set up for the event.

It was just an hour before guests would be arriving. I sat down in the middle of the empty theatre and took a selfie, posting it to my social media with the caption, *Have the whole place to myself. Isn't life grand!*

I was just slotting my phone back into my pocket when Neil appeared. He carried two small paper plates on which he'd placed a selection of finger foods. He handed one plate to me and kept the other for himself. Was this his version of an olive branch?

"See? I'm not a total slave driver," he said grudgingly, and I couldn't help the way my lips twitched. I wanted to smile but held it back. He might be a bit too buttoned-up, but Neil was a decent sort. At the very least, he worked hard and took pride in his job. I'd observed that today, despite my comments about his soft hands.

He surprised me when he took the seat next to mine, and we ate in companionable silence. After a few minutes, his phone buzzed, and he put his plate down to pull it out.

Being the nosy person that I was, I read it over his shoulder. It was that Annabelle lady again. It looked like they were chatting through a messenger app.

Annabelle: I wish I could be at the screening tonight. I'd love to finally meet!

I pretended to focus on eating a small cracker with hummus while I watched Neil type a quick reply out the corner of my eye.

Callum: I wish you could be here, too. We'll meet one day. I'm sure of it.

Wait a second ... Callum?! What the hell? Callum Davidson was one of the stars of *Running on Air*. He was also Neil's boss. Why was Neil messaging some girl and pretending to be him? I didn't breathe a word, but when Neil went to put his phone back in his pocket and his eyes met mine, the colour drained from his face.

He knew I'd seen.

I slowly raised an eyebrow as my mouth curved into a smile. I'd been right about him. Strait-laced Neil had a whole lot more going on under his professional exterior.

"I can explain," he said.

I couldn't hide the mirth in my voice. "Please do."

I watched as he sat forward and dropped his head into his hands, swearing profusely under his breath. Oh, shit. This was serious. My smile dropped. Neil was stressed out, and I suddenly felt bad for him. What had he gotten himself into?

I reached out and placed a hand on his shoulder. "Hey, it's okay. I won't tell anyone. Your secret's safe with me." A short silence fell before I asked, "Do you want to talk about it?"

He sat back and cast me a troubled look as he shook his head. "You wouldn't understand."

I kicked my feet up on the chair in front of me. "Try me."

Another silence fell. He blew out a breath. "Jesus Christ. I can't believe I'm considering telling you of all people. I must really be going mad."

I tried not to be offended by the *you of all people* or the *going mad* bit of what he just said. I knew I wasn't exactly his favourite person. Plus, we barely knew each other. But sometimes, it was easier to tell secrets to strangers than to those close to you.

"I used to have a really big crush on Leanne," Neil blurted.

My eyebrows jumped at his confession. What did Callum's girlfriend have to do with this? The little tomboy was the last person I expected Neil to fancy. I imagined him going for delicately feminine blondes who wore dresses and cardigans and shit. There was nothing delicately feminine about Leanne, but she was still all woman. Being a fan of the show, I looked up to her a lot, actually. I was kind of impressed that Neil had crushed on her. He really was full of surprises.

"I never stood a chance with her, obviously," he said, gesturing to himself. "I mean, look at me and look at Callum."

"Hey, don't be so down on yourself. You're a good-looking chap," I said, feeling like he needed the compliment right then. Sure, Callum Davidson was sex on a stick, but Neil wasn't unattractive. He was hot in a nerd boy sort of way. If Callum was Superman, then Neil was Clark Kent, and I'd always had a soft spot for men who wore glasses.

His cheeks coloured a little at my compliment. "Thanks," he said shyly. "But I know what I look like. I'm not the sort of man women notice."

I wasn't sure I entirely agreed with that statement, particularly since I had noticed Neil had a nice, pert little backside on him. What? It wasn't a crime to glance at a bottom from time to time, especially one as visually pleasing as Neil's. Still, I didn't argue with him. Instead, I got straight to the point. "So, you decided to pretend to be Callum online? How did that happen?"

He rubbed his jaw. "It's complicated. When I realised Leanne was never going to choose me over Callum, I was in a really bad place. I was depressed. It was around the same time that Callum started having me run his social media accounts. He had thousands of unread messages from fans, and he wanted me to pretend to be him, just composing a few polite responses, saying thanks for the support and all that. A few months into it, I came across a message from Annabelle," he sighed, his head falling back against the seat as he stared up at the high ceiling. He had a handsome profile, I noticed.

"And?" I prodded, nudging his elbow. I was hooked on his story and wanted to know more.

"She was a fan of the show and had sent a long message about how she was into parkour and hoped to be as good as Callum one day. She talked about how she looked up to him and would love any advice he could give about improving her free running. I sent her the usual response, thinking I'd leave it at that, but she kept responding, and before I knew it, I was pulled into a full-blown conversation where I was pretending to be Callum. I hadn't meant for it to happen, but now I really like her, and I hate the fact that I've been lying about who I am all this time. I haven't had the courage to come clean."

I gave his arm a soft squeeze. "Shit, Neil, that's tough." I'd heard my fair share of catfishing stories over the years, but none like this. Neil hadn't intended to fool this girl. He'd simply been doing his job, and his willpower slipped. It must've been especially hard replying to all those messages and pretending to be the guy Leanne chose instead of him.

"I'm going to have to ghost her," he said. "I can't keep pretending."

I studied him a moment. He looked so forlorn, and I happened to be a sucker for lost causes.

"Not necessarily."

He glanced at me. "What do you mean?"

"Well, you clearly have it bad for this girl. And going by what you've said, you two have really hit it off in your conversations. You might've been pretending to be Callum at the start, but you've still been you behind the mask, and if she's still chatting with you, then that means she likes your personality. You could come clean. If she's genuinely into the person she's been talking to and isn't just some fame chaser who wants to date a celebrity, then maybe she'll understand and give you a fair chance."

Neil stared at me, not looking convinced. "I'm pretty sure if she knew the truth, she wouldn't want anything to do with me."

"If she doesn't, then that's her loss."

"Why are you being so nice? You weren't this nice when we first met." He folded his arms, eyes narrowing slightly.

"Believe it or not, I actually am a nice person. But I tend to get a little argumentative when I get going on a topic, and that isn't always a good thing when I'm meeting new people. I guess you have the first-hand experience of that."

Some of his defensiveness faded as he unfolded his arms. "Well, be that as it may. I still think ghosting Annabelle is the best thing to do. It's too risky to come clean."

"I disagree. Nothing ventured, nothing gained."

"Okay, then, if you think it's such a good idea, how do I go about telling her the truth?"

I stood from my seat, folding up my now empty paper plate to throw in the bin. "Let me ruminate on it for a few days and get back to you with a plan."

Both his eyebrows rose right up into his forehead. "A plan?"

I nodded. "Yes, a plan."

"Why would you help me? What's in it for you?"

I shrugged. "I think you're interesting. I'm also invested in this real-life episode of *Catfish* now, and I won't be able to rest until there's a happy ending."

With a parting grin and a wink, I turned and left him sitting in the empty theatre, my mind awash with ideas. I'd never tried my hand at playing Cupid before, and I was oddly excited to get shooting my bow and arrow. Besides, being a gamer, I could never resist a challenge, and helping Neil win over the girl he's been lying to would be the perfect real-life sidequest.

3.
Neil

When Afric mentioned she livestreamed while gaming, I couldn't help taking a look. A simple online search brought up her channel, and my heart jolted when I saw she was live right this very moment. I hit play and braced myself. I needed to know what sort of person I was getting involved with.

Less than a second later, she was on my screen, her hair up in a messy ponytail and large hoop earrings dangling from her ears. She was playing a game called *Greenforest,* where her avatar was a squat, impish-looking creature with batlike wings, a bulbous nose, and bushy eyebrows. In the far corner of the screen sat Afric, controller in hand as she simultaneously gamed and sang, making up her own lyrics to Garth Brooks' "Friends in Low Places." She wasn't too bad of a singer, and I had to admit her lyrics were funny.

Behind her, you could see what appeared to be a bedroom, which was lit by a multitude of neon lamps. It looked like the inside of a futuristic arcade. I glanced around my own bedroom, which was decorated in a navy, black, and magnolia colour scheme. It seemed bland by comparison.

This wasn't the kind of thing I normally watched, but there was something oddly compelling about her.

"Ah, what a tune," Afric said with a chuckle when she finished singing. "My mam went to see old Brooksie in '97 and she still has a picture of her and all the aul ones from our street in their Garth T-shirts on their way to the concert. She says it was the best day of her life. Kind of offensive if you ask me since she's given birth to eight children.

Anyway, enough about my mother. That's me signing off for the night. See you all tomorrow, same time, same place."

She made a peace symbol with her fingers then gave a little salute before the screen went blank. I shut the lid of my laptop and worried I'd made a terrible mistake. I'd confessed my biggest secret to someone who broadcasted to possibly thousands of subscribers every day live on the internet. What if she had a whim and told her viewers what I'd done? Everybody watched *Running on Air*, and my catfishing story would make for a salacious bit of content.

I lay back in bed, tossing and turning for half the night. I needed to talk to Afric again, make certain that she'd keep my secret, but I didn't even have her number. I could ask Michaela for it, but that would lead to questions. She might even decide to quiz her friend, and I had no clue how good Afric was at keeping secrets. She could be a blabbermouth for all I knew. Going by what I did know of her, she likely *was* a blabbermouth.

What was I thinking?

In the end, I didn't need to get Afric's number from Michaela because she found me first. I was working at a café near the gym where the cast trained daily, laptop open, when someone slid into the seat opposite me. Glancing up, I found Afric with her elbows resting on the table, hands steepled under her chin as she studied me. Her hair was different from the last time I saw her. She'd somehow gotten rid of the blue and dyed the ends to match the natural blonde of her roots.

"You changed your hair," I commented. She'd actually look normal if she weren't wearing an overly large Minnie Mouse jumper and enough jewellery to drown a person.

Every finger sported several rings, and around her neck were a number of silver chains.

"What?" she questioned, then her hand went to her head. "Oh, right. Yeah, I did. Made a video of the process and everything. I was mostly just trying to get Brad Mondo to notice me."

I scrunched my brow. "Brad Mondo?"

"Never mind about him. I came here because I have some questions for you."

"How did you find me?"

She twirled a strand of hair around her finger. "Michaela mentioned you come here most mornings for breakfast. Speaking of which, I'm starving. I'm going to order something to eat. Be back in a sec."

With that, she left and went up to the counter. I watched as she relayed an order then returned to sit across from me. "You know," she began, eyeing my set-up. "Maybe it's a poor person thing, but I've always been fascinated by people who are comfortable enough to sit in a café and work on their laptops without a care in the world. Aren't you afraid of getting robbed?"

I glanced at my MacBook then back to her. "Not really. I have everything backed up to the cloud."

She waggled her eyebrows. "Do you now?"

"Yes, and I'm not sure why you're acting like I just made a double entendre because I definitely did not," I replied in a flat tone.

Afric shrugged. "I've just always found the term 'backed up' to be very provocative. It evokes images of well-endowed ladies shaking their arses on night club dance floors."

"Personally, it makes me think of toilets in need of plumbing," I countered and she barked a laugh, her blue eyes sparkling.

"Ha! Oh my God, you're right. I stand corrected. Anyway, what was I talking about before? Oh yes, you with your MacBook out begging to be robbed. I just find it so extravagantly confident. It's like you're daring the gods to defy you."

"I assure you, I'm far from extravagantly confident. My lack of confidence and self-esteem is half the reason you're here."

She clapped her hands together. "Right, yes, we should start discussing that. So, you really like this Annabelle girl, huh?"

I nodded, my shoulders tensing as I glanced about. Like I said, this café wasn't far from the gym, and one of my bosses could decide to pop in at any moment.

"How much do you think she likes you?"

"What do you mean?"

"Well, do you think she has real feelings for you? Feelings that are strong enough to counteract the deception of finding out who you really are?"

I frowned at her question. I really liked Annabelle. In fact, our chats were the highlight of most of my days (pathetic, I know), but was *I* the highlight of *her* day? Hard to say. She thought I was Callum Davidson, a man who was more or less my polar opposite, so even if she did like me, she liked the me that looked like Callum.

"I don't know," I answered truthfully.

Afric's eyes softened, and I bristled. I didn't need her to feel sorry for me.

She drew in a deep breath and unfolded a napkin before placing it on her lap. "Well, in that case, we should try to find out, because if her feelings aren't strong enough, then there's always the danger that she'll throw a tantrum and out you to your bosses. That's the last thing we want to happen."

Just like that, the eggs I ate for breakfast turned sour in my gut. Afric voiced a worry that had been gnawing away at me for months.

"Fuck," I muttered under my breath. This whole thing was stressing me out.

"Neil Durant, did you just swear?" Afric whispered, her eyes alight with humour.

"How do you know my last name?"

"Michaela mentioned it."

"Michaela mentions an awful lot."

"She likes you. Have you ever noticed how alike you both are? You could be twins, the non-identical kind."

"We're not that alike," I countered.

"Yes, you are. You're both really prim and proper, maybe a little anal retentive, though that's not a bad thing. I'm the opposite of anal retentive and am currently in the horrible situation of having my accounts audited. The joys of self-employment." She made a bug-eyed expression and mimicked putting a gun to her head.

I lifted my eyebrows. "You're being audited?"

"Sadly, yes. I really regret deciding to do my own taxes these last few years. I'm trying to find an accountant with a penchant for masochism to sort things out for me." She gave a self-deprecating laugh. "So far, I haven't had any luck."

I picked up my coffee and took a sip. I wasn't an accountant, but I had a head for numbers and was excellent at taxes and personal finance. "I could help you. I'm very good at keeping tidy accounts," I offered.

Her eyes widened. "Seriously?"

I nodded. "I can certainly take a look." I'd blurted the offer, but now that I was thinking about it, this could be a good exchange. Afric was assisting me with Annabelle, and in return, I could organise her accounts.

"Are you certain?" she went on. "Because, believe me, it's a lot of work."

"I don't mind the work," I said, then cleared my throat. "I'd actually like to make a formal agreement. Just so things are clear."

Her brow furrowed. "What do you mean?"

"Well, helping you with your accounts could be my way of paying you back for your advice on my, um, situation. This way, we're both getting something out of it."

She stared at me, the beginnings of a smile shaping her lips. "You're one of those people who insists on paying back loans as soon as possible, aren't you? If someone gave you a pound for a cup of coffee, you'd be forcing that pound back into their hand the very next day, right?"

I pursed my lips because she wasn't wrong. That's exactly how I was. "Where exactly are you finding cups of coffee in London for a pound?" I shot back, and she smirked.

"Fine. I agree to the exchange. Want to shake on it?"

A part of me would prefer a written contract, but in this case, a handshake would have to suffice. Afric reached across the table, and we shook hands, her soft palm sliding against mine. I was momentarily aware of the sensation of her skin before she let go and asked, "Are you free later today?"

"Um … I'm not sure."

"Let's exchange numbers so that I can text you directions to my flat," she went on, not giving me time to protest. She pulled out her phone and looked at me expectantly, waiting for me to call out my number.

Reluctantly, I recited the digits, and a moment later, my phone buzzed with a text. I opened it and grimaced, then glanced at Afric in annoyance. "Did you just send me a dick pic?"

She chuckled in amusement. "I like to think of it as redistribution. I'm a female streamer, so I get an inordinate number of dick pics sent to me daily. I do the arseholes a favour by sending the pictures to my friends so that we can judge them. I mean, look at that one. It has a bend in it. I wonder if that's a positive or a negative with the ladies."

I was certain my face showed my disgruntlement as I swiftly deleted the image from my phone. "Please don't send me any more of those."

"Why not?"

"Because I didn't ask for them."

At this, she slammed her hands down on the table dramatically. "Well, neither did I!"

Several people from nearby tables cast us curious glances. I looked to Afric and frowned again. Everything about her was so loud and brash that I failed to realise how young she actually was. If she was Michaela's age, that would make her mid-twenties at most. I had just turned thirty. I needed to be the grown-up here.

"I'm sorry. You're right. The men who send you those pictures are out of line, and you shouldn't have to deal with that. Isn't there any way you can block them?"

"Not really, no," she answered glumly. "But thank you. I appreciate the sentiment." She cleared her throat before continuing. "Anyway, you can stop by my flat sometime this week. Whenever suits. I'm normally home in the evenings. We also need to assess how Annabelle feels about you. Do you two ever talk on the phone, or is it always by direct message?"

"We don't talk on the phone. If we did, she'd easily figure out the truth. I don't sound anything like Callum."

"Hmm," Afric eyed me a moment just as the waitress arrived with her food. She'd ordered waffles with maple syrup, blueberries, bananas, and a plate of bacon on the side. I watched in awe as she immediately dug in.

I'd always found sweet things unappetising in the morning, never mind the mix of sweet and savoury she was currently indulging in. The woman must've had a gut of steel. I, on the other hand, inherited IBS from my father's side of the family, which meant I was always careful about what I ate. I was also intolerant to dairy. The bright side was that I kept a trim, athletic figure and rarely put on weight.

"Afric," I said, trying to snag her attention. She looked up, chewing on a bite of waffle as she waited for me to continue. "You're not going to tell anyone about this, are you?" I asked, ducking my chin.

She put down her fork and reached out to touch my hand. The contact was unexpected, and a jolt of awareness went through me. People didn't touch me very often, which was probably why I was having a visceral reaction to her hand on mine.

"Of course not," she replied, her expression sincere. "Swear on my own life. We're friends now, Neil. You can trust me."

"We are?"

She let go of my hand and picked her fork back up. "Look, I know I can come across a little abrasive at first, but I swear, it's not intentional." A pause as she smirked. "Most of the time, I can't help it, but I think you're interesting, Neil Durant. You've got secrets, the juicy kind, and only the most intriguing people have secrets like that."

I was a little taken aback by her compliment. I'd never considered myself particularly interesting. "I don't like having secrets, though. And I really don't want to be intriguing. I just want to be normal."

She pointed her fork at me. "Well, it's lucky you met me. If it's the last thing I do, I'll make Annabelle fall in love with you, and you two will be the most normal couple in the world."

I wasn't convinced, but I'd give her a shot. It wasn't like I had many other options. Besides, there was always a chance that it could work, even if it was a slim one. Afric could turn out to be my very own genie in a bottle, granting me a wish that could make my life normal and boring again.

I returned my attention to my laptop while Afric finished her food. When she was done, she used a napkin to dab her face, placed some money down on the table, then slid out of the booth. I eyed her warily as she approached, reaching out as if to touch me again. I drew back because I wasn't prepared for the odd zing I'd felt when she'd put her hand on mine a few minutes ago.

"Relax. Your collar is stuck inside your jumper," she said, clearly noticing my stiffness. "I was just going to fix it for you."

I reached up and fixed the collar myself. She shot me a crooked grin. "Do you not like being touched or something?"

"Why would you ask that?"

"You just backed away like I have the plague. I know gamers get a bad rap for hygiene, but I swear I'm clean. I always shower before I leave the flat, at least."

"I'm sorry. I didn't mean to offend you. I'm just a little ..."

"Stiff? Awkward?" she suggested. "We're going to need to loosen you up before you meet Annabelle. Women like to be touched, ya know."

My gut dropped. I just couldn't imagine meeting Annabelle, seeing the disappointment in her eyes when she took me in. Then, I thought about touching her, and my throat dried up. I was a lying piece of shit, and I definitely didn't deserve to touch someone as angelic as Annabelle.

"Well, I need to get going," Afric said, interrupting my thoughts. "Text me if you plan on stopping by my flat this week."

With that, she left. I stared back at my laptop screen, and it took me a long while to remember what I'd been working on.

4.
Afric

"You need to shut up and let me concentrate," I complained as I sat in my gaming chair several hours into a livestream.

I was trying to pinpoint where the troll was hiding, and TheBigSix was being way too distracting. The troll was a sneaky little bastard. I planned to clobber him with my truncheon, but he kept hiding behind boulders and rocks. The virtual violence was going to win me a whopping two hundred points.

"I didn't say anything," TheBigSix argued.

"You're talking right now, aren't ya?" I countered. "And when I said you need to shut up, I meant you're breathing way too heavily. What's going on over there anyway?"

Yellowshoes gave a boisterous chuckle in the background while TheBigSix protested, "I'm not up to anything. This is slander."

"All I'm saying is, none of us can see you. You could be going to town on yourself, and nobody would be any the wiser," I continued to tease.

"I am not ... Ugh. Just kill the troll, will you? I've got a frozen pizza in the oven, and it's going to be ready in five minutes."

"Fine. But you need to learn how to take a joke."

The troll peeked his head out from behind a boulder, and I grinned as I muttered to myself, "I've got you now, my pretty." I pulled out my truncheon and swung it high in the air before bringing it down on the troll's head.

"If we ever meet in person, remind me never to get on your bad side," Yellowshoes said with a low whistle, her husky American accent in my ears.

I gave an evil laugh. "Only the wise know never to cross me."

There was a knock on my bedroom door and my flatmate, Sarita, poked her head in. "There's a man at the door for you. He said his name is Neil."

"Oh!" I exclaimed in excitement. "Send him in." Sarita nodded and disappeared.

"Who's Neil?" Yellowshoes asked.

"Yeah, who's Neil?" TheBigSix added, sounding a little disgruntled. I suspected he had a crush on me. It wasn't something he'd ever expressed in words, but we'd been online friends for years, and I just got a certain vibe from him. Like whenever I mentioned going out to find a hook up, he'd get all quiet and grumpy about it.

"Never you mind," I said before I turned my attention to the camera. "That'll have to be all for today, everyone. I hope you enjoyed my murderous antics. See you all tomorrow!"

I switched off my stream, shut down my computer, and turned to face the door just as it opened. Neil ran a hand through his dark brown hair and cautiously stepped inside like he was entering a radioactive zone. We really needed to work on his demeanour, loosen him up a little. The man was stiff as a board.

"Hi, your flatmate said to come in."

"Yes, yes, step inside my lair," I replied, motioning him farther into the room. "I'm so glad you came."

I stood and led him to my desk, where several haphazard piles of bank statements and receipts were stacked. I liked to think of it as organised chaos, though really, it was just chaos. He eyed them in a weirdly eager way like he was actually excited by how messy everything was. Oh, yeah, Neil was a neat freak. Evidently, he got a thrill out of organising messes, which was probably a good thing considering his job.

"So, this is what we're working with," I said, noticing he still hadn't looked at me, his eyes on the unruly stacks. "Do you need me to explain anything, or do you want to just get stuck in?"

He began to roll up his shirtsleeves as he pulled out my gaming chair and sat down. Okay, so he had really nice forearms. I filed the information away for later ponderance.

"I'll get started and will let you know if I have any questions," Neil replied as he picked up one of my bank statements and scanned it.

"Okay, good. Do you want a cup of tea or coffee? I have a fancy Nespresso machine and a milk frother that makes a mean cappuccino."

"It's too late in the day for coffee," Neil answered. "I'll take a cup of tea, though."

"Coming right up," I said, saluting him as I went out into the combined kitchen slash living area.

Sarita and her girlfriend, Mabel, both sat on the couch watching *RuPaul's Drag Race*.

"You bitches! I told you to call me when *Drag Race* started," I complained as I went to turn on the kettle.

"It literally just started," Sarita shot back. "And anyway, you have a guest. Isn't that the same Neil Michaela works with?"

"Yes. He's helping me with my accounts."

"Thank God. I thought you were gonna try to do them yourself again."

"Hey! I'm not that bad."

"You wouldn't be getting audited if you were good, Afric."

I chewed my lip as I placed a tea bag in a mug then poured in hot water. "Make me feel good about myself, why don't you," I said glumly.

Mabel elbowed Sarita in the side, and my flatmate rolled her eyes. "I'm sorry. All I'm saying is, I'm glad he's helping you. From what Michaela says, the bloke is great at pretty much everything."

"Here's hoping," I said as I went to bring Neil his tea. When I entered the room, I found he'd already started re-organising my bank statements into neat, orderly piles and was going through them one by one. He'd brought his laptop and had it open in front of him as he entered numbers into columns in an excel sheet.

"Your tea, good sir," I announced as I set it down in front of him.

He barely glanced up as he pointed to an entry on one of my bank statements. "What's Night Owl Accessories? It's only come up once so far, and you have it marked down as a business expense."

My brow furrowed as I eyed the name. I bought something for £150 last September, but I couldn't for the life of me remember what it was. "I'm not sure. Let me check." I pulled out my phone and Googled "Night Owl Accessories," laughing quietly to myself when I saw it was the name of a parent company that owned an online store where I bought some sex toys.

Neil glanced at me, waiting. "Well?"

"Never mind. It's not a business expense. Just put it under personal."

"Are you certain? These accounts need to be perfect, Afric. You can't afford any errors."

Oh, well. I tried to let him off easy, but he did ask. "If you must know, the purchase was for a dildo and one or two items of a similar ilk."

Neil

I couldn't look her in the eye as I returned my attention to the screen of my laptop. I was certain my cheeks were flaming red at this point. Afric's accounts were a delicious mess, but in the future, I'd just Google items I wasn't sure about instead of asking her directly. Anything to avoid awkward moments like this. Then again, *she* didn't seem awkward at all. On the contrary, she seemed to enjoy my embarrassment.

"You're right," I replied soberly. "That should definitely be under personal drawings."

I continued transcribing, hoping she'd leave me to it, but instead, she came and leaned against the edge of the desk, arms folded as she studied me.

"Could you turn on some normal lights? All the neon is giving me a headache," I complained, feeling more uncomfortable the longer she studied me.

"Do you know who you remind me a little of?"

I shrugged, wishing she'd just go and let me work. "I don't know. Who?"

"Tom Holland."

"The actor? I don't see it, but okay."

"Well, obviously, you're a bit older than him," Afric allowed. "But the resemblance is uncanny." Her lips formed a little smirk.

"Why are you smirking?"

"No reason."

"There's obviously a reason," I stated flatly, getting annoyed now.

"Next time you have a moment, go and look up his performance on *Lip Sync Battle*. It's pretty much my favourite thing on the internet."

"Okay, I'll do that," I replied.

"I think it'd be a good Halloween costume idea for you. Anyway, I'll leave you to it." Praise Jesus. "I'm going to watch *Drag Race* with Sarita and Mabel but give a call if you need anything." Before she left, she turned off her many neon lamps and flicked the switch for the regular ceiling bulb.

I returned my attention to my computer and tried to focus on Afric's bank statements, but my curiosity got the better of me. I navigated to Youtube and searched for the video she mentioned. Hitting play, I stared wide-eyed as Tom Holland lip synced to Rihanna's "Umbrella" while wearing a wig, corset and hot pants. There was something oddly entrancing about the whole thing, though it was safe to say I'd never be confident enough to wear that as a Halloween costume.

I realised I'd neglected to turn the volume down when Afric poked her head into the room again. "You're watching it!" she exclaimed happily.

"Uh huh," I replied, sheepishly exiting the page and clicking back to my excel sheet.

"So, what do you think?"

"I think I don't look anything like him," I responded stiffly.

"I meant what do you think of the video? Does it make you question your sexuality?"

I pursed my lips, shooting her an uncomfortable look. "A little bit, yes," I admitted grudgingly.

Afric barked a laugh. "Ha! I knew it. It makes everyone question their sexuality. That's the magic of that video."

"I should get back to work," I said, turning away from her.

"Right, yes, you work. I'll be out here if you need me," Afric replied, ducking back out of the room.

I got a good two hours work in and was packing my things when she returned.

"You're leaving?" Afric asked as she leaned against the doorframe.

"Yes, I promised my grandma I'd stop by for dinner."

"Aw, that's nice. Are you two close?"

I nodded. "Pretty close. She raised me and my sister, Rosie, after our parents passed away."

"Your parents died? Oh, my God, Neil, why didn't you tell me?!"

I shot her a perplexed look. "Um, it didn't come up during the three brief occasions we've spent time together."

Afric came farther into the room, sitting on the edge of her bed as her bright blue eyes met mine. "I'm so sorry for your loss."

I frowned, something about the sincere look in her eyes hitting me right in the chest. I cleared my throat. "It was a long time ago. Listen, I need to get going." I wasn't too keen on having a heart-to-heart. I was exhausted and hungry and not in the mood for anything deep and meaningful, especially not with her. Afric already knew way too much about me.

"Right. Sure," she replied, looking up at me when I stood. My eyes were drawn to the cute smattering of freckles across her cheeks. "When will I see you again?"

"I'll stop by tomorrow after work."

"Great, see you then."

***

By the time I arrived at Grandma's house, it was almost seven-thirty.

"You're late. That's not like you," she commented when I entered the kitchen. She sat at the table with a cup of tea, a magazine open in front of her.

"Sorry about that. I was helping out a friend."

"You're a good lad, always doing favours for people, so much like your father," Grandma said wistfully. "Rosie and I have already eaten, but there're some lamb chops, potatoes, and carrots in the oven. Oh, and I made my special rosemary gravy."

"That sounds like heaven. I'm starving," I said as I pulled out the plate, grabbed a knife and fork from the drawer, then sat down across from Grandma to eat.

"So, which friend were you helping?"

"She's a new friend," I replied. "Her name is Afric."

"That's a pretty name. How did you meet?"

"Through Michaela. They used to be flatmates before Michaela moved in with her partner, James."

Grandma gave a thoughtful frown. "This isn't the same friend of Michaela's you said was particularly unpleasant, is it?"

I was surprised she remembered me saying that since it was a few weeks ago now. Then again, Grandma was a shrewd woman with a memory like a steel trap. Very little evaded her. "Actually, yes, but I was wrong about her. Mostly. I thought she was unpleasant, but I'm beginning to learn she's just a bit eccentric. It takes a little getting used to."

"First impressions aren't always correct," Grandma nodded. "What were you helping her with?"

"She's self-employed, and her accounts are being audited. I offered to lend a hand sorting through the mess."

Grandma's lips curved in a smile as she lifted her mug for a sip. "You must like her to make an offer like that."

"Don't give me that smile. I don't like her in the way you think. She's not my type at all. And besides, you know tidying messes is my favourite pastime. I'm doing myself a favour more than anything else."

Grandma laughed. "That's true. You do love a good tidying up."

She returned her attention to her magazine while I cut into the lamb chops. Rosie entered the room and took a seat at the table. "Hey! I didn't hear you come in."

"He was late because he was doing a favour for his new friend Afric," Grandma said, still with that faint curve to her lips. She thought she knew something, but she was dead wrong. My friendship with Afric was pure convenience. She was helping me with Annabelle, and I was helping her with her accounts. It was that simple.

Rosie's eyes widened with interest. "Oh, really? You know there's this girl online I follow called Afric. I didn't think it was a very common name, but that always happens, doesn't it? You learn a new word you never heard before, and then suddenly, you're hearing and seeing it everywhere."

I glanced at my sister as I chewed a bite of carrot. What were the chances it was a different Afric? Especially since *my* Afric was an online personality, or whatever it was you called people who did what she did.

"Who's the girl you follow?"

Rosie grinned. "It's this Irish girl. She livestreams while playing video games. I'm not really into the games, though. I watch mostly for the funny banter. There's a Scottish guy and an American girl who she plays with, and the three of them are just hilarious together."

Hmm. I didn't remember there being a Scottish guy when I checked out her stream. I must've been wearing my thoughts on my face because Rosie gave an excited gasp.

"Oh, my God! Is your friend the same Afric? This is so cool. Can you get me her autograph?"

"I never said it was the same person," I countered, but my sister waved me away.

"Your expression said it all."

"She's right," Grandma added. "Rosie has always been great at reading expressions."

"If I weren't a librarian, I'd become one of those fake psychics who use cold readings to pretend they know stuff about your dead relatives."

"Do that, and we'll all disown you."

"So, what's she like in real life?" Rosie went on.

"Who?"

She rolled her eyes. "Afric. Who else? Is she as funny as she is on her stream?"

"I'm not sure funny is the right word. The woman doesn't have a filter. I suppose some people find that sort of thing amusing."

"Oh, don't act like your sense of humour is so highbrow. I saw you chuckling away at an old episode of *Faulty Towers* last week."

"I was not chuckling," I argued. "I might've smiled in mild amusement, but that's all."

"Please get me an autograph. *Please*," Rosie begged.

"Fine," I relented grudgingly, suspecting Afric would be unbearable when she discovered what a huge fan my sister was of hers. "I'll see what I can do."

5.
Afric

"Okay, everyone. I need to grab a shower. See you all tomorrow."

"You're showering at six p.m.? Do we need to stage an intervention?" Yellowshoes asked as I turned off my stream. She and TheBigSix were still online, and since she was so used to interacting with us, calculating the time difference between the U.K. and Florida had become second nature.

"Sometimes I shower late. What of it?" I countered as I pulled off my hoodie. I wore only a tank top underneath, something I never wore when I was streaming because that was just asking for trouble. But Yellowshoes and TheBigSix were my pals. I trusted them enough to see me in something that wasn't three times too big.

"Is Neil coming over again?" Yellowshoes went on, and I could practically feel TheBigSix's silent disapproval simmering through his mic.

"Yes, he is. He's helping me with some personal stuff."

"Personal, eh?" There was a smile in her voice now.

"Not *that* kind of personal, gutter brain. It has to do with my finances. Neil's a numbers whizz."

"What's wrong with your finances?" TheBigSix asked, finally joining the conversation.

"Nothing for you to worry your pretty little head about," I answered. "Now, I better go. He'll be here soon, and I stink to high heaven. Seriously, I think it might be a health and safety hazard at this point," I continued jokingly.

Yellowshoes laughed. "Okay, girl. Go shower. Talk tomorrow?"

"Yep, talk to you tomorrow. Bye, you two," I said and logged off before TheBigSix could channel any more annoyance at me. His current profile pic was a quote from some fantasy novel he was obsessed with, but I'd seen a picture of him when he first started playing *Greenforest* and remembered he wasn't bad looking. He seemed tall, with dark auburn hair and brown eyes. That was as much as I could remember. He typically gamed with only his mic on. Yellowshoes turned her camera on every once in a while, but normally, she preferred just to use her mic, too.

Sarita was staying at Mabel's tonight, so I had the place to myself. I would've indulged in a bubble bath, but I didn't have time since Neil already texted saying he was on his way. He worked in Shoreditch, so it'd take him at least half an hour to get here by the Tube, if not longer since it was rush hour.

I turned on the shower and stepped under the spray. I'd just finished shampooing and conditioning my hair when there was a knock at the door. What the hell? How had he gotten here so fast? I quickly rinsed myself off, threw on my enormous fluffy bathrobe, and went to answer the door.

"You're early," I said when I found Neil standing there, his satchel bag over his shoulder.

"And you're dripping," Neil replied, eyeing my wet hair before his attention drifted down to my robe.

"That's because you caught me mid-shower. I didn't expect you to arrive so quickly."

He shifted uncomfortably from foot to foot, eyes on the floor. "Well, go and finish. I'll wait here."

"Nonsense," I said, reaching out and grabbing his arm to pull him inside the flat. "Go into my room and get started. I'll be with you in a few minutes."

I shooed him inside my room, noticing he was wearing jeans today. They showcased what I already knew was a very nice backside. Neil glanced back at me, catching me clearly checking out his arse. He seemed to flush then went to sit down at my desk. I flicked on the ceiling light, knowing he wasn't a fan of the neon lamps, then went to finish my shower.

When I returned to the bedroom, clad in thick fleece pyjamas, Neil was quietly working, his back to me. I picked up my tablet and began checking through my emails and various social media accounts. I was scrolling through my brother Billy's latest pictures. With eight kids, my family was big, but I was closest to Billy since he was the youngest and I was the second youngest.

Billy was a bit of a wild card. You never knew what new job he was working at or what he might be up to, which was one of the reasons why I loved him. He was unpredictable, his mop of curly brown hair as chaotic as the person it sat atop. Missing him, I sent a quick message.

Afric: Like the new pics. Where were they taken? Also, you better be coming to visit me soon!

It didn't take long for him to reply.

Billy: Me and some of the lads went to Lough Derg last weekend. Beautiful spot. As regards coming to visit you ... Go and check outside your front door.

My heart skipped a beat. I wouldn't put it past Billy to surprise me with a completely random visit. Neil cast me a quick glance as I rose from the bed and went to the front door of the flat. I threw it open, letting out a disappointed sigh when I found the doorway empty.

Afric: You bastard! You got my hopes up!

Billy: Muah ha! Just know I could appear at any moment. You better be ready for me.

Afric: I was born ready.

"Everything okay?" Neil asked, pulling my attention away from my tablet.

"Yeah, just my brother Billy being an arsehole and tricking me that he'd come to visit. He lives in Dublin, so we don't get to see each other often."

"Are you close?"

I nodded. "There were less than two years between us, so growing up, we always did everything together."

"It must've been nice to have a sibling near your age. My sister, Rosie, is six years younger than me. I've always felt more like a parental figure than a brother."

"That's probably because of your parents passing away," I said in a soft voice, noticing a hint of sadness behind his eyes. "You became the dad. My oldest brother, Ryan, was like that. Our parents were always working, so he was the one who took care of us younger ones."

"How many siblings do you have?"

"Seven."

Neil's eyes widened. "Wow, that's a lot of kids."

"Yep. My parents are a pair of absolute horndogs, obviously," I joked, and Neil's lips gave the barest hint of a twitch.

"Was it hard living in such a big family?"

"Not really. At least, if it was, I didn't know any better. But it gave me a thick skin. My brothers and sisters were endlessly slagging each other off."

"That would certainly give you a thick skin," Neil agreed, falling silent a moment. He looked like he was building up the courage to say something as he bounced his knee. "Speaking of siblings. My sister is actually a big fan of yours. She was wondering if I could get her an autograph?"

My grin spread wide across my face. I could tell it bothered Neil to make such a request, and I couldn't resist the opportunity to tease him. "Your sister is a fan of moi?" I asked, preening as I placed a hand to my chest.

Neil's lips formed a straight, disgruntled line. "I just found out. Apparently, she watches your stream."

"Well, in that case, I'd be more than happy to give her an autograph, but if you want, I can do you one better. How about a video call?"

He shook his head. "Rosie's very shy. She might have a heart attack if you video called her."

I found it cute that he was protective of his sister's shyness. "Okay, an autograph it is then." I went to grab a pen and paper. Neil returned his attention to his laptop, but I sensed him surreptitiously watching me out the corner of his eye. I was tempted to write something cheeky to his sister, like, *sorry your brother has such a big stick up his arse*, but I tried to summon some maturity. After all, we were being nice and cordial with one another today. Instead, I asked him, "Does she spell her name with a 'y' or an 'ie'?"

Neil cast me a quick glance. "With an 'ie'." There was a pause before he continued, "Don't write anything ridiculous."

I shot him a fake offended look. "Well, I wasn't going to, but now that you've warned me—"

"Forget it. Don't bother. I'll tell Rosie you said no."

"Hey, don't be so prickly. I was only going to write, *Dear Rosie, thanks for being a fan. P.S. Your brother has a lovely bottom. Yours sincerely, Afric.*"

At this, Neil's cheeks flamed bright red, and it was silly how much I enjoyed embarrassing him. In fact, he seemed a little tongue-tied, and it was absolutely adorable.

"What?" I asked. "I know you caught me looking earlier. You've got a nice arse, and being that I spend most of my days cooped up in this room live streaming, I noticed. No need to be all weird about it."

"I'm not being weird."

"Yes, you are. Your shoulders are all hunched, and your cheeks are like two big raspberries."

"My cheeks are not like raspberries," he objected. "I'd just appreciate it if you didn't sexually objectify me like that." I sensed he was trying to cover up his embarrassment. "This might not be a place of work, but I am doing you a professional sort of favour, so please, keep your ogling to a minimum."

"Oh, so now you're gonna play the sexual harassment card?" I teased. "Fine, I shan't cast my covetous gaze upon your fine derriere ever again. Happy?"

He glowered at me. "Yes, now, please, could you be quiet so I could actually get some work done?"

I made a show of zipping my lips before scribbling down a very normal message for his sister, followed by my signature. I folded it in half and got up from the bed. Neil's fingers were typing, his eyes on the screen as I slid the piece of paper into the little pocket on the breast of his shirt. I heard him inhale a sharp breath at the contact.

"There you go. Oh, crap, was that more sexual harassment? I just can't seem to keep my crazy libido in check around your potent masculinity."

"Funny," Neil deadpanned, not bothering to look at me.

Well, it seemed his humour had died a gruesome death. I returned to my bed and answered a few more emails, all the while sneaking peeks at him here and there. Over an hour went by, and his cool façade never broke. Maybe I'd gone too far with my teasing. I was so bad at knowing whether or not I'd stepped over the line from entertaining to offensive.

Finally, Neil blew out a breath and sat back, powering his laptop down.

"All done for tonight?" I asked.

He nodded, finally deigning to look at me. "I'll have to do the rest remotely if that's okay? The new season of *Running on Air* starts filming in a few days, so I'll be in New York for the next six weeks."

Six weeks? That was ... Well, it was a long time. Kind of. I guess I just felt sad that I wasn't going to see him for so long. I'd strangely gotten used to his prickly self.

"I don't mind you finishing the accounts up remotely, but what about our plan to make Annabelle fall in love with you?"

Neil raked a hand over his cleanly shaven jaw, a hint of self-deprecation in his voice when he replied, "Right, *that*. We can message back and forth, I guess, and you can give me pointers, but any in-person meeting will have to wait until I get back."

"Okay, that's doable," I agreed, again feeling that weird pang that I wasn't going to see him again for ages. It was probably why I asked impulsively, "Are you busy tomorrow?"

Neil's eyebrows rose. "Tomorrow?"

"I'm going to watch a tournament over at the Red Bull Gaming Sphere. You should come. It'll be a good opportunity for you to practice flirting for when you finally meet Annabelle in person."

"Are there typically many women at gaming tournaments?"

"Okay, so there might be a *slight* gender imbalance," I allowed, "but there'll definitely be women there. I promise. And if not, you can just practice on me."

Neil chewed his lip, his eyes running over me. "I'll think about it."

I bobbed my head. "Cool." Why did I suddenly feel so awkward? Maybe it was a bit weird to suggest he use me to practice flirting. He hadn't commented on it, though. "Are you excited about the trip to New York?" I asked, changing the subject.

He shook his head. "Not really. Travelling all the time gets old very quickly. I like my routine, and it's constantly being broken when I have to jet off to South Africa for eight weeks of filming."

"Oh, yeah, it sounds terrible," I said, heavy on the sarcasm.

He eyed me now, the tips of his ears turning pink. "I didn't mean to sound so ungrateful. I do love my job. I'm just a creature of habit. I'm pretty much a granddad in a thirty-year-old's body, set in my ways. Plus, being around the cast, they're all so adventurous and wild. It makes me feel, well, the opposite, mainly because I *am* the opposite."

"It's not a bad thing to be how you are," I countered. "Not everyone wants to be around someone who's constantly jumping off buildings and putting themselves in danger. That would get old very fast. Sometimes we underestimate the appeal of a nice, even keel."

"Annabelle obviously likes someone who embraces danger. She thinks she's messaging with Callum Davidson," Neil said.

Well, then, maybe Annabelle isn't the right one for you, my mind argued, but I was impressed when I didn't voice the sentiment. I scratched the back of my head. "Yeah, about that. Haven't you ever found it a little weird that she's messaging with 'Callum' when Callum has a girlfriend?" I asked, unable to resist. It was something that had been bothering me for the last few days.

Neil's expression turned perturbed. "I don't think she knows he's with Leanne. They try to keep their relationship out of the public eye as much as they can these days."

At that, I laughed. "*Right*. If she's a fan of the show, then she knows Leanne and Callum are together. And I'm saying that as a fan of the show myself. We've all watched their tumultuous relationship play out on screen."

Neil frowned. "Okay, true, but I think because they were so at odds with one another for the first few seasons, Annabelle believes they aren't right for each other. Seeing Callum and Leanne on TV only gives you half the picture. I know that because I see them every day, and they're one hundred percent in love. But if all I saw was what happened in the show, I'd probably have my doubts about them being right for each other, too. Nowadays, they try to keep most of their relationship off air. They learned that lesson the hard way in the early seasons."

Hmm, it sounded like he was trying to rationalise it to himself, but I had a feeling Annabelle wasn't the sweet girl she wanted Neil, or should I say 'Callum', to believe she was. Neil might've been the one doing the catfishing, but I suspected that when it came down to it, Annabelle was the guilty party.

6.
Neil

I stood outside the gaming sphere waiting for Afric. The place wasn't too far from my work, so I was able to walk over once I clocked off for the day. I checked my watch. She was running a few minutes late. A part of me was relieved because the thought of practicing flirting with random strangers sent a chill down my spine. Maybe Afric wouldn't show.

Flirting wasn't my strong suit. This was a fact I knew about myself. It was something I tended to avoid at all costs.

I was about to call Afric to check where she was when I spotted her approaching. Her long blonde hair was down around her shoulders, and she wore a loose-fitting black and white striped shirt with burgundy coloured leggings, Converse, and large hoop earrings. It was the most normal outfit I'd seen her in yet. She even wore a little bit of make-up, the black eyeliner highlighting her startlingly blue eyes. My chest did a weird flip-flop, and I wasn't sure why.

Okay, maybe I did know why, but I was trying to ignore it. It was only yesterday that I was at her place, and I still didn't know how to feel about her admitting to checking out my arse.

Women rarely checked me out, so to have Afric compliment me like that was, well, it wasn't unpleasant. I'd spent so long seeing myself as this plain, unnoticeable bloke that it was kind of shocking to have her compliment me. Even if it was only my backside she'd been complimenting. It gave me hope that once Annabelle discovered the truth, she wouldn't be completely horrified by the real me. Perhaps I wasn't as plain and unnoticeable as I thought I was.

"Hello! Sorry, I'm late. There was a delay on the Tube. Typical," she said as she reached me. "Have you been waiting long?"

"Not long. You look nice."

She patted her windswept hair. "I do? Oh, well, there's no particular reason for that."

I frowned at her odd statement. "Shall we go inside?"

Afric nodded, glancing at the entrance and biting her lip. She seemed nervous, which was unusual. "Just give me a minute."

I studied her. "Is everything okay?"

She was still staring intently at the entrance. "What? Yes, I'm perfectly fine."

"You sure? You seem—"

"What do I seem?"

"Tense?" I hedged.

She deflated, blowing out a heavy breath. "I just haven't been here in a while."

"Are you taking part in the tournament or something?"

"No, but my ex, Dev, probably is, and I haven't spoken to him since our break-up."

Oh. She was nervous about seeing her ex-boyfriend. Now it all made sense. Something about the show of vulnerability warmed me to her. "When did you two break up?" I asked.

"About six months ago."

"We don't have to go in if you don't want to," I said in a gentle voice.

Afric shot me a determined look. "No, I want to go in. I have to. He's not stealing this place from me. I just need to reclaim it."

"Well, in order to do that, you'll need to actually step inside."

She narrowed her gaze. "I know that." Still, she didn't move. I gave her a moment to prepare herself, and as we stood there, a man in a suit strode by, bumping into Afric without stopping to apologise. I caught her by the elbow and made sure she was okay. Then, feeling strangely bothered by his rudeness, I walked after the man and tapped him on the shoulder. He turned around, shooting me a questioning look. "What?"

"You should watch where you're going," I said. "You almost knocked my friend over back there."

He glanced at Afric, then at me. "Whatever, mate. You two were blocking the path."

With that, he turned and left. "Dickhead," I muttered as I returned to Afric.

She smiled up at me. "That was rather chivalrous."

"I just can't stand rude people," I said.

"You live in London, Neil. This city is full of rude people."

"Well, it bothered me how he didn't even stop to apologise. Are you okay?" I asked, looking her over.

"I'm fine, but thank you." She took a deep inhale and straightened her shoulders. "Right, let's do this," she said, but she still didn't move.

I bent my head to look her in the eye. "Do you want me to go in first?"

She swallowed then nodded, and feeling protective of her at that moment, I led the way into the gaming sphere. Afric followed close behind me, and I took the place in as we entered. A good number of people were gathered for the tournament, and computers were set up all about being used by lots of people with headsets on, completely absorbed in their gaming. I eyed the race car simulators surrounded by large screens, impressed with the setup. This place certainly meant business.

"Do you want a drink?" Afric asked. "I'm getting one."

"A drink sounds good." Strangely, her nervousness about bumping into her ex made my nervousness about flirting fade a little.

Afric grabbed us two Red Bulls, and several people waved to her. She said hello, but she didn't stop to chat with them. Instead, she led us over to sit on a bench. I took a swig of the tangy-sweet drink. "I probably shouldn't be having this. It tends to give me heart palpitations."

"Right?" Afric agreed. "It's good for staying alert during a gaming marathon, though."

"Ah, I see how that could help," I replied just as three blokes appeared in front of us. Two of them carried some sort of handheld gaming devices, their eyes intent on the screens as their thumbs pounded the buttons. The third was a dark-skinned guy with close-cropped hair and a beard who seemed to be eyeing Afric intently. He had a nose ring and wore a black hoodie with a skull design and ripped jeans. I was ninety-nine percent certain this was her ex.

"Afric. It's been a while," he said with a smile.

"It has," she replied, lifting her chin. "Hello, Dev."

"I was beginning to think you were avoiding me."

"Nope. Just been busy. My stream has been gaining a lot of new viewers."

"Really? I went to tune in the other day, but you were offline. It actually feels like you've been streaming less," Dev commented, and Afric's shoulders tensed. She didn't reply right away, and some instinct pushed me to come to her defence. Without fully thinking it through, I slid my arm around her waist. I heard a small, sharp breath escape her, and I was acutely aware of the curve of her hip under her loose shirt before I glanced at Dev.

"That's probably my fault. I've been keeping her busy," I said. "I'm Neil, by the way."

Dev's attention finally came to me, one eyebrow shooting up. "Oh, hey," he said, then glanced back at Afric. "He doesn't seem like your usual type."

She shot him an arch look. "Maybe I decided to change my type."

Dev narrowed his gaze. "Maybe you did."

A short silence fell. Afric shot a look at Dev's friends, who were still completely absorbed in their devices. "Do those two ever shut up? I can barely get a word in."

I chuckled quietly, and Dev scowled, not responding to her joke as he replied, "I better get going. The tournament is starting soon." He motioned to his two mute gamer friends to follow him.

"Break a leg," Afric called after him, making a rude hand gesture to his retreating back before grinning up at me.

"That was the best. Thank you for pretending to be my boyfriend. I can't believe I didn't think to suggest it earlier. Dev was so pissed off."

"He was?"

"Oh, yeah. He always goes all quiet and frowny when he's angry."

"Well, I'm glad I could help you put it to your ex," I said before realising my arm was still around her waist. I carefully removed it, but not without again noticing she was hiding some devastating curves under her baggy clothes. I filed the information away under the heading: Things I didn't need to be thinking about.

"I know how awkward it can be seeing someone for the first time after a break-up," I went on.

"The bloody gall of him, too," she exclaimed quietly, turning her body towards me on the bench. "One of the reasons he broke up with me was because he said I gamed too much, and now he has the cheek to comment that I'm not streaming as often as I used to."

"That is kind of shitty," I agreed.

"He said he wanted a girlfriend who was into normal stuff. In other words, he wants someone who will cook and clean and dress up nice, while he sits on his arse gaming all day and being treated like a prince."

"Sounds like you're better off without him."

"Oh, I definitely am. It's crazy what a few months will do to give you clarity on a person," Afric said as she blew out a breath. She fell silent a moment, looking around. "There are fewer women here today than there normally are. I'm sorry. I know I promised you people to practice flirting with."

"Don't apologise. I've actually been a nervous wreck thinking about it. I hate flirting."

"Me, too. It's such a performance. Whatever happened to just having a natural conversation with someone?"

"Exactly," I agreed. "I think once you have a connection, the flirting just becomes a part of the conversation without being forced."

Afric nodded and folded her arms. "Will you still stay and watch the tournament with me? It's fine if you want to leave."

I stared at her, a weird tug in my chest. Funnily enough, I didn't feel like leaving. I actually wanted to stay and hang out with her. "Sure, I can stay for a while."

Now she smiled. "Great." She nodded to the drink in my hand. "Want another one of those?"

"Absolutely not."

She chuckled. "Okay, then. Let me show you around instead. I'll give you the grand tour."

She stood from the bench, and I followed her down a row of computers.

***

I was standing behind the film crew in Central Park when my phone buzzed with a message. I pulled it out, spotting Afric's name on the screen, and smiled automatically. What was this? It appeared I'd started to enjoy our budding friendship. I could at least admit that I had fun with her last week at the gaming sphere. Afric and I had spent over an hour playing a race car game. She beat me every time, of course, but I still enjoyed it.

I glanced down to read her message.

Afric: How's everything going over in the Big Apple?

Neil: I'm a bit jet-lagged but getting by. I'm in Central Park atm. The cast is shooting.

Afric: OMG, that sounds fun! Send me a pic.

I hesitated. She wanted a picture? I rarely took selfies, and more often than not, I was the one behind the camera. I glanced around. Everybody was busy working, not paying me any attention. Navigating to the camera app, I put it in selfie mode and lifted the phone. I made sure to get some trees and greenery in the background, as well as the buildings beyond, and attempted a smile. The first few shots weren't great. My smile was wooden. But after a few more tries, I loosened up and managed to take a reasonably good selfie. I went back and forth over whether to send it, then, feeling impulsive, I hit 'send'.

Instead of a text response, my phone lit up with a call. "Hello?" I answered.

Afric was already chuckling. "My goodness, you're too cute. I meant a picture of the cast filming, not a selfie of you, ya big eejit."

I stiffened, slamming my palm into my forehead as I held the phone to my ear with my other hand. "Oh, right. Sorry, I thought—"

"Don't apologise. You look lovely, Neil. Thank you for gracing my phone with your heavenly visage."

"Okay, there's no need to make fun. I thought young people sent each other pictures of themselves all the time. Isn't that what people your age do? They send selfies drinking coffee, or selfies with ice-creams, or other mundane things that certainly don't require documenting."

"First of all, you just called me basic, which I'm prepared to overlook because I'm not. And second of all, you're not that much older than me, Neil. I'm twenty-five. You're thirty. We're hardly a Boomer and a Gen Z. Pretty sure we're both Millennials, so ..."

"I didn't mean to offend you. You're the one who called me up, laughing your arse off at my selfie, which, might I add, I happen to think I look well in. At the very least, it was the best of a bad bunch—"

"Hold up, how many pictures did you take?" Afric asked, her voice full of amusement.

"A few," I admitted grudgingly. "But that's neither here nor there."

"Oh, my God. I'm going to die," she chuckled. "I would've loved to see you standing there taking selfies when you're supposed to be working."

"Well, enjoy the visual because I won't be sending you any more photos of my time in New York."

"Wait, no fair! I want more pictures. That way, I can live vicariously through you. In fact, I think you should send me a selfie every day to show me what you're up to. No, I demand it. I am, after all, stuck in my bedroom in Brixton live streaming video games to teenage boys while wearing gigantic hoodies to give them as little as possible to wank over."

"Okay, I'm not sure where to start because there's a lot to unpack there. Besides, it's not all teenage boys who watch you. My sister, Rosie, watches your stream all the time."

"That's good to know. Tell her I said hi. Also, speaking of your sister, did she like the autograph?"

I smiled, thinking of how excited Rosie was when I gave it to her. "Yes, actually, she was made up about it. Thanks for that, by the way."

"No problem. But back to the daily selfies. I seriously think you should consider it. Think of it as a confidence-boosting exercise. You clearly have some self-esteem issues—"

"I do not have self-esteem issues," I protested weakly before amending. "Well, okay, I may have some, but it's not a huge deal."

"You're pretending to be someone else online to a girl you're infatuated with," Afric said, and I deflated.

"Fair point."

"So, here's my suggestion. You take a picture of yourself once a day in front of some cool landmark or other. You're in New York, so it won't be difficult. Taking selfies can be kind of awkward, especially when some passing stranger looks at you and rolls their eyes all, *God, they're taking a selfie, how embarrassing, how vain …*"

"Well, now I really want to do it," I deadpanned.

"No, hear me out. It's a good thing. You have to not give a shit what strangers think of you. The most confident people don't care what anyone thinks of them. I remember walking through Trafalgar Square one time, and there was this lady in a ballgown having a photoshoot, but it wasn't a modelling shoot. It was like she'd paid someone to take pictures of her just for her own personal photo album. I remember thinking to myself, *wow, that woman does not give a single shit, and I am here for it.* That's who you need to be, Neil. You need to be the lady in the ballgown in Trafalgar Square."

"I'm not putting on a ballgown, let alone in Trafalgar Square of all places."

"I'm not asking you to, though if you did, you'd look amazing, but that's beside the point. Selfie taking in public requires confidence and a zero-shits-given attitude. And both of those are things you could do with having more of, especially if you want to impress Annabelle."

At the mention of Annabelle, I stiffened, spotting James, Michaela, and Callum walking towards me. "Listen, I'll think about it, but I'm making no promises. I have to go now."

"I look forward to tomorrow's photo," Afric said, a smile in her voice.

"Hey, I haven't agreed—"

"Can't hear you. The signal's breaking up." With that, she hung up. I shook my head. Why was I even humouring her? I was busy pondering this question when I realised Michaela was right next to me, a curious expression on her face.

"Okay, am I going mad, or did I just hear Afric's voice on the other end of that phone call?" she asked.

"Pretty sure you're going mad," I said, shoving the phone in my pocket. Luckily, Leanne was on the other side of the park, waving me over. "Oh, looks like I'm wanted," I said and quickly departed, though I sensed my co-worker's suspicion as I walked away.

7.
Afric

"Okay, folks, I think you're all gonna love this, especially those of you who have a soft spot for nostalgia," I said as I started my evening stream. "I've decided that from henceforth, Fridays are now vintage themed, which means every Friday, I'll be playing something from the nineties. I've managed to get my hands on a second-hand Sega Mega Drive, alongside a copy of *Sonic the Hedgehog*. Yes, that's right. Get ready for some dancing with your gameplay because the soundtrack for this has some absolute bops on it!"

I fired up the game, the old-school "SEGA" theme tune filling my headphones. *Sonic* was one of the first games I'd ever played. My parents were too cheap to fork out for a new console, so I had to resort to playing my eldest brother's beat-up old Sega when all my friends at school had Nintendos.

The music for Green Hill Zone came on, and I began humming along and bobbing my head as the little blue cartoon hedgehog ran across the 2D scenery, diligently collecting gold rings and bonus points.

Just like always, the comments began to roll in. I cast them a cursory glance, grinning when I spotted one that said, *You need to make up lyrics to this music. I'm still laughing at your interpretation of* Friends in Low Places.

And another.

Omg! What a blast from the past. I'm a 90's kid so this is right up my alley.

Then there were the usual few unpleasant ones.

This game is shit. Turning off stream.

Show us your tits.
U r soooo ugly.
Negative comments like these were par for the course. My tough skin was primed for them. Still, when I was having a bad day or feeling particularly low, they sometimes managed to sneak past my defences. Today wasn't one of those days. I was feeling good about myself, so the negative comments had no effect. Instead, I focused on the positive ones.

RosieTheLibrarian: This looks so fun! I think I might need to find a second-hand Sega for myself.

The name gave me pause. Neil had said that his sister was called Rosie, and it was certainly possible that she was a librarian. A small grin touched my lips as I gave her a shoutout.

"RosieTheLibrarian, if you live in London, you should try hitting up N1 Games on Baron Street. They'll be able to sort you out."

She wrote another comment.

RosieTheLibrarian: Thanks, I'll try that!

I smiled to myself, wondering how Neil was doing over in New York. I'd requested he send me daily selfies, but since our phone call yesterday, I had yet to receive one. Then again, I was a few hours ahead of him.

Two hours later, I finished out my stream and headed into the kitchen to grab some dinner. The living area was empty, but I could hear Sarita and Mabel giggling over something in Sarita's bedroom. They were probably cosied up in bed together watching funny videos.

As I poured some pasta into a pot, an uncommon feeling struck me. I almost felt ... jealous of them. Every so often, a jolt of loneliness would hit me, and I'd contemplate re-entering the dating scene. Then I'd remember how much I enjoyed my sanity and think better of it.

Ever since Dev and I broke up, I went out to clubs or used Tinder to find a hook-up when the need arose. But what if I was missing out? What if there was some perfect man out there just waiting for me to find him while I was too busy having meaningless sex or sitting in my bedroom live streaming in my PJs?

When my food was ready, I sat down on the couch, scrolling through my phone as I ate. I was almost done eating when a message popped up from Neil, and I smiled. He'd sent a picture of himself standing in a park across the water from Manhattan, the iconic skyline in the background. Neil's black-rimmed glasses sat perched on his nose, his white shirt buttoned all the way up, his hair neatly combed. He had an awkward grin on his face as he pointed a thumb over his shoulder to the skyscrapers behind him.

I swear he was too adorable for words. Also, his outfit was giving me serious *Book of Mormon* cast member vibes, and honestly? I wasn't hating it. Seeing all those perfectly done-up buttons weirdly made my fingers itch to rip them open.

Last week, when Neil had accompanied me to the gaming sphere and we'd bumped into Dev, I'd been shocked (and a little bit thrilled) when he put his arm around my waist and pretended to be my new boyfriend. It was a kindness I hadn't expected from him, and his closeness when he put his arm around me was a reminder of how much I'd been missing physical contact.

I pushed the thought aside and brought my attention back to my phone. Yesterday, when I'd requested a picture of the shoot and Neil sent me a selfie instead, I just about died from how cute he was. He could be uptight, but there was a refreshing lack of pretension about him that was incredibly endearing.

What do you think? He asked in a text under the picture.

Afric: Good effort. I give you a B+. Your smile isn't as confident as I'd like it to be, though. I want to see those pearly whites!

Neil: Guess I'll have to try harder tomorrow.

Afric: I guess you will ;-)

Neil: We're about to go eat pizza at some place close to the hotel. What are you up to?

Afric: I just finished streaming for the day and ate a lacklustre bowl of pasta for dinner. I'd kill for some New York pizza. Very jealous of you right now.

Neil: Shall I send you a picture? Or would that be rubbing it in too much?

Afric: Send one. I can lick the phone screen and pretend it works like the flavoured wallpaper in Willy Wonka.

Neil: Please do not lick your phone screen. Studies have shown they have more germs than a toilet bowl.

Afric: Pfft. Germs are good for you. My parents let me go around licking everything when I was a kid, and I rarely ever got sick.

Neil: Please stop texting me about licking things.

Afric: Okay, fine. Wouldn't want you getting all hot under that perfectly buttoned-up collar.

Neil: I assure you the opposite is true.

Afric: The gentleman doth protest too much.

Neil: I'm going now. Have a good night.

Afric: You, too! And don't forget I want another selfie tomorrow.

Neil: We'll see.

I put my phone down, a weird sensation in my chest. I had one of those odd feelings, like I could text with Neil for hours, just chatting about random, ordinary stuff.

With him still at the forefront of my mind, I went into my bedroom and opened my laptop. I hadn't had a chance to do a deep dive on Annabelle yet, and there was no time like the present.

I typed her full name "Annabelle Carlino" into the search bar, and she came up right away. Hmm, she was very pretty. I could see why Neil was smitten. Annabelle had long, straight red hair and looked to be medium height. Her feed was of the fitness/inspirational persuasion, with lots of goal-setting quotes and photos of her working out in the gym. The woman had a *fantastic* body, like Ripley from *Aliens*. She and Leanne were similar in that regard. It seemed Neil had a type, and that type was sporty, super buff ladies.

Aside from my fondness for leisurewear, I wasn't buff or sporty at all. I'd always been too lazy to fully embrace regular exercise. Oh, well. At least my joints wouldn't get worn down by the time I was thirty. You had to look on the bright side.

There were a few girlfriends in her pictures, all of them pretty and fit like her. Her profile stated she was a personal trainer, which explained why she was at the gym all the time. I looked up the place where she worked and found it wasn't too far from my flat.

A crazy idea struck.

I could sign-up for a free pass and check her out in the flesh. See what kind of person Miss Annabelle was in real life. I entertained the thought for a few minutes. Annabelle might not be the perfect angel Neil imagined her to be, but

I wasn't going to discover the truth from a selectively curated social media grid. I had to see how she acted in real life. Doing some sleuthing could be fun. Then again, if Neil found out, he'd likely burst the blood vessel I had a knack for getting pumping in his forehead.

Unable to make a clear choice, I decided to sleep on it and decide for certain in the morning.

Neil

I shoved my phone in my pocket, unable to rid the visual of Afric licking my neck from my brain. Where the hell had that come from? Tingles skittered down my back at the imagery. I wasn't sure what was going on with me lately, but somehow the content of our texts had caused my mind to wander to an unexpectedly sexy place.

And now, the image refused to leave.

It had clearly been way too long since I last had sex. Yes, that was why I was suddenly having erotic thoughts about Afric of all people. Not that she wasn't attractive in her own unique way, but she certainly wasn't *my* type.

We'd just reached the pizza place when my phone buzzed. I pulled it out, expecting another teasing message from Afric. Instead, I found a DM from Annabelle.

Hey stranger! How's everything going with filming the new season? I'm so jealous you get to be in New York right now. x.

I scanned the message before doing something I'd never done to her before; I left her on read. I felt awful, but I just couldn't interact with her right now. My head was too messed up, and pretending to be Callum was beginning to take its toll on me. I didn't want to do it anymore, but unfortunately, it was a part of my job. And yes, okay, what

Afric said to me about Annabelle pursuing Callum when he was in a relationship with Leanne had been bothering me a lot. I'd tried reasoning it out, telling myself she might not even know they were together, but the more I thought about it, the more unlikely that explanation seemed.

To be honest, I didn't know how to feel about her anymore.

I decided not to think about the whole thing until I returned to London. There was way too much work to be done over here, and I didn't have the headspace for anything else.

"You okay, Neil?" Leanne asked as she approached me.

I rubbed the back of my neck. "Yeah, I'm just a little tired. Still adjusting to the time difference."

"It's rough, isn't it," she said with a sympathetic smile. "On our last trip, it took forever for my body clock to adjust." She held out a slice of pizza. "Here, I got you a slice with vegan cheese since I know you can't eat dairy."

"Thanks," I replied as I took the slice, touched by her thoughtfulness. I was so hungry I'd intended on eating the normal cheese, but at least this way, I could avoid a sick stomach later tonight.

I sat down at a table for two, and Leanne joined me. The rest of the cast and crew were sitting at tables nearby. We ate in silence for a minute or two before Leanne commented, "I saw you taking pictures of yourself earlier. What was that about? Have you started a new social media feed I'm not aware of or something?"

A small measure of embarrassment pinched at me as I cleared my throat. "No, uh, a friend back home challenged me to take a selfie every day while I'm here and send them to her. She thinks it's a good confidence-building exercise."

Leanne's mouth curved into a smile. "She?"

"Yes, I have a female friend. Is that so shocking?"

"Of course not. Don't be silly. At least now I know the reason why I've caught you grinning at your phone so often lately."

"I haven't been grinning at my phone," I protested.

Leanne threw her hands up. "Okay, my mistake. You weren't grinning. Maybe you were gurning, and I was just standing too far away to tell."

"Funny," I deadpanned.

We ate the rest of our pizza in quiet, but what she said stuck with me. Had I been grinning at my phone? I guess texting with Afric could be kind of amusing sometimes.

When we got back to the hotel, I took a long, hot shower then crawled into bed. The following day was a blur of activity. I barely had a chance to grab a bite to eat, never mind take a selfie for Afric. I was reminded of this when I got back to the hotel, called for some room service, and found a message on my phone.

Afric: It's 10 p.m. here, and still no picture. Have you chickened out on me?

Neil: Work was crazy today. I didn't have time.

Afric: Sounds a lot like an excuse.

Neil: No, seriously. It was mayhem. I'll send you two selfies tomorrow to make up for it.

Afric: Okay, I suppose I can allow for that. I hope you're not working too hard! I'm about to call it a night and watch an episode of North and South before bed.

Neil: North and South?

Afric: It's an old period drama Michaela's been on at me to watch. She swears it's one of her favourites.

Neil: Well, my co-assistant has good taste, so I'm sure it's worth a watch.

Afric: Hey! Why don't you watch it with me? We can sync up our screens on Netflix.

I stared at her text, unsure of how to respond, when there was a knock on my door announcing the arrival of my room service order. I went to grab it, tipped the porter, then set it on the table next to the bed. I pondered Afric's offer again and thought maybe it would be nice to watch a show together, even if it was only virtually. I'd always found hotel rooms particularly lonely. It was one of the main reasons I didn't always enjoy travelling. I picked up my phone and shot off a text.

Neil: Sure. My dinner just arrived, so I need something to watch while I eat anyway.

Afric: Great! Log in to your Netflix account and pull the first episode up. I'll do the same, and then I'll send through a video call link.

I changed into a T-shirt and some lounge pants before getting comfortable on the bed with my food and laptop. A minute later, Afric's video call link came through, and her face appeared on my screen.

"Hey, you!" she said with a smile. "Oh, you look so cosy and tired in that big hotel bed. What are you eating?"

She craned her neck to see what was on my plate, and I couldn't help my small grin. "Just a chicken salad and some potato wedges."

"Is that sweet chili dip?" she asked, eyeing my plate. "I love sweet chili. Great, now I'm hungry. Can you wait a minute while I go grab some snacks?"

I chuckled. "Sure."

A minute or two later, she was back with a bag of Doritos. "Okay, now I'm ready," she said, climbing under her duvet. We made sure to both press play at the exact same moment before settling in to watch the episode. It was one of those BBC period dramas, but I hadn't seen it before. The main character was a woman, Margaret Hale, who had moved from a picturesque country town in the south of England to an industrial town in the north called Milton. She makes the acquaintance of the owner of the local cotton mill, Mr Thornton, and they strike up an antagonistic relationship.

"Okay, I was sceptical at first, but I'm totally into this. Mr Thornton is an absolute ride," Afric said a little while into the episode.

"Mr Thornton is a what?" I asked, bemused.

"He's a ride. It means I'd gladly bang his brains out," she clarified.

I quickly pushed thoughts of Afric banging some actor's brains out from my head. "Isn't he the same guy who plays a dwarf in *The Hobbit*?"

"Yes, and if I were Smaug, he could plunder my treasure cave all night long."

I almost choked on a sip of water. Then I laughed. I laughed so hard it hurt my stomach. Afric was chuckling, too.

"Technically, it was a treasure mountain," I pointed out.

"Even better. He can mount my treasure mountain anytime."

I shook my head, unable to disguise my amusement. "Okay, I need to stop encouraging you. Let's just watch the episode, shall we?" I said once I finally gathered my composure.

"By all means," she said, a smile in her voice.

Later, during a particularly intense scene between Margaret and Mr Thornton, Afric let out a long sigh. "The way he looks at her. I want that," she said longingly.

"I'm not sure people look at each other that way anymore. We're all too busy looking at our phones and laptops," I replied.

"Wouldn't you look at Annabelle that way if you ever met her in person?" she queried.

Her question caused me to stiffen. "I don't know. Maybe."

"I was checking out her pictures on social media today," Afric went on.

I stiffened further. "You were?"

"Don't be so concerned. I wasn't stalking her or anything. I just wanted to get a feel for the kind of person she is. She seems really into health and fitness."

I ran a hand down my face, suddenly feeling more tired than I'd been in a while. "She is. She likes parkour, too. That's why she's so obsessed with the show."

"She's very pretty," Afric said, and if I wasn't mistaken, I sensed there was something else she wanted to say but was holding back.

"You think so?"

"Anyone with a pair of eyeballs can see that she's pretty, Neil."

"I guess you're right," I said, focusing back on the episode and worrying my lip.

"She has that whole slim but muscular look going on. You must be really into that. Leanne has a similar body type," she said.

I frowned, thinking about it. "It's not that I particularly favour it. I developed feelings for Leanne mainly based on her personality and our close friendship. The same goes for Annabelle. Our conversations are what made me start liking her."

"Oh," Afric said, an odd note in her voice. "Well, that's good to know."

It was? Why? I didn't voice the question, and both our attentions quietly drifted back to the episode.

Afric yawned softly when the end credits rolled. "I'm tempted to watch the next part, but I know I'll only end up staying awake all night to watch the whole thing, so I should probably go to sleep."

"We can watch the next episode tomorrow night if you want?" I offered impulsively.

I wasn't sure why, but I'd really enjoyed this. Just virtually spending time with someone instead of sitting alone in my hotel room was surprisingly pleasant.

She granted me a pleased smile. "Seriously? I'd love that. Okay, I'll call you around the same time tomorrow. Will you be free?"

"I should be."

"Great. Talk to you then."

"Goodnight, Afric."

"'Night, Neil."

With that, we ended our video call, and I lay back in bed, staring at the ceiling. I had a long day of work ahead of me tomorrow, but knowing that I'd get to watch *North and South* with Afric at the end of it oddly made the prospect far more bearable.

Afric

Neil was going to murder me if he ever found out about this. Well, it was a good thing I didn't plan on telling him. I'd followed the devil on my shoulder and decided to hell with it. I had a free afternoon, and I was going to do a little reconnaissance.

It had been easy enough to sign up for a free pass at the gym where Annabelle worked. The trouble was, I'd had to endure a one on one with a personal trainer named Derek and explain my health and fitness goals to him. I was a little disappointed I hadn't been assigned to Annabelle. That way, I could've really picked her brain.

I'd given Derek some made-up spiel about wanting to lose a stone, and he'd drawn up a workout plan for me. He was so nice that I felt a little bit guilty for wasting his time and was actually considering joining the gym now.

What? They had a competitive yearly rate, and to be honest, I could do with getting into shape. My sedentary lifestyle was starting to affect my ability to climb the stairs to my flat these days. Huffing and puffing up several flights of stairs was not a good look, at least not at my age.

Once Derek released me to explore the gym on my own, I wandered from section to section until I spotted Annabelle standing with another of the personal trainers next to a row of elliptical machines.

I took a sip from my complimentary water bottle and eyed her while stepping onto a nearby treadmill. I was too far away to hear what she was saying to her co-worker, but I didn't want to risk getting too close and arousing suspicion. I set the treadmill to a medium speed and started a slow jog. I figured I might as well get a workout in while I was here.

After a few minutes, two middle-aged women entered the elliptical area, each climbing onto a machine. They chatted as they began exercising, both a little overweight. My attention went to Annabelle as she whispered something to her co-worker, a tall, muscular guy in a sleeveless shirt that displayed his gun show, which I guess was the point.

I narrowed my gaze, suspecting they were making fun of the two women in some way by their grins and conspiratorial whispers. Thankfully, the women were oblivious to whatever was being said about them, too busy chatting away as they exercised.

A small brick settled in my stomach. I mean, I could've been wrong. Annabelle and Mr Muscles could've been talking about something else entirely, but my gut told me otherwise.

I'd come here hoping to assuage my misgivings, but all I'd managed to do was make those misgivings even worse. I hadn't known Neil long, but he was such a cutie pie, and I felt protective of him. He was my adorable little Clark Kent, and I suddenly couldn't stand the thought of Annabelle getting her claws into him.

I was having, shall we say, nefarious thoughts.

Nefarious thoughts that were urging me to ensure Neil and Annabelle never met at all.

I'd find him a nice girl. Someone worthy of him. After all, I knew lots of great gamer ladies online who would eat Neil right up like a scoop of double chocolate chip ice cream with sprinkles on top. If she didn't live an ocean away, I might've even considered introducing him to Yellowshoes. My girl was beautiful and had a cracking sense of humour.

Annabelle and Mr Muscles left, and I wound things down on the treadmill. I wiped down the machine, dabbed the sweat from my brow, and took a long gulp of water. I walked by the two ladies on the ellipticals, gave them a wink, and told them they were looking fab. They both chuckled and shook their heads at me as I headed for the showers.

I was on the bus on my way home when two new messages came in from Neil. The first showed him standing with the Statue of Liberty behind him. The second was him on Fifth Avenue, surrounded by pedestrians, the road full of those recognisable yellow taxis.

Looking good, I replied.

I never realised the skill required to take a decent selfie, especially in a city as crowded as this one, he sent back.

You'll be a pro by the time your trip is over, I promised.

Later that night, I ordered Thai food in preparation for my video call with Neil. I changed into my PJs and had everything set up before I sent him a text.

Afric: I'm about to call you!

Neil: Go ahead. I'm ready.

I grinned as I sent through the call. Seriously, I loved this new arrangement. I enjoyed annoying him by swooning over Mr Thornton and making lewd comments about what I'd let him do to me.

The call connected and Neil appeared on my screen. He wore a long-sleeved T-shirt, his hair a little rumpled, eyes tired. From what Michaela had told me, their work trips tended to be very demanding. Neil was likely exhausted after a long day running around after all those reality TV stars.

"Hey!" I said. "What did you order from room service today? Inquiring minds would like to know."

He held up his plate to show me. "I treated myself to a steak. Callum fell off a wall this morning and almost broke his ankle. Luckily, we just needed to ice it, and the swelling went down, but he gave us a scare there for a minute."

"Sounds stressful. You feeling okay?"

"I'm fine. Nothing a good night's sleep won't cure."

"Well, I decided to delay my dinner so that we could eat together. I ordered Thai green curry."

"Perfect. Shall we start the episode? I'm oddly curious to see what Miss Hale and Mr Thornton get up to next," Neil said.

"Let's do it," I replied with a grin.

We ate quietly and watched the episode for about ten minutes before I said, "You know, I have this online friend. She lives in Surrey, I think. Her name's Alice. Pretty sure she works in IT, but she's also a huge *Greenforest* gamer. She's a redhead, too, if that's what you're into."

"If that's what I'm …" Neil said, sounding like he'd only been half-listening. Somehow, I felt like he was even more into *North and South* than I was, which only caused the fondness I already felt for him to expand.

"I just feel like you should widen your horizons," I went on. "You know, Annabelle's not the only woman in the world."

He let out a heavy sigh. I had our call minimized, but I saw him run a hand down his face in the tiny square in the corner of my screen. "So, this is your angle now," he said.

"What angle?" I asked, feigning innocence. "I don't have an angle."

"You've set your mind against Annabelle and are now trying to interest me in this Alice person as a distraction."

"Neil, I'm only looking out for you—"

"Well, you don't need to. I'm perfectly capable of looking out for myself."

"Are you, though?"

"What's that supposed to mean?"

I blew out a heavy breath, nerves building. I hadn't intended on telling Neil about my visit to Annabelle's gym, but maybe he needed to hear it. Maybe he needed a cold splash of reality. "Pause the episode for a second. I need to tell you something."

Neil frowned and did as I requested. I paused the episode, too, then sent him an anxious look through the screen. "What's going on? Why do you have that weird look on your face?"

I bit my lip, then blurted, "I did a bad thing."

"What did you do?"

"Remember how I mentioned checking out Annabelle's social media?" I asked, tucking some hair behind my ear. Neil nodded. "Well, I noticed she works at a gym that's only a ten-minute bus journey from my flat. So, I thought I'd go check her out in person."

Neil stared at me, eyes wide with horror. "Please tell me you didn't talk to her."

"Of course, I didn't talk to her. I merely observed."

At this, he seemed to relax a little, but he still looked perturbed. "And what did you observe?"

"Not a lot, honestly."

"Okay, well, please don't ever do that again," Neil said, exhaling in relief.

"It's just that—"

Neil's eyes flashed to mine. "What?"

"I may have seen her and one of her co-workers making fun of two overweight women while they were working out. I'm not one-hundred percent certain, but it seemed like Annabelle was laughing at them."

His frown returned. "I can't imagine Annabelle doing something like that."

"Yes, but you hardly know her, not in person. For all you know, she could be the one catfishing you into believing she's a nice lady when in reality she's the type who—"

"Can we not talk about this until I get back to London?" Neil interrupted gruffly, and I fell silent. "I just want to enjoy watching this show with you because honestly, I've been looking forward to it all day. Let's leave Annabelle out of the conversation for the time being."

"Oh." I was taken aback, blinking as I asked, "You've really been looking forward to this all day?"

Neil sighed again. "Yes, I have. It's come as a great surprise to me, but I actually enjoy your company, Afric."

I fell silent again. I had no words, which was a rare occurrence for me. A warm, tingling sensation took up residence in my chest. Finally, I whispered, "Neil."

"Yes?"

"I enjoy your company, too." A pause. "And I'm sorry for spying on Annabelle. I won't do it again."

In the small square in the corner of my screen, I saw his lips twitch in a smile. "I'm glad to hear it." A pause. "Now, can you be quiet? I'm about to press play, and I'm sick of you talking through all the good bits."

I chuckled, making a show of zipping my lips before setting my empty plate aside, burrowing under the covers, and hitting play at the same moment Neil did.

8.
Neil

"What?! It can't just end there," Afric exclaimed.

"What do you mean?" I asked.

She threw her hands up into the air. "I mean, after all that longing, I thought they'd at least give us a decent sex scene. I feel like writing a strongly worded letter to the BBC."

"Their period dramas aren't exactly known for having graphic sex," I pointed out, mildly amused. Afric and I had just finished watching the final episode of *North and South,* and she wasn't impressed with the ending.

"True, but I still think it's ridiculous that all we get is a kiss. I feel short-changed. My flatmate, Sarita, and I binge-watched *Bridgerton* at Christmas, and I'm telling ya, they didn't pull any punches. Neil, your glasses would've fogged up at the absolute *raunchiness.*"

I smiled in bemusement. "Well, sadly for you, this isn't *Bridgerton.*"

"You can say that again!"

"You're surprisingly worked up about this. It might've been just a kiss, but don't you think it was still a very romantic one?" I asked.

"Well, sure, it was romantic, though personally, I've never been big into kissing."

I furrowed my brow. "Seriously?"

Afric shrugged. "It just doesn't float my boat."

I was perplexed. "But ... when you're with someone, what do you do? Just ... avoid their mouth?"

"Pretty much. I mean, if push comes to shove, I'll endure a kiss, but my preference is not to do it at all."

"That is so bizarre," I said, shaking my head at her. *And her lips were far too pretty not to be kissed.* I pushed away the errant thought, no idea where it had come from.

"It really isn't. Some people don't like chocolate cake. I don't like kissing."

"So, you'll let a man put his penis in you, but you won't let him kiss you?" I blurted, then instantly regretted it when I saw the mischievous glint in her eye.

"Say 'put his penis in you' again," she encouraged. "That was rather sensual."

I felt warmth heat my cheeks. "I'm being serious. Why don't you like kissing?" I was unexpectedly bothered by her preference, and some part of me needed to get to the bottom of it.

"I don't get why you're so shocked. It really isn't a big deal."

I was stumped as to the reason, too. But I simply couldn't abide by her not liking kissing. It was one of life's true pleasures, especially when you found someone you shared a connection with. The first kiss had the potential to be mind-blowing.

"What about when you're in a relationship? Do you like kissing then?" I went on.

"I don't do relationships. Not anymore."

"You don't? But what about Dev?"

"Dev was the last straw. I'm sick of being broken up with all the time. It's obvious I'm just not suited to being in a couple."

"Just because you were dumped doesn't mean you should completely write-off relationships," I countered. I was no stranger to being dumped myself.

"Right, but what if every single relationship you'd ever been in ended with your partner breaking things off, never the other way around? Whether it's the fact that I game for a living, or I talk too much, or I don't dress sexy enough, men get tired of me after a while and decide to move on. I'm not the sort of person people want to deal with long-term, and I honestly can't blame them. I can be a lot sometimes. Don't deny it because I know you thought the same thing about me when we first met. Anyway, now I just find someone to satisfy my sexual needs when the urge arises instead of getting into relationships. It's a whole lot easier."

I stared at her face on the screen, then blinked. "Afric, that's—"

"Kinda mercenary, I know, but it suits me."

"That's not what I was going to say. I was going to say that if the men you're with don't stick around, then that's on them, not you. It doesn't mean you'll never find someone who wants to spend forever with you. It just means you need to keep looking."

"But looking is so time-consuming," she complained.

"Everything worthwhile in life is time-consuming."

"Well, I'd much rather spend my time at home playing computer games than going out on bad first dates and suffering through boring, stilted or awkward conversations."

"Okay, you have a point about first dates. I'm not a fan of them either." I wanted to quiz her further on her dislike of kissing, but I didn't want to come across obsessed. And sure, random hookups could fulfil a sexual need, but what about her emotional needs? One of the biggest reasons people entered into couples was for the emotional connection and companionship. And I knew she was lying when she said she wasn't suited to being in a couple. Obviously, it was something she longed for deep down.

She wouldn't have expressed her desire for someone to look at her how Mr Thornton looked at Margaret Hale if she didn't. She simply wasn't admitting it to herself.

"I bet you're adorable on first dates," Afric said, distracting me from my train of thought. "Do you show up in a shirt and tie, brandishing a bunch of flowers?"

"There's nothing wrong with trying to make a good impression," I said defensively because that was *exactly* how I showed up to first dates.

"I wasn't being critical. I love how smart you always look. You're so ..." she trailed off, pausing as she thought about it. "Clean."

I shot her an incredulous look through the screen. "Clean?"

"Yes. It's a compliment. You never look scruffy." She gave a self-deprecating laugh. "I, on the other hand, am always scruffy. And my room is always a mess. I bet your bedroom is neat as a pin."

It was, but I didn't admit it. "You're not scruffy. You're just a little chaotic. But I like chaos. I like getting the chance to turn it into order."

"Oh, you don't have to tell me. I swear you almost jizzed in your pants the first time you saw my haphazard pile of bank statements," she said, cackling.

My shoulders stiffened. "I did not ... almost do what you just said I almost did. I merely enjoy organisation. It's not a crime."

"Never said it was, Neilio. Never said it was."

"Please don't start calling me Neilio."

"Too late. I'm already taken with it," she replied with her usual cheeky grin. "Anyway, it's late here, so I better log off. I was thinking of watching the first episode of *Sanditon* tomorrow? Care to join?"

"Okay, but you can't complain if there isn't any softcore porn involved," I said, and Afric gave another cackle.

"I'll make no promises, Neilio. There's a good chance I'll complain, and you'll just have to sit back and endure it." With that, she ended the call before I could tell her to quit calling me Neilio again.

I slid my laptop onto the nightstand and lay back, unable to stop thinking about the fact that Afric didn't like to kiss. I wondered if it was a phobia or a germs thing. She had mentioned that she liked how clean I always was. Then I considered that it could be due to a bad experience and my jaw clenched instinctively. Had someone forced themselves on her? Had she gone through something awful and was now forever traumatised by the experience? For some reason, I really wanted to get to the bottom of her strange aversion.

Turning over, I clicked off the lamp and closed my eyes. Afric's pretty lips and cute smile filled my mind as I drifted off to sleep.

Afric

It was only three p.m., and I was already impatient for my nightly video call with Neil. I'd just finished up streaming for the day and decided to go out and treat myself to some sushi at my usual haunt. Instead of taking the bus or a taxi, I decided to stretch my legs and walk since the weather was decent. I could always do with getting a little extra vitamin D since I spent way too much time indoors.

I stopped by my mailbox on my way out of the building and found several bills and one or two items addressed to Sarita. I was busy sorting through them and sticking them in my bag when a familiar raucous laugh caught my attention.

"I'm telling ya, those nuns are like bloodhounds," the familiar voice proclaimed. "I took a girl from St. Mary's to her Debs last week, and this one nun got all up in my face when we were dancing. She told me to leave room for Jesus. I tried to explain to her the ridiculousness of the statement. Jesus is an important man. He has far better things to be doing with his time than making sure I keep a respectable distance from the girl enthusiastically backing her arse up against me on the dancefloor."

I smiled wide as I turned around, beaming as I took in the sight of my younger brother, Billy. His curly hair was an unruly mop, and his hazel eyes shone bright with mischief. He'd teased that he might come for a visit, but I hadn't expected him to turn up so soon. The only luggage he had was a backpack slung over his shoulder.

Billy's eyes caught mine, and he smiled right back, his phone held to his ear.

"Listen, bud, I better go. I'm visiting my sister in London. Yeah, I'll give you a call as soon as I'm back home."

He hung up and slid his phone in his pocket before opening his arms wide. I dove right into them, and he swung me around with a chuckle. "You came to visit!" I said in delight when he let me go.

"I told you to keep an eye out for me, didn't I?"

"Yes, you did, and I'm so happy you're here. How long are you staying for?"

"Not sure yet. I only bought a one-way ticket. You know me, I like to play it fast and loose."

"And it's why I love you. I was just heading out to grab something to eat."

"Perfect timing. I literally stepped off the plane an hour ago, and I'm famished."

With that, I grinned then gave him a clip round the ear.

"Hey!" Billy exclaimed. "What was that for?"

"That was for giving cheek to a nun. Have a little respect."

"She was the one who started it. I was only defending myself!"

I shook my head at him. These antics were typical of Billy. "I can't believe some silly girl was crazy enough to ask you to escort her to a dance in the first place," I said in mild amusement. "That's just asking for trouble."

"It was Anne-Marie O'Dwyer from around the way. Remember her?"

"Yes, I do. I didn't think she was your type."

"She's not really, but I was bored enough to accept the invitation."

"Maybe you should focus on girls your own age."

"She's nineteen, and I'm twenty-three. I'm hardly out snatching cradles."

"Still, I think you need an older woman. Someone with enough spirit to handle your wildness and keep you on the straight and narrow."

"The Straight and Narrow is what they've started calling the alley at the back of Hennessy's pub," Billy countered. "Couples do be riding in that alley like the clappers on a Saturday night, so if that's the sort of place you think I should be frequenting—"

"Don't be cute," I interrupted. "You know what I meant."

"I do, but it's far more fun to be wilfully obtuse."

I shook my head at him, grinning as I replied, "They should've called it Pump Alley instead."

Billy gave a hoot of laughter as we reached the restaurant, pulling open the door before motioning me in. We managed to snag my favourite table by the window, and I realised it was the exact same spot where I shared that first lunch with Neil and Michaela. I thought about our discussion last night. I'd been in high spirits complaining about the lack of a sex scene in *North and South* when I'd blurted out my dislike of kissing and history of break-ups. It wasn't something I generally went around telling people, mainly because it was none of their business. But the more I thought about the way Neil had looked at me with a mixture of surprise and sympathy, the more I regretted my confession.

I didn't want him feeling sorry for me because there was nothing to feel sorry about. It wasn't that I'd always hated kissing; experiences had simply moulded me in such a way that my stomach now turned at the idea of locking lips with anyone. I wasn't traumatised, okay? I just didn't enjoy it. I could still have a full and active sex life minus the kissing.

"So," I said to Billy after we'd both given our orders to the waiter. "How's everyone back home? It's been a while since I last chatted with Mam and Dad on the phone."

"Hmm, let me see," Billy replied, rubbing his chin. "Ryan's busy with the wife and kids, as per usual. Maura works every hour God sends. Sharon and her partner just got approved for a mortgage. Patrick is still single and living his best bachelor life. The twins' restaurant is doing well, and as you know, Helen is still at home with Mam and Dad. I'm not sure she'll ever move out, but they like having her there all the same."

"Well, if she's happy and they're happy, then there isn't really anything wrong with it," I said, thinking of my older sister. She was twenty-seven and suffered from severe anxiety, which meant she'd shied away from many of life's milestones in favour of staying at home with our parents. She found solace in the repetition of the familiar, and that was fine by me. Whatever keeps you sane.

"And what about you? Where have you been living? Have you been working at all?" I asked, bringing my attention back to Billy.

"Ah, you know me. I'm a piece of driftwood floating down the stream," he replied, making flowing motions with his hands. "I go where life's crazy path decides to take me. I did a stint at Electric Picnic over the summer, but right now, I'm in between gigs."

I pursed my lips, studying him more closely. "So, you aren't living anywhere in particular?"

"I've been sleeping on friends' couches mostly. But sure, it's grand. I always have a room at Mam and Dad's that I can go back to if worse comes to worst."

"You can't couch surf forever, though. Why don't you think about moving over here? We can find you a job and a room to rent. It'll be great. That way, we can see each other all the time." It'd also give me the chance to keep an eye on him. Billy had a reckless streak, and the rest of my family were often too busy with their own lives to realise when he needed help.

"You know, that doesn't sound half bad. I do love this city."

"London's a great place to live. There's always something happening here. I think you'd fit right in."

"Okay, I'll think about it," Billy agreed just as our food arrived. He dug into his sushi rolls while I was distracted by my phone vibrating with a message.

I opened it up, my mouth shaping into a smile when I saw Neil had sent another selfie. It appeared to have been taken next to the steps leading down into a subway station. Neil smiled confidently into the camera, and for a second, something warm and fuzzy filled my chest. He looked so … well, he looked *hot* in a professional, office clerk sort of way. Neil wore his usual buttoned-up shirt and glasses, but there was something in his eyes, a comfort in his own skin that wasn't always present.

I only got glimpses of it from time to time, like when that bloke bumped into me outside the gaming sphere and he'd chased him down. Or later, when he'd slid his arm around my waist and confidently informed Dev he'd been keeping me busy. The memory sent a rush of butterflies through me.

I typed out a reply.

Afric: Wow, you really knocked it out of the park with that one, Neil. Seriously, I have no notes.

Afric: NO NOTES.

Neil: Honestly? This isn't some elaborate ruse to lull me into a false sense of confidence before you tear me down?

Afric: I promise there's no ruse. You look great! I'm a proud mama bear.

I hit send before I had the chance to read it back. Oh, God … Did I really just type … "mama bear?" Who says that? I spent several moments freaking out before I snapped myself out of it. I wasn't the type to second guess myself. And it wasn't like I was texting someone who'd sneer at me. This was just Neil. I'd spent the last few nights in my PJs stuffing my face in front of my laptop screen with him while watching a period romance.

Neil: Pretty sure that's not possible since I'm several years older than you ;-)

I chewed my lip, deciding to double down instead of admitting embarrassment.

Afric: It is possible. I birthed you from an insecure little babe into the confident selfie-taking professional you are today.

Neil: The image of you birthing me has left me feeling rather uncomfortable ...

I grinned as I read this message.

Afric: Stop picturing it then, ya big perv!

Neil: You're the one who created the picture in the first place!

Afric: I planted the idea. You're the one who took the time to visualise it.

Neil: This is such a weird conversation.

Afric: I know. And you're welcome.

Afric: And I meant what I said. It's a great photo of you :-)

Neil: Thanks. I'm glad my selfie-taking has finally passed muster.

"What are you smiling about?" Billy questioned. "More to the point, who are you texting with?"

I put my phone down and glanced at my brother. "I'm texting my friend, Neil. He's in New York at the moment for work."

Billy tilted his head. "Neil? Neil? I don't recall you mentioning a Neil before."

"He's a new friend," I said as I plucked up a sushi roll before dipping it in some soy sauce.

Billy waggled his eyebrows. "A special friend?"

I smirked. "No, he's just a regular friend. But I love talking to him. He's so prim and proper, so easy to rile. I have great fun teasing him."

"Interesting," Billy said with a knowing little smile.

"What's interesting?"

"You fancy him."

"No, I don't," I said, then paused to think about it. "Well, I do think he's cute and handsome, but not in a way that makes me want to jump into bed with him. Besides, he's besotted with this bitch called Annabelle, so—"

"A *bitch* called Annabelle," Billy mused. "It gets better. You definitely fancy him."

"I haven't finished talking, have I? I called her a bitch because she works in a gym and makes fun of overweight people when they're working out. I went to her gym on one of those free day passes and saw her doing it with my own two eyes."

Billy laughed loudly. "My god, you have it bad. What were you playing at going to her place of work? Were you spying?"

"Well, yes, but it's not what you think. You know my friend Michaela who works for the *Running on Air* TV show?"

Billy nodded, still with that annoying smile on his face.

"Neil and Michaela work together. That's how I met him. At first, he found me annoying and I found him dull, but when we got to know each other better, we both changed our minds. Well, I changed my mind. Neil might still find me annoying, but he suffers it because I'm helping him out."

"How are you helping him?"

"I'm helping him to become more confident, and that has a lot to do with Annabelle. I can't tell you all the details because it's Neil's business, but Annabelle doesn't actually know Neil's true identity. He's been catfishing her. I promised him I'd help him come clean to Annabelle, but the more I learn about her, the more I don't think she's right for him."

"Are you sure this Neil fella's a good bloke? Catfishing is a bit shady, especially in this day and age."

"Like I said, I can't tell you all the details, but if you knew how it all came about, you'd actually feel sorry for him. He didn't intentionally set out to catfish her. It's complicated. And I think he was a little lonely at the time. But the person he's pretending to be is the exact opposite of Neil, which makes things even worse. If Annabelle is the vain, narcissistic type I suspect she is, then she could break Neil's heart when she sees the real him."

Billy took a sip of his drink. "Poor bloke."

"I have a plan, though. I'm going to try and set him up with someone else before he ever gets the chance to meet Annabelle."

Billy's smirk re-emerged. "And would this someone else happen to be you?"

I rolled my eyes. "No, I'm not setting him up with me. I already told you I don't fancy him. I'm going to find him a nice, kind, pretty lady. Someone who will appreciate what a gem he is."

"Sure, sure," Billy said, clearly not believing me for a second.

I frowned as I focused on my food. Did I fancy Neil? Was that why I felt so passionate about keeping him away from Annabelle? I mean, I did think he was handsome, and as had already been established, he had a *fantastic* backside that I enjoyed ogling. But it wasn't just how he looked. I liked Neil's personality on a fundamental level. I looked forward to talking to him at the end of each day, hearing his opinions and takes on things, and arguing with him when I disagreed.

Even sitting here now, it was hours until our video call, and I was already wishing those hours away. Had chatting and watching period dramas with Neil somehow become the highlight of my day?

Ah, hell, maybe Billy was onto something after all.

9.
Neil

A soft, delicate hand ran down my bare stomach, and my gut swam with desire. She laughed softly, and it vibrated through me, lighting me up from the inside out. Her hand went lower, taking me fully into her grasp. I turned over, and a flash of blue hair filled my vision. I threw my head back as she fisted me, pumping once, twice …

When I glanced at her again, her hair was no longer blue, but blonde, and now she was lowering herself down my body, tugging at the waistband of my jeans …

I woke on a gasp, blinking at the clock on the bedside dresser. It read 6:07 a.m. My alarm normally went off at 6:30 a.m., but I'd woken early, probably due to the intensity of the dream I'd just had. One part of me wished to go back to it, but another part wished to avoid it altogether. The woman in my dream had held a striking resemblance to …

No, I refused to delve too deeply into whatever that meant. It was just a silly dream. Nothing to be concerned about.

Climbing out of bed, I headed straight for the shower, setting the water temperature to slightly cooler than normal. It did the trick to temper the heat that had been burning under the surface of my skin. Once out of the shower, I dressed, checked my agenda for the day, then set off to start work. I had a busy schedule to contend with, but I welcomed it since it allowed me to avoid analysing my unexpectedly erotic dream.

Later on, I'd just finished grabbing lunches for the cast when my phone rang with a call from my sister. "Hello, Rosie," I answered.

"Hey, thought I'd give you a bell, check how things are going over there," she replied.

"Things are good. The filming is on schedule, and no one's managed to injure themselves too badly so far," I said before taking a sip from my coffee as I leaned back against a wall. I'd been on my feet all day, and this was the first chance I'd had to grab some caffeine.

"That's great to hear. I'm at work, too. We're just about to close up for the day," Rosie said. "I'm nervous because I had the wild idea to set up a book club and the first meeting is later this week. I'm worried nobody will turn up."

"I'm sure people will show. Book clubs are hugely popular these days," I said to reassure her. "What book are you going to be discussing?"

I heard Rosie blow out a breath on the other end of the line. "*Eleanor Oliphant is Completely Fine*. Do you think it's too quirky for a first pick?"

"No way. That's a great book and it has a fantastic twist. People love twists. You chose well."

"I hope so. The head librarian, Noleen, will be only too thrilled to shove the failure in my face if it isn't a success."

"I didn't realise working in a library could be so cutthroat," I said just as I spotted Callum headed my way.

Rosie sighed. "You have no idea. Listen, I better go, but I'll call again later in the week. Grandma's been wanting me to set up a video call. She misses you. She always does whenever you have to travel for work."

"Well, tell her I miss her, too. And let me know when you want to do the video call. I'll make sure I'm available."

"Will do! Talk soon," Rosie said.

I hung up just as Callum reached me. He had sunglasses on, so I couldn't tell what kind of mood he was in. We were currently camped out in one of the many city parks we'd been filming in. Right now, everybody was having lunch, though Callum was always the fastest eater of the bunch.

"Neil, I was hoping to have a word with you," he said, and my stomach lurched. A sense of dread set in as I imagined he'd discovered my online relationship with Annabelle and was about to tell me I was fired.

"Oh?" I replied, reaching up to nervously tug at my shirt collar. "What about?"

"Mine and Leanne's anniversary is coming up, and I was hoping you could help me plan something special," he said, and just like that, relief flooded me.

I set my coffee down and pulled out my tablet, all business as I started searching for the best-rated restaurants in the city. "Right, yes, I'd be happy to. What did you have in mind?"

Callum eyed me a moment, pushing his sunglasses down to pierce me with his bright green stare. "You okay, mate? You seem a little tetchy."

I tried to affect a casual demeanour as I cast him a quick glance before returning my attention to the tablet. "I'm perfectly fine. Now, there are some Michelin star restaurants that come highly recommended—"

"Don't change the subject. You're not fine, I can tell. Come on now. You can talk to me. We're friends, right?"

"Technically, you're my employer."

"But you've worked for me for years. You've worked for all of us for years. We consider you a part of the gang, a part of the family even."

Something about what he said caused a sharp stab of guilt in my middle. "That's very kind of you to say, but this is still my job." And I definitely didn't deserve his friendship, not after what I'd done.

"Is this about Leanne?" Callum questioned abruptly, and I tensed.

"What do you mean?"

"I know you used to have a thing for her, and I know I was kind of a dick about it at the time, but it's all water under the bridge as far as I'm concerned."

"It's not about that," I said, shaking my head.

"But it is about something?" Callum countered, and I realised I'd just inadvertently dug myself a hole.

"It's a personal matter. Nothing you need to be concerned about."

At this, Callum threw his arm around my shoulders and led me over to sit on the bench a few yards away. "Did I not just say we were family? Come on, Neil. You can trust me. You work for me, but I also consider you one of my closest friends."

My eyebrows shot up. "You do?"

Callum barked a laugh. "Bloody hell. Maybe I should be offended that you sound so surprised."

"I just didn't think you thought of me in that way."

"Course I do! You're one of the most trustworthy people I know. Why else would I let you run all my online accounts for me?"

Again, the guilt stabbed. Only this time, it hurt more. I wondered briefly if a person could die from the sheer weight of the guilt they carried. "Right, yes. Actually, about that. I'm not sure if I'm—"

"Ah, I know it's a pain in the arse, but if it were left to me, none of it would ever get done. I'm shite at all that social media stuff. Don't have the attention span for it at all."

"It's really not very complicated," I said.

Callum grinned. "Call me lazy then. So, you're really not going tell me what's bothering you?"

I considered opening up to him. Not about the Annabelle stuff, but about the things that were frying my nerves in general. Mainly, there was the fact that I'd had a sex dream last night that had completely thrown me for a loop. Sure, my view of the woman in my dream had been hazy, but her hair was telling. There was only one blonde woman who also used to have blue hair in my life right now. The idea that I was having sex dreams about Afric left me more than a little discombobulated. She was too young for me, too out there, her personality too loud and boisterous. Basically, we were chalk and cheese. It would never work. Not that she'd ever be interested.

"What's the longest you've ever gone without sex?" I blurted, and Callum's grin widened.

"Ah, so that's why you're tense. I get it," he said, rubbing his chin. "Let me see. I'm not sure I've ever counted the months, but there were definitely some long stretches when Leanne and I were on the outs. Why? How long's it been for you?"

I winced as I replied, "Over two years."

Callum let out a low whistle. "Fuck, mate, that's rough."

"Yes … It's been quite rough," I agreed, though it wasn't the end of the world. It wasn't like a person could die from lack of sex.

"Just you and your hand for two whole years. Poor bastard," Callum went on in commiseration.

I chuckled self-consciously. "Make me feel better about it, why don't you."

"Sorry, sorry, I just feel your pain, you know? Hey, how about I take you out tonight? It's been a long while since I've been anyone's wingman. I'll ask Paul to come, too. He's the last of the group who's still single since Isaac's been seeing a girl back in London."

"Oh, you don't need to do that," I said. I was trying my best to be polite because, honestly, the thought of Callum Davidson being my wingman was too painful to think about. No woman would even bother to look at me with him by my side.

"I want to do it. You're the backbone of our group," Callum said. "We'd all be lost without you. It's about time I did something for you for once."

Yet, again, the blade of guilt slid deep. If Callum had a clue of what a piece of shit I really was, he wouldn't be making this offer. He'd probably break my jaw if he knew, and I'd probably deserve it.

"Seriously, we've still got the afternoon shoot to contend with. You're going to be exhausted by tonight. I doubt you'll have the energy to go out."

"You let me worry about that," Callum said as he stood. "I'll meet you in the hotel lobby at eight."

With that, he went, and I was left sitting there, dreading whatever the night had in store.

Afric

It was just after seven p.m. when my phone rang. Billy was taking a nap on the couch while I gamed in my bedroom. Quickly logging off, I glanced at the screen and spotted Neil's name. My lips formed a grin.

Would you look at me? Grinning just because Neil was calling me. It had crept up on me, but I'd obviously developed a little bit of a crush on him. It wasn't a big deal. I had crushes on people all the time. I'd just about gotten over my obsession with Michael Sheen.

What? He had a cheeky smile and a smashing personality.

"To what do I owe the pleasure of a phone call at this hour?" I answered. With the time difference, Neil was probably still in the middle of his workday.

"Hey, I just wanted to let you know that I can't make our video call tonight," he said reluctantly.

Just like that, disappointment set in. I'd been looking forward to our call all day. "Oh? Is everything all right?"

"Everything's fine. Something just came up."

"What came up?"

There was silence on his end for a moment before he replied, his voice tight, "Callum and Paul are taking me for a lads' night out in the city."

I noted the weariness in his voice. "Well, that's going to be a boatload of fun. Why do you sound so stressed about it?"

I heard him exhale a heavy breath. "Callum's gotten this idea in his head that he's going to be my wingman. Sometimes I wonder if he has any clue what he actually looks like."

I barked a laugh. "Callum Davidson knows exactly what he looks like. I can't count the number of times he's been conveniently topless on *Running on Air*."

"Right, well, either way, it's going to be a disaster. Any woman I try to talk to will only be interested in him."

My smile vanished as my eyebrows drew into a frown. "If that's the case, then none of them have an ounce of taste. You're a catch, Neil. When are you ever going to realise that?"

"You think I'm a catch?" he asked, sounding surprised.

"Of course I do. You've got a steady job, your own flat, a smart dress sense and impeccable personal hygiene. You're organised, reliable, and kind. Need I go on?"

"You're forgetting that I'm also stiff, uptight and a little bit awkward," he argued.

"Oh hush. You're only stiff and awkward when you're uncomfortable. Once people get to know you, you're great. I can personally vouch for that."

"That's very kind of you to say, but it's not that simple."

"Why isn't it?"

"Well, for a start, you're not like most women."

"Hey!"

"It's not a criticism. I think it's wonderful how you see the world. You don't dismiss people because of their imperfections. In fact, you seem to enjoy people far more because they're imperfect. But in my experience, the women I meet in bars are looking for tall, dark, and handsome men with six-figure salaries."

I was shaking my head as I listened to him. "I disagree. I think that a lot of women *think* they want tall, dark, handsome, and rich. And sure, money can help make life more comfortable, but what they really want is a man who's kind, a man who listens and is genuinely interested in who they are, a man who cares about their happiness and wellbeing. That's you, Neil," I said, feeling somewhat breathless at my declaration. "You are the ideal catch for the person who actually takes the time to look beneath the surface."

He didn't say anything for several seconds, and I started to worry I'd said too much, revealed something I hadn't meant to reveal. But then Neil spoke, "I can't believe I'm saying this, but the world would be a better place if it had more people like you in it, Afric."

A smile graced my lips as I lifted my chin. "That's very true."

He laughed softly, and I loved the sound. "How are you? I hope you don't mind me cancelling our call tonight."

"Not at all," I lied. "And I'm fine, really good, actually. My brother Billy is visiting. Currently, he's taking a nap and snoring his head off on my couch. He said the flight took a lot out of him. I told him if a one-hour flight takes a lot out of him, then he's not going to last long in this world," I paused to laugh. "Speaking of siblings, how's Rosie? I think I spotted her commenting on my live stream the other day. She wouldn't happen to be a librarian, would she?"

"Yes, she's a trainee librarian. I actually had a call with her earlier. She's been fretting about this new book club she's hosting at the library where she works. She's worried nobody's going to show up."

"Well, Billy and I can go if you like?" I offered impulsively. "Fill out the numbers. Plus, Billy can talk for Ireland, so he'll be only too happy to fill any awkward silences."

"Seriously? You'd do that for Rosie?"

I'd do it for you. I also couldn't resist the chance to meet Neil's sister in person and quiz her about her brother.

"Sure, I haven't got anything else on this week, and I do love a good book discussion. Send me all the details, and I'll be there."

"Rosie might faint if you show up. She's such a fan of yours."

"If she faints, I'll make sure to catch her," I said with a chuckle.

Neil laughed again, and again, I loved the sound of it. "Right, well, I'll give her a heads up that you're planning on going. Hopefully, that way, we'll be able to avoid any fainting."

"Hopefully. Good luck with your lads' night," I said, though somewhere deep down, I didn't entirely mean it. The idea of Neil hooking up with a random woman didn't sit well with me at all. God, I really needed to get a handle on this silly crush. Maybe if he'd quit being so adorably self-deprecating, I could manage it.

"Thanks," he said, a hint of foreboding in his voice. "I need all the luck I can get."

Neil

The bar Callum selected was too loud, too busy, and far too stylish for my liking. I would've much preferred a quiet little pub somewhere, but Cal insisted I'd have a better chance of meeting someone in a place like this.

Actually, if I were being honest, I'd much rather be back in my hotel room video chatting with Afric.

"Can you get your head in the game?" Callum asked, nudging me with his elbow where we sat by the bar drinking our pints. "You look a million miles away."

"Sorry. I was just thinking about work," I lied.

"Well, that's the first thing you need to knock on the head. You're already in danger of becoming a workaholic. Don't let it cock block you, too."

"Didn't you say Paul was going to join us?" I asked in an effort to change the subject.

"Yeah, he begged off, though. I think he's got some secret hook-up going on here in New York. He's been disappearing every night this week and won't tell anyone where he's going."

"Definitely sounds like he's seeing someone," I agreed. "What about Leanne? Does she mind you going to a bar without her?"

"No, she thought it was a great idea. You know Leanne loves you, and she's well aware I wouldn't stray." He paused, eyeing me a moment as he took a sip of his drink. "She did mention something about a girl back home who you've been texting."

Right. I'd forgotten Leanne caught me sending selfies to Afric that day. "Yes, I have been texting someone, but she's just a friend. It isn't romantic."

"You sure about that?"

No, especially not if she really is the woman from my hazy sex dream.

"Yes, I'm sure."

"Good. That means we can put operation 'Get Neil Laid' into action. Have you seen anyone you like?"

I gave the bar occupants a cursory glance. The place was full of attractive women, but I just wasn't interested. I wasn't sure if it was due to a fear of being turned down or because my thoughts were already focused on someone else.

Worryingly, that someone wasn't Annabelle. I still hadn't messaged her back, and I feared she might be angry at me, or well, angry at fake Callum, but I just couldn't think of what to say to her, how to let her down gently. I'd realised that I wasn't as invested in meeting her as I had been the day I confessed everything to Afric in the empty cinema. The day she'd promised to help me. She hadn't wanted anything in return at the time. Was that because she found my predicament entertaining, or because she just genuinely wanted to do something nice for a stranger?

"Not yet," I finally replied, turning my attention back to Callum.

"Well, sit up straight and at least try to act a bit more confident. There's nothing women find more attractive than confidence."

"I'll try," I told him, lifting my head and straightening my shoulders just as a pretty blonde appeared at Callum's side.

"Hey, my friends and I were just talking about how awesome your tattoos are," I heard the blonde exclaim.

"Thanks. Very kind of you to say," Callum replied.

"Oh em gee, are you British? I love your accent."

"Yep. My friend Neil and I are both from London," Callum said.

I turned slightly and gave her a small nod. Her attention momentarily flicked to me before returning to him. I didn't think I'd ever been so instantly dismissed before. It was almost comical.

"That's so cool. How long are you here for?" she asked Callum.

"Just a few more weeks. Neil is actually—"

"Do you know what," she cut in before he could finish, "I should give you my number. If you're going to be here for a few weeks, then maybe we could meet up, grab dinner together or something."

My mouth settled into a grimace because this was going exactly as I'd predicted. If Callum and I were on a buffet table, he'd be the succulent chicken everybody wanted and I'd be the day-old dry bread roll in the corner.

"I'm sorry, but I'm not actually single," Cal replied firmly.

"Oh," the blonde breathed before a seductive grin shaped her lips. "Well, your girlfriend back home doesn't ever have to find out."

"His girlfriend isn't back home," I cut in, my tone surprisingly confident. I felt bad that Callum was stuck trying to fend off some stranger's advances just because he was trying to help get me some action. "She's here in New York, and if she knew you were flirting with her man right now, she wouldn't be pleased."

The blonde frowned at me in annoyance while Callum shot her an apologetic smile. "He's right. My Leanne is incredibly possessive." He said it like he was proud of the fact, and I briefly wondered how it would feel to have a woman love you that much, so much that she couldn't even stand the thought of you talking to someone else. Must be nice. I wasn't sure any of my previous girlfriends had ever felt so passionately about me. Sure, they liked me well enough, but I was fairly sure they wouldn't be overcome with jealousy if a random woman in a bar tried to chat me up.

The blonde cleared her throat. "Well, it was nice to meet you all the same." With that, she returned to her friends. I actually felt a little sorry for her. She'd been brave to come over and introduce herself to Callum, much braver than I was since I wasn't sure I wanted to talk to any of the women in this bar tonight.

"That wasn't awkward at all," Callum said as he returned his attention to his pint.

"I hate to break it to you, Cal, but you aren't wingman material. Not for the likes of me, anyway."

"What are you talking about? I can be a good wingman," he protested.

"I think it only works if the person you're a wingman for is better looking than you," I said.

Callum scoffed. "Bollocks. Anybody can do it."

I shook my head. "If you introduce me to any of the women in this bar, they're not going to want to talk to me, I promise."

"But you're a good-looking chap," he argued.

"Maybe, but I'm not *you*. There's a reason why you're the TV star and I'm the assistant is all I'm saying."

He leaned his elbow on the bar, studying me now. "Are you depressed, Neil? You sound a little depressed."

"I'm not depressed. I'm just not deluded, and I …" I trailed off. Had I actually been about to tell him about Annabelle? A part of me just wanted to get the truth out, lay my misdoings on the table, and let Callum decide how to punish me for them. The other part was way too scared to take the chance. If I lost my job, what would I do? No one at *Running on Air* would give me a reference once they discovered the truth.

For years I'd toyed with the idea of setting up my own event planning business. Helping to organise events was my favourite part of my current job as an assistant, and I was good at it, too. Perhaps coming clean to Callum was the push I needed to step out of my comfort zone and finally take a chance at that little dream.

"And you what?" Callum prodded, still studying me closely.

I blew out a long breath, my courage mostly fleeing when I replied, "And there is actually a girl back home, but it's complicated."

"How so?"

I swallowed tightly, impulsively choosing to tell him the truth while leaving out the incriminating details. "We met online, but she has no idea what I look like."

"So what? You're hardly ugly. It's not like she's going to be horrified when she meets you."

I stared at my beer. "When I described myself to her, I wasn't exactly honest."

"What kind of person did you describe?"

Christ, why was I even telling him this? It was like taking a step dangerously close to the edge of a cliff. "Someone a little like you."

"Ah," Callum said, sitting back on his stool. "I see."

"Do you?"

He nodded, a thoughtful expression on his face as he fiddled with a cardboard coaster. "When Leanne and I got together, I mean, when we got together properly, that must've fucked your head up a little, right?"

"Well, I wouldn't exactly say that, but—"

"But it obviously did a number on your confidence. You probably thought to yourself, if only I were more like him, maybe she would've picked me instead."

"I don't think I want to be having this conversation," I said, a tension headache forming at my temples.

Callum pointed the coaster at me. "Well, it's a conversation we need to have. Leanne and me ending up together has nothing to do with you, Neil. It doesn't reflect on your worth or what a great bloke you are. We just always had that spark, that connection where we couldn't leave each other alone. The rest of the world might as well not exist."

"Sounds really nice."

"It is nice. It's more than nice, but what I'm saying is, you could've been the most perfect man in the world, and she still would've had her eyes fixed on me. As I said, we had the spark. And one day, you're going to meet someone. Maybe it won't be completely clear to you at first, but there'll be something about her, something that will refuse to let you leave her alone. Like, when I first met Leanne, she rubbed me up the wrong way entirely. We didn't get along at all. But then, over time, I realised why she annoyed me so much. It was because she'd burrowed her way under my skin."

What he said sparked a memory of me sitting at the table in the sushi restaurant across from Afric. I'd been so incredibly annoyed by her, yet she had my undivided attention all the same. I dismissed the thought. Afric and I were nothing like Callum and Leanne. They were soulmates; while we were … Well, I wasn't entirely sure what we were, but I certainly didn't think we were soulmates.

"The only way to know if this internet girl is the one for you is to meet her in person. If she doesn't like the real you, then she's not worth another second of your time."

"Yeah, you're right," I said, even though I just couldn't imagine actually meeting Annabelle. And though I'd told Callum about her, she wasn't the woman who had thrown all my current thoughts and feelings into disarray.

"You sure you don't want me to set you up with someone here?" Callum asked. "Give your hand a night off. The poor bastard must be run ragged."

At this, I laughed. "He's definitely run ragged, but no, I don't think a one-night stand will help in what's troubling me."

Callum patted me on the shoulder. "Let's finish these pints and get our arses back to the hotel then because I'm absolutely knackered."

10.
Afric

"Tell me again why we're going to a book club when we could be out doing, oh, say absolutely anything else?" Billy asked as we rode the bus to the library where Neil's sister worked.

"Because I promised Neil we'd go to fill out the numbers. His sister organised the book club, and she's worried no one's going to turn up."

"Oh, even better. So, we could be the only two people there, and I haven't even read the book."

"I gave you a rundown of the story, didn't I?"

Billy might not have read the book, but I had. Every couple of months, I did a weeklong gaming detox where I spent zero time online and only read paperback novels. I always knew when I needed to take a break from the internet because there'd be this pit of anxiety in my belly and my thoughts would constantly race. It was a clear sign I needed a hiatus. Since streaming was my job, I factored the detox weeks in as time off. Most of my followers were understanding about it.

"Yes, but I'm not sure I can discuss a book I haven't read. Maybe I should just sit there and keep my mouth shut."

I laughed loudly. "You keeping your mouth shut. Now that's something I haven't witnessed before, and I've known you since you emerged from the womb."

"For your information, Mam says I was a very quiet baby."

"Maybe you were, but I don't remember it."

"She said I slept all the time, and it was a chore to wake me up even for food."

"Now that I can imagine. You sleep twelve hours a night."

"Don't be ridiculous. I sleep the requisite eleven and a half just like everyone else," he joked.

"You have the sleep schedule of a newborn puppy," I said just as the bus approached our stop. We hopped off and made the short walk to the library, an old red brick building with a blue-painted door. It was very quaint. I hadn't seen any pictures of Rosie, but I'd just been imagining a female version of Neil. It might've been a bad idea because now I was in danger of developing a minor crush on Neil's sister, too.

I mean, if Neil appeared in front of me now wearing a sexy librarian get-up, aka, pencil skirt, heels, tight blouse, and glasses hanging off the tip of his nose, I'd still fancy him.

Maybe I'd fancy him more …

"What are you thinking about? You've gone all quiet," Billy prodded.

"Nothing. Come on, let's go inside."

I linked my arm through his, and we stepped into the main lobby area of the library. It was after hours, but there were a good few people about. I hoped that meant Rosie's book club had attracted more attendees than she expected. I was surprised that I cared about Neil's sister's feelings since we hadn't even met yet. Perhaps it was because he cared about her, and I cared about him, so if she was happy, then that meant he'd be happy, too.

I cared about his happiness.

How odd.

On instinct, I pulled out my phone and shot off a quick message.

Afric: Just arrived at the library. Happy to report a bunch of people have shown up.

His response was immediate.

Neil: That's a relief. Rosie really wants this to be a success. Thanks for letting me know. And thanks for going along. It means a lot.

Afric: As I said, I've nothing else on. How did everything go last night?

I was more than a little eager to hear how Neil's night on the town had panned out.

Neil: Exactly as I predicted.

Afric: Meaning?

Neil: Next to Callum, I was invisible.

You're not invisible to me. The thought came unbidden. I frowned at my phone, worrying my lip as I typed out a reply.

Afric: I'm sure you're overexaggerating. After all, you do have an arse that won't quit, and women notice these things ;-)

Neil: You're just trying to make me feel better.

Afric: Yes, but it's also the truth.

Neil: Okay, I'll have to take your word for it since I find it impossible to properly see my own backside in a mirror. I always end up straining my neck and pulling a muscle.

Afric: Did you just admit to checking out your own butt?

Neil: Not in the way you're implying.

Afric: It is exactly in the way I'm implying.

Afric: I better go. The book club's about to start.

I grinned as I shoved my phone back in my pocket, not giving Neil the chance to respond. I could just imagine him getting all flustered and worked up over my teasing, the vein in his forehead popping.

Billy and I entered the moderately sized reading room, where chairs had been arranged to form a circle. A number of people were already taking seats, some with dog-eared copies of the book, others with new, pristine paperbacks. There was something about libraries that always made me feel cosy. I was a sucker for the smell of old paper mixed with the faint hint of mildew and the atmosphere of enforced silence. I wasn't even being sarcastic. That shit was pure *soulful*.

A woman who appeared to be in her mid-twenties stood by a table fussing with a stack of note cards. She didn't wear a pencil skirt and blouse but instead wore jeans and a navy wool top. She had the same brown hair and eyes as Neil, and she even wore similar glasses. Her hair was tied back in a neat bun.

She must've sensed Billy and mine's approach because her gaze flicked up, her eyes widening when they fell on me. She seemed to do a double-take as a shy, shocked smile graced her lips. "Oh, my God, it's you! I mean … You're Afric, right?"

"That's right, and you're Rosie?"

"Yes. Hello. Goodness, I can't believe you're here. Neil said you were going to come, but I didn't believe him."

"Well, I hope you didn't bet on it because here I am," I replied with a smile.

Rosie gave a soft laugh, and I noticed my brother eyeing her up. She was a cute little thing, and Billy would eat her for breakfast. I gave him a subtle elbow in the ribs to warn him she was off-limits. He scowled at me in return.

"No bets were made, thankfully," she replied as she set her note cards down on the table and took a step closer. "Will you be honest with me about something?"

"Sure."

Rosie gestured to the chairs that had been placed around the room. "Do you think the seating arrangement was a poor choice? I'm beginning to worry it makes this look like an AA meeting rather than a book club."

At my side, Billy gave an amused chuckle. "I'm pretty sure AA meetings don't have the trademark on circular seating arrangements," he said, drawing her attention to him for the first time. "I'm Billy, by the way. Afric's brother."

I suspected Rosie had been so stunned by the sight of me that she hadn't even noticed Billy standing beside me. Now, her eyes rounded, and her cheeks displayed the slightest hint of rouge. It wasn't a surprising reaction. Billy was a bit too tall and a bit too skinny, his nose slightly too large and his curly hair a smidge too unkempt. Despite this, he was still a handsome son of a bitch. Women had always flocked to him, especially with his mischievous smile and twinkly hazel eyes.

"It's a pleasure to meet you, Billy," Rosie replied politely. "So, you think I should leave the chairs as is?"

"It's a little late to change them now. Almost everyone is already sitting down," I said.

She shook her head at herself. "You're right. I don't know why I'm overthinking this. And I'm sorry for being weird and anxious. We've just met, and I'm fretting to you about chairs of all things."

"Don't apologise. Neil talks about you all the time, so I feel like I know you already," I said to reassure her.

Her eyebrows shot up. "He does? Well, that's not very surprising. He's always been the protective, reliable older brother who likes to worry over me. I'm not sure what I'd do without him."

The way she spoke about Neil warmed my heart. What was happening to me? The more I learned about him, the more sentimental I seemed to become. I'd never been particularly soft or emotional, but somehow Neil brought out that side of me. And for crying out loud, all this was happening, and he wasn't even in the country right now.

Rosie cleared her throat. "Well, I'd better start the proceedings. Wish me luck."

"Good luck," Billy and I both said in unison as she went to greet the people who were seated.

We took two of the last remaining empty seats, Billy sliding in next to me as he whispered, "She's fucking adorable."

"It must run in the family. Neil is also adorable," I replied before I properly thought through what I was saying. Billy grinned knowingly, and I swiped him on the arm.

"Quit it with the grinning. Also, hands off Rosie. She's not for the likes of you."

He feigned offence. "And whyever not? I'm your brother. You should be supporting me in my sexual endeavours, not holding me back."

"Your words are telling. You just said sexual instead of romantic. Rosie is a romance girl, not a passing sexy times girl."

"I can do romance," Billy protested.

I scoffed at that. "I'll believe it when I see it. But you won't be practicing on Rosie. I mean it. She's off limits.

134

Neil would have my guts for garters if you besmirched his baby sister."

"Fine, fine, I'll keep my filthy mitts off her. You're probably right. She's far too angelic and innocent for me. I shall leave her *unbesmirched*."

I laughed. "Now you're getting it."

Billy shot me a mock scowl, and we quieted down as the book discussion began. It was such a success that neither Billy nor I were required to fill any awkward silences. Rosie held her own the entire evening and managed to direct the conversation through the themes and subject matter of the book with finesse. It was clear that literature was her passion. As soon as she started talking about the story, she practically lit up and glowed. My brother seemed to notice the same thing because he barely took his eyes off her for the entire hour.

I had a feeling I was going to have to reiterate my warning for him to stay away from her.

As the meeting drew to a close, I headed over to Rosie to congratulate her on how well things had gone.

"That was fantastic!" I exclaimed as I reached her.

"Thanks. Everyone seemed to enjoy it well enough," she replied, glancing at me and then Billy. "If you both don't have other plans, you should come back to my place for dinner. As a thank you for coming tonight, I mean. I live with my grandma, and she always cooks way too much. With Neil away, there'll be even more extra food than usual."

"Oh, um, sure," I replied. Her offer took me by surprise, especially since we'd just met. I had to remind myself that she was an avid watcher of my stream and considered me something of a pseudo-celebrity. I glanced at Billy. "You don't mind, do you?"

"Why would I mind? I never turn down a free meal, especially not a free meal homecooked by a grandmother. Those are the best kind."

Rosie shot him a shy smile. "Right, well, I'm just going to finish tidying up in here, and then we'll go. My house is only a short walk away."

"We'll help you tidy," I offered.

Fifteen minutes later, we were walking towards Neil and Rosie's grandmother's house for dinner. I wondered if he'd be annoyed that I'd accepted the invitation. He could be a bit awkward and private about certain things. Maybe he'd think this was overstepping a boundary. But I didn't have any ill intent. I genuinely wanted to meet his grandma and get to know Rosie better.

The house was one of those post-war numbers, and I could just imagine Neil growing up here. I pictured a prim and proper little kid with glasses, a sad little kid whose parents had died. My heart clenched. I couldn't remember if he said what age he was when it happened, but he had mentioned that his grandmother raised him and his sister, so he must've been on the youngish side.

Rosie, who Billy had been bombarding with questions during the short walk, pulled a key from her bag. As soon as she opened the door, I was assaulted by the homely scent of roast chicken and what I suspected was freshly made gravy. My mouth began to water as she motioned for us to enter the hallway, and I took in the old but well-loved furniture and the slightly scuffed wooden floor with a Persian rug running down the middle.

Rosie hung up her coat and bag before offering to take ours.

"Grandma," she called out. "I hope you don't mind that I brought some guests for dinner."

At this, a woman with short grey hair appeared at the top of the hallway. She looked to be in her seventies and wore a polka dot apron.

"Well, hello," she said, dusting her hands on the apron as she took in Billy and me with a warm smile. "Are you friends of Rosie's from the book club?"

"No, Grandma, this is Neil's friend, Afric, and her brother, Billy," Rosie introduced. "Neil mentioned the book club to Afric, and she was kind enough to come along. I asked them to dinner to thank them." She paused to glance at Billy and me. "This is my grandma, Philomena."

"But you can call me Phil," Neil's grandmother amended as she came to greet me. "It's so lovely to meet you, Afric. Neil has mentioned you a few times, though he didn't tell me quite how pretty you are."

I placed a hand on my hip. "Are you trying to butter me up, Phil?"

She gave a hoot of a laugh. "Oh, I like you," she replied before turning her attention to Billy. "And you're a fine-looking chap, though you look like you could do with a good meal. Come on into the kitchen. I've made chicken, roast potatoes, carrots, and green beans."

"Sounds delicious," I said as we all followed her into a well-appointed kitchen, with a table in the far corner for dining. Billy and I sat while Rosie helped her grandma dish up the food. I couldn't resist pulling out my phone and shooting off a quick text to Neil.

Afric: Don't freak out, but I'm in your grandma's house right now about to have dinner.

Neil: What? Please tell me you're joking.

Afric: Not joking. Rosie invited Billy and me back after the book club to thank us for coming.

Neil: My sister is too nice for her own good sometimes. You'd better behave.

Afric: Hey! I'll have you know I'm on my best behaviour. Phil and I have really hit it off.

Neil: Dear lord ...

Afric: Relax. I'll be good as gold. I promise.

Neil: Why do I get the impression you're smiling mischievously right now?

Afric: Probably because I'm already figuring out a subtle way to suggest we peruse your baby pictures?

Neil: I'm going to murder Rosie for this.

Grinning, I slid my phone into my pocket just as a plate heaped with steaming, delicious-smelling food appeared in front of me. Phil placed a large jug of gravy in the centre of the table before taking a seat next to Rosie.

"So, remind me, how did you and my Neil meet again?" she asked, directing her question at me. Something in her smile told me she already knew the answer to this. Perhaps she was fishing for extra details her grandson might've purposefully left out.

"His co-worker, Michaela, is one of my closest friends. We used to live together before she moved in with her boyfriend, James," I explained. "I was meeting her for lunch one day, and Neil tagged along. Let's just say, we didn't hit it off right away. He wasn't too fond of me that first time we met. I have a bad habit of teasing people who I find interesting."

"If you grew up in our family, you'd know that teasing is practically an Olympic sport," Billy put in.

"Obviously," I went on. "It's my fault that Neil was unimpressed with me that first time. Then our paths crossed again a few weeks later, and it went a little better. I think he realised I wasn't as bad as he first thought. Anyway, we've been pals ever since."

"Well, I'm glad to hear you two found a way to get along," Phil said. "I must admit I have seen a bit of a change in Neil since you two became friends. He can be somewhat uptight."

"Grandma!" Rosie exclaimed. "That's not fair. You know Neil feels responsible for taking care of us. It's why he works so hard."

"Yes, and I love him for that," Phil agreed. "All I'm saying is that Neil has been acting like a thirty-year-old since he was only a boy. Lately, I've noticed him be a little less strict with himself, and I suspect it might be your doing, Afric."

"Well, I'm not sure if it's all down to me, but Neil's been a good influence on me, too. He's certainly taught me how to be more responsible, especially with my finances."

"Oh, yes, he did mention something about assisting you with your accounts."

"He's an absolute whizz," I said. "I'd have been lost without him."

"Then I'm glad you both managed to make your friendship work," Phil said. "I think we often avoid those who aren't the same as us, but if we just gave those people a chance, we'd realise how inconsequential the differences are in comparison to how much they can improve our lives."

"Here, here," Billy said. "My life has certainly been improved by this gravy. What on earth do you put in it to make it taste so good?"

Phil tapped the side of her nose. "It's a secret family recipe. I'm afraid I can't reveal it. Though, you are welcome to come back for dinner any time. Rosie and I love having guests. It's always just the two of us when Neil travels for work."

"Doesn't he have his own flat in the city, though?" I asked.

"Oh, yes, he does, but he comes here most evenings for dinner. He doesn't like eating alone."

Right. I remembered him mentioning something about that. "Well, I can't blame him. Your cooking is delicious."

"At my age, I've certainly had time to perfect it," Phil said.

"Very true," I replied. "A woman in her, what, late-forties could definitely gain the experience to be an excellent cook."

Phil gave a hoot of laughter as she nudged Rosie. "She's a charmer, this one. I can see why Neil is so fond."

Her statement ignited a warm glow inside me. It started as a tiny flicker but quickly spread to encapsulate my entire body. Neil often acted like he reluctantly put up with my friendship, but he'd obviously spoken highly of me to his grandma if she thought he was fond of me.

While Billy, Rosie, and Phil chatted about how the book club had gone, I pulled out my phone again and found another text from Neil.

Neil: What's happening? You haven't said anything weird to my grandmother, have you?

Afric: Would you stop. Phil loves me already. She said I was a charmer.

Neil: She's obviously getting on in years and losing her sense of proper judgement.

Afric: The cheek! The insolence! The gall! Your grandma's judgement is perfectly fine. I am incredibly charming. She also mentioned understanding why YOU are so fond of ME. I'm feeling rather touched, to be honest.

Neil: Again, her judgement is declining. Poor woman. She's clearly mistaking reluctant friendship for fondness.

Afric: If you don't admit you're fond of me right this moment I'm going to show these texts to Phil.

Neil: FINE! I'm fond of you. Now shut up about it.

Afric: Don't be so embarrassed. I'm fond of you, too ... Kind of how a person gets fond of the mangey dog that follows them around every day :-P

Neil: Funny.

Afric: Phil's cooking is amazing, btw. She's also given Billy and me an open invitation to come for dinner anytime, so get ready for me gate-crashing your nightly dinners when you get back from New York.

Neil: You will not. I'll barricade the door ... out of curiosity, what did she cook today?

Afric: Chicken, homemade gravy, roast potatoes, carrots, and green beans. I'm happily stuffed to the gills.

Neil: God, I'm jealous. I've been getting really sick of room service and eating out.

Afric: Aw, poor baby, having to tolerate living in a five-star hotel with freshly prepared meals just a phone call away.

Neil: Piss off. You know what I meant.

***

I didn't manage to bring up the topic of Neil's baby pictures that evening, but I had every intention of doing it next time. I thoroughly enjoyed getting to know Phil and Rosie, and it was surprising because I wasn't always such a sociable person. In fact, I often went through phases of barely leaving my flat, especially if I was deep into a gaming marathon.

I'd sit by my computer morning, noon and night, ordering in food and constantly streaming to my growing audience of fans. By no means was I someone who made a ton of money from streaming, but I made a liveable wage, which was enough to pay for rent, groceries, and utility bills, plus a little extra.

The little extra usually went towards my penchant for buying expensive clothes. Whenever I got a big payout, I went on an online shopping spree from my favourite designers. I was particularly fond of oversized, boldly coloured jumpers paired with equally boldly coloured leggings that cost an arm and a leg.

My favourite items, though, were what I called the "Emperor's New Clothes" pieces. I loved it when designers created clothing that looked kind of ridiculous, but because it came from a lauded brand, everyone acted like it looked amazing. There was a dissonance that appealed to me, an ugly/beautiful aspect to those items that always drew me to buy them. Neil had been scolding me for said purchases while he'd worked on my accounts, but I couldn't help it. They brought me joy.

Speaking of Neil, over the course of several weeks, our friendship fell into a regular pattern of nightly video calls. We'd finished several great period dramas together, and I was constantly on the lookout for new ones I thought we'd both enjoy. I loved how much of a romantic he was and sometimes suspected he enjoyed the intimate parts of the shows even more than I did.

Intermingled with the nightly calls were daily text messages where we chatted about all manner of subjects. If a random thought crossed my mind, I always knew I could text Neil about it. And okay, often, these random thoughts annoyed him, which was an activity that entertained me immensely.

    Afric: I have a question.
    Neil: Okay.
    Afric: wHY iS iT iNfiniteLy mOre dIsturBing wHen yOu caPitalise rAndom lEtterS iN a sEnteCe?
    Neil: Not sure. It just is. Thanks for that. Now I'm creeped out.
    Afric: MayBe the rAnDom caPitalisaTion inDicaTes a PsyChoTic staTe of miNd?
    Neil: Will you please stop? I feel like I'm texting a serial killer.
    Afric: buT sCarinG yOu iS sO mUcH fUn.
    Neil: STOP. IT.
    Afric: SorRy caNt. oOh lOok, a sHinY kNife ...
    Neil: Seriously. Stop.
    Afric: Muah ha! Okay, sorry for scaring you. Normal Afric is back. Hello.
    Neil: Thank heavens.
    Afric: oR iS sHe??
    Neil: Afric!

***

Afric: Tell me something no one knows about you.
    Neil: Why?
    Afric: Because I find your secrets fascinating.
    Neil: I don't have secrets. Aside from the one you already know about.
    Afric: There must be something. Here's one of mine: I once fashioned myself an adult nappy out of household items so that I could keep gaming without needing to stop for bathroom breaks. I was trying to break a world record.

Neil: That is ... incredibly odd and disturbing. A little gross, too.

Afric: I know. Technically it's not a complete secret because Sarita and Michaela found out.

Neil: Seriously, Afric, that's not normal behaviour.

Afric: What about me ever gave you the impression I was normal?

Neil: Okay, I stand corrected. Did you break the record?

Afric: Sadly, no. Some teenager in the Philippines pipped me to the post. Luckily, I'm not obsessed with any games right now, so I haven't felt the urge to do anything extreme lately. It's only when I'm obsessed and don't want to stop that I do crazy things like that. I've actually been working on being more moderate with my gameplay. I feel much healthier for it.

Neil: I'm glad to hear it.

Afric: Soooo ... have you thought of a secret yet?

Neil: No.

Afric: Oh, come on. There must be something.

Neil: There's nothing you'll find interesting.

Afric: I find everything about you interesting.

Neil: Why?

Afric: I'm not sure. Probably because you're my opposite. Isn't there something in science about opposites attracting?

Neil: That's about magnets, not people.

Afric: Either way, it's true about us.

Neil: We're not as opposite as you think.

Afric: No?

Neil: No. We both seem to enjoy period dramas.

Afric: I'm not sure that one similarity makes us alike.

Neil: It still shows that we're not complete opposites.

Afric: Oh, my God, tell me a secret right now before I die of frustration!
Neil: Okay, let me think. Far be it from me to leave you frustrated.
Afric: Neil Durant, are you flirting?
Neil: Absolutely not.
Afric: Liar.
Afric: Anything?
Neil: How's this? Sometimes I browse homes on estate agent websites and imagine myself living there with a wife and kids. Like fantasy house hunting for my fantasy family.
Afric: I think I might cry. That is adorable.
Neil: I am not adorable. Take that back.
Afric: Sorry, I can't. You're a fucking adorable man, Neil. It's a simple fact.
Neil: Um. . .thanks, I guess.
Afric: You're so awkward with compliments. I love it.
Neil: And you're annoying.
Afric: So, when you picture your wife, does she look like Annabelle or ...
Neil: I told you I didn't want to discuss her until I get back.
Afric: Okay! Don't bite my head off. I was just wondering.

***

Afric: I have a new pet peeve.
Neil: Oh?
Afric: You know when someone gets castrated in a TV show?
Neil: Happy to report I don't watch those types of shows.

Afric: It usually happens in horrors and thrillers.

Neil: Can I remind you there's a time difference between us, and I just woke up. Please don't put me off my breakfast.

Afric: In that case, I'll apologise in advance because I have to get this out.

Neil: Don't.

Afric: So, anyway, a character gets castrated by some psychopath, then skip to the next scene, and someone's either cooking a sausage or eating a sausage or slicing a sausage in half. I hate it. I hate it so much.

Neil: Great. Now I won't be eating anything until lunch. Definitely won't be touching sausage for a while.

Afric: I'm sorry, but someone had to hear my complaint. I'll buy you the fanciest breakfast in town when you get back to London.

Neil: I'll hold you to that ... Now you have me thinking about my own TV pet peeves.

Afric: Do tell.

Neil: I hate it when a character wakes up in hospital and pulls out their IV. It makes me feel physically ill.

Afric: Oh, I hate that, too! I feel weak when I see it.

Neil: I also hate it when two characters are so desperate to have sex that they push everything off the table and onto the floor. Makes my skin crawl.

Afric: I could just imagine you losing your stiffy right away if a woman did that. You'd stop everything and get down on the floor to pick all the stuff up and put it back in its rightful place.

Neil: You're 100% correct. I would do exactly that.

Afric: I know you too well.

Neil: I better go. Duty calls.

Afric: Don't forget to message me later!

***

Neil: Okay, so that movie last night definitely wasn't a romance. What was the title again?

    Afric: Quills. *And I know, okay? I was duped by a top 100 list.*

    Neil: How could anyone categorise a film about the Marquis de Sade as a romance anyway?

    Afric: Agreed. Whoever made that list needs their head checked. I'll be haunted by images of Geoffrey Rush's bare backside for weeks.

    Neil: Weeks? It'll take me years to get over it.

    Afric: LOL. Disturbing scenes and lack of romance aside, you have to admit it was a good movie, though.

    Neil: It was decent, but I insist on choosing the next one. It might be a while before I can trust you again.

    Afric: Understandable.

***

Afric: Billy's gone home, and now I'm lonely.

    Neil: I'm sorry.

    Afric: I wanted him to move here, but he says he has too much going on in Dublin.

    Neil: Do you miss your family a lot?

    Afric: Yes and no. I love them, but growing up in a house with so many people was claustrophobic at times. I need my own space nowadays. I do enjoy going to visit them, though.

    Neil: I feel the same way. I love my grandma and Rosie, and I like seeing them most days, but I don't think I could live with them, not at this age anyway. My flat is my sanctuary.

Afric: Speaking of your flat, you need to invite me over when you get back.

Neil: Invite you over for what?

Afric: To watch period dramas together. Our nightly ritual still needs to be maintained.

Neil: Yes, but we don't have to stop doing it via video call.

Afric: Are you afraid to watch romances with me in person, Neil? Will you be overcome by the sexy scenes and try to ravish me out of sheer horniness?

Neil: Aside from Quills (which I'm still not sure I've forgiven you for), nothing we've watched has contained graphic scenes. And no, I won't be overcome. There's this thing called self-control.

Afric: Well, I still want an invite to your flat. You've seen mine. It's only fair that I get to see yours.

Neil: I'll take it under consideration.

Afric: If you don't invite me, I'll turn up when you aren't expecting me.

Neil: You don't know my address.

Afric: I'll wheedle it out of Michaela.

Neil: I won't open the door.

Afric: You'd leave me out in the cold? :-(

Neil: For Christ's sake. Fine. You can come over some night when I'm back.

Afric: Yes! I can't WAIT.

Neil: Why do I feel like I'm already regretting this?

Afric: Don't regret it. I'll be a saint. I won't even sneak a peek in your knicker drawer.

Neil: You're the worst.

Afric: I'm the best, and you know it.

11.
Neil

It was my final night in New York. In the morning, we all flew home to London, and I couldn't wait to sleep in my own bed again. I missed the familiarity of my flat, even though it could be a little lonely sometimes. Aside from eating meals alone, I mostly enjoyed living by myself, though. Sure, one day I wanted to have a big house and a family of my own, but for now, my flat was where I could relax and be myself.

At the very least, it was where all my stuff was.

I'd just finished yet another room service dinner when a video call came through on my laptop. After the craziness of the final day of shooting, I'd almost forgotten about my nightly ritual with Afric. Yes, it was an unusual arrangement, but I'd become attached to it. We seemed to be in almost constant contact these days.

No one could be more surprised by how much I'd ended up enjoying her friendship than me.

I enjoyed the random thoughts she messaged me about at all times of the day and night. And I enjoyed how much it amused her to tease me. Sometimes I had the urge to reply to her messages with something a little less stiff and uptight, but it was like we'd taken on these roles, with her being the provocateur and me being the irritable grouch who reacted.

I'd gotten so used to interacting with her virtually that I was slightly apprehensive about seeing her in person again. I feared it was going to be too intense. I'd developed a real affection for her during these weeks apart, and it was very different from how I'd felt about her before I left. I wasn't sure how to handle the change.

Not to mention, there was Annabelle to deal with when I got back.

I definitely wasn't looking forward to that.

Walking over to the bed, I sat down and accepted Afric's call. When she filled the screen, I blinked. Then I did a double-take.

"Hey, so I actually think we might have watched every decent period drama out there. I've been at a loss to find something new that has good reviews," she said, but I barely heard her. I was too struck by the sight of her.

"Neil?" she said, frowning. "Are you okay?"

I cleared my throat. "Yes, I'm fine … Just, what are you wearing?"

She glanced down at the tight, pale vest top she wore, a bright purple bra evident underneath. I'd never seen her wear anything like that. She always had on baggy pyjamas or oversized jumpers. I'd even wondered if she was self-conscious about her weight. She certainly didn't need to be. Afric was curvaceous in a way that would make most men's jaws drop, and her breasts were … God, I felt like a pervert even looking at them, but they were perfect. Definitely more than a handful. And that was something I wished I didn't know. There was a certain bliss to ignorance because the feelings I'd been having and the closeness we'd developed now had the added bonus of me being undeniably sexually attracted to her. Maybe I always had been and had just been lying to myself all this time. She had a pretty face, well, a beautiful face, actually, and now I knew her body was just as beautiful.

I was in so much trouble.

"Oh!" she exclaimed with a laugh. "Sorry. I've probably scarred you for life by wielding my road frontage in your face. Sarita left the heating on for too long, and the flat is absolutely boiling. You're lucky I'm not in the nip, to be perfectly honest."

Thank heavens for small mercies.

Still, I really didn't need *that* imagery in my head. Also, did she just use the term "road frontage" to refer to her ample bosom? I stifled a laugh, grateful that she could only see above my waist because my pants had grown distinctly tighter.

"Neil, you've gone bright red," she went on. "Do you want me to put something on? I think I have a pashmina lying around here somewhere."

"Yes, put on the pashmina," I said stiffly. "I feel like I've just logged onto your OnlyFans."

I immediately regretted saying that when she grinned into the camera, placing a hand on her hip.

"Oh, come on. This top isn't that revealing. It's a simple vest. It's hardly a see-through bra with nipple peekaboos."

"What on earth are nipple peeka—No, never mind, I don't want to know."

Her wonderfully cheeky laughter filtered through the speaker. "You are such a prude, and I love it! Hold on. I'm getting the pashmina."

"Thank Christ."

When she reappeared, she was thankfully covered, though the item of clothing she now wore was made of black silk dotted with pale pink cherry blossoms. It was arguably sexier than the low-cut vest, but at least now I didn't have to avoid looking at the most glorious cleavage I'd ever seen.

"This better?"

"Yes, thank you."

"Well, I'm blaming you if I die of heatstroke. Also, can we discuss the fact that your cheeks are still flaming? What on earth, Neil? It's just me. You don't need to be embarrassed by a pair of boobs. Actually, you should be flattered. I only let people I trust see my body."

Now, I frowned. "Why is that?"

She shrugged. "When I first started streaming, I was a little naïve and used to wear normal clothes. Nothing even remotely risqué, mind. Just normal-sized T-shirts and tops. Well, unfortunately, I was blessed with my mother's giant knockers, and the comments were almost ninety percent boob-related. That's why I now wear tops that cover them up. Not because I'm ashamed of them. They give me back pain from time to time, but other than that, I think they're fantastic." I knew of a few other choice words to describe them. "I just don't want to attract viewers who are only interested in sexualising me. Sure, I might have a bigger audience if I did, but mentally, that kind of commentary starts to weigh on you. It makes you overly critical about your appearance, and I don't want to spend my time obsessing over what I look like."

It was enraging that she had to go to such lengths to cover herself, but I understood the nature of the internet. Being the only female cast member of *Running on Air*, Leanne had to deal with some horrifically demeaning comments from time to time. Luckily, she had a great support network to help her deal with things like that when they happened. Afric had been all on her own, and the thought of her being emotionally mature enough to go through that and come out the other side intact was impressive. It was times like these I was glad that my sister shied away from dating apps.

"I fucking hate that you had to go through that," I said, my jaw tense.

Her eyebrows shot up. "Did you just swear?"

"Yes, because what you just told me makes me angry. You were what, a teenager when all this happened?" Michaela had mentioned Afric was pretty young when she started online.

"I was eighteen."

"See? That pisses me off."

"I have to say; I quite like it when you're pissed off on my behalf. It's very sexy alpha male."

"Don't do that."

"Don't do what?"

"Don't brush off what happened by pretending to flirt with me."

"Who says I'm pretending? Anyway, it was a long time ago. I'm over it."

"It's obviously still affecting you psychologically. You don't just wear baggy clothes to stream. You wear them all the time. And for some reason, you hate kissing, which is also concerning—"

"The kissing thing has nothing to do with the clothes. That's a separate matter entirely."

"Even so, I don't like it. You're young and beautiful and funny and kind and brilliant, and you shouldn't miss out on a lifetime of kisses," I clamped my mouth shut when I realised how much I'd rambled.

Onscreen, Afric stared at me. For once, she looked speechless. Then she finally spoke, "You think I'm kind?"

It surprised me that kindness was the compliment she'd decided to focus on. "Yes, you've been kind to me at least."

"I didn't realise bothering you with random text messages day and night was considered a kindness," she said with a surprisingly shy laugh.

I looked her in the eye. "The texts don't bother me, Afric. I like them." Not only that, I looked forward to them on an unhealthy level. I refrained from mentioning that to her, though.

"Oh ... Well, that's good to hear." She fell silent again. Her eyes levelled on something on the other side of her room when she whispered, "Thanks for the other part as well."

"What other part?"

"You called me beautiful. I can't remember if anyone's ever called me that before."

A moment of honesty struck me. "Well, they should because you are. You've got incredible eyes, a cute nose, and gorgeous ..."

At this, her lips began to curve in a grin. "And gorgeous what?"

I swallowed, forcing myself to answer. "Gorgeous lips. Don't go getting a big head about it."

Her grin widened. "Too late. I can already feel it expanding. Please don't be too distracted by my gorgeous lips. I wouldn't want you getting turned on by the idea of me wrapping them around your gorgeous—"

"Afric!"

"Gorgeous cheek," she finished. "What did you think I was going to say?"

I sighed and rubbed my forehead. "Go on, lap it up because that's the last time you'll ever get a compliment from me."

"Aw, not fair! I want more compliments, Neil. I love how embarrassed you get when you give them."

"I know you do, you sadist."

"So, we should probably branch out and watch a new genre since we've exhausted the available selection of period dramas. How do you feel about romcoms?" she asked, and I was relieved for the change of subject.

"I have no aversion to romcoms. What did you have in mind?"

"I was thinking we could go by decade. Start with the best romcoms of the eighties and work our way up from there."

"Sounds like a plan," I replied and settled in while she searched for a movie.

***

The following morning, after I'd gone through security and had an hour to wait for my flight, I grabbed a coffee and found a quiet spot to do some work. When I logged into one of Callum's social media accounts, I found a message from Annabelle.

Hi Cal,

I hope you're doing well. I don't want to be that whiny, insecure girl who complains about stuff like this, but you've gone real quiet on me lately, and I'm just worried I said something wrong. Did I? Or have you simply decided to ghost me? I wouldn't blame you if you have. I'm just some random person on the internet, and you're a famous TV star. I get it. If you don't want to keep talking to me, that's fine. I won't bother you anymore. But if it's something else, if it's something I've done to upset you, please let me know. I've been driving myself crazy wondering.

Love Annabelle.
xxx.

Guilt sliced through me as I read her message. I was a pathetic excuse for a human being. I'd led this woman on and gone silent on her out of nowhere. I needed to fix the mistake. I needed to come clean to her. She deserved that much. Drawing in a deep breath, I drafted a reply.

Hi Annabelle,

First, please let me apologise for the silence on my end. I've been working through some things, but that's no excuse. I've clearly hurt your feelings, and that was never my intention. I'm about to board a flight back to London, and once I get settled after I land, I'd like to meet up to talk in person. I have something important that I need to tell you, and I feel it would be a further disrespect not to explain everything face to face. If you're free someday this week, please let me know. I'll pay for whatever transport you need to come and meet me.

Sincerely, Callum.

Afric

My phone vibrated with a call from Michaela, and I picked it up right away.

"Hello, stranger! How are you? How was New York?" I asked, excited to hear from her.

"Hey, it's so good to hear your voice," she said. "New York was wonderful but exhausting. We got home last night, and I slept for thirteen hours."

Nervous energy fluttered through me. If Michaela was home, that meant Neil was home, too. I figured he'd been sleeping after the flight as well because he hadn't called or texted in over a day. It was the longest we'd gone without communicating since he'd left for the trip. The thought of seeing him gave me way too many feelings, the most prominent being anticipation.

"Oh, I love a long, delicious sleep after getting home from travelling. So, when can I see you?"

"Actually, I was hoping we could hang out today, but I have a favour to ask."

"A favour?"

"It's Isaac's birthday, and Neil and I have been given the task of organising a small, impromptu surprise party. We've rented a private roof bar, but because it's so last minute, we can't get any staff except for a barman. Would you mind helping set everything up? Sarita and Mabel have already agreed to help, but I need one more person. Please say you'll do it? There'll be free drinks and snacks involved."

"You had me at roof bar. What time do you need me there?"

"Can you make it by four? The party starts at six."

"I can make it. But there's something you should know before I arrive."

"Oh?" she said, a note of curiosity in her voice.

"Drumroll, please ... Neil and I have kind of become friends. Really good friends, actually."

There was a pause on her end. I expected her to express surprise and shock, but instead, she exclaimed, "Oh, my God, I bloody knew it! I knew he was hiding something. Are you two ...."

"No, no, we're just friends. We hit it off that time I covered for you at the private screening."

"That's so unexpected. I thought you both rubbed each other the wrong way."

"We did, but then he realised how amazing I am, so here we are."

"You are definitely amazing. I can't wait to interrogate Neil about keeping secrets from me. Okay, I better go, but I'll see you later. I'll text you the address of the bar."

"See you later."

As soon as I hung up, butterflies filled my stomach. After all these weeks, I was going to see Neil in person. A memory from the other night surfaced. I'd been so eager to call him that I'd completely forgotten what I was wearing. I'd never revealed much skin in front of Neil before, and when he got a load of me in my tight, low-cut top, I swear he almost burst a blood vessel. It was clear he was embarrassed, and it was also clear he hadn't disliked what he saw. The idea sent a fresh wave of butterflies through me.

You're young and beautiful and funny and kind and brilliant, and you shouldn't miss out on a lifetime of kisses.

No one had ever spoken to me like that. Dev, nor any of my previous boyfriends, had ever expressed such sentiments. I couldn't believe that was what Neil thought about me. I never expected him, of all people, to think of me so favourably. The bit at the end about a "lifetime of kisses" had me unconsciously lifting my fingers to lips.

Would I still hate kissing as much as I did if Neil was the one kissing me?

I wasn't so sure.

All I knew was I didn't despise the idea the way I did when I thought about kissing anyone else.

I'd just showered, but I still needed to find something to wear. Day to day, I never gave much thought to dressing up fancy, mainly because I spent most of my time in my bedroom. Today was different, though. Some part of me yearned for Neil to look at me in the way he had over our last video call. I wanted to see the flushed cheeks paired with the flash of heat in his dark brown eyes.

For once, I regretted my wardrobe of comfortable yet stylish designer items. I didn't own anything that would be considered "sexy." But for the first time in a long time, I felt like wearing something that wasn't three sizes too big.

Rifling through my wardrobe, I finally found a black skater dress that I hadn't worn in forever. It was conservative since it had a high neckline and long sleeves down to the wrists, but it was also tight around the bosom before flaring out over the hips. I grabbed the dress, then found some purple tights and paired them with my red Converse. Next, I styled my hair into space buns, put on a little make-up as well as a pair of large gold hoop earrings, and I was ready to go.

I studied my reflection and smiled. Yes, this outfit would do nicely.

Sarita and Mabel were waiting in the living area when I emerged from my bedroom. They'd both agreed to help Michaela with the party, too. Sarita eyed me up and down.

"Okay, who are you, and what have you done with Afric?"

I put a hand on my hip. "I'm wearing a dress. What's your problem?"

"No problem. I'm just wondering who you've dolled yourself up for," she shot back. "Is Michael Sheen going to be at this party or something?"

"You leave Michael out of this. And no, he isn't. I haven't dolled myself up for anyone. It's a party. I can hardly go in pyjamas."

"Well, I think you look lovely," Mabel said, shooting me a kind smile.

"Thank you, Mabel."

Sarita blew out a breath. "Fine, keep your secrets. We'd better get going if we don't want to be late."

A little while later, Sarita, Mabel, and I entered the private rooftop bar in Shoreditch, where Isaac's surprise party was being held. He was the newest and youngest member of *Running on Air*. Originally from South Africa, I read that the group had discovered him while filming one of the earlier seasons and subsequently recruited him to be on the show. I thought it was nice how they all welcomed him into the fold and threw him birthday parties even though he hadn't been with them very long. Michaela always said that working on the show felt like being in a big family, and I sometimes felt a little jealous of that.

I was a dichotomy because I adored being alone, working for myself and answering to no one, but I also craved companionship.

Michaela was there to greet us when we arrived, though I didn't spot Neil anywhere. She must've sensed I was searching for him because she shot me a secret smile and whispered, "He's out back taking drinks inventory."

I grinned and headed in the direction Michaela had pointed. There was a small hallway at the end of which appeared to be a stock room. I approached the threshold, and there he was. His back was turned to me as he held a clipboard and pen, scribbling down numbers while counting bottles of alcohol. I allowed myself a moment to take him in and also to admire his backside in the navy slacks he wore. Then, quite impulsively, I launched myself forward and wrapped my arms around his middle. A startled breath gushed out of him as he stiffened.

"Guess who?" I whispered, and he instantly relaxed. A deep, amused chuckle escaped him.

"Afric," he said, still facing away from me. My name on his tongue sent a tingle down my spine. God, I really had it bad. "You almost gave me a heart attack," he went on.

On instinct, I rested my head in the space between his surprisingly broad, firm shoulders. "Sorry. I was excited to see you. You smell amazing, by the way. What cologne are you wearing?"

I felt him melt into the backwards hug like he needed the connection just as much as I did.

"Um ... I think that's just my fabric softener."

I took a deep inhale. "Whatever it is, it smells great."

A small sigh escaped him. "Thanks."

"How was your flight home?"

"Long. I'm glad to be back."

"I'm glad you're back."

"Are we ever going to turn around and face each other?" There was a smile in his voice.

"I don't think so. I'm enjoying this hug too much."

"Me, too."

"For a rangy bloke, you're surprisingly huggable."

He laughed, and the sound vibrated through me. He began to twist around, but I didn't loosen my hold as I looked up. Our eyes met. There was a tenderness in his gaze that took me off guard. His eyes travelled over my face, taking in my every feature before settling for several seconds on my lips. My belly fluttered. Neil brought his eyes back to mine, and I finally released my hold and stepped away. His gaze swept down my body and his eyebrows rose.

"You're wearing a dress," he stated.

"That is correct," I replied with a smile.

"You look ... nice."

My smile widened. "Nice? Is that the best you can do?"

"Fine, you look fantastic." There was a pause as his cheeks reddened ever so slightly, and he amended, "Then again, I've been staring at you through a computer screen for weeks, so anything is a step up from that."

I swiped him on the shoulder. "Hey! Don't ruin it."

He chuckled deeply. "Sorry. I couldn't resist." He gave my body another perusal. "It really is good to see you."

"It's good to see you, too. I missed seeing your stupid face in person."

Now he smiled, his eyes not leaving mine. I couldn't look away either. It just felt so exhilarating to finally be standing in the same room as him. To anyone else, it probably seemed mundane, but I might as well have been on a rollercoaster my heart was beating so fast.

"How are you?" he asked, breaking the intense moment.

"I'm good. Excited for the party."

"Don't get too excited. We still have to set everything up, and Leanne's been nagging me all day to make sure Isaac doesn't find out."

"Even if he does find out, I'm sure he'll fake his surprise when he walks in," I replied and noticed Neil glancing over my shoulder at the open doorway.

"Do you mind if I close the door?"

I shook my head. He stepped past me and went to close it. My eyebrows shot up questioningly as he turned back around.

"I have something important to tell you, and I didn't want anyone to overhear," he said, and my heart started to pound. Was he about to express his unquenchable desire for me? No, that couldn't be—

"I'm meeting Annabelle tomorrow," he blurted, and everything inside of me deflated.

12.
Afric

I stared at him, eyes wide. "You are? In person?"

Neil nodded. "I've left her messages unanswered for weeks. Ghosted her, basically. I kept telling myself I'd deal with her when I got home, but if I'm being honest, a part of me was just hoping the problem would go away. Then I read a message from her before my flight, asking for an explanation. She thinks she did something wrong and is beating herself up about it. I have a feeling I've really hurt her, and I just need to tell her the truth. It's the right thing to do."

"I guess," I said, glancing at the floor.

"You think it's a mistake meeting her, don't you?" Neil said, worry in his voice.

"Not necessarily. It's certainly ballsy."

"No one's ever called me ballsy before." I brought my eyes back to him. There were stress lines on his forehead indicating he'd been fretting over this a lot.

"I think it's brave. I certainly wouldn't have the courage to do it," I told him.

Neil ran a hand through his neatly combed hair. "I just need to draw a line under the whole thing, you know?"

"I completely get it," I replied, pausing a moment before I asked, "So, do you not have feelings for her anymore?"

He looked away, some indecipherable emotion passing over his features. "Even if I did it wouldn't matter. I can't start a relationship with someone based on a lie this big."

Hmm, that wasn't exactly a straight answer. I reached out and took his hand into mine. I wanted to be supportive because he'd clearly agonised over this, but I couldn't help voicing a concern. "What if she gets mad and decides to go public with the story?"

"If that happens, then so be it. It'll be my fault anyway. My conscience won't allow me to just ignore this." He glanced down, staring at our interlocked fingers as though they fascinated him.

"Where are you meeting her?"

"At the café near the gym."

"Isn't that a little close to home?"

He scratched his head. "I don't know ... Yes, probably. I panicked when I messaged her the location, okay? Anyway, it's done now." He paused, eyeing me desperately. "Will you come?"

"Come with you to meet Annabelle?"

He nodded. "You don't need to actually sit at the table while I talk to her. You could sit somewhere close by. I just think I'll feel more confident facing her if someone's there in my corner."

I'll always be in your corner.

"Okay, sure, I'll come. That café makes incredible waffles, and I've been fiending for more."

Neil smiled, falling silent as he exhaled a heavy breath. "Thank you. You're a good friend."

"And you're a good person. You just made some unwise decisions and got yourself into a shitty situation. It happens. Don't beat yourself up about it."

"How do you know I'm beating myself up?" he asked, curious.

I reached up with the hand that wasn't currently holding his and stroked a finger over the fine line between his eyebrows. "When you're stressed, this line deepens."

Neil's expression turned thoughtful. "I've never noticed that."

"That's because you don't look at your face as often as I do. I've been staring at it through a screen for weeks, and I can always tell when you've had a stressful day at work, depending on how deep this line is."

"Makes sense," he murmured, eyes following the movement of my hand as I lowered it. Several moments of quiet passed before he spoke. "Michaela was pleased to inform me that you told her about our friendship." He raised a questioning eyebrow.

"Was I supposed to keep it a secret?" My tone was teasing as I tugged on his hand. "Are you ashamed of me, Neil?"

He tugged back, effectively plastering my chest to his front, and a soft, surprised gasp escaped me. An unexpected wave of arousal shot through me at the contact. "Never. Don't ever think that." His eyes flickered back and forth between mine, and my breathing stuttered.

"Okay," I said, my voice uncharacteristically breathy now.

For the second time in however many minutes, we were locked in a stare-down. I yearned to know what he was thinking. There were secrets in his eyes that called to me. And I hadn't been lying earlier; he really did smell good. It wasn't just his fabric softener, either. Everyone had their own unique scent. It was hard to pick out the notes and determine what exactly Neil's was made up of, but it was now ingrained in my memory. It caused a visceral reaction in me.

Footsteps sounded down the hallway, and Neil let go of my hand. He turned around swiftly and picked up his clipboard and pen. The door opened, and Michaela poked her head in. Her attention went from me to Neil, and it looked like she was attempting to suppress a grin.

"There you two are. Afric, I need your help out front."

I cast Neil one last glance, my insides still all aflutter after the forceful way he'd tugged me close to him. He looked at me briefly, a certain brooding intensity about him that I hadn't seen before. Then he returned his attention to his clipboard, and I followed Michaela out.

Two hours later, the bar was decorated, and everything was ready for the party. As people started to arrive, Neil appeared in front of me.

"The place looks amazing," I exclaimed. "You and Michaela really pulled it off, especially given how little time you had to prepare."

"Don't forget you and your friends helped, too. But thanks. I love party planning. It can be stressful at times, but it's also one of my favourite parts of the job."

"You planned the screening in Notting Hill, too, didn't you?"

"With Michaela's help, yes," he replied.

"Well, you certainly have a knack for planning events. If I ever decide to throw myself a big, splashy birthday party, I'll know who to come to."

Neil smiled. "Can I get you something to drink?"

"Sure. What would you recommend?"

"Well, there's beer, prosecco, or wine. There are also some cans of premixed cocktails that may or may not be disgusting. The jury's still out."

"You haven't tasted any of them yet?"

He shook his head. "Not sure I'm brave enough."

"Why don't we both try them together then?"

A grin tugged at his lips. "Fine, but if they're horrible, I'm blaming you." He disappeared, and I found a seat at the edge of the terrace. I couldn't spot Sarita or Mabel anywhere, and I didn't really know anyone else here.

Michaela was over at the bar next to James and several other people I didn't recognise.

When Neil returned, he took the seat right next to mine, which left us both facing out with our backs to the wall. His arm brushed mine as he offered me a can that purported to be a margarita, alongside a glass with ice. "Here you go."

"Thanks. Which one did you go for?"

"Whiskey sour."

"Ambitious choice. Okay, moment of truth," I said as I opened my can and poured its contents into the glass while Neil did the same. We were quiet as we each took a sip.

"Well, it's not disgusting, but it isn't delicious either," I said. "How's yours?"

"It's okay. I'm a bit jetlagged, so I don't plan on drinking much tonight anyway. I tend to fall asleep when I get drunk, so don't let me have anything else after this."

I nodded and fell quiet as I took another sip. Then, my curiosity got the better of me. "So, did you go on any other nights out while you were in New York? Other than the night you already told me about?"

Neil shook his head. "When would I have found the time? I spent most of my evenings video calling with you."

"That's true. I'm quite an awesome distraction, aren't I?"

He glanced at me, his eyes seeming to trace down the slope of my nose. "You're certainly distracting."

Tingles filled my chest. "Good distracting or bad distracting?"

"I haven't decided yet," he teased, and I scowled at him playfully.

"Thanks for finishing my accounts, by the way. You did an amazing job. I passed my audit with flying colours."

"You did? That's great. Let me know if you need a hand for next year."

"That's okay. I should probably get myself a real accountant next year. If I'd done that from the beginning, the audit might never have happened."

"You're right. You should get an accountant, though I'm going to miss tidying up your messes."

"At least you won't have to worry about going bright red figuring out whether my expenses are business or personal," I said with a wink.

Neil shook his head, not meeting my gaze as he sipped his drink. "Why would you bring that up?"

"Because it's funny. It's also funny that you're still embarrassed about it. Everyone buys sex toys, Neil. It's perfectly normal."

"Not everyone," he said in a quiet voice.

I blinked at him. "You've never bought a sex toy?"

"It's not the same for men. When women buy dildos, it's a symbol of eroticism and empowerment. Some bloke going into a sex shop and buying a fleshlight has much seedier connotations."

I tilted my head as I sat back. "I don't know. The image of you going to town on a fleshlight is very erotic, in my opinion."

Neil gaped at me. "Afric!"

I chuckled loudly. "What? I'm joking. Well, kind of. But you're right. There is definitely a discrepancy between men and women in that area, but there shouldn't be. Everyone is someone's cup of tea, you know?"

He glanced at me, an odd expression on his face when he said, "Yeah, I know."

"Neil, introduce us to your friend," came a voice, and we both looked up. Leanne and Callum stood before us, a handsome couple if ever I saw one. They had that glossy attractiveness that marked them as celebrities. I suspected it was down to being able to afford fancy skin treatments and personal stylists the rest of us didn't have access to.

Next to me, Neil sat up a little straighter.

"Oh, hi, um, this is Afric," he said as both of them took me in with interest.

"I'm actually a friend of Michaela's," I said. "I met Neil through her. It's great to meet you both, though. I'm a big fan of the show."

"That's very kind of you," Leanne said, her eyes going from me to Neil and then back to me. "You wouldn't happen to be the friend Neil's been sending selfies to?"

I laughed and looked at Neil. "You've been telling people about the selfies? That was supposed to be our little secret."

Neil rolled his eyes. "Don't listen to her. There's no secret."

"Or is there?" I went on, waggling my eyebrows, and Leanne and Callum both laughed.

"Well, it's nice to finally meet you, Afric," Callum said. "Neil hasn't shut up talking about you the whole time we were in New York."

"I was not—" Neil began to protest then gave up when he realised Callum was just trying to embarrass him.

"I'm not surprised. You are kind of obsessed with me," I said.

At this, Neil laughed and shook his head. "You're all horrible. I'm going to get another drink."

"You said I wasn't to let you have anymore because of the jet lag, remember?" I said as he stood.

"I know, but one more won't kill me. Do you want another?"

"Yes, but no more canned cocktails. I'll have a beer this time."

Neil looked to Callum and Leanne. "What about you two?"

"I'll come help you," Callum said, ushering Neil away while Leanne sat down across from me. I had a feeling I might be in for a bit of an interrogation. It was clear that both she and Callum were protective of Neil.

I watched as she leaned forward, resting her elbows on the edge of the table as she surveyed me. "So, how long have you two been friends?"

"Not long. Three months, maybe?"

"Do you like him?"

"Yes, I like him a lot," I answered honestly.

"Good."

I started to smile. "Anything else you'd like to know?"

"No, just don't hurt him. Neil's a sweetheart."

"Um, we're just friends. This isn't—"

"It's none of my business what it is or isn't. Just be kind to him. He deserves someone who's kind because he's the kindest, most generous person I know."

I glanced across to the bar where Neil and Callum were grabbing our drinks. "Yeah, he is," I whispered before looking back at Leanne. She smiled at me.

"I like you."

"I like you, too. Well, I like what I've seen on TV."

"Then you like the highly edited version of me. Maybe by the end of tonight, you'll discover whether or not you like the unedited version," she quipped just as Neil and Callum returned. Neil slid in next to me, and again, his arm brushed mine. I wished I could keep my arm resting against his. The contact was shockingly addictive.

"You okay?" he whispered, his breath washing over my cheek.

I nodded. "I'm great."

"What did Leanne say to you?"

I tapped the side of my nose. "Sorry. I can't break the girl talk code of silence."

He narrowed his eyes. "There is no such thing."

"Oh, yes, there is."

"Okay, everyone," Michaela announced loudly from where she stood by the bar. "Isaac's on his way up, so we need to all be quiet."

I made a show of zipping my lips as I grinned at Neil. He didn't look impressed that I wouldn't tell him what Leanne had said. The entire place hushed, and someone dimmed the lights. I felt Neil's attention in the darkness and glanced at him again. His eyes were on my profile, and there was a look on his face I hadn't seen before. It was a sexy look like he was imagining doing sexy things to me, but that couldn't be true … Could it?

"Why are you looking at me like that?" I whispered.

"No reason," he whispered back, leaning towards me a little. The whiskey sour must've had a higher alcohol content than my margarita.

"Are you tipsy already?" I asked, amused. "You've only had one drink."

"It's hitting me harder because of the jet lag, I think," Neil replied just as Isaac climbed the stairs to the roof bar, and everyone leapt up, bursting into a chorus of "SURPRISE!" He jumped back, startled, and I could tell it was a genuine reaction. He hadn't been expecting the party. He probably thought that since they'd all just gotten back from such a long trip, they wouldn't have the time to plan anything.

People all flocked to him to wish him a happy birthday while I remained seated next to Neil, and we quietly drank our beers. Over the course of the next three hours, I was introduced to most of the people who worked on *Running on Air*, as well as many of their significant others. I think a lot of people assumed I was Neil's girlfriend since we were both glued to each other the entire night. Every time I met Michaela's gaze, she was practically brimming over with mirth. She clearly enjoyed the idea of Neil and me forming a connection. I'd have to reiterate the fact to her soon that we were only friends.

Then I grimaced, remembering I'd agreed to go with Neil when he met Annabelle tomorrow. I was so nervous for him, and honestly, I was worried because I got the sense Annabelle was the kind of person to freak out over what Neil had done. If she was as shallow and mean as I suspected, then she might go crazy at him when she discovered the truth. Well, at least I'd be there to protect him if she did.

I had a feeling Neil's nerves for tomorrow were getting the better of him, too, because he hadn't stopped at those two initial drinks. I was pretty certain he was now on his fifth drink and working towards a sixth. I had also consumed several drinks myself and was feeling tipsy.

"I don't think you should go," I blurted.

We were sitting in our seats by the wall again while most of the other party-goers danced in the middle of the roof terrace to some catchy pop song.

Neil tilted his head to me, a shine of inebriation in his gorgeous brown eyes. Had they always been gorgeous or was I just now noticing them? His normally perfect hair was a little mussed, his glasses a little askew, and my fingers itched to reach out and fix them for him.

"You don't think I should go where?"

"To meet Annabelle tomorrow. I'm worried."

"Me, too."

"Is that why you're getting shitfaced?"

"I don't know. Probably."

"Why don't you just cancel?"

"I can't. I have to do this. I have to come clean."

"No, you don't," I said emphatically before lowering my voice to a whisper. "Catfishing is a lot more common than you'd think. And the vast majority of people who do it never have some big moment of confession, and certainly not face to face."

"The lie is weighing on me. I have to get it out," he said, his words slightly slurred as he brought his gaze to mine. "You'll still come with me, won't you?"

I blew out a breath. "Of course, I'll still come. I'll even take out my hoops for you if it comes to it."

His brow furrowed. "Take out your—"

I motioned to my earrings. "I'll take these out and fight her if she's cruel to you. I mean it. I don't care if it's the middle of the day in a busy café. If she doesn't realise what a gem you are, then I'm liable to lose it," I said, rambling tipsily.

At this, Neil smiled. Then he surprised me when he tiredly rested his head on my shoulder. "I think that might be the nicest thing anyone's ever promised to do for me."

"Well, I'm bordering on drunk, so don't get used to it," I replied with a chuckle, enjoying his warmth on my shoulder. The next time I glanced down, I found him fast asleep, his breathing slow and steady. "Poor boy, you're exhausted," I whispered as I finally gave in to the urge to fix his glasses.

He wasn't lying when he said alcohol made him sleepy because, judging from his breathing, he was completely conked out.

I was busy admiring his face while he slept when someone cleared their throat, and I looked up to find Michaela standing over us with James at her side. "Is he asleep?" she whispered.

I nodded. "He's still jet-lagged, and I think he drank a little too much."

"We should call a taxi to take him home," Michaela said. "I can't leave, though. I have to hand the keys over to the clean-up crew once the party is over."

"I can bring him," I offered impulsively. "I haven't had too much to drink."

Michaela eyed me a moment, then glanced at James, who shrugged at her in return. She looked back at me. "Okay, let me write down his address."

And that was how I found myself in the back of a taxi with Neil dozing against me. James and Callum had assisted me in getting him down and into the cab, both of them thoroughly amused since neither had witnessed their prim and proper assistant get blackout drunk before.

"Are we almost there?" I asked the driver about fifteen minutes into the journey.

"Almost. You might want to try waking your friend up. No offence, but a little thing like you isn't going to be able to carry him."

The driver was right. I definitely couldn't carry Neil, especially not since his flat was several storeys up. Michaela said it was on the fourth floor. I nudged his arm, and he groaned in response, but he didn't open his eyes.

"Neil," I said softly, "you have to wake up."

He groaned a second time, but instead of moving his head off my shoulder, he snuggled closer, effectively resting his head on my boobs. I glanced down at him, and my breathing stuttered. He looked so boyish and handsome, and I didn't dislike him resting on me. In fact, I liked it more than I should have.

I stroked his hair away from his face and shook him again. Finally, his eyes opened as he blearily took in his surroundings. "Afric, where are—"

"We're in a taxi. We're almost at your place, but you need to wake up because I can't carry you up four flights of stairs."

"Oh," he said, still drunk but not entirely unaware of where his head was resting. A faint redness touched his cheeks as he withdrew. The taxi came to a stop, and I paid the driver before ushering Neil out. I slung his arm around my shoulders as I made my way towards the entrance to his building.

"Do you have a key fob to get in?" I asked.

"In my pocket," he said, fumbling for it to no avail. I batted his hand away before sliding my own into his back pocket and pulling out the fob as well as the key to his flat. We entered the building, and thankfully, there was a lift. Neil lived in a nice place, much nicer than where I lived. I led him inside the lift, and his head sagged to the side as I pressed the button for his floor.

"I'm sorry. I drank too much," he slurred.

"It's okay. We all drink too much from time to time."

"You shouldn't have to bring me home like this," he went on. "It's embarrassing."

"No, it isn't. I can't count the number of times I've gotten shitfaced and Michaela or Sarita have had to escort me home. It's what friends do for each other."

"Right, *friends*," he said, and there was an odd note in his voice, but I put it down to his lack of sobriety. The lift opened, and we stepped out, Neil's arm still around my shoulders. I found his door and slid in the key before pushing it open.

We entered a moderately sized combined kitchen and living area. It was just as neat and tidy as I expected it to be, with a large bookshelf next to a comfortable-looking grey sofa, a coffee table, and a flat screen TV on the wall. For a second, I imagined us having our movie nights all curled up together on that sofa, and a swell of want bloomed within me. I wanted to watch movies here with Neil. I wanted to laze on his sofa reading novels from his bookshelf while he whipped something up for us in the kitchen.

Man, I really did have it bad. Pretty sure I'd never drunkenly lusted after cosy domestic bliss before.

Neil finally let go of me before leaning back against the wall as he kicked off his shoes.

"Thanks for getting me home," he said. "How are you … going … to get …"

"Home?" I finished, and he nodded. "I'll order a taxi."

Neil frowned and glanced over at the sofa I'd just been ogling. "You can sleep over there if you want. I have some extra pillows and blankets … somewhere."

His offer sent a flutter through me. I was on the verge of accepting when my phone buzzed in my bag. I pulled it out and quickly read the text before bringing my attention back to Neil.

"That was Sarita. She and Mabel are in a taxi now. They're going to stop off here and pick me up. This building is more or less on their way, so—"

Before I could finish the sentence, Neil closed the distance between us. I stood frozen as he lowered his face to my neck, his nose nuzzling at the sensitive hollow below my ear as he breathed, "I wish you could stay."

For a second, I swear my heart stopped beating. "I wish I could, too, but I'm drunk, and you're even drunker. It's a bad idea."

His nose moved, drawing a line from my neck up to my jaw. "I love how soft you are," he said, and a shiver trickled down my spine. "I love you in this dress." His hand came to rest on my ribs, just below the swell of my breast. The heat of it seared into me, warming me up from the outside in.

"Neil," I said his name, a weak protest.

"I want to kiss you. I can't stop thinking about it."

"You know I don't do kissing." My heart hammered a mile a minute as my subconscious added, *but for you, I might*. The realisation was startling. I honestly hadn't wanted to kiss anyone since I was fourteen years old.

"Do you have any idea how much that kills me?" he asked, his breathing heavy against me as he finally withdrew. I couldn't believe he just said that. Had he been thinking about kissing me? Did my preference bother him so much because he'd been wanting to kiss me as badly as he seemed to want to right now?

He lifted his head, his eyes so bright and intense I would've fallen over if he didn't have me backed up against the wall. "I know I'm going to … regret saying all this in the morning."

"Don't. It's nice to be wanted."

Now his eyes practically blazed. "Want is too tame a word."

I stared at him, just stared and stared until the annoying vibration of my phone interrupted the moment. Sarita and Mabel were obviously outside in the taxi, and I wasn't enough of an arsehole to leave them with the meter running just to prolong this epic moment of honesty between Neil and me.

"That's probably Sarita," I said. "I should go."

He didn't move away, instead pressing even closer. "I can't understand why I want you so much," he murmured, and I became aware of a stiff length against my thigh.

I swallowed tightly. "One of life's strange mysteries."

Neil blew out a long breath. "I should let you go."

"Yes, you should."

"But I don't want to."

"Me neither."

Now his eyes met mine again, and they were practically undressing me. "Text Sarita and tell her you're staying here."

I lifted a hand and stroked his cheek. "If you weren't drunk right now, I would." *I'd do it in a heartbeat.*

"I'm not that drunk."

"I practically had to lift you out of the taxi, Neil."

He huffed an amused breath. "Fine. I'm drunk. But that doesn't mean—"

"It means you're not thinking straight. I'm not thinking straight either. Now go and drink some water before you go to bed. You don't want to have a hangover in the morning."

"Okay," he said, looking at me like I was torturing him by leaving. I moved away and toward the door.

"I'll see you tomorrow," I said as I left.

"See you tomorrow, Afric," he reluctantly replied.

13.
Neil

I woke up with the mother and father of a hangover. The tail end of last night was a little blurry, though I did recall flashes of Afric coming back here with me in a taxi. Freaking out, I sat up in bed, trying to recall what happened, what I'd *said* to her. There was a half-finished glass of water on my nightstand. I picked it up and downed it in one long gulp, just as the memories resurfaced.

Oh, God.

I'd told her I wanted her.

I'd rested my head on her perfect breasts, nuzzled her neck, backed her up against the wall, and inhaled her scent. But … wait, had she said something about wanting me, too? The memory was too hazy to recall her exact words, but she certainly hadn't been disgusted by my advances.

I was so full of regret and sick with a hangover that all I wanted to do was stay in bed all day and feel sorry for myself. I couldn't do that, though, because I'd stupidly arranged to meet Annabelle. Not only that, I'd asked Afric to accompany me. So, now I had to meet Annabelle face to face with a hangover, and I also had to do it while being mortifyingly embarrassed for practically groping my newest friend last night.

Maybe deep down, I was a truly despicable person.

I sat there, wallowing for a long few minutes before I finally dragged myself out of bed and into the shower. I scrubbed my entire body clean while trying to figure out how to act in front of Afric when I saw her. Perhaps I should feign amnesia? People got too drunk to remember things all the time, right? At least that way, we wouldn't have to discuss it.

I want to kiss you. I can't stop thinking about it.
I winced. I couldn't believe I'd told her that. What on earth had possessed me? I was normally so good at keeping my feelings and impulses to myself, but a few beers and a bit of jet lag and I was spilling my guts to one of the few people I truly enjoyed spending time with.

I wouldn't be surprised if she didn't show up today. I'd probably scarred her for life with my drunken advances.

It was almost time for me to head out to the café when my phone buzzed with a text.

Afric: Hey! How's your head? I'm outside your building, and I brought coffee. Thought you could do with some caffeine before you face Annabelle.

Just like that, relief hit. I hadn't scarred her for life. At the very least, I hadn't scared her away completely. Now I just needed to worry about what she remembered me saying to her.

Neil: My head is pounding. It's my own fault, really. Stay where you are. I'm on my way down.

I grabbed my keys and wallet, then made my way to the lift. One of my neighbours, an elderly woman with curly, plum-dyed hair, was bringing her Pomeranian for a walk. The little dog emitted a tiny growl when I passed, and I made sure to give it a wide berth.

"Sorry about him," the woman said. "He's terrified of everything, so he growls."

"No worries," I said, thinking the little dog probably had the right idea. Maybe if I growled at everything that scared me, the world would give me a wide berth, too, and I wouldn't have to face days like this.

The doors to the lift opened when we reached the ground floor, and I motioned for the woman to leave first.

"Such a polite young man," she chirped approvingly as she exited the lift.

As soon as I emerged, I spotted Afric standing outside, two takeaway coffee cups in hand. Her hair was pulled up into a high ponytail. She still wore the hoop earrings from last night, the ones I distinctly remembered her saying she'd take out to fight Annabelle for me. A faint smile touched my lips at the memory.

She wore an oversized black hoodie that appeared to have epaulets on the shoulders boasting studs, spikes, and diamante. On her legs were forest green leggings. Her clothing choices were always unusual, though I'd come to appreciate them. I'd noticed she spent quite a bit of money on clothes when I'd gone through her accounts. Far too much, actually. So, these strange outfits had to be designer, given how much they cost. Maybe my taste was so basic that I couldn't spot style when I was looking at it.

The woman and her little dog passed by Afric, the dog growling at her, too. She grinned down at it. "Tell me about it, buddy. Feckin' ridiculous if you ask me."

My neighbour gave a chuckle before continuing on her way.

"Morning," I said, "I didn't realise you could converse with animals." She turned around with a tired smile. I was glad I wasn't the only one feeling worse for wear.

"Just one of my many talents," she replied and held out a coffee. I took a long sip, eyeing her because she appeared to be acting like everything was normal. She hadn't brought up last night, but some impulse had me needing to clear the air. "Afric, if I said anything to offend you last night, I'm deeply sorry. I was drunk and jet-lagged, and that's no excuse, but I'd still like to apologise."

She gave a small, fond chuckle. "Would you ever stop? We're friends, Neil. You don't need to apologise for getting drunk and letting loose. In fact, I highly approve of it. Everyone needs to let their hair down once in a while."

I scratched the spot behind my ear. "Still, I shouldn't have been so—"

"Horny?" she cut in. "It happens to the best of us, especially when alcohol is involved. You were horny and drunk, and I was the only one there to receive said horny drunkenness. I get it. It's been a while since I've gotten some action myself. Anyway, can you please wipe that guilty look off your face? We're good. I actually think I like you more now. You're an adorable, horny drunk, and in my book, that's far better than an angry drunk or a mean one."

"I still feel bad about it," I said while pondering her statement.

It's been a while since I've gotten some action myself.

The urge to rectify that situation hit me like a sledgehammer.

"Well, don't," she insisted. "There's nothing to feel bad about. Now, how are your nerves for today? You sure you don't want to cancel on Annabelle? I won't judge you for it if you do."

I inhaled a deep breath. "No, I want to get this over and done with. If worse comes to worst and I lose my job, I can always go on the dole and move back in with Rosie and Grandma until I figure things out."

"You're not going on the dole, and you won't lose your job. I met most of the people you work for last night, and Neil, you probably don't realise this, but they all completely adore you. I suspect that even if they found out about Annabelle, they'd still forgive you for it."

"I don't deserve their forgiveness."

She shook her head at me. "It goes to show just how good you are that you think this is the worst thing a person could possibly do on the internet. I've basically lived online since I was a teenager, and I've seen some seriously foul shit. Your little catfishing episode is barely the tip of the iceberg."

What she said made me feel a tiny bit better, but not by much. We rode the Tube together, and Afric was kind enough to distract me by talking endlessly about the mission she and her gaming friends, Yellowshoes and TheBigSix, were currently undertaking in her favourite game, *Greenforest*. Most of the details went right over my head since I'd never been into computer games, but the way her eyes lit up with passion as she spoke was what held my attention.

There was magic to this woman. The more I got to know her, the more evident it became. She lived in her own world, made up her own rules, and I was almost envious of her. I'd always lived in other people's worlds. I facilitated their lives, made sure everything was planned for and running smoothly. Perhaps the possibility of Annabelle outing me to Callum was a good thing. Maybe it meant I'd finally quit being someone's assistant and start chasing my own dreams for a change.

But what were my dreams?

The idea of branching off and starting my own event planning business was certainly appealing. I'd even done research and sketched out a business plan, but that didn't mean I'd ever go through with it. It was just so much easier to stay put, keep working as an assistant and let my life go on as normal. Sometimes, I felt like I was drowning in the status quo and I'd never find the courage to try and build something of my own. I was paying my bills. I was putting money away in savings, but was I actually living? Was I fulfilling my potential? Did I want to? Did I have it in me to be my own boss and possibly other people's boss?

I had to admit, the thought of being the one in charge was invigorating.

When we reached the café, Afric grabbed a table in the corner while I went to sit by the window. I ordered some green tea because my stomach was too queasy for actual food. Several minutes went by, and I glanced over at Afric's table. She'd just been served a plate of waffles, and I envied her appetite. She shot me a wink and a thumbs-up, and I noticed she'd seated herself in a position so that she could discreetly keep an eye on my table.

Then, the café door opened, and in walked the prettiest redhead I'd ever seen. Seriously, her pictures didn't do her justice. Annabelle was beautiful, though strangely, that didn't affect me like it used to. Something had changed. She'd once occupied a pedestal inside my head, but no longer. I didn't see her as this perfect, angelic being anymore, and I was glad for it. She was just a normal human woman to me now. It made facing her far more bearable.

She glanced around the café, clearly searching for Callum. Nerves thrummed through me as I stood from my seat, glancing at Afric one last time. She had a bite of waffle halfway to her mouth as she gave me an encouraging nod.

Deep breath in, deep breath out.

I approached Annabelle and opened my mouth to speak. Nothing came out. She glanced at me for a second, then instantly dismissed me, instead looking over my shoulder. When I didn't move, she glanced at me again.

"I'm sorry, can I help you?" she clipped, and something stabbed in my gut.

"Yes, um, are you Annabelle?"

At this, her dismissiveness waned. "I am. Did Callum send you? Is he not able to make it?"

I motioned to the table I'd been occupying. "Can we sit for a moment?"

Warily, she nodded and walked to the table before taking a seat. I could practically feel Afric's avid attention as she watched us, but it didn't make me feel self-conscious. There was something reassuring about her presence.

When I met Annabelle's eyes, there was a light of recognition in her. "Hey, I think I know you. Aren't you one of the assistants from *Running on Air*? I've seen you on the show a few times."

I sometimes appeared in the background of scenes, but I didn't realise anyone paid much attention to me. "Yes. My name is Neil. I work for Callum. I actually run most of his social media accounts."

Now she smiled. "Oh, you must know all about me then. Callum and I message each other a lot. Where is he, by the way? Is he running late?"

I didn't answer her question. Instead, I sent her a meaningful look. "Callum doesn't go on his social media accounts. That's why I run them for him."

Now she frowned. "What are you talking about? Of course he …" she trailed off as she stared at me for a long, long moment, the penny finally dropping. There was a flash of horror in her eyes, and my gut sank. She glanced out the window, fidgeted with her hands, then turned back to me, leaning closer and lowering her voice.

"Do you mean to tell me that you're the one I've been messaging with all this time?"

I nodded. "I'm so sorry. Callum has me reply to all his messages, but before I knew it, we were having these full-blown conversations, and I didn't know how to come clean to you."

Annabelle's eyes narrowed with a quick, brief flash of fury. "You could've told me the truth at any time."

"You're right. I could have. But I found I liked you so much that I didn't want to lose your friendship. I feared that if you knew the real me, you wouldn't be interested."

At this, she studied me intently but didn't say anything for almost a full minute. It was clear she was thinking very hard, sorting through the information.

"Is this why you went quiet on me for weeks?" she finally asked.

I nodded, and silence fell yet again. I eyed her anxiously, dying to know what she thought. Across the café, I met Afric's gaze, and she widened her eyes pointedly as if to say, *Stop looking at me and focus on her!*

Annabelle lowered her head, closed her eyes, and inhaled a deep breath. Then, she opened her eyes and looked right at me. I was shocked when she gave me a small smile. "You're wrong, you know. Yes, I would've been mad that you'd been lying to me, but I wouldn't have been uninterested."

I blinked at her. "You wouldn't?"

"Of course not. You're cute."

"I am?"

She nodded, and a strange warmth filled my chest. She thought I was cute? She wouldn't have been uninterested? Perhaps my lack of self-confidence had been misplaced. It gave me a boost to know I wasn't quite as unnoticeable and bland to the opposite sex as I thought I was.

I cleared my throat. "Well, thank you, that's very kind, but I still can't justify what I did. It's inexcusable, and I can't apologise enough for not responding to your messages these past few weeks. You have no idea how awful I feel about that. It's why I asked to meet with you today. I wanted to finally be honest with you face to face. It's the least you deserve. I can never undo what I did, but I can at least offer you the respect of being truthful."

Annabelle arched an eyebrow. "So, that's it? You came here to tell me the truth and walk away?"

"Well, yes. Obviously, you'd never possibly be interested in anything more after the way I lied."

"What if I am interested?" she blurted.

Uh, what?

She reached across the table to take my hand in hers. "Neil, I might've thought you were Callum all this time, but that doesn't change the fact that you were the one I was talking to. You were the one whose messages I looked forward to. The one whose personality made me laugh and smile and brightened my days."

My mouth wouldn't work. Shock. I had to be in shock. I'd been so convinced that once she discovered I wasn't Callum, she'd run a mile. But she hadn't. Not yet, anyway. She was still sitting across from me, staring at me with wide, kind eyes. "I looked forward to your messages, too," I said at last.

"I have a bold suggestion."

"Oh?"

She squeezed my hand. "How about we put the lies behind us and start fresh?"

"So, you want to—"

"I want to date you, Neil."

Her statement soothed a wound deep inside me, one whose presence I hadn't been completely aware of. Annabelle accepting that I wasn't Callum and wanting to give me a chance bolstered my confidence. It healed an infection that had been festering, made me feel like I had worth. And that was probably why I replied with a simple, "Okay, yes."

Afric

I watched Neil and Annabelle from across the café, and a brick sank in my belly. From all outward appearances, she seemed to be taking his confession rather well. I realised belatedly that some part of me hadn't wanted her to take it well. I wanted her to storm out and say that she never wanted to hear from him again. That way, Neil and I could resume our friendship without her shadow looming over it.

But that wasn't to be.

They were over there chatting away, the conversation flowing like any successful first date. Jealousy swarmed within me, an expanding, shadowy beast. I was suspicious, too. Something about the ease with which she'd taken Neil's revelation made me wary. Any normal person would've at least yelled or displayed some form of indignation. But not Annabelle. She was taking this all in stride, and I wasn't entirely convinced it was genuine.

Then again, that could've just been my jealous shadowbeast talking.

I'd decided to go easy on Neil and act like his advances last night were nothing out of the ordinary. He was clearly chagrined by his actions, and for once, I didn't feel like teasing him. The truth was, I couldn't stop thinking about his words and the lustful way his eyes had consumed me.

I wanted him to look at me like that again. Instead, he was over there with Annabelle, the two of them getting on like a house on fire.

I hated this. I hated absolutely everything about it.

Why hadn't I tried harder to convince him not to come this morning? That way, I could've kept him all to myself. Oh, my God, now she was holding his hand. I wanted to stab something. Preferably her.

Picking up my fork, I skewered a piece of waffle and bitterly shoved it into my mouth. When I'd woken up this morning, the soundtrack in my head had been "Lovely Day" by Bill Withers. Now it was "Ain't No Sunshine," also by Bill Withers.

A little while later, Neil and Annabelle both stood from their table. She came forward, pulling him into a hug. The stabby instinct returned. They exchanged words, and then she left. Once she was gone, Neil made his way over to me. His expression was one of pleasant surprise.

"That looked like it went a lot better than either of us expected," I said, trying hard not to sound as unhappy and jealous as I felt.

He ran a hand through his hair. "Yeah, she, um … she said she wants to date me."

WHAT?!

My eyebrows shot up, and my chest burned with the fire of a thousand suns. It wasn't a fun feeling, let me tell you. "Do you … do you want to date her?"

A fleeting shadow crossed his features. "Well, yes, I suppose I—"

"Great," I said, cutting him off sullenly as I stabbed my remaining piece of waffle with my fork. Was it possible for one's stomach to spontaneously drop out of one's body? That was the sensation I was feeling right then.

Neil frowned. "What's wrong with you?"

"Nothing," I replied, unable to disguise the irritation in my voice.

He folded his arms, tilting his head in curiosity. "Well, that's obviously a lie."

I let my fork fall to my plate with a loud clatter. "I just don't think you can trust her," I blurted, and his frown deepened.

"Okay, why not?"

I made a dramatic hand gesture. "Well, for one, there's what I observed of her at the gym."

"Afric, you don't even know if what you saw was correct. You said yourself you were too far away to hear her conversation."

"So? Her snickering and body language told me all I needed to know. And to be honest, there's a good chance that she's only asked you on a date to get closer to Callum."

Neil's lips pressed together, dismay colouring his features. "Right, so you don't think she could ever genuinely be interested in me, is that what you're saying?"

"No, of course not, but this is an unusual circumstance, and I care about you, Neil. I won't stand by and watch you get taken advantage of."

"You think I'm naïve, then?"

Oh, hell. I was messing this up completely. Where was my tact when I needed it? Then again, it had never been my strong suit.

I levelled my eyes on his. "Look, I just feel like someone who thought they were conducting an online relationship with Callum Davidson wouldn't take to being catfished quite so graciously. Maybe if she'd gotten a little angry first, then yes, I would've believed her acceptance, but the way she behaved is way too suspicious to me."

I left the other part of what I wanted to say unsaid. The fact of the matter was that I was upset by how easily he'd agreed to a date with Annabelle when there was clearly some attraction and feelings brewing between us. He might've been drunk last night, but that didn't mean there wasn't some truth to what he'd said. It seemed I was destined to repeat old patterns, developing feelings for men who, for various reasons, discarded me in the end. The sad thing was Neil and I hadn't even been in a relationship.

He didn't respond for a long moment, and a shadow fell over the table. "Listen, I have to go. I have to check in at the gym. Callum and James wanted me to run some errands for them."

I gaped at him. "So, you're just going to run off and leave things like this?"

"I can't see what good will be achieved by sitting here arguing."

I frowned, a little piece of my heart breaking in two. "Fine, go then."

"Afric—"

"Just go. You've won the lottery. Annabelle wants to date you. Congratulations."

He frowned back at me, but he didn't reply. Instead, he left, and I wandered up to the counter to order another plate of waffles.

I was about to eat every last one of my feelings.

14.
Neil

Two days went by. Afric and I still hadn't spoken. I missed her more with every passing hour, but I was also still angry at her. I was angry at her for poking holes in Annabelle's easy acceptance, for being so suspicious, and for arousing my own suspicions in return. She'd broken the momentary spell Annabelle had cast over me and inserted stirrings of doubt.

And the fact of the matter was that I couldn't stop thinking about her. Not Annabelle. *Afric.* Interpret from that what you will.

A few hours after I departed the café, I accepted the fact that I wasn't as excited about dating Annabelle as I wanted to be. When we'd been sitting across from each other and she said she wanted to date me, I'd felt a certain amount of gratification. It had soothed me to think a woman like her would actually want me, despite my lie. A few months ago, I wouldn't have believed that she could accept the real me, not even in my wildest dreams. But now that I had some time and space to think about it, the happiness I should be feeling fell flat. Annabelle wasn't the one who sent my pulse racing.

No, that award went to the frustrating Irish girl whose bright blue eyes, cheeky smile, and curvy body wouldn't get out of my head.

I was busy working at the gym when I received a message. My stomach flipped because for a second, I thought it might be Afric, but it wasn't.

Annabelle: Hey, want to meet up for coffee?

On the surface, it was a simple question, but I wasn't ready to see her again so soon. Not with how Afric's suspicions still had me all twisted up.
Neil: Sorry, I can't right now. I'm working.
Annabelle: Why don't I bring the coffee to you then? If you're scheduled for a lunch break soon, I could also bring food ...?
Her offer had me stumped as to how to respond. Then, staring at my phone, an idea sprung, and my resolve firmed. It pained me to think it, but there was a very good chance Afric was right and Annabelle only wanted to date me to get closer to Callum. What better way than to invite her to the gym and see how she reacted to being around him in person?

Impulsively, I texted her back, agreeing to lunch and sending her the gym's address before I returned my attention to my laptop. When I worked here, I typically camped out close to the entrance, where there was a small lobby with a coffee table and a comfortable couch. Michaela was off today, so I was the only one on duty to run errands for the cast while they trained. So far this morning, none of them had asked for anything, so I was free to deal with emails and correspondence.

I was focused on reading one particular email about a magazine photoshoot for the cast when the buzzer went off for the door entry system. My heart leapt right into my throat. It had to be Annabelle. Sure enough, I checked the security camera, and there she was. It was a warm day by London standards, and she appeared to be wearing a denim jacket over tight workout gear. She worked as a personal trainer, so the workout gear made sense.

I pressed the button to let her in, and a moment later, she emerged through the door, her red hair tied up in a neat bun.

"Hi," I said awkwardly. "Thanks for coming over."

"Of course! I've been looking forward to seeing you again. I brought coffee and two veggie bowls. I hope you don't mind that there's oat milk in the coffee. I'm vegan, so it's second nature to me to order the milk substitute," she said, then grimaced. "You probably wanted normal milk."

She seemed a little nervous, and it warmed me to her slightly. "I'm actually dairy intolerant, so the oat milk is perfect."

"Oh, you are? Well, that's a relief."

I motioned to the couch where I'd just powered down my laptop and packed away my things. "Welcome to my place of work. We can eat here. The cast is training inside. I can give you a quick tour of the gym before we eat if you like?"

Her eyes wandered to the glass door that led inside. There was a light in them for a second before she shook her head. "Maybe later? I'm starving, and I work in a gym all day long, so it won't be anything new to me."

Well, at least she didn't appear overly eager to go inside and meet everyone. And by everyone, I meant Callum.

"Are you sure? It's not a regular sort of gym. There are lots of ramps and jumping walls kitted out specifically for practicing parkour. I remember you saying you dabbled in freerunning from time to time."

She carried the lunches over to the table and set them down before taking a seat on the couch. "Yes, I do, but I'm nowhere near the standard of the *Running on Air* cast. I'd only end up embarrassing myself in front of them," she said with a hint of self-deprecation.

She offered me one of the coffees alongside a veggie bowl. "Thanks. Next time I'll buy."

The polite statement was second nature, but it was only after it left my mouth that I realised I'd insinuated there'd be another lunch date.

"It's no problem. I've always loved buying meals for others. It's one of those simple kindnesses that make people happy, you know?"

"Hmm, I never thought of it like that, but you're right. It's always nice when someone decides to treat you, though being the man, I should probably insist on paying you back."

She waved me away. "I don't go in for all that. So long as things are fifty-fifty, I'm okay with it."

"That sounds very reasonable."

Now she smiled. "So, there's going to be a next time?" she asked, circling back to my earlier foolish remark.

"Uh, sure," I replied, trying not to grimace. I'd made it seem like I was dying to see her again, and she'd barely been here a few minutes.

"Cool," she said, her smile deepening. "I was beginning to worry you'd lost interest in me since I hadn't heard from you in two days."

I scratched my head. "Right. Sorry about that. I've been busy with work." And fretting over whether or not you're using me to get close to the man you really want. "I also wanted to let you decide if you really wanted to see me again without being pushy. Honestly, I'm surprised you want anything to do with me after what I did," I said, hoping that if she were concealing a hidden agenda, then this might lead her to reveal some of her true feelings about the situation.

"Well, maybe I'm crazy, but when you explained everything, it just made so much sense to me. And I could relate. If I'd been in your position, perhaps I would've done the same thing."

"I doubt you've ever had to pretend you were someone else. You're beautiful," I said because it was the truth.

"Thank you, that's very kind, but I didn't always look like this. I was very overweight as a teenager. I still have to exercise all the time and watch what I eat to maintain a healthy balance."

My eyebrows rose, and a few things became clearer. Was this why she hadn't outright rejected me at the café the other day? She knew how it felt not to fit society's conventional beauty standard? Or, in my case, to not be over six feet tall with a jawline that could cut glass and muscles bigger than my head.

"I guess we're not necessarily what people think we are when they look at us," I finally replied.

"Definitely not," she agreed.

We continued chatting and were almost done eating when the door that led to the gym opened. Callum and Isaac emerged, looking like they'd both just showered after a morning of exercise. I glanced at Annabelle, but she didn't seem to display any kind of overt reaction to seeing Callum.

"Hey, Neil," Isaac said, looking from me to Annabelle. "Who's your friend?"

"Isaac, Callum, this is Annabelle. Annabelle, this is Isaac and Callum," I said, introducing them.

Annabelle shot me a little smile. "You know I already know who they are, Neil." She stood and reached out to shake both of their hands. "I'm a gigantic fan of the show."

Callum shot her the practiced smile he used during interviews and events. "It's always a pleasure to meet a fan."

"Oh, the pleasure is all mine. I actually started doing parkour because of you guys. Obviously, I'm nowhere near your skill level, but it's a fun hobby."

"Well, I'm glad we inspired you," Callum replied, then glanced at me. "We're heading out for lunch. I was going to ask you to join us, but it looks like you've already eaten."

"We could always grab dessert, couldn't we, Neil?" Annabelle said sweetly, then chuckled. "Those tiny veggie bowls never satisfy my hunger." There was a note of eagerness in her voice that set off some alarm bells, but I tried to give her the benefit of the doubt. She was meeting two of her idols. Of course, she'd want to go and have lunch with them.

Annabelle glanced at me then in a sort of pleading way. "Sure," I said. "Dessert sounds good."

"Great, let's go. I'm starving," Isaac replied.

We grabbed our things and made the short walk down the street to the same café where Annabelle and I had first met two days ago. When we were seated at a booth in the back, I noticed she was quick to slide in next to Callum. She removed her denim jacket, revealing the tight, low-cut workout top that matched her sculpted leggings. I watched as she picked up the menu and scanned it.

"Oh, wonderful, they have vegan desserts. I think I love this place already."

"We eat here a lot since it's so close to the gym," Isaac told her.

"Is that so?" Annabelle chirped.

"Yes, and Neil practically lives here," Callum added. "If he's not at the gym, I always know where to find him." A pause as his attention went between us. "So, how did you two meet?"

It was probably stupid of me, but I hadn't been ready for this question. Luckily, Annabelle swooped in with an answer. "We met at the supermarket. I was looking for the oat milk, and Neil was happy to point me in the right direction. We hit it off from there."

"That sounds like something that happens in romcoms rather than in real life," Isaac commented, and Annabelle laughed softly.

"I know, right? It was the perfect meet-cute."

I noticed Callum's brows furrow a little in confusion. I'd told him I met a girl online but that we'd yet to meet in person. Clearly, he presumed correctly that Annabelle was this girl and that we'd finally taken the plunge to meet. Her fake story about bumping into each other at the supermarket didn't match up.

He shot me a questioning look, but I just shrugged. It was possible, after all, that she was a completely different person to the internet girl since I'd never told him her name.

"What about you and Leanne?" Annabelle asked, snagging his attention. "Did you both meet on the show, or did you know each other from before?"

So, she *was* aware of their relationship. That benefit of the doubt I'd given her earlier was wavering thin.

Callum's easy demeanour grew somewhat wary. I knew he liked to keep details of his relationship as private as possible these days. Though, he had asked her the same question, so it didn't come too out of left field. I, on the other hand, was beginning to wonder if Annabelle's lack of enthusiasm to tour the gym and meet the cast earlier was carefully woven to lure me into a false sense of security. There was just something about how she looked at Callum that deepened my suspicions. She seemed far more alert when she spoke to him than when she spoke to me.

"We met on the show," Callum answered, not giving any further details.

"It must be difficult to have your relationship viewed and judged by millions of people. I'm in awe of how you both manage to make it work."

"It certainly wasn't easy in the beginning," he replied.

"Shall I go up and put in our orders?" I said, wanting to change the subject. This whole situation was weird enough without Annabelle interrogating Callum about his and Leanne's relationship. I looked to Annabelle as I explained. "Ordering is self-service here."

"Oh, okay. I guess I'll get the vegan apple pie with cashew cream."

Callum and Isaac both told me what they wanted, and I went over to put the order in. When I returned, Annabelle had somehow managed to sidle even closer to Callum and was peppering him with parkour-related questions. I slid back in next to Isaac as he bent to whisper in my ear, "I'm sorry to break it to you, but I think your girl has a thing for Callum."

I stiffened and sighed. So, Afric had been right all along. She had to have been if Isaac had come to the same conclusion and he'd barely spent half an hour in Annabelle's company.

"Yeah," I replied in a quiet voice. "I think you might be right about that."

Isaac shot me a commiserating grimace as I racked my brain for ways to make a clean break with Annabelle and also make things up to Afric. I never should've doubted her.

Afric

"I'm so jealous," Yellowshoes complained. "You have no idea how much I wish I could join you guys this weekend."

"I wish you could, too," I replied. "We'll meet in person one day, though. I promise."

"If you're so desperate, why don't you book a last-minute flight?" TheBigSix suggested. "Life is all about being spontaneous."

"I can't. I have to work. If I didn't, I might actually be tempted to book that flight, no matter how costly."

A few weeks ago, there'd been a reported UFO sighting in a rural part of Cornwall. This weekend, me, TheBigSix, and several of our U.K.-based extra-terrestrial enthusiast online friends were going to travel down there, camp out for a night, and see if we could catch a glimpse of said UFO. I was glad for the distraction since Neil had been giving me nothing but radio silence for two days now. And sure, two days wasn't long in the grand scheme of things, but it was when it came to Neil and me. I'd gotten far too attached to our constant communication, and I missed him like crazy. Though, admittedly, I was still hurt and upset that he didn't believe me about Annabelle. That he'd *chosen* her. Maybe it was silly of me to think that whatever bond we'd built over the last few weeks could be more important to him than his precious Annabelle.

Okay, so I was harbouring some bitterness.

I guess sometimes people simply refused to see the truth even when all the signs were staring them right in the face. They wanted the lie far too desperately. It was probably why all those online romance scams managed to lure people in.

The thought of Neil desperately wanting a picture-perfect happy ending with Annabelle cut through me like the new sword TheBigSix had just won for himself after a wager with a ghoul in Greenforest Tavern. My minor crush had clearly transformed into something much, much more serious, and I was feeling particularly morose about it.

I chatted some more with TheBigSix about our planned trip to Cornwall, then logged off for the evening. I had a headache, and my mind was racing, which usually meant I needed some time offline to clear my head. I'd just hit play on my guided meditation app when there was a knock on my door, followed by Sarita announcing, "You have a visitor."

I bolted upright in my bed. "Who is it?"

"It's Neil," came a voice I hadn't heard in two days.

Just like that, my body filled with nervous energy as I forced myself to lie back down. Feigning nonchalance, I replied, "It's okay, Sarita, you can send him in."

"I'm not your butler," she grumbled while I closed my eyes and followed the mediation, taking measured breaths in and out. I heard my door open and close a moment before Neil asked, "What are you doing?"

"I could ask you the same question," I replied evenly.

I heard him emit a tired sigh before I felt a weight lower onto my bed. "I came to apologise. I was an idiot, and I'm prepared to grovel for forgiveness."

Well, that was quite the statement.

I opened my eyes. Neil sat on the edge of my bed, his shoulders slumped. My phone continued to emit the sounds of a trickling stream, leaves rustling in the wind, and birds chirping in the distance.

"Oh?"

He looked like he hadn't gotten a wink of sleep. He'd clearly been agonising over something, our argument most likely, and I had to resist the urge to pull him into my arms and hug him tight. I hated seeing him so sad.

"You were right about Annabelle," he said, looking forlorn.

By contrast, relief filled me, but I kept my composure.

"What brought you to this conclusion?"

His gaze finally met mine. I'd missed those brown eyes. "She came to the gym today to share lunch with me."

A brief, sharp stab of jealousy went through me, but I tamped it down. Clearly, their lunch date hadn't gone well, given the fact he was here now apologising.

"I designed it as a bit of a trap if I'm being honest. I couldn't stop thinking about what you said about her using me to get close to Callum, so I decided to test the theory. I invited her to the gym for lunch, and things were going fine. Then, Callum and Isaac came out having just finished their training and invited us to join them at the café down the street. It was clear we'd already eaten, but Annabelle practically jumped at the chance, saying she was in the mood for dessert."

I scoffed. "I'll bet she was."

Neil frowned. "Again, I feel like such a fool for not going with my gut and listening to you in the first place. I was too busy being flattered by her acceptance like an idiot. We arrived at the café, and Annabelle sat right up close to Callum, peppering him with endless questions and even asking him about his relationship with Leanne. I was mortified. Even Isaac said it was obvious that Annabelle had a thing for Callum. Callum didn't seem to notice, probably because he's used to women being all over him. Anyway, after we ate, we parted ways. Annabelle mentioned coming to the gym for lunch again next week, and I panicked and agreed. She's clearly using me to spend time around Callum, and now I have no idea how to cut ties with her. She has too much dirt on me."

"Well, if you ask me, she sounds like an absolute bitch."

"Afric, I'm still the one in the wrong—"

"You came clean to her, and now she's using the situation to her advantage. She's a manipulative bitch, plain and simple. She clearly sees that you're too nice and too scared of her outing you to refuse her."

"Maybe I should just tell Callum the truth and face whatever consequences come after."

"You could do that. I'd advise you to take a few days to think about it first, though. Confessing is a big step."

Neil nodded, his face drawn in thought. A long moment of quiet fell before he asked, "What can I do to make it up to you?"

"Nothing. I've been fuming mad, of course, but I do get why you didn't listen to me. You wanted the fairy-tale." Bitterness pinched at my gut. "Annabelle is beautiful and sexy, and she said she wanted to date you. I can't fault you for saying yes."

"That's not why I said yes."

A flutter of hope went through me. "It isn't?"

Neil shook his head. "I'll admit it felt good to think she might like me enough to forgive my lies. It stroked my fragile ego, and that's probably why I said yes. But all those feelings I thought I had for her simply weren't there when we met in person. I didn't feel any kind of connection, not like ..."

"Not like what?" I asked, a little too eagerly. I was still lying down, but my heart was hammering in my chest. It filled me with an unnecessarily large amount of relief and giddiness to know that Neil hadn't fancied Annabelle when he met her in real life. He hadn't felt a connection to her, and for whatever silly, sentimental reason, that made me ridiculously happy.

"Not like I should have felt if I truly cared about her," he finished, and something about his tone told me that wasn't what he'd been about to say. He paused to eye me, a look of agony on his face. "Can you forgive me? I promise I'll never doubt you again."

"You should doubt me. I'm not perfect. I just so happened to be right about this. And yes, you're forgiven. I'm glad you came here. I've missed you."

Neil reached out and traced a finger along my arm. I held my breath for a moment, the simple touch lighting fireworks in my belly. "I've missed you, too," he murmured, then quietly continued to stroke my arm with his fingertips. A few moments passed, nature sounds filling the room before he said, "This is really nice."

"It's a meditation app. This one is my favourite. Nature sounds of the forest."

"It's very peaceful."

"Come and lie down. Meditate with me. After the day you've had, you obviously need some relaxation."

There was a flash of heat in his eyes, there and gone in less than a second, and a little thrill simmered through me. Silently, he slipped off his shoes and walked around the bed before lowering himself into the empty spot next to me.

His head rested against the spare pillow, and I turned my head slightly to the side to take him in. Our shoulders were touching, but I didn't move away. I savoured the barest hint of contact. Neil stared at the ceiling while my eyes traced the faint lines on his forehead, the swoop of his nose, and the jut of his chin. Without thinking, I reached out and removed his glasses. He finally looked at me, his expression questioning.

"You should take these off. They must give you tension on the bridge of your nose and behind your ears."

"They do, actually. How did you know?"

"Lucky guess."

"Thank you," he whispered, and I felt like he was thanking me for more than just removing his glasses. I placed them behind me on the nightstand, then rested my head on my pillow again and closed my eyes.

"I'm going on a trip to Cornwall this weekend," I said.

"Why are you going to Cornwall?" Neil asked, sounding curious.

A faint smile shaped my lips. "One of the locals claims they spotted a UFO the other week. I'm meeting up with a few of my online friends to see if we can catch a glimpse of it for ourselves."

I sensed him shaking his head, though his voice held only affection. "Of course, you are. What exactly did this local see?"

"Unidentified flying object. He says there was a lit-up, spinning object in the sky above the field where his cows graze. He claims it darted clear across the sky, faster than any man-made aircraft could possibly travel."

"So, this is the account of a farmer?" Neil asked, his tone teasing. I remembered the first time we met when he claimed the only people who ever saw UFOs were those who lived out in the middle of nowhere who were bored and trying to drum up some entertainment for themselves.

"Just because he's a farmer doesn't mean he isn't credible."

"It definitely doesn't make him credible either, though."

"You should come with me," I blurted on impulse, then opened my eyes to look at him. His eyebrows shot up. "I mean, we need at least one sceptic to balance out the group, so you'd be doing me a favour."

"I don't know. I might not be able to take the time off work at such short notice," he said.

"I'm sure Michaela will be happy to cover for you."

He rubbed his chin, thinking about it. "Hmm, getting out of London and away from Annabelle for a while does seem like a good idea. How are you getting there?"

"I was going to take the train."

"I could drive us," he offered.

My heart leapt. "So, you'll come?"

"Sure. Someone has to prove to you that aliens don't exist."

"Ha! I think you'll find *I'll* be the one proving *you* wrong," I said, pausing for a moment before I continued. "I didn't know you owned a car."

"I keep it at my grandma's house because the parking is terrible at my building. I don't drive it very often since traffic in this city is a nightmare. It might actually be enjoyable to get out on the open road. Sometimes, I feel like all the crowded Tube journeys I take will eventually suck away my soul."

I laughed at that. "Okay, you can drive us, but before you commit fully, you should know that we'll be camping out for the night. A friend of a friend has an uncle who owns a farm close to the original UFO sighting. She's gotten us permission to camp in one of the empty fields."

Neil went quiet as he thought about it. "I couldn't convince you to stay at a B&B instead, could I?"

I swallowed tightly. Visions of Neil and me holing up in a bed & breakfast for an entire night was giving me premature hot flashes.

"That would defeat the purpose. If we stay in a B&B, we won't be able to spot the UFO."

Neil emitted a heavy sigh. "Fine. Do you at least have a tent?"

I shook my head. "I was going to go to Lidl tomorrow and see if I could find a cheap one in the middle aisle."

"We're not staying in a Lidl tent. James has some good quality camping gear that I'm sure he'll let us borrow."

"Okay, that sounds like a better idea," I said, a small smile tugging at my lips. Neil and I were going camping together. We were going to be sharing *a tent*. The thought made me unreasonably giddy. I was so happy he came over and that we were now talking again.

"Neil?" I whispered, feeling vulnerable.

"Yes?"

"Let's never fight again."

There was a hint of a smile in his voice when he replied, "Okay."

A warmth spread through me, and we fell into silence. I closed my eyes and tried to bring my focus back to the meditation. Neil and I followed the lady's voice, interlaced with nature sounds as she instructed us on our breathing. Somehow, the sound of Neil's deep breaths going in and out was far more relaxing to me than the meditation. I enjoyed his closeness, the moment of quiet peace and serenity between us. And I guess it might've been a little too relaxing because somewhere along the way, I fell asleep.

15.
Neil

When I woke up, the first thing I noticed was that I wasn't in my own bed. A moment later, I became aware of the woman wrapped in my arms, her head resting gently in the centre of my chest. Emotion swelled within me as I gazed down her. She looked so peaceful.

Through the window, I saw it was fully dark out. The clock next to Afric's computer read 10:35 p.m. We'd been asleep for *hours*. Her soft, deep breathing filled my ears. I didn't know whether to try and extricate her from my arms or simply wake her.

A part of me didn't want to move a muscle.

Okay, so it wasn't just a part. It was all of me.

Having my arms around Afric felt right. I couldn't explain it. It just did.

You should probably move, my brain urged.

Stay right where you are, my heart countered.

Finally, I decided to go with my brain. Afric might not appreciate waking up with me like this. She certainly hadn't invited me to fall asleep in her bed. As gently as I could, I unwrapped my arms and deftly slid out from under her. She made a noise of complaint as I settled her onto the pillow, but then her breathing evened out again.

I climbed from the bed and found my shoes. I sat on the chair by her computer desk to slip them on. Next, I grabbed my glasses and jacket and was just putting both on when a sleepy voice asked in amusement, "Did we take a nap together?"

I turned to the bed, and the sight of her tired eyes and puffy lips made something tighten in my chest. *She was so beautiful.* I couldn't believe I didn't see it right from the first moment we met. How blind I'd been. "Yes," I replied. "Sorry about that. I didn't mean to fall asleep."

"Why are you apologising? I fell asleep, too." She stretched out like a lazy cat, and my eyes were inexplicably drawn to her body. She was curvaceous and well-endowed in a way that made my blood heat.

I forced myself to look away. "Well, I'd better get going."

"You don't have to. It's late. Just stay here."

"No, I really should go." I stood firm. She had no idea how difficult it would be to spend an entire night in her bed and not do something that would jeopardise our friendship irreversibly. Somehow, she'd become one of the most important people in my life. Far more important than Annabelle had ever been.

Looking back, I saw our online courtship for what it truly was; empty and hollow compared to the kaleidoscope of feelings and frustrations Afric seemed to provoke in me.

"Okay, well, text me and let me know when you get home safe. Otherwise, I'll worry."

"I will," I replied, zipping up my jacket and heading for the door. I was halfway there when I stopped. Some foreign urge took over as I turned back around and approached Afric's bed. I swear I heard her breath hitch when I bent and pressed the softest kiss to her temple.

"I know you don't like kisses, but I just want you to know how glad I am that we're talking again. The last two days have been miserable."

A faint smile touched her lips. "It's a good thing we agreed never to fight again. And it's mouth kisses I have a problem with. You can kiss my forehead all you like."

I laughed gently and shook my head. "I better go."

"Don't forget to text me," she called as I left her room.

"I won't," I called back.

***

The following day I was busy with work and organising our road trip to Cornwall. I told Afric that I'd take care of everything, and she seemed happy to leave me to the preparations. It was a four-to-five-hour drive, and luckily James had agreed to loan me his tent, gas cooker, cooler box, and two sleeping bags.

I didn't share Afric's hope and excitement for spotting UFOs, though I was looking forward to spending time with her. I even went shopping for food so that I could cook dinner while we camped. I was also looking forward to getting out of London, clearing my head, and figuring out how to tell Annabelle I didn't want to see her again.

I arranged for Michaela to cover for me at work, then collected my car from my grandma's. On Friday afternoon, I parked on the street outside Afric's flat before shooting off a text.

Neil: Are you ready? I'm outside and parked on double yellow lines.

Her response came promptly.

Afric: Say no more. I'm coming down now.

A minute later, she appeared. Her hair was down, and she wore a pale pink knitted top with a loose neckline, causing it to fall over her bare shoulder. It wasn't supposed to be provocative, but something about the sight of her bare skin made my throat thicken. I emerged from the car and took the backpack she had slung over her shoulder.

"I'll put this in the boot for you," I said.

I hadn't intended for it to happen, but my knuckles brushed her exposed shoulder, and she inhaled sharply. Her skin was so *soft*. I couldn't get the feel of it out of my head as I withdrew, and oddly, Afric wouldn't meet my gaze. Instead, she muttered, "Thanks," before going to sit in the passenger seat. I returned to the driver's side, put the car in gear, and we set off.

I was aware of her unusual silence and wanted to ask her about it, but I bit my tongue. Had I made her feel awkward by taking her bag like that? I'd thought it was a chivalrous move, but she seemed to have reacted weirdly to it. Some women didn't like men to do stuff like that for them anymore, opening doors and such, which I completely understood. I just had no idea if Afric shared those preferences.

"You look nice today," I said, glancing at her briefly before bringing my attention back to the road.

"Thank you," she replied. "You look nice, too."

A warmth filled my chest. I liked that she liked how I looked. "Thanks."

She leaned forward and tapped on the touch screen radio. "Do you mind if I sync my phone up with this so that we can listen to some music?" she asked, breaking through my thoughts.

"Sure, go for it."

She played around with her phone, then tapped the radio screen before an unusual electro song came on.

"What is this?"

"Yellow Magic Orchestra. They're a Japanese electronic band who've been going since the late seventies. I love their stuff. It reminds me of the music from video games in the nineties."

"Weren't you a foetus in the nineties?" I asked, wryly amused.

"Technically, yes, but my parents were cheapskates, so they made me play my older brothers' and sisters' hand me down consoles instead of buying me a new one."

"What age were you when you started gaming?"

She touched her chin. "Hmm, let me see. I was definitely under ten when I played my first video game, but it wasn't until I was a teenager that I became obsessed, and it wasn't a healthy obsession either. I often lost months to gaming. Nothing in the real world could compete. Then eventually the spell would break, and I'd realise I hadn't showered in so long my skin had developed a film." She gave a self-deprecating chuckle. "I have more of a healthy relationship with it now, though. I know when I need a break, and I'll give myself an entire week off."

"That does sound healthier. And I, for one, am glad that I didn't know you during the non-showering phase of your life," I said, and she chuckled again before falling quiet, her gaze focused out the window. It took forever for us to get out of London traffic, but once we hit the motorway, it was smooth sailing for a while.

Finally, I built up the courage to ask her about the bag incident. "Did I make you feel uncomfortable when I took your bag earlier?"

Her shoulders tensed. "Why would you think that?"

"You just seemed weird about it."

She shifted in her seat. "I wasn't weird about it."

She seemed adamant that she didn't want to talk about it anymore, so I dropped the subject. We let the music drift over us before I pulled into a rest stop so we could use the bathroom and grab something to eat. When we got back on the road, Afric didn't put her music on, happy to sit and be quiet for a while instead.

"Do you think it will be cold tonight?" she asked after a stretch of silence. "I've never gone camping the normal way before, only at music festivals, and those are always too noisy to actually bother trying to sleep."

"It might be a little bit cold, but James loaned me a great quality tent and sleeping bags, so we should be able to keep warm. He also gave me a gas cooker, and I brought some food so I can cook us dinner."

At this, she cast me a surprised glance. "You're going to cook me dinner?"

"I'm going to *attempt* to cook you dinner," I corrected.

"Are you a good cook?"

"I'm decent, though I've never cooked in the outdoors before, so it could go either way."

"Well, even if it's terrible, I'll still eat it. None of my past boyfriends have ever cooked for me." She fell quiet for a second, then frowned. "Not that ... I mean, not that you're my boyfriend or anything, I just meant ..."

She was rambling, and it was almost shocking because she was always so unabashed about things. Nothing seemed to embarrass her, but now it appeared something had. I smiled gently. "Relax, Afric. I know what you meant."

"You do?"

"Well, we don't have a typical sort of friendship."

"Don't we?"

"No. I think you might actually be my best friend now," I confessed, glancing briefly from the road to her to weigh her reaction. A bright, pleased smile graced her lush lips.

"I'm your best friend?"

"Yes. Aren't I yours?"

She thought about it a moment. "I always considered Sarita and Michaela my best friends, but both of them have been preoccupied with their other halves lately." She paused, and I sensed her eyes on my profile. "I guess you are my best friend now. Huh."

"You sound surprised."

"Aren't you surprised? Don't get me wrong, I love that we're friends, but I never would've expected this for us."

"Me neither," I said, smiling faintly as my thoughts wandered back to what she said about none of her previous boyfriends ever cooking for her. "A man's really never cooked for you before?"

She shook her head. "Most of my boyfriends were gamers like me. We're not exactly known for our culinary skills. Picking up the phone and ordering pizza is probably the most effort we'll put into a meal."

"My grandma taught me how to cook. She always said it was a good life skill to have."

"If Phil taught you, then you must be good. That woman's food is pure heavenly comfort. You're so lucky you get to eat there every day."

"I do recall her giving you an open invitation to dinner any time you want."

"And I recall you saying you'd barricade the door if I turned up," she shot back, and I laughed.

"Okay, perhaps I was being a tad dramatic. Besides, I'd have to let you in since we're now best friends."

"That's true."

A few beats of silence fell.

"So," I hedged, "these boyfriends of yours, which one made you hate kissing?"

She narrowed her eyes. "Don't be a sneak. I never said it was a boyfriend who made me hate kissing. Did you ever consider that it might just be a natural preference?"

"Is it?"

She blew out a breath, folding her arms as she brought her attention to the window. "No."

"If you don't want to talk about it, that's fine. I'm being nosy."

"You are being nosy. But I'll tell you if you really want to know. It's nothing deeply shocking or disturbing. It's all very mundane, actually. When I was fourteen, I had my first boyfriend. His name was Gary, and he lived down the street from me. He was a year older, and I had a crush on him for a while. He had pale blonde hair and green eyes, and I thought he was just *sooo* handsome. Anyway, one of my friends asked him if he wanted to go out with me, he said yes, and I thought all my dreams had come true. Sadly, the dream didn't match reality. Gary barely ever spoke a word to me. He'd just tell me to meet him at the back of one of the sports pitches near where we lived. We'd exchange hellos, and then he'd put his arms around me and start kissing me right away. I suppose that's all being a boyfriend means to a fifteen-year-old, kissing and groping."

"I'm guessing the kissing wasn't so great then?" I asked, and Afric grimaced, like even the memory of it made her ill.

"It was terrible. Gary was gorgeous, but his breath was atrocious. I was too young and in awe of the fact that he even agreed to be my boyfriend to request that he brush his teeth or at least chew some gum before he kissed me. And his kissing technique was all tongue and slobber. Absolutely no finesse. I hated it, but I didn't want to lose him as my boyfriend. All the girls at school were so impressed that I'd managed to snag him, so I went along with the meeting up and kissing thing for weeks and weeks until, eventually, I couldn't take it anymore. I finally found the courage to break up with him."

"Did you tell him why?"

At this, she chuckled. "Yes, I did. I told him he needed to start brushing his teeth regularly and to get some tutorials on how to kiss. He said I was wrong and just being a frigid bitch. Anyway, I was glad to be rid of him, but then a year later, when I started going out with another boy, the idea of kissing him literally turned my stomach. I just couldn't do it. It was like that original experience with Gary had given me a phobia, and I've been this way ever since."

I was frowning now, my attention on the road ahead. "I'm sorry. That's awful, Afric."

"My brother Ryan got sick once from eating some gone off chicken, and he hasn't eaten poultry since. I guess it can happen with anything."

"Did any of your boyfriends ever complain or find it odd that you wouldn't kiss them?" I asked, then winced. "Sorry, that was intrusive. Forget I said it."

"It's fine. You're just curious, and I get it. It's a weird preference. And just so you know, there hasn't been a long string of boyfriends. I've had four. Four after Gary, that is. Dev was the most recent. And no, none of them seemed to be bothered about not kissing so long as I'd do, you know, everything else with them."

"Well, I would be bothered," I blurted.

"You couldn't be in a relationship without being able to kiss?"

"Definitely not," I said adamantly.

"I shouldn't be surprised. You are terribly romantic."

"I am?"

"Sure. Our friendship was forged on our mutual enjoyment of period romances, and I'm pretty sure you enjoy them even more than I do."

"I like stories about people falling in love. It's not a crime."

"I never said it was. All I said is that you're a romantic. It's one of my favourite things about you."

"Well, I'm glad you appreciate that side of me. Few of my past girlfriends ever have."

Afric gasped. "They took your romantic side for granted? The ungrateful hussies!"

I chuckled. "Everybody has their preferences. It's not their fault if I'm not what they desire. My first girlfriend, Richelle, said I was too nice, and she really just wanted someone who was prepared to …" I trailed off, suddenly realising this topic wasn't something I wanted to discuss with Afric.

"Someone who was prepared to what?" Afric questioned, leaning forward and eyeing me curiously.

"Someone who was prepared to be more vigorous in the bedroom," I finished.

"She wanted to be fucked hard then," Afric surmised.

I frowned. "Do you have to be so crude?"

"Yes, I do, especially when it makes you blush so handsomely," she said, reaching out to pinch my cheek. I shrugged her off.

"The thing with Richelle was that I was only nineteen, and she was the first person I'd ever been with. If she'd only given me a chance to mature and learn, I might've gotten around to … doing that to her, but I was just so inexperienced. I had no clue what I was doing."

"And did you figure out what you were doing by the time the next one came along?"

"Yes. Kirsty was my longest relationship. We were together for three years. I was older then, twenty-two, and had several one-night stands under my belt. I was more confident by the time I met her. I definitely thought she was the one, was even ready to propose to her, but then we had a conversation about children, and she knew for definite that she didn't want them. I do want children, eventually, of course, so we ended up parting ways."

"That's tough. Some people want kids; some people don't."

I cast her a quick glance. "What about you?"

"Me? Oh, well, in a perfect world, yes, I'd love to have kids, but my failed past relationships suggest it'll be hard to find someone who'll put up with me long enough for that. I mean, I get it. My job is unusual. It can be annoying to be with someone who becomes so distracted by virtual worlds when you just want them to live in the real world with you. Maybe once I'm financially stable enough, I'll adopt on my own or find a sperm donor." She paused then, and her expression turned mischievous. "Hey! Perhaps you could donate some sperm to me? I bet your kids would be cute as buttons and so well-behaved."

The suggestion of donating sperm placed several lewd images in my head, and none of them involved medical procedures. I was quick to push them away since I didn't need to be getting an erection while driving. "I don't think so."

"Not even if I let you impregnate me the old-fashioned way?" she teased, and I was certain I'd gone bright red again.

"Are you trying to make me crash this car?"

"I don't know. Does the idea of old-fashioned impregnation make you lose your concentration?" she purred.

"No," I lied. "Don't be ridiculous."

She gave an amused cackle. "Sorry, I'm being mean, aren't I?"

"Yes, you are."

I felt her studying me now. "So, were there any others after Kirsty?"

I shook my head. "It was soon after we broke up that I got the job with *Running on Air* and immediately fell head over heels for Leanne. She had no idea, of course, not until years later when I finally drummed up the courage to confess my feelings and she turned me down in favour of Callum."

"That has to have been rough," Afric said. "Do you still have any feelings for her?"

"No, not at all. Don't get me wrong, I was heartbroken for a while, but I eventually pulled myself together and got over it. That's when Annabelle came on the scene. And now you're up-to-date with the history of my unsuccessful little love life."

"Aren't all love lives unsuccessful until people eventually find the right partner?"

"I guess so. And maybe all the failures are necessary to learn."

An impish grin graced her lips. "Kind of like how your several one-night stands taught you how to pleasure women in the bedroom?" she teased.

I suppressed a smile. "I should've known you'd want to bring that back up."

"I'm quite shocked, to be honest. You didn't strike me as a one-night stand type."

"I'm not. That period also taught me that I don't enjoy meaningless sex."

"You're my opposite then. Nowadays, the only sex I have is meaningless," she said, and something twisted in my gut.

"Right. I'd almost forgotten that you don't do relationships."

"Not anymore," Afric sighed.

I swallowed tightly. "Hypothetically, though, if someone came along who didn't care that your job was unusual and was prepared to stick around, would you enter into a relationship then?"

Something flickered in her expression. Something that looked a lot like self-consciousness. "Hypothetically, yes," she replied quietly, not meeting my gaze. Her answer caused me a ridiculous amount of elation, but I kept my expression neutral.

"Well, you never know. Perhaps one day this hypothetical man will appear."

"Perhaps he will," Afric agreed, her gaze fixed out the window.

16.
Afric

It was late evening when we arrived in Cornwall, and I had to take my phone out to get directions to our camping location. The rural village landscape wasn't so well signposted, but Google eventually brought us to where we needed to be.

I spotted the farmhouse first, a white, two-storey structure with old-fashioned paned windows fronted by an ancient-looking oak tree. It belonged to the uncle of TheBigSix's friend, Milly. I should probably start using his real name, which was Adam, because it'd be a little weird to call him TheBigSix in regular conversation. We'd never met in person before, and I was excited to see him, especially since he'd come all the way down from Scotland.

Neil and I had shared, shall we say, an interesting drive. For a start, he'd clearly noticed my odd behaviour when he'd taken my bag. His knuckles had inadvertently grazed over my bare shoulder and collarbone, and I'd had the most disturbingly intense reaction to his touch. It sent a charged, deeply erotic stirring right through my stomach, and I'd needed a moment to gather myself.

I'd never had such a strong reaction to anyone before. This attraction to Neil hadn't appeared right away. Instead, it had grown and expanded slowly over time into this uncontrollable organism that now lived and breathed inside of me.

Its only sustenance was Neil. Yep, kind of awkward.

I wasn't sure how I was going to feed said orgasm—I mean organism!—without tipping Neil off that I was lusting after him.

The conversation about our past relationships had certainly been eye-opening. And when I'd asked if he'd consider being my future sperm donor, the blood vessel in his forehead had started to pump. I had no clue whether it meant he hated the idea so much it stressed him out, or if it meant he liked the idea so much it equally stressed him out.

Either way, sharing a tent with him tonight was going to be an experience.

Neil turned his car down the narrow dirt road that led to the farmhouse. All around us was farmland. In the distance, there was a view of the sea alongside a lighthouse, its stark white colour in contrast with the vibrant green of the grassy cliffs and the deep blue of the sea beyond them. It was an amazing spot. A place I never would've discovered without the friendships I made online.

There were several cars parked outside the farmhouse. Neil parked next to a silver SUV. Then, before I had the chance to do it myself, he was at my side, opening my door for me.

"Thanks," I said, my eyes flicking up to meet his before both our attentions were drawn to the house. The front door flew open, and a tall, burly ginger appeared. TheBigSix, or Adam, certainly lived up to his online name. He was well over six feet tall and had one of those husky bear physiques. He wasn't what I'd call fat, but he wasn't thin either. He wore jeans and an open work shirt with a T-shirt underneath, and a giant smile spread across his face as our eyes met.

Before I could react, he strode forward, picked me up, and surrounded me in a tight hug. "You made it!" he exclaimed, his Scottish accent rumbling through me. "Look at the wee size of ye. I didnae know you'd be so tiny in person."

I pushed him off, scowling playfully. "I'm not that small. You're just a feckin' giant."

Adam gave a boisterous laugh. "Aye, true. It really is good to see you. I'm only sad Winona couldn't make it."

"Winona?"

"Yellowshoes. That's her real name," he explained.

I smacked my forehead. "Right. I forgot. Well, she was hardly going to fly all the way over just to spot a few UFOs. You know she's not into all this stuff as much as we are."

"At least her flight wouldn't have been as long as my drive. It took me the guts of a day to get down here," he said, and his attention finally fell on Neil. I glanced at my friend and found him staring at Adam as though he was trying to figure something out.

"And who's this?" Adam asked.

"This is my friend, Neil. I think I've mentioned him to you a few times. Neil, this is Adam."

Adam nodded as he stepped forward, holding his hand out to Neil in a friendly manner. A beat of silence fell before Neil took it, and they shook hands, both eyeing one another as though trying to get the other man's measure. "It's good to meet you, Neil."

"And you," Neil replied, his demeanour a little stiff.

Adam stepped back. "Well, come on inside and say hello to the others. You two are the last to arrive, so we'll head out to set up camp soon."

Neil fell into step beside me while Adam led us inside. "He fancies you," Neil murmured with his hand at my elbow.

"What makes you say that?" I asked. I'd suspected Adam's crush for a while, but I'd always considered it harmless, mostly because I never expected to meet him in real life. But now, well, now we had met. I wasn't sure what made Neil spot that he fancied me, though. Aside from scooping me into a hug, Adam had behaved perfectly ordinary.

"I can just tell," Neil replied, a slight rumble in his voice that I hadn't heard before. I couldn't say I hated it. A thrill went through me at the thought of him being jealous.

"Well, I guess we'll just have to wait and see if he makes a move," I said, testing the waters of his possible jealousy.

He frowned hard. "He better not."

"Why? It's been a while, and I deserve some action."

Something ticked in Neil's jaw. My God, he had to be jealous. This was priceless. I loved how intense and broody he'd suddenly become. "Because we're sharing a tent," he grunted. "And I don't wish my sleep to be interrupted."

I reached out to touch his arm. "Relax, darling man. Your beauty sleep won't be interrupted. Whatever Adam feels for me, it isn't reciprocated. I only see him as a friend. If he makes a move, I'll kindly inform him of that."

Neil's gaze fell on me, and I tried to read his thoughts, but his expression was too hard to decipher. His only response was, "Good."

We entered the farmhouse, and Adam introduced us to the rest of the group. Some of them I knew from the internet, while others were new to me. There were twelve of us in all. After the introductions were made, we lugged our camping gear across several fields to the spot where we'd supposedly have the best view if any UFOs were to make an appearance.

Neil carried our tent, his backpack, and the rest of our belongings, only allowing me to carry the sleeping bags, which weren't very heavy. When we arrived at the camping spot, he spread a blanket out on the grass before handing me a water bottle from the cooler box and instructing me to sit and take a load off. He was treating me all special, and I was quite overcome. If he wasn't careful, I might swoon.

I watched as he read the instructions before going about erecting our tent. He'd taken his jumper off, leaving him in a plain navy T-shirt that gave me a good view of his biceps and forearms. The way they flexed as he held a metal pole in each hand before inserting one into the other. Oh, no, a swoon was upon me. It was happening!

Neil was completely oblivious as he finished putting up the tent before placing our backpacks and sleeping bags inside.

Several yards away, everyone else was still setting up their tents when Neil had finished. I was impressed. He came and sat down next to me, his breathing a little laboured as he grabbed the water bottle from my hand and took a long gulp.

Um, *okay*.

I was momentarily transfixed by the fact that his lips were pressed where my lips had been seconds ago. A pleasant shiver trickled down my spine as I watched his throat bob while he swallowed.

"Thirsty work?" I asked as he placed the empty bottle on the ground.

"Yes. It wouldn't have been if I were a little more fit."

I disagreed with his statement since Neil was fit as a fiddle from what I could see. There didn't seem to be an ounce of fat on him. Granted, I'd never seen him topless, but from the few brief times we'd hugged or been physically close, I could feel that he was muscular. Not in an overt way, but he was definitely in good shape.

"Do you ever work out at the gym with the cast of *Running on Air*?" I asked him.

"I do. Michaela and I often use the treadmills and the weights, but we don't go anywhere near the ramps or jumping walls."

"If you work out, then you must be fit enough. You certainly look it," I said, my gaze wandering over his chest and down to his trim waist.

"Thanks," he said then, seeming pleased with the compliment. "What about you?"

"If you're asking if I work out, the answer is no, but I do go on lots of long walks. And since I don't drive, I typically have to carry my groceries all the way home, so that kind of counts as lifting weights, right?"

Neil chuckled. "I can't see how it's much different," he agreed.

I sighed. "I should probably think about starting more regular exercise, though. The women in my family tend to pile on weight after they turn thirty. I'm only twenty-five, and I've already started to gain."

Neil looked like he disagreed. "I think you look great just as you are."

At this, I shot him a grin. "Are you flirting with me?"

I expected him to deny it. Instead, he ran his eyes over me, "Maybe I am."

His gaze met mine, and he didn't look away. My chest began to flutter as I shoved him lightly on the shoulder. "Oh, my God, stop that."

He tilted his head. "Stop what?"

"Stop staring at me with those eyes. You're making me come over all peculiar."

He didn't reply. Instead, his attention dipped to my mouth before coming back up. He reached out to tuck a stray strand of hair behind my ear, and I inhaled sharply.

"Afric," he breathed.

"Hey, do either of you want a drink?" came a voice, and I looked up to see Adam approaching us. I frowned in annoyance. Seriously, I was so mad at him for interrupting. I needed to know what Neil had been about to say more than I needed my next breath.

"Um, sure, I'll take one," Neil replied before glancing at me.

"I'll take one, too," I said, my voice coming out a bit huffy.

Adam nodded, his expression curious as he looked between the two of us.

"Be right back," he said, and I returned my attention to Neil.

"You were saying?"

His brow furrowed. "I was saying ... Eh, what was I saying? Right, I was going to say that if you want, you can always come to the gym and work out with Michaela and me. Though, like I said, I don't think you need to lose any weight. You're perfect."

I suspected that wasn't what he'd been going to say, but I let him off the hook, especially given that last part. He thought I was perfect? My heart didn't know what to do with that information.

I lifted my eyebrows at him, my pulse pounding. "Perfect?"

His stare was heated. "I'm sure you're aware you have a body that could launch a thousand ships."

A thousand ships? I was officially swooning again.

"What about my face, though?" I asked, veritably preening.

"Quit fishing for more compliments," he chided playfully, falling quiet a moment as he eyed me intensely, "But, yeah, your face is pretty spectacular, too."

I stared at him, not knowing what to say, and then Adam was back with our drinks. Bloody Adam! King of the poorly timed interruption. "Here you go. I hope you like Bud. I consider it piss water myself, but I made the mistake of letting Steve bring the drinks," he said, shooting an irritable glance over at a skinny, long-haired guy who was still trying to wrangle one of the tents.

"This is fine," I replied, taking the proffered can while Neil did the same. I could barely focus on Adam because Neil's voice kept replaying in my head.

I'm sure you're aware you have a body that could launch a thousand ships.

Your face is pretty spectacular, too.

I really was feeling peculiar now. My breathing was all uneven, and there was a heat beneath the surface of my skin that simply refused to abate.

"Nice tent, by the way," Adam went on, making conversation. "You must be a regular camper. Looks high quality, and you got that thing up faster than any of us."

"I actually borrowed it from my boss. I only got it up so fast because I read the instructions," Neil replied, and Adam gave a good-natured chuckle.

"Right, that always helps."

I started to reconsider my theory about Adam fancying me. He wasn't acting at all jealous about Neil. Instead, he seemed completely casual and laidback. Perhaps I'd been wrong about him.

"Well, I'd better go start on the food. We brought a portable barbecue, and I'm going to cook burgers and hotdogs for everyone. You both are welcome to share."

"I actually brought a gas cooker and supplies," Neil said, and Adam nodded.

"You came prepared. I like it. Okay, I'll leave you to it then. Give a shout if you need anything."

He left, and Neil and I fell into silence. He turned his attention to me, and I realised he was sitting so close that our shoulders were almost touching.

"So, you think my face is spectacular?" I asked, raising an eyebrow.

"You're well aware that you're pretty," Neil huffed. "Quit being smug about it."

"I think I like being smug about it," I teased, nudging his shoulder with mine.

"Of course, you do."

"Look, you're blushing. Have you gone shy?"

"Stop it, Afric."

"Or what?" I challenged.

In a flash, he was on me, his chest hovering above mine as I lay flat on my back. Words died on my tongue while heat filled my body. Neil leaned over me, his hands circling my wrists and pressing them into the blanket. "Or I'll kiss you," he threatened, "and we both know how much you'd hate that."

My breathing stuttered. "You're right. I w-would hate it. *So much.*"

His eyes blazed. "Maybe I should do it then."

"Go ahead," I goaded, and his attention went to my parted lips. He leaned a fraction closer. I was stunned to discover the lack of distress I felt at the prospect of him kissing me. There was no sickness in my gut, no sense of revulsion. Only anticipation. Only *want*.

I was nervous, though. Anxiety mixed with need, practically paralysing me. All of the feelings I'd suppressed for so many years converged and swirled inside me, so much so that I could barely stand it.

"If you try to kiss me, I'll vomit in your mouth," I warned, panting.

"Will you?" he asked. He didn't sound like he believed me.

My breasts rose and fell, pushing into Neil's lean chest. He seemed to become aware of that, too, and I gasped when I felt a brush of stiffness in his pants. Then, dismay flickered behind his eyes. I must've given him some indication of nerves because he withdrew, instead bringing his mouth to my temple, the same spot he'd kissed after we'd shared a nap in my bed the other evening.

His kiss was delicate. When his mouth left my temple, he brought his forehead to mine and rested it there, a slow, minty exhalation leaving him and washing over my face. I wasn't turned off by his breath. I relished everything about him, it seemed. No part of him was unappealing to me. Perhaps for the first time in my life, I actually wanted to explore someone else's mouth with my tongue. I wanted to *taste* him.

The thought stunned me. It was revelatory.

All these years, the very idea of locking lips turned my stomach. Now I wanted it more than anything.

A second later, he rolled off me. It was my own fault that he'd stopped. I'd obviously given some non-verbal cue that the idea of kissing him scared me half to death. And it did, but not for the reasons he might've thought.

I missed his heat, the delicious pressure of his hands as he held my wrists down. The weight of his forehead resting against mine. The shocking brush of his obvious erection against my leg. Ugh! Why did I have to show him I was nervous?

Now I have become Disappointment, the destroyer of sexy times.

"It's almost dark. I better get started on the food," Neil said, his voice weirdly blank.

I didn't speak, choosing to remain seated on the blanket while Neil went about setting up the gas cooker. It looked like he was making us steaks, and my mouth watered at the prospect. The last few minutes had played havoc with my hormones, and now I was absolutely famished.

Neil was busy cooking when Adam appeared again. He brought over two more cans of lager, handing one to Neil as he cooked before coming and sitting next to me on the blanket. Neil eyed him intently before grudgingly focusing back on what he was doing.

"Looks like your boyfriend is making you a slap-up meal," Adam commented. We were far enough away from Neil that he couldn't hear our conversation. At least I didn't think he could.

"He's not my boyfriend," I said as I opened the can and brought it to my lips.

"He wants to be, though," Adam replied, and I glanced at him speculatively.

"Are you mad about that?"

His brow furrowed. "Why would I be mad?"

I shrugged. "Not sure. I always wondered if you had a crush on me." He barked a laugh, and it was a little too amused for my liking. "What's so funny?"

"Christ, you've an ego."

"I don't have an ego. You just always seemed jealous whenever we were gaming and I mentioned going out to find a hookup."

"I wasnae jealous, Afric. I was worried. I think of you as a younger sister, and London is a dangerous city. I didnae enjoy the thought of you going out there and having sex with random blokes who could turn out to be serial killers."

"Oh," I said and took a long gulp as chagrin took hold. "That actually makes sense."

"Aye, it does. And anyway, I thought it was obvious that I like Winona."

I gaped at him. "Yellowshoes?"

"Aye," he replied sombrely.

"But you two are always arguing."

"Arguing is akin to foreplay for some."

I laughed at that. "You're such a perv. Have you ever told her that you like her?"

He shook his head.

"Why not?"

"She's not gonna be interested in the likes of me, and besides, she lives too far away."

"I still think you should tell her, see what she says. You never know. She might decide to move to Scotland. She's always complaining about the unbearable heat in Florida and how much she'd love to live somewhere cold and rainy."

His eyebrow arched. "You think she'd move to Scotland for me?"

"I don't know. It's possible. You'll never know until you tell her how you feel."

Adam fell silent after that, the two of us drinking in quiet contemplation. He said that Neil wanted to be my boyfriend. The very idea sent butterflies flitting around inside my stomach. And the way Neil had looked at me earlier. He definitely wanted to kiss me. I just wasn't sure if his feelings matched mine. Was he merely sexually attracted to me, or did the very essence of who I was appeal to him the way the very essence of who he was appealed to me?

Eventually, Adam went to re-join the others, and Neil approached with two paper plates. He handed one to me, and I peered down. He'd cooked us steak, mushrooms, peppers, and diced potatoes with some kind of gravy sauce drizzled over the top.

"Wow, how did you manage all this on that tiny little cooker?"

"I prepared the vegetables and the sauce this morning, so I only had to throw everything into a pan and fry it up."

I grinned. "You're a genius. And thank you for planning this whole trip. It should've been my job to plan it. I was the one who invited you, after all."

He shrugged and lowered to sit next to me. "I'm a bit of a control freak when it comes to planning."

"I noticed that."

We ate quietly for a few minutes before Neil asked, "So, what were you and Adam talking about?"

"Are you trying to find out if he made a move on me?"

Again, he shrugged and focused on eating.

"He didn't make a move. Turns out he doesn't fancy me at all. He fancies our online friend, Winona. That's what we were talking about. I was encouraging him to tell her how he feels."

"Oh," Neil replied, and I noticed his shoulders loosening at this information.

"So, now there's egg on my face. He laughed so hard when I asked if he had a crush on me. He said he thinks of me as a little sister."

"Well, you said you didn't fancy him either, so at least you don't have to go through the awkwardness of turning him down. Unless, of course, you were lying and you do like him?" He glanced at me questioningly.

"I wasn't lying," I replied. "Besides, I actually like someone else."

Neil frowned so hard the familiar line between his eyebrows deepened. "Who?"

"You wouldn't know him," I lied.

He exhaled a breath, still frowning as he aggressively chewed his steak. When we finished dinner, Neil produced two red velvet cupcakes. "Grandma made these. She was kind enough to let me steal two for the trip."

"As if I needed any further cause to adore your grandmother," I said, taking a bite from the cupcake with relish.

"She likes you, too. She thinks you're a hoot," Neil replied, a fond note in his voice.

I smiled wide. "I am a hoot. They should put that on my gravestone and credit Phil with the quote. I can't wait to come to dinner at her house again, though I'm trying to be polite and wait for an actual invitation," I said, shooting him a pointed look.

"You're welcome any evening. Just text me first to let me know, and I can pick you up on my way over."

The offer gave me a warm shimmer in my chest. "How chivalrous. Okay, I'll do that."

"Grandma will be thrilled. She rarely has visitors. After Mum and Dad passed away, a lot of our family and friends started keeping their distance. It was like some of them thought the tragedy was contagious. Or maybe they feared being asked to help care for Rosie and me."

I glanced at him, a sadness hanging over his handsome profile. "That's awful. Why are people such arseholes?"

Neil shrugged. "I don't know. They just are."

I took another bite of my cupcake as silence fell between us. A few moments later, I asked, "How old were you when it happened? When your parents died, I mean?"

His eyes were looking out into the distance at the darkening horizon. "Thirteen. Rosie was only seven. Grandma had been minding us while Mum and Dad went to Paris for the long weekend. On the drive home from the airport, they had a collision with a truck."

My stomach hollowed listening to him speak. I had a big family, and they were all busy with their own lives, but I never really thought about how quickly and easily something terrible could happen to them. A simple drive home from the airport had snatched Neil's parents right out from under him.

On instinct, I placed my hand on his, my palm resting over his knuckles. "Rosie said you work so hard because you feel the need to take care of her and Phil. I think it's admirable how you stepped up and filled the role your parents left behind."

Neil let out a small breath. "I didn't have another choice, but I wouldn't have it any other way either."

"They're very lucky to have you."

He shook his head. "I'm lucky to have them. I love them both so much. They're my rocks."

My gaze met his, and so much affection for him filled my chest that I felt like I might burst. He was such a wonderful person, and I had so many feelings for him now it was dangerous. They were going to come spilling out someday, and I would be helpless to prevent it from happening.

A little while later, we joined the others. Neil and I sat side by side, drinking a few more cans and staring up at the sky in the hopes of spotting something. Well, *I* hoped to spot something. Neil hoped to prove me wrong. He seemed to be on his best behaviour, though, because he didn't try to argue with the group as we discussed the possibility that an extra-terrestrial life form might've visited earth. And I could tell he was itching to point out the flaws in our logic. I reached out and squeezed his knee, thanking him for playing nice. His eyes met mine, and there was heat there, the kind of heat that came with the consumption of three cans of lager while sitting in a field in the middle of nowhere, Cornwall.

It was almost two in the morning before we eventually decided to call it a night. Everyone was disappointed that we hadn't encountered any flying saucers, but I knew it was always going to be a long shot.

"I need to pee," I said as Neil and I made our way over to our tent.

"I brought a roll of toilet paper if you need some," he offered.

"That's okay. I brought my own, but, um …"

"What is it?" he asked, frowning.

"It's just that it's dark, and I don't want to pee too close to the tent, for obvious reasons, but I also don't want to go too far away on my own."

"I'll come with you then."

"But you'll hear me peeing," I complained.

"For crying out loud, I'll put my hands over my ears if you want."

I smiled. "Yes, do that. Thank you."

I grabbed my toilet paper, and we walked a little distance away from the campsite until we found some bushes that would afford me enough privacy.

"Do you need to go?" I asked.

"No, I went earlier."

"Okay." A pause. "Are you sure you don't need to go? Because I'm not coming back out here if we get back to the tent and you suddenly feel the urge."

"Afric, stop temporizing and pee. It's getting cold out here."

"Fine," I huffed. "But you better cover your ears as you promised."

"I'm covering my ears," he said, and I watched as he brought his hands up to cover them.

I quickly did my business, snapped off a few sheets of toilet paper, then used some of the hand sanitiser in my pocket before re-joining Neil. We were both quiet on the walk back to the campsite, and Neil seemed to be stewing on something. I could tell by how he kept frowning and acting like he wanted to say something but didn't know if he should.

Finally, he asked, "So, who is he then?"

I shot him a confused glance. "Who is who?"

He heaved an irritable breath. "This bloke you fancy."

Oh. *Oh.* I'd mentioned liking someone while we ate dinner, and I'd made it sound like there was some mystery man when, in fact, the person I liked was Neil himself. There was something about the dark and being miles away from civilisation that made me feel like I could speak freely. At long last, I wanted Neil to know how I felt about him. Then he could decide what he would do with the information, and it would be out of my hands. The ball would be in his court, so to speak. And besides, it wasn't like he was completely indifferent to me. He was obviously attracted to me given what he'd said about my looks and the very obvious erection he sported when he pinned me to the blanket earlier.

"I'm not sure how to put this," I said, and he groaned.

"Christ, don't tell me it's someone I know."

"It is, actually."

He raked a hand through his hair then stared up at the sky as if talking to a higher power. "This is a sick joke, isn't it? You're going to keep on doing this to me, aren't you?"

I reached out and grabbed his arm. I met his gaze, and my voice was sincere when I said, "Neil, it's you! You're the bloke I fancy."

He blinked. Then he blinked some more. Then he just stood there, dumbstruck.

I laughed awkwardly. "Say something."

He swallowed thickly. "You fancy me?"

I more than fancied him, but tonight wasn't the night for *that* conversation. I lowered my gaze. "Yes, I do."

"I didn't know."

"Duh. That's why I told you."

He fell quiet again. I nudged him with my elbow. "This is the part when you tell me you fancy me back."

His eyes flickered between mine, and there was such intense emotion in them that I felt taken aback. He moved closer, and my breath caught. His hand came to rest on my shoulder, and his eyes practically blazed. My throat thickened, and just like that, he didn't need to say a word. He was channelling his attraction at me so intensely I felt like my skin might burst aflame.

Neil's hand moved from my shoulder and slid all the way up to cup my cheek, "I fancy you," he breathed, and my insides heated. He glanced at my mouth, and I thought he wanted to kiss me, but then his eyes traced my features before he exhaled reluctantly. "We should get back."

I nodded, a little disappointed that he didn't kiss me, but my skin still tingled with awareness as we made our way back to the campsite. The atmosphere between us had changed. It felt lighter and heavier all at once.

Outside the tent, we quietly used bottled water and toothpaste to brush our teeth. Neil had even brought a tiny bottle of mouthwash. He always thought of everything. For a second, I imagined us as an old married couple with one of those His and Hers bathrooms, the two of us standing side by side as we completed our night-time rituals.

After my unexpected confession, Neil was looking at me differently. He seemed charged like a battery overflowing. Once we were done brushing our teeth, he politely offered to wait outside while I changed into my sleep clothes. A part of me wanted to reply and say I didn't mind at all if he came in and watched.

"You can come in now. I'm decent," I called as I shimmied into the toasty sleeping bag. I noticed with delight that when Neil had gone to relieve his bladder earlier in the evening, he must've snuck in here and placed a hot water bottle inside my sleeping bag.

"Where did this come from?" I asked, showing him the hot water bottle as he entered the tent.

"I boiled some water on the gas cooker. You said you were worried about being cold."

"Is there one in your sleeping bag, too?"

He shook his head. "I only brought one. I don't mind if you have it."

"Nonsense. We should share it."

"How could we possibly share it?"

"We could unzip both our sleeping bags to make one big sleeping bag. Then, we could put the hot water bottle between us," I suggested brazenly. I certainly wouldn't have suggested it if I didn't have several cans of lager in my system and if I hadn't just confessed that I fancied him and vice versa.

Neil started to pull his jumper up over his head, and I watched with rapt attention, not even bothering to look away. Sadly, he still had a T-shirt on underneath, so I didn't get to glimpse what I was certain was a very nice male chest.

"We're not doing that," he replied stiffly as he began to work on the fly of his jeans.

"Why not?"

Now he seemed tense. "I've already set everything up. I'm not going to rearrange our whole sleeping situation just so we can share a hot water bottle. I'm sure I'll be warm enough without it." There was a pause as his attention came to me. "Can you turn around for a minute? I'm trying to undress."

I frowned at him. "Why are you being so testy all of a sudden?"

His shoulders stiffened. "No reason."

"Are you freaked out about what I said?" I asked, a flicker of self-consciousness rising.

He huffed a breath. "Yes, I'm freaked out, but not at all in a negative way."

"Oh."

His eyes met mine, and they softened. "Sharing a sleeping bag with you would be a lesson in torture," he said, and understanding dawned. He didn't trust himself to behave with me. Didn't he realise how much I wanted to misbehave with him?

"I suppose we should stick to individual sleeping bags then," I said as I held myself up on my elbows.

Neil frowned, then nodded in agreement before shimmying into his own sleeping bag. Once settled, he glanced at me, looking like he was about to say something but then thought better of it. Without a word, he flicked off the torch, and the tent was encased in darkness.

I closed my eyes and tried to fall asleep, but it was no use. There was a tension between us now, and I had no idea how to break it.

All I knew was that I was never going to be able to sleep with him right next to me, close enough that all I had to do was reach out to touch him.

17.
Neil

I couldn't sleep. My thoughts were a tangled mess of sexual frustration. It was my own bloody fault, too, since I'd come dangerously close to kissing Afric today. What was I thinking holding her down like that? She probably thought I'd lost my marbles. But now, well, now we'd both admitted to being attracted to one another. It felt like neither of us knew the next step. Normally, I might've kissed her, but obviously, that wasn't the right move with Afric. It pained me, though, because I wanted to kiss her so badly; it was a physical ache in my chest.

I heard her emit a heavy sigh before she whispered, "Neil."

"What?" I whispered back.

"I can't sleep. Do you mind if I turn the torch back on for a while?"

"No," I replied eagerly. "Turn it on. I can't sleep either."

She reached across me, and the flowery scent of her shampoo filled my senses. She clicked the torch on, and a low light lit the tent. I glanced up as Afric hovered over me, shadows striating her elfin face. She was moving back to the spot she'd been lying in when I caught her upper arm. She didn't speak, just stared at me expectantly. I had no clue what to say. I just needed her close. We stayed like that for several long seconds, our gazes locked, before Afric broke the quiet.

"W-why are you giving me Mr Thornton eyes?" she asked, her words staccato.

Because I'm falling in love with you, a startling voice in my head answered.

It was a sobering thought, one that had my blood pumping to claim her. I didn't say it, though. It was clearly way too soon for declarations of love, even though I'd never felt this way about a woman before. Finally, I replied, "I bet I could make you like kissing."

Her eyebrows shot up, and her breathing became uneven. "How?"

"I have excellent attention to detail."

Her eyes lowered to my mouth, and a hazy look crossed her features. Was she ... turned on by the idea? She certainly didn't appear disgusted by it. I could almost believe that she wanted me to kiss her. Like the idea intrigued her.

"I'm not ..." she said, then faltered, frowning to herself.

"You're not what?"

"I'm not very good at kissing," she blurted. "I've spent my entire life avoiding it. There's a good chance I'm terrible."

I gripped her arm more firmly, tugging her closer. We were still in our individual sleeping bags, the thick material separating us, though she was currently half on top of me. "Let me be the judge of that," I said thickly.

"Okay," she replied, and everything inside of me came alive, like a hundred light bulbs flicking on at once. I was Oxford Street on Christmas Eve, merrily aglow.

"Seriously?"

She shrugged. "It can't hurt to try. Maybe I've been missing out and I don't even know it."

I swallowed as she closed her eyes, waiting for me to make the first move. My pulse pounded. Now that the pressure was on to perform, I was hesitating. She opened her eyes, a puzzled look on her face.

"What's wrong?"

I shook myself. "Nothing, just ... give me a minute." I unzipped the top of my sleeping bag then shifted positions, moving us so that I was braced above her. I unzipped the top of hers, and she watched in silence, a vaguely amused look on her face.

"Why are you unzipping our sleeping bags? Do you need a full range of motion for a kiss?"

"Yes, actually, I do," I said, shooting her what I hoped was a smouldering glance, and she immediately quieted. I took her in, my heart pounding a wild rhythm in my chest. She was ridiculously beautiful with her messy blonde hair and impossibly blue eyes. She wore a loose-fitting T-shirt to sleep in, the dipped neckline affording me a view of her rounded cleavage.

I wanted to bury my face in it.

Time seemed to become slow and thick like honey as I leaned down and pressed my lips feather-light to her throat. A strained gasp escaped her. I moved up, kissing her chin. My hand cupped her cheek as I finally brought my lips to hers. The moment of truth. I pressed my mouth to her lush, soft lips delicately at first.

Fireworks shot through my body, and I felt her tremble.

I was scared that she might startle and push me away if I kissed her as roughly and passionately as I wanted to, so I kept the pressure of my mouth light. I recalled what I'd said to her the night of Isaac's surprise party.

I want to kiss you. I can't stop thinking about it.

Now it was happening, and I felt like I was dreaming. I pressed my lips to hers, this time with a little more pressure, and I heard her whimper. The sound pulled me out of my trance as I drew back. I stared at her and was stunned to find several tears streaming down her face.

She was *crying*.

"Oh, God, I'm sorry. Have I upset you?" I asked with worry as I gently caressed her wet cheek.

She shook her head, her hands coming up to touch her tears. "No. I don't even know why I'm crying. The kiss brought all these suppressed emotions I didn't even know were there to the surface, and I'm just ..." she trailed off as she brought her eyes to mine, "completely discombobulated."

"I shouldn't have kissed you."

"I wasn't crying because I disliked it," she said, and I blinked.

"Why then?"

"I think I was just feeling way too much."

I studied her. "So ... does that mean you liked it?"

"I don't know." A pause as she glanced away shyly, her voice lowering almost to a whisper. "Maybe you should kiss me again. That way, I'll know for definite."

"I don't want to upset you."

"You won't. I promise."

Hesitantly, I lowered my body to rest next to hers. She stared at me while I bought one hand up to stroke her cheek and the other to cup her neck. She released a shaky breath as our gazes locked, and I pressed my lips to hers once more. I kept my eyes open, gauging her reaction. Hers fell shut almost immediately. She whimpered again, but this time it was accompanied by her hands tugging feverishly at the collar of my T-shirt, pulling me closer. I accommodated her, my chest pressing against hers as I continued to kiss her featherlight. After a few moments, she started to respond, her lips pressing against mine with building fervour.

My cock stirred, and I knew there was no possibility of me not getting an erection right now. Even this chaste kissing was giving me all sorts of depraved impulses. I wanted to strip her bare and lay waste to her with my tongue. I wanted to taste every inch of her and give her endless orgasms just to watch her writhe for me over and over again.

I was kissing her more forcefully now, and if the small moan she emitted was anything to go by, she seemed to welcome it. My breathing was laboured, my pulse erratic. Before, I'd had the willpower to stop, but now, I was lost. I loved the taste of her, the lush softness of her lips.

Her mouth opened for me, and her tongue dipped out. It ventured tentatively, stroking along mine, and I couldn't contain the low groan that rumbled from my chest. I needed more of her, more of this. I was dying of thirst even while I was drowning. Afric's hands drifted down then snaked under my T-shirt. Her delicate fingers drifted across my lower stomach, and I jolted. Pleasure shattered through me at her touch.

"Is this okay?" she whispered into the kiss.

"Yes. More than okay. Don't stop," I replied, my words guttural as I shifted us so that I was half lying on top of her, cupping her face in my hands as I deepened the kiss. Her mouth opened fully, welcoming me in. I couldn't believe this was happening. After fantasising about it, the fantasies had nothing on reality. This was the greatest, most intense kiss of my life. I never wanted it to end, but I also didn't want to overwhelm her.

Eventually, I broke away to catch my breath, studying her closely as I weighed her reaction. Her lips were puffy, her eyelids half-mast as she reached for me.

"Come back," she begged, and at that moment, she was the sexiest woman I'd ever laid eyes on.

I was about to kiss her again when there was a loud shout outside followed by hysterical yelling. Afric and I stared at one another in confusion before we both leapt into action, climbing out of the tent to investigate. Adam's friend, Steve, the one who took forever to get his tent up, was running around waving his hands in the air, very obviously drunk off his arse.

"Look! Look! It's them! They're trying to make contact," he cried out. Several others were gesticulating at a light shining in the distance, all of them as drunk as Steve.

Adam emerged from his tent wearing nothing but a pair of boxer briefs. He looked like a cranky bear with his hairy auburn chest out as he glanced up at the sky, shook his head, then grabbed Steve by the elbow.

"Good God, man, how much have you had to drink? That's not a bloody UFO. It's the lighthouse over on the coast."

At this, Steve frowned and rubbed his forehead, looking drunkenly chagrined. "Oh," he said, realisation dawning.

I glanced at Afric, and just like that, we both burst into laughter. Adam looked over at us and started laughing, too. Moments later, we were all in hysterics. I nudged Afric with my elbow, my voice affectionate when I said, "I told you it was all fake."

She scowled up at me playfully. "Just because we didn't see anything tonight doesn't mean it's fake."

I noticed her shiver and moved closer, wrapping my arm around her waist, "Come on. Let's get back inside before we catch our death."

She nodded, and I led her back to the tent. I wanted to continue what we'd started before being interrupted by Steve's drunken shouting, but I also had a bit of a dilemma. Afric was important to me, more important than any woman I'd ever been with before, and I wanted to do things right. I needed to set Annabelle straight, for real this time, and tell her I wasn't interested in dating her. If she then decided to tell Callum the truth, so be it.

Afric

I woke up with my face mashed into Neil's chest. After the UFO false alarm last night, we'd gone back to bed, but he hadn't reinitiated the kissing. Instead, he reached out and pulled me close, and I'd fallen asleep while he held me, both of us in our individual sleeping bags.

Neil was a perceptive man, and he must've known that the sheer intensity of kissing him had been jarring. Life altering, you might even say. I definitely needed time to process it.

Before I met Neil, I would've happily gone without kissing for the rest of my life. Now I wasn't sure if I could survive a single day without kissing him, and that was a terrifying thought. What if somewhere along the way, he came to the same realisation as Dev and my other past boyfriends? What if he decided I was too annoying or that my gaming demanded too much of my attention?

I'd survived those past rejections with my head held high, but if Neil rejected me, there were no two ways about it. I'd be devastated. How I felt for him was stronger than how I'd ever felt for anyone else, and I didn't know if I'd get over it if he didn't want to be around me anymore.

Neil still slept as I moved away from him and shuffled out of my sleeping bag. The hot water bottle had long gone cold, and the chilly morning air hit me fast. I grabbed a hoodie from my bag and pulled it on over my head.

When I emerged from the tent, I quickly went to pee and freshen up as best I could. I'd only slept outdoors for one night, and already, I felt like I could do with taking an hour-long shower when I got home. The survivalist life certainly wasn't for me.

When I returned, Neil was up and dressed. I found him outside, sitting on the ground while he tied his shoelaces. The tent had already been partially disassembled, and oddly, I was relieved. It meant he planned on leaving soon, and that was fine by me. I was all up in my head, almost paralysed by my fears of rejection and of losing him. The tent was a reminder of all the ways my heart had lit up and soared last night when he pressed his lips to mine.

"Morning," he said cheerfully as he came and walked towards me with a warm smile. He bent and pressed a kiss to my temple, his hand coming to rest on my shoulder. "I hope you don't mind that I started packing up early. I have a few things to take care of back in London, so I wanted to get on the road as soon as possible."

"No, that's fine. I have to stream later today, so I should be getting back, too."

He glanced down at me, and he must've sensed something was off because his eyebrows drew together. "Are you feeling okay?"

"I'm fine," I lied. "I think sleeping on the flat ground has just made me feel a little worse for wear."

"Right. Me, too. Next time, we'll have to invest in an air mattress or something."

"Next time?" I asked. "You actually intend on going camping again?"

"Of course. I've enjoyed this," Neil said, eyes focusing on me curiously. I stepped away from him a small distance, clearing my throat.

"Well, just give me a few minutes to say goodbye to Adam and the others, and then I should be ready to go," I said, and he nodded, eyebrows furrowed as he returned his attention to packing away the tent.

"Take your time. We're not in a big hurry."

When I went over to Adam's tent, he was sitting inside chatting with his friend, Milly.

"Hey, Neil and I are going to head off now. I just wanted to say goodbye."

"You're leaving already? Was it something I said?"

"No, nothing like that. I wish we could stay longer, but Neil needs to get back for work."

"Well, in that case, come here and give me a hug," Adam said, drawing me into a tight embrace before releasing me. "Neil seems like a good bloke. Hang on to him."

"I'll try," I said while my heart gave a sharp thud. Adam had no idea how difficult it was for me to hang on to people, specifically boyfriends. I told him I'd talk to him soon, online obviously, then headed back to Neil.

Half an hour later, we were on the road on our way home to London. The drive was silent, but my mind was loud. I'd never been so freaked out over a man before. Last night, he'd gazed at me like I hung the moon and stars, and the prospect of losing his adoration was paralysing. My feelings for him had grown in an insidiously quiet way, and now, he was in my heart and soul. He was a vital part that I couldn't bear to lose.

We were back in the city when Neil's phone, which he'd placed in a holder near the gear stick, silently lit up with an incoming text. He didn't see it because he was focused on driving, but I did, and the preview that showed on the screen made my heart sink.

It was from Annabelle.

Hi Neil! So good to hear from you. I'd love to meet up again. Just name the time and place. xxx

After the night we'd shared, he'd messaged Annabelle asking to meet up? What the actual fuck? I was horrified. Heartbroken. *Bereft*. Normally, I might have yelled at him and demanded to know what had turned him off me so completely that he was running back to a woman who was only using him to get to someone else. But right now, I wasn't in a normal state of mind. I was too upset to speak.

When we arrived outside my building, I fled the car like my arse was on fire.

"Afric, wait," Neil said, emerging, too.

I paused and glanced back at him. He opened the boot and removed my bag before holding it out to me. "You almost forgot this," he said, eyes searching mine.

"Right, thanks," I mumbled.

Neil sighed, placing his hands on his hips. "Okay, what's going on? You've been quiet for most of the car journey, and now, you're running into your flat like you can't get away from me fast enough."

Impulsiveness and fear had me deciding to distance myself from him at that moment. If only to protect my heart from further pain. "I just need some space," I said, making a concerted effort to keep my voice even.

Neil studied me, his features drawn in thought. There was silence for several moments before he ran his hand over the stubble on his cheek, a look of understanding on his face. "Okay, I get that last night might've been too fast for you. Can I come over later to talk?"

"I'll probably be streaming."

He frowned. "Well, let me know if you finish early, and I'll stop by."

"Okay," I said and turned to go.

I didn't look back as I went inside, doing my best to hold in the tears that were welling behind my eyes and in the back of my throat.

18.
Neil

So, Afric was freaking out over the kiss; that much was clear. I didn't want to be pushy, so I gave her the space she requested. Besides, once I got this meeting with Annabelle over and done with, I could focus all my attention on Afric and figure out what exactly had her acting so out of character.

Currently, I was sitting at a table in the café waiting for Annabelle to arrive. Several minutes ticked by before the door opened, and in she walked. She wore a thick duffle coat, her long hair up in a ponytail. Windswept strands framed her pretty, feminine face. I took a nervous sip of my coffee, then stood as she approached.

"Hey!" she greeted. "How are you? How's your week been?"

"My week's been good. And you?"

She lifted a shoulder. "Can't complain."

"Would you like anything to drink? Perhaps a bite to eat?"

"I already ate, but I'll take a mint tea," she replied.

I nodded and went to the counter to put her order in before returning. My mouth grew dry as I retook my seat. "So," I said, clasping my hands together. "I actually asked you to meet me today for a reason."

Her eyebrows rose curiously. "Oh?"

I plastered what I hoped was an apologetic expression on my face. "I'm so sorry, Annabelle, but I can't see you anymore."

Now, she frowned. That clearly wasn't what she'd expected me to say. She looked vaguely hurt, and guilt nipped at me. "Why? I thought we were getting on well," she said.

I'm fairly certain I'm in love with someone else, my subconscious replied, but I sensed that wasn't what Annabelle wanted to hear, and I didn't want to discuss Afric with her. This thing between us was too new, too delicate to talk about with anyone else yet.

"We were getting on well, but it's not going to work between us. I'm not right for you."

She stared at me for a long moment, and just like that, the hurt expression vanished, replaced with a look of malice. "Well, that much is obvious."

"Pardon?"

She gave a cruel scoff. "You pretended to be Callum Davidson to get with me. Obviously, I never would've looked twice at you if it weren't for that."

"Yes, but you did say you were willing to give things a shot anyway."

Annabelle rolled her eyes, and I suddenly felt quite ill. It was like in the movies when a nice character reveals they're the villain. It's shocking, but on some level, it makes sense. You see their previous behaviour more clearly. Not that I didn't already suspect she was using me.

"Come on, Neil, let's be real here. I *was* never and *could* never be interested in you. You're not hideous or anything, but I like alpha males, and you're the most beta male I've ever laid eyes on. And to be perfectly honest, it's kind of pathetic how you used your access to Callum's accounts to chat up women."

I gritted my teeth, gripping tightly to the handle of my coffee mug to keep from saying something unkind. "That wasn't my intention, and you know it."

"You say it wasn't your intention, but how can I know you aren't just some pervert taking advantage of his position to lure women in. For all I know, the polite nerd-boy thing is all an act."

Her words struck like a blow, but I didn't give her the satisfaction of responding to the putdown. "So, what was your plan? Use me until you got your chance to steal Callum from Leanne? Have you any idea of how in love they are?"

Annabelle's eyes flashed with venom. "They think they're in love, but it's patently obvious they're terrible for each other. They were on and off again for years, and now, they're just settling."

"That might be how things seem on the telly, but believe me, their love is real. I see it first-hand every day."

Annabelle was shaking her head. "You're wrong. They're a terrible match. Callum will soon realise that. He just needs the chance to get to know me better, see that he has other options, and you're going to help me with that."

I folded my arms. "I hate to break it to you, but from here on out, I want absolutely nothing to do with you."

Her smile was malicious. "If you want me to keep your catfishing a secret, then you'll do whatever I say for as long as I say it."

"Reveal my secret if that's what you want, but I won't be helping you," I told her, my tone final.

A waiter arrived with Annabelle's mint tea, and it was almost comical how she thanked him with an angelic smile before replacing it with a glower that she levelled directly at me.

She leaned in close, her voice little more than a whisper, low and threatening. "I have screenshots of every single one of our conversations, Neil. You might not care about me revealing what you did, but how would you feel if I posted them on the internet? They make it look like Callum Davidson was cheating on Leanne by messaging with a fan. His reputation would be in tatters, and it would be all your fault."

My entire body drew taut at her threat. Annabelle was far cleverer and more manipulative than even Afric had given her credit for, and she'd seen through her act much earlier than I had. Somehow, Annabelle had realised that I cared about Callum. He wasn't just my boss, he was my friend, and she knew I couldn't live with myself if I were the reason his reputation was destroyed.

I stared at her with narrowed eyes. "What do you want?"

Her features settled into a look of satisfaction. "I'm in the mood for a night on the town. I think you should message Callum and ask him if he wants to join us. You can invite some of the others, too, just to make it seem less obvious that I'm specifically interested in Callum. Not Leanne, though."

I shot her an incredulous look. "If I invite Callum, Leanne will most likely want to come along."

Now she shrugged. "Fine. I don't care if she's there, but you'll need to distract her while I chat with Callum. I want at least thirty minutes uninterrupted conversation with him."

I ran a hand down my face, stress building. "You're insane."

"No, I'm not. I'm simply a woman who knows what she wants and will stop at nothing until she gets it."

I stared at her in awe of her sheer audacity. Why hadn't I listened to Afric and simply ghosted her? All I knew was bringing Annabelle into my life was the worst decision I'd ever made, and I wasn't the only one who was going to suffer for it.

Afric

I'd just finished applying my make-up when my resolve broke. I lowered myself to my carpeted bedroom floor, my head thumping back against the wall. *Ouch, that hurt.* Well, I probably deserved it.

I was being an idiot. In my crazy, insecure mind, I'd formulated a plan to avoid pain and push Neil away by getting dressed up, going out, and possibly finding a stranger to flirt with. I couldn't go through with it, though. My heart wasn't in it. I needed to act like a grown-up and simply ask him about the text I saw from Annabelle. There could be a perfectly reasonable explanation for it, after all.

As I reached for my phone to call him, I heard a knock on the door to my flat. Sarita was out, so I went to answer it. My eyebrows shot up when I found Neil standing there. He looked absolutely wretched. His hair was unkempt, like he'd been running his fingers through it in agitation, and there were grey bags under his eyes.

"What the hell happened to you? You look like you've aged a decade since this morning."

"I probably have," he replied listlessly. "Stress can cause premature aging, right?" He looked past me and into the empty flat. "Sorry for turning up without calling first. I've had a really bad day. Can I come in?"

Just like that, guilt flooded me. For all the spiteful pep talks I'd given myself, Neil didn't deserve my bitterness. Even if he had hurt me by secretly meeting up with Annabelle, it was petty to do the same thing and hurt him back. I should've tried to be the bigger person.

"Sure, come in," I said, stepping aside.

He walked in and flopped down onto the couch. I sat on the armchair opposite him and continued to take him in. He looked so exhausted that all I wanted to do was pull him into my arms and hug all his worries away.

"I went to see Annabelle today," he said. "I wanted to set the record straight and tell her I couldn't see her anymore. You're too important to me to start anything new without making a clear break with her."

I swallowed tightly as more guilt swept in. The meeting with Annabelle had been about putting an end to their dating, not some grand attempt to win her over like my insecure little mind had conjured up.

"Oh," I said, shame threatening to drown me as Neil's gaze rose and he seemed to properly take me in for the first time. His attention ran up my legs, taking in the black skinny jeans, before stopping at the tight, lowcut lace top I wore.

"Why are you dressed like that?"

I lifted my chin, but my voice was wobbly. "I was planning on going out."

"Planning on going out where?"

"To a bar."

His eyes narrowed. "Why?"

I shifted awkwardly in my seat, chewing my lip as I replied, "So, I might've gotten the wrong end of the stick this morning." Neil stared me down, his eyes once again running over my form-fitting outfit and vampy make-up. "I'd been freaking out over our kiss and how much it meant to me and how hurt I'd be if you ever decided you didn't want to see me anymore. Then, on the drive home, I saw a text pop up on your phone from Annabelle, which just sent all my insecurities into overdrive, and—"

"You thought …" Neil interrupted before trailing off, shaking his head as he swore under his breath. "No, Afric. Good God, no. I would never—"

"I know that now. I was an idiot. Egg all over my face again. Ha! Typical."

He sat forward, reaching across and taking my hand into his. "You have to know that what I thought I felt for Annabelle can't hold a candle to how I feel for you. And as for the other thing, you have no need to worry about me not wanting to see you." He paused, his throat moving as he swallowed. His brown eyes met mine with an intensity that was almost a physical force. "I can barely stand the wait in between your text messages, so it's safe to say there's no chance of me randomly deciding that I don't want to see you."

I met his gaze, my heart flip-flopping inside my chest cavity. "You really mean that?"

He squeezed my hand. "Yes. I hate being away from you. It's torture. I would gladly live on the shelf in your bedroom if you let me."

I gave a watery laugh. "Even with all the neon lamps glaring at you?"

"Even with them," Neil replied.

I sent him a sincere look. "Ever since I woke up this morning, I've been letting my worries take over. I should've just talked to you. I'm sorry."

"Yes, you should have, but there's no need to apologise. I understand why you freaked out. The kiss was a big deal," Neil said, his eyes so soft with understanding and empathy that I thought I might melt. "You shouldn't ever feel the need to run from me, Afric. I'm not some arsehole who won't listen."

"Okay," I said, my cheeks heating. "That's good to know." I studied him again, curious as to what had made him look so stressed and dishevelled. "So, tell me what happened with Annabelle."

Neil ran a hand through his hair. "Christ, don't remind me. The woman is psychotic. It was really bizarre. When I told her I didn't want to see her anymore, her attitude changed completely. It was like an angel turning into a devil. Now, she's blackmailing me into setting up a group night out so that she can get to know Callum better in a casual setting."

I gaped at him. "What the actual fuck?"

"My sentiments exactly. She's so bloody shady I can't believe I didn't see it sooner."

"Why don't you just tell Callum the truth? Beat her to the punch. If she's as nutty as you say, then she'll end up telling him eventually. Going along with her blackmail will only make things worse in the long run."

"I was going to, but now she's threatening to publish screenshots of our chats to the internet. Those screenshots make it look like Callum was genuinely flirting with her behind Leanne's back. It could ruin his reputation. I need to keep her sweet for a little while until I can figure out the best course of action. I know Leanne will believe me when I tell her it was me behind the messages, but their relationship has already suffered enough public scrutiny. I can't be the reason it's put under further strain. I have to think of some way to fix this without it affecting Callum and Leanne."

His features were overwrought, and I hated what all the stress of this was doing to him. I sat back, my thoughts racing as I tried to come up with an idea. I couldn't just sit there and allow Annabelle to blackmail Neil like this.

"Perhaps I should just tell Callum. Like you said, keeping him in the dark will only make things worse in the long run," Neil sighed.

I held a hand up. "Shush for a second. I'm thinking."

"What are you thinking?"

I lifted my gaze to his. "Adam is an incredible hacker. So is my other online friend, Winona. There could be a way for them to hack Annabelle's computer and phone and wherever else she's saved copies of the screenshots and delete them. Then, she'd have no evidence. It'd be her word against yours."

Neil didn't look convinced. "I don't know. It seems risky. And illegal. And what if she has them backed up on a USB or a separate hard drive?"

"Okay, true," I said, pretty sure neither of us was prepared to break into her home and steal this hypothetical hard drive.

Neil blew out an exhausted breath. "I don't want to break the law anyway. If it weren't for what she could do to Callum, I'd end this right now. I hate that I was too weak to resist messaging with her. I never should've entertained it for a single moment. Fuck, I'm such an idiot."

I reached out to soothingly rub his arm. "We all have moments of weakness. Don't beat yourself up. It's counterproductive at this point."

"I guess." He blew out a breath, his eyes yet again running over my outfit. "You look amazing, by the way." A pause as he frowned. "Why exactly do you look amazing?"

Damn. I was hoping he wouldn't go back to this. My stomach tensed. "Um … Don't I always look amazing?"

"Yes, but not like this."

My throat ran dry.

"Afric?" Neil's eyes were questioning, and my belly flooded with guilt.

"So," I said, my voice meek. "I was really mad at you. I thought you'd chosen Annabelle over me, so I was going to …" I couldn't finish. I already hated the flicker of betrayal in his eyes.

"You were going to what?" he asked, jaw tight.

"I was going to go out to a bar and try to flirt with a random stranger to get back at you," I blurted rapidly, throwing my hands out. "It was a stupid idea. I already decided against it before you even arrived."

Neil's eyes darkened. His eyebrows were angry slashes across his forehead as he stared at me. He leaned forward, resting his elbows on his knees. "Fucking hell, I'm mad at you," he said in a low, gruff voice.

"You have every right to be."

A second later, he reached forward, yanking me over onto his lap. I gasped as his hands smoothed over my hips, then ran possessively up my spine before sinking into my hair.

He met my gaze, his eyes hard and passionate. "You can't just run off and do crazy, irreversible things without talking to me first. That's not you, Afric. You don't bury stuff. You say it to my face. What changed?"

I looked away, unable to handle the intensity of his eyes when I responded. "I guess I was just so hurt at the idea of you going to Annabelle because I let you kiss me last night, and that's not something I agreed to lightly." I paused and lifted my gaze, hoping my meaning hit home.

His fingers weaved through my hair, kneading at a tight spot at the base of my skull. God, that felt good. His eyes lowered to my mouth. "It's partly my fault. I should've just told you I was going to see Annabelle, but I saw that you were already stressing about the kiss, so I didn't want to overwhelm you."

"Can we forgive each other and move on?"

"Yes," he replied fervently. "But first, if anything like this happens in the future, promise me you'll ask me about it first before drawing your own conclusions, and I'll promise to do the same."

I brought my hand up and wrapped my pinkie around his. "I promise."

Neil's expression heated as he brought my hand to his mouth and dragged his lips over my knuckles.

A swift bolt of desire shot through me. Shivers skittered down my spine. "*Neil.*"

His eyes blazed when I said his name, and his head tilted, a confidently masculine look on his face when he replied teasingly, "Afric."

"You're making me come over all peculiar again," I said breathily.

He smirked. "So long as I make you come, I'm good with that."

I laughed shyly. "I've created a monster."

He continued massaging my skull, his mouth close when he whispered, "I want to kiss you."

"Then what are you waiting for?"

Less than a second later, his mouth crashed onto mine with crushing intensity. There was nothing soft or tentative about this kiss, not like the ones he'd given me last night. This kiss held the sheer ferocity of his passion, and it knocked me sideways. I couldn't remember ever being wanted like this before.

Neil's tongue dipped out, a silky caress, and I moved my legs, climbing astride him until I felt the delicious thickness in his pants. It slid against my core, and I trembled into the kiss. Neil's hand tightened in my hair while the other moved down to cup my backside.

He broke the kiss, breathing fast as he growled, "You're so fucking sexy." Then, he bent and gently nipped my jaw with his teeth. "I'm obsessed with you."

His words made my heart feel like it was lit up in a shimmery glow. This time, I was the one to kiss him. I dragged my lips teasingly across his before deepening it, tasting him. I'd never kissed anyone like this. Up until this point, I'd only ever tolerated a man's mouth on mine, but not now. Now, I was an active participant.

Neil had come into my life unexpectedly, and it was just as unexpected how he'd slowly become an intrinsic part of my reality. I'd once thought him dull and unimaginative. Now when I considered living in a Neil-less world, all I saw was grey. He was the glow that lit up my days, the colour that painted the canvas of my existence.

We kissed for countless minutes, exploring every inch of each other's mouths before a brazen impulse struck. Sarita wouldn't be home for at least a few more hours, which meant there was no chance of anyone walking in on us.

I broke the kiss, gulping down a lungful of air while Neil stared up at me, his eyes hooded, cheeks flushed. I wanted to make him feel good. I wanted to drive him *wild*.

And that was why I started to climb off him, my knees hitting the floor. He watched me, chest rising and falling.

"What are you …" his voice trailed off as I reached for his fly, and his eyes followed the movement of my hands as I pulled down the zip. I swear he stopped breathing when I slipped my hand inside and cupped him. He was hot and hard and silky, and I gasped at the feel of him. Neil's head fell back against the couch as he muttered strangled words under his breath.

"You're so hard," I said, gripping his firm length. My thighs trembled, clenching at the thought of him inside me.

He didn't speak, just stared at me with starved, fascinated eyes like he couldn't look away if he tried. I bent closer, pulling his cock free as I bent my lips to him. He hissed. I made sure to lock eyes with him as I slowly took him into my mouth. One of his hands gripped the arm of the couch while the other reached down to stroke my hair.

"I don't know what I did to deserve this," he said, his voice hoarse. "But thank you."

I smiled as I took in more of him, and he swore profusely. I swirled my tongue around the head of his cock, and a violent shudder went through him. I knew from the small details he'd mentioned here and there that it'd been a while since he last had sex. It had been a couple of months for me, too, and I wanted to make this good for him. For both of us.

I bobbed my head, increasing my rhythm and watching him, savouring all his little reactions and loving being the one to do this to him. I relished the control of it, the power of being able to render him so completely mindless.

He was mine. Always. After last night and today, I wasn't sure I'd ever be able to let him go. He was a part of me now, had made a place for himself in my heart and soul. He had no idea how much his reassurances meant to me. I needed to know that he wasn't just going to cast me aside, and Neil had no reservations about letting me know he was here for the long haul.

I tasted a salty spurt of pre-cum, and his body tensed. He stared down at me, and I made sure to hold his gaze as he came with a strangled grunt, his hand caressing my cheek as he watched me, his features etched in awe.

He said he was obsessed with me, but I was just as obsessed with him.

And then, like an annoying fly buzzing in our faces, his phone vibrated in his pocket.

"Ignore it," I urged.

Neil frowned, his regretful eyes wandering over me. "I have to go."

"What? Right now? Why?"

"Remember what I said about Annabelle blackmailing me into organising a night out with Callum?"

I gaped at him. "That's tonight?"

He nodded, looking vaguely ill.

"Well, then," I said determinedly. "I'm coming with you."

"Afric, it's going to be a nightmare."

"So why would I let you face it alone?" I countered.

"You really want to come?"

"Yes. I really do. Let me be the person in your corner, Neil."

His eyes caressed me like I was the most beautiful, wondrous thing he'd ever seen. "I don't deserve you."

"Yes, you do. We deserve each other. Now, come on, let's get this awful experience over and done with so that you can take me back to your place tonight and return the favour I just bestowed upon you."

At this, his eyes heated. "I want to return it right now."

I shot him a coy look as I stood and headed to the bathroom to brush my teeth. "Patience is a virtue, baby boy."

Neil groaned. "You're going to be the death of me."

19.
Neil

If a higher power were trying to punish me, then they'd curated this night perfectly.

Annabelle had chosen the venue, and it was the sort of place I actively avoided. Loud music. Flashing lights. Overcrowded bar.

When the bouncer recognised Callum and Leanne, he insisted on sorting us out with a private booth in the VIP section. He was a huge *Running on Air* fan. None of the others had been able to make it at such short notice, which meant it was just me, Annabelle, Afric, Callum, and Leanne seated at the booth. Callum and Leanne sat on one side while I was wedged between Afric and Annabelle on the other.

Safe to say, this was one of my least favourite outings to date.

When we arrived, Callum had given me an impressed look, like I was cultivating some sort of harem for myself. It killed me to lie to him as I insisted Afric was just a friend. Nothing could be further from the truth. Afric was so much more than a friend to me now.

I'd been furious when she revealed her plan to go out to a bar alone and flirt with strangers, but I couldn't stay mad at her for long, not when I saw the hurt in her eyes when she told me she'd thought I'd chosen Annabelle over her.

Speaking of Annabelle, she hadn't looked pleased when I turned up with Afric. She clearly didn't appreciate the competition of another woman being present. Annabelle might've been attractive, but she didn't have Afric's spirit, her liveliness, her incandescent glow. There was simply no comparison.

Annabelle was even more annoyed when she spotted Callum with Leanne on his arm. I hadn't failed to notice the split-second scowl she threw my way like I was somehow supposed to convince Callum to come alone. As if that wouldn't arouse suspicion.

Now, we were having drinks and discussing our favourite countries to visit. A typically benign topic of conversation, but not so when Afric, who had no qualms pointing out people's mistakes, was present.

"I just adore Spain," Annabelle said. "I have such fond memories of Corfu. I've been there a couple of times now."

"Isn't Corfu in Greece?" Afric questioned as she leaned forward, resting her elbow on the table.

Annabelle blinked, then waved a hand through the air as she sipped her cocktail before primly placing it back down. "Spain, Greece, it's all sunny skies and sandy beaches, right?"

"Um, no," Afric shot back. "They're not even beside each other. There are, like, a bunch of other countries in between."

"Well, geography isn't my strong suit," Annabelle chuckled, shooting a smile across the table at Callum. "So, sue me."

"Human decency isn't your strong suit either," Afric muttered under her breath, and I knew she'd had one too many drinks. When I looked at Annabelle, it was clear she'd heard. Her eyes darted to mine in accusation. Great, now she knew I'd told Afric all about her and the real reason we were here tonight.

"Pardon me?" Annabelle said, her gaze narrowed on Afric.

"I was just saying that for someone who claims to have been there a bunch of times, didn't you notice the people weren't speaking Spanish?"

"I was there with friends. I didn't spend much time with the locals," Annabelle replied cuttingly.

"Don't tell me you're one of those people who go abroad and immediately look for the British pubs?" Afric shot back.

Okay, this was in danger of turning into a full-blown argument.

"I really enjoyed South Africa," I cut in. "It's not somewhere I ever would've have gotten the chance to visit if it weren't for my job."

"I loved South Africa, too. Remember that wildlife reserve we visited?" Leanne said. "It's still one of the most beautiful places I've ever been."

"You guys are so lucky. You get to travel all the time," Annabelle pouted.

"It's definitely one of the perks of the job," Callum said. "Though flying isn't my favourite."

"Oh, you poor thing. Do you have a fear of flying?" Annabelle asked sweetly.

Callum chuckled. "No, nothing like that. It's just boring trying to fill all those hours stuck on a plane."

"Neil," Leanne said, sending me a pointed look across the table. "Come help me get another round of drinks in."

Great. She obviously sensed something was up. Leanne was far too shrewd not to pick up on the weird vibes between me, Annabelle, and Afric. Not to mention Annabelle was making bedroom eyes across the table at Callum every chance she got. I cast Afric a look that said how much I adored her and how much I hated putting her through this as I followed Leanne from the booth. When we reached the bar, Leanne turned and pointed her finger right into my chest.

"Ow! That hurt," I complained.

"What is going on with you, Neil? Are you enjoying having two women compete for you or something?"

"No, of course not."

"Don't give me that. The last time I saw you with Afric, you two were so cute together, and now you've brought this Annabelle person along as your date when you clearly have nothing in common with her and zero chemistry. It doesn't compute. This isn't like you."

I rubbed the back of my head. "I know it's not like me, but it's complicated."

"How complicated can it be? A blind person would be able to tell you're besotted with Afric. You've barely been able to take your eyes off her all night, and the poor girl's been knocking back drinks like it's going out of fashion. It clearly pains her to see you with Annabelle. Also, Annabelle keeps flirting with Callum, and it's beginning to piss me right off. If she shoots him one more secretive little smile, I swear to God—"

"Leanne, I'm so sorry," I said just as a snappish voice interrupted.

"Neil, can I have a word?"

I turned and found Annabelle behind me, a murderous expression on her face. I stepped away from Leanne as she pulled me to the other end of the bar.

"That girl back at the table, Astrid—"

"Afric," I corrected.

"Afric, whatever. She clearly knows about our ..." she paused, glancing about to make sure no one was listening before she finished, "*arrangement*. How dare you tell her!"

"She's my best friend. Of course, I told her. I needed advice."

"*You* needed advice? Shall I remind you that I'm the one who's been wronged here?"

"Maybe at first, but not anymore. Now you're insisting on deluding yourself," I replied, speaking my mind for a change.

"I am not deluded," she said, reaching inside her handbag and withdrawing a small object. A second later, she was wielding it in my face. It was a USB drive. "If you don't start playing along better, I'll hand this over to Leanne. Every last one of our conversations is on there. I'll tell her the messages were from Callum and that you've been arranging things for us, helping Callum keep our affair a secret."

"Affair? There was no affair!"

"That's not what I'll tell her."

She was a sociopath. An actual sociopath.

My gut twisted into knots from stress. At the other end of the bar, Leanne was leaving with a tray of fresh drinks. She shot me a questioning look as if to ask, *You need saving, mate?*

I shook my head, and she nodded, continuing on her way. I brought my attention back to Annabelle.

"Are you even hearing yourself? This is madness. If you do that, Callum will never want you."

"Yes, he will," she spat. "You made me fall for him, and now you're going to make it real. You owe me that much."

I stared at her, mouth agape. She'd ... fallen in love with him? "You can't fall for someone through messages, especially not if you haven't even met in person," I said.

"It felt like I had met him, though, through watching the show. And then the messages." Her voice cracked, and for a second, her vulnerability shone through. My defensiveness dropped as guilt flooded in.

"I can't tell you how sorry I am."

"No! You don't get to be all sorry and apologetic. You made me fall in love with someone who doesn't even exist. This is all your fault."

Finally, I truly understood. Annabelle was heartbroken and latching at straws. She was trying to force something to be real, even though a part of her must've known it never could be. I knew how that felt. Before I met Afric, I would sometimes wish that I was Callum. I'd convinced myself that life would be so much easier if I were him.

"Listen, let's just go back to the table, have one more drink, and then call it a night. This isn't going to work. Leanne has already noticed you've been flirting with Callum."

Just like that, the vulnerability vanished, replaced with flinty determination. "No way. I'm not letting you off the hook that easily. You're going to see this night through and as many other nights as it takes for Callum to finally drop that bitch."

"Annabelle, you can't be serious. Just think about this for a second," I said, but she was no longer listening. She strode back to the booth, and wearily, I followed.

This night was no longer merely a nightmare. It was actual hell.

I slid into the booth, my arm brushing Afric's, and our gazes met. Leanne was right. Afric had been drinking way too much. She was already halfway through the fresh drink Leanne had just gotten her from the bar.

"Are you okay?" I murmured to her quietly, my hand gently brushing her knee. A shiver seemed to go through her, and I felt it just the same. The connection between us was pulled taut, vulnerable to snapping at any moment. With this whole Annabelle situation, everything was still very much up in the air.

"I don't think anyone here is okay," she whispered back candidly. "Well, aside from Callum, who miraculously seems clueless that Annabelle has been undressing him with her eyes all night."

I couldn't help the smile that tugged at my lips. "Well, they do say ignorance is bliss," I replied just as Annabelle's voice cut through our conversation.

"I love being a personal trainer, but my long-term goal is to own my own gym one day."

"Wow, that's ambitious," Callum replied.

"Yes, and I pride myself on that. I can't stand it when people have no ambition, you know? Or worse, when they have potential but are too lazy to tap into it. I know so many people who never bothered to leave my hometown. They're just stuck there working in these dead-end jobs."

"That's a very judgemental thing to say," Afric interjected loudly, drawing Annabelle's attention.

Annabelle shook her head. "I disagree. I'm being honest. If more people were honest, the world would be a far better place."

Afric was already shaking her head. "You have no idea what you're talking about. I livestream to thousands of people daily." I could tell from the way she spoke that she was drunk, and I wondered if I should intervene.

Annabelle scoffed. "Sure, you do."

"I do! It's my job. I'm a gamer. Ask Neil."

"It's true," I said before reaching out to touch Afric's arm. "Perhaps I should get you a glass of water."

"No water! I'm trying to make a point." She jerked away, turning her attention back to Annabelle. "There's no lack of honesty out there, *believe* me, especially not online. I deal with the brutally honest opinions of people in the comments section every single day. If anything, people are far *too* honest."

"She's not wrong," Leanne agreed. "I came to a point where I had to stop reading the comments. They were messing with my head."

"Exactly," Afric exclaimed. "That kind of critical honesty can be helpful in small doses, but when it's a constant onslaught, your mental health suffers. And about the other thing, not everybody gets joy out of being ambitious. Some people find happiness in the familiar. Take my older sister, Helen, as an example. She suffers from anxiety, but the way she manages it and lives a fulfilling life is through routine. She's always lived at home with my parents, hates travelling, has slept in the same room her entire life, but she's happy. She's a homebird. Our parents are her best friends, and they adore her company. Some people might see her situation and feel sorry for her, but that's just because they're judging her by their own desires and ambitions. I always aspired to live in a big, diverse city like London, but I don't judge the people who still live in the town where they grew up. Just because you live in one place doesn't mean exciting things don't happen. It doesn't mean that you don't still have stories to tell and things to talk about. I think if we all accepted that it's fine to want to live a big, flashy life just as much as it's fine to live a small, quiet one, then *that's* what would make the world a better place."

I stared at Afric, my affection for her expanding exponentially. She defended the underdog, and I was certain that was the reason she'd wanted to help me with my predicament in the first place. It was what drove her to pursue a friendship with me at a time when I'd been far from friendly. I wanted to say so many things to her at that moment, but I couldn't with our current audience.

"We'll just have to agree to disagree on that one," Annabelle said. "I'm sorry, but I refuse to believe your sister can be truly happy still living at home with her parents."

Afric stared at her, and I tensed, worrying she might say something insulting, but then she simply stood and stated, "I need to pee."

"I'll go with you," Leanne said and followed her from the booth.

Afric

"Okay, you have to tell me what's going on with Neil," Leanne said as we entered the bathroom. "I seriously can't understand what he sees in Annabelle. She's completely unlikeable."

My chest filled with that feeling of vindication you get when someone doesn't like the same person as you. "Thank you!" I exclaimed. Admittedly, I was very tipsy as I rambled, "And who insists on everyone calling them Annabelle? Surely, any decent person would at least shorten it to Anna or Belle. But no, she wants everyone to wrap their tongue around all three syllables. Who does she think she is? A heroine from a Jane Austen novel or something?"

Leanne chuckled as she walked into an empty stall and closed the door. I entered the one next to hers. "I can't argue with you there. But seriously, you clearly know something I don't. I've seen the way you look at her," Leanne went on, still talking while she did her business.

I stared at the navy stall door in front of me. "What way do I look at her?"

"Kind of like you want to tear her perfect, glossy red hair out."

I cackled loudly. "Yes, that's exactly what I want to do every time she starts talking."

"Is it because Neil chose her over you? Do you fancy him?"

"What? No! I mean, yes, I do fancy him. Neil's my sexy little Clark Kent, but it's not that simple," I replied, flushing the toilet before I emerged from the stall and walked over to wash my hands.

Leanne emerged, too, and proceeded to wash her hands in the sink next to mine.

"Sexy little Clark Kent! Oh, my goodness, that's the perfect description of Neil. How isn't it simple, though? You like him, and I've known him long enough to see that he likes you, too. I just don't get why Annabelle is even in the picture."

I blew out a breath, the many drinks I'd consumed making me feel much looser-lipped than usual. I eyed Leanne through the large mirror hanging on the wall over the sinks. "How much do you care about Neil?"

"A lot. He's like family," Leanne replied without missing a beat.

"I guess that means you'd forgive him if he did something really bad," I said.

Leanne frowned. "Well, yes, within reason. I'd forgive Neil most things bar murder. He's been the backbone of our group for years. Every time there's an emergency, Neil is there with a clear head and a cool reserve to handle things. There are so many times when I've relied on him, times I'm sure I wouldn't have gotten through without him." She paused to eye me, a hint of concern on her face. "Afric, is there something I should know?"

"What about Callum?" I asked, avoiding her question. "Does he feel the same way?"

"Yes, he values Neil just as much as I do. Every member of the cast adores him. He's been with us through thick and thin."

"Okay, that's ... that's good to know," I said, my thoughts racing. Was I really doing this? Was I actually going to tell Leanne the truth?

"Afric, talk to me. You're freaking me out."

I met her gaze, the buzz of alcohol fuelling my honesty. "Neil probably won't forgive me for telling you this, but I'll take the hit because I care about him so much and he's too nice a guy to tell Annabelle where to shove her blackmail."

"Blackmail?" Leanne gasped, gripping my upper arm and ushering me over to the fancy velvet couch at the far end of the bathroom. She sat us down and levelled me with a serious look. "Tell me everything and start from the beginning."

So, I did.

20.
Neil

I watched Afric and Leanne walk in the direction of the bathrooms when Callum spoke, drawing my attention.

"I've actually been meaning to discuss something with you," he said to me before casting an apologetic glance in Annabelle's direction. "Sorry, love, I hope you don't mind if we talk about work for a minute?"

"Not at all," she replied, demurely flicking her hair over one shoulder. "Go ahead."

Callum brought his attention back to me. "James and I have been working on a business idea for a while," he said, and my eyebrows rose.

"You have?"

He gave a self-deprecating smile. "Neither of us is going to be fit enough to be jumping off buildings the rest of our lives. My knee is already fucked up. I swear it gets an ache right before there's a rainstorm these days. But anyway, my point is that both of us aren't the young whippersnappers we used to be. We need more long-term financial security."

"Seems smart," I said, nodding as I took a gulp of my drink.

"So, we've come up with a plan to start our own sportswear brand."

"Oh, that's so cool. I would definitely buy your sportswear if you had a women's line," Annabelle put in.

I really, really wish you weren't here, a voice in my head complained. Every time she spoke, I thought of what she said over at the bar and the USB drive she had in her handbag that she'd clearly brought along to threaten me.

"It's early days yet, and there's still a lot of planning to do," Callum went on, "but both of us have been in agreement about one thing, and it pertains to you."

"To me?" I asked, not entirely sure what he was working up to. I was too busy fretting over Annabelle.

"We want you to be our COO," Callum said, and I blinked. "It'd be a big step-up from your current job, and there'd be a significant pay rise."

"Wow, what a fantastic opportunity for you, Neil," Annabelle chirped with false sincerity, and just like that, turmoil set in. I remembered all the reasons why I didn't deserve such a wonderful offer.

"Yes, it is," I agreed, glancing at Callum. "Are you sure you don't want someone more experienced?"

"Nope. We want you. It's a new venture, and the three of us will be learning the ropes together."

I rubbed my jaw. In any other circumstance, I'd jump at this offer, but guilt and remorse swarmed within me. I didn't deserve the respect nor the opportunity Callum was offering me.

"Can I think about it?" I asked.

"Of course. Take your time. There's no rush," Callum said just as Leanne and Afric returned from the bathroom. In the space of a second, the atmosphere changed. Leanne looked ready to commit murder as she glared at Annabelle. Afric stood behind her, a sheepish expression of drunken guilt and worry on her face, and just like that, I *knew*.

I knew she'd told Leanne everything, and I was in danger of puking up every last scrap of food I'd eaten today.

"You should leave," Leanne said, her furious gaze intent on Annabelle.

Annabelle shot her an incredulous look. "Excuse me?"

"Are you hard of hearing, love? I said you should leave," Leanne practically growled, and Callum reached out to take her hand.

"Leanne, what's the matter?"

"I'll tell you what's the matter," Leanne snapped. "This bitch has been blackmailing Neil, and I'm putting a stop to it here and now."

I was frozen in place. I couldn't believe this was happening. I cast Afric an accusatory look, and her eyes were filled with a thousand *sorrys,* but it wasn't good enough. This wasn't her secret to tell. It was mine, and she'd taken away my chance to do it at a time and place that suited me. I certainly wouldn't have chosen to tell Callum and Leanne the truth in a flashy, crowded nightclub while Annabelle herself was present.

Finally, I stood. "Listen, I can explain."

"No, you don't need to explain anything," Leanne said, her expression full of sorrow. Oh no, this was worse than anger. *She felt sorry for me.*

"Can someone enlighten me because I'm completely in the dark here?" Callum asked.

"Yes," Leanne replied. "I'll explain everything after this bitch leaves."

"What did you just call me?"

"You heard me."

Annabelle's gaze cut to Afric. "You told her."

Afric's attention went from Annabelle to Leanne and then finally to me again. She looked like she regretted what she'd done, and I knew she was drunk, but that was no excuse. She shouldn't have told Leanne, not like this. This was about to turn into a shitshow; I could already feel it.

Some sort of determination formed in Annabelle's eyes as she dug into her bag and pulled out the blasted USB drive. "We're in love. We have been for months. I have all the evidence here," she said, a wild expression on her face as she wielded the drive at Leanne.

"Eh, who's in love?" Callum asked, bewildered. He was still the only person present who didn't understand what was happening and also the one who had been wronged the most. Every organ in my body pulsated with guilt. He was going to be so angry at me for this.

"Do you think I'm an idiot?" Leanne asked. "Afric told me the truth."

"It's a lie," Annabelle said. "They're trying to cover for Callum. We've been seeing each other behind your back for nearly a year."

Callum stood. "Who in the what now?"

My head started to pound. "She's lying," I said. "She's obsessed with you. I'm sorry for bringing her here."

"I am not—" the words died on Annabelle's tongue when Afric leapt toward her and plucked the USB drive from her grasp. She threw it on the floor and stomped on it with the heel of her shoe. It cracked right down the middle.

"You idiot," Annabelle droned. "Do you think that's the only place the screenshots are saved?"

"Nope, I certainly don't, you absolute madwoman," Afric said before she came to me, hands gripping my shoulders. "I'm so sorry, Neil. I did this because I care about you so, *so* much. Callum and Leanne love you. They'll understand." Then she crashed her mouth to mine and kissed me as though her life depended on it. Despite being furious at her, my body responded, a tidal wave of pleasure going through me at the sensation of her lips on mine. Too soon, she pulled away, looking to Annabelle one more time before returning her attention to me. "Now, I have to go. There's not a moment to lose. I'll explain everything later."

I stared after her in confusion as she turned tail and ran out of the club. "Where the hell is she going?" Callum asked.

"I have no idea," I replied before finally bringing my attention to Annabelle. "You should go."

"I'm not going—"

"Yeah, I second that. *Leave*," Callum said, and there was no mistaking the threat in his voice. The words rumbled out of him like a growl. Callum could be an easy-going bloke, but when someone tried to mess with his relationship, he took no prisoners.

Annabelle's eyes shone with tears as she realised her plan had failed epically. I had no illusions that she wasn't going to share the dirt she had online, but at least now she couldn't blackmail me anymore or try to break up Callum and Leanne.

She hitched her handbag over her shoulder and glared at the three of us. "You'll regret this. All of you will."

With that, she left, and I stood there feeling worse than I'd ever felt. I wished to be invisible because this entire situation was painfully mortifying.

"I'll hand over my resignation in the morning," I said, unable to look either Leanne or Callum in the eyes. "I'll work as many weeks' notice as you need, but I completely understand if you don't want to see me. If that's the case, I can organise for a temp to replace me in the meantime. I'll do my best to minimise the damage I've caused. There's no way for me to ever make it up to you, but just know I hate myself for what I did more than anything."

"Good Christ, Neil. Will you quit falling on your sword for a second and sit down? Explain to me what's going on because I'm still very, very confused," Callum ground out.

I didn't want to explain anything, but I knew it was my duty. I owed him this much. I nodded soberly and went to take a seat, but before I could sit, Leanne was there. She threw her arms around me and hugged me tightly. I froze from the unexpectedness of it. Why on earth was she hugging me?

"I wished you'd talked to me about this. You could've told me. We used to talk about everything," she said. Something about her hug crumpled me. Emotion swelled in my throat, but I refused to cry in this situation. It was already humiliating enough as it was.

Leanne drew back, and I finally sat down. Callum sat across from me, clearly waiting for a full explanation. I cleared my throat and forced myself to meet his gaze.

"A few weeks after you had me start running your social media accounts, there was a message from Annabelle. She was a fan of yours. I replied to her in the usual polite, reserved manner, pretending to be you. I had no intention of a long, drawn-out interaction, but she continued to send messages, and before I knew it, we were having a full-blown conversation. That conversation turned into regular messages, and before long, I'd developed feelings for her, or at least for the person I thought she was."

"Christ," Callum said, his thick eyebrows drawing together. "So she's the woman you told me about? The one from the internet who didn't know what you look like?"

I nodded, seeing full understanding dawn on him.

"I hated the deception, but I knew a woman like Annabelle would never be interested in the real me. She wanted a bloke like you, with the tattoos and the muscles—"

"Fuck's sake, Neil, you make me sound like a twat."

"Not at all. You have no idea how many times I actually wished I was you during all this. Life would be so much easier. I think all the messaging people and pretending to be you screwed with my head. I lost a real sense of who I was."

Now Callum's eyes clouded with sympathy. "I had no idea."

"You shouldn't have had him doing that in the first place," Leanne put in, her voice scolding. "Not after …" she trailed off, and I knew what she'd been about to say. Not after how I'd told her I had feelings for her, and she'd rejected me in favour of Callum.

Callum looked at her, then ran a hand down his face. "*Fuck*, I'm an idiot."

"You aren't. Regardless of the personal struggles I was dealing with, what I did was wholly unprofessional. I completely understand if you fire me. In fact, I insist that you do. I broke your trust in the most abhorrent manner, and Annabelle has screenshots saved of our conversations. Conversations that make it look like you were cheating on Leanne with a fan. If she publishes them online, it'll cause you no end of bad press."

"Actually, about that," Leanne said. "There's a reason Afric ran off just now. She and I were talking in the bathroom, and we hatched a plan."

"What sort of plan?" I asked.

"Yeah," Callum added, eyeing his partner. "What sort of plan?"

Afric

"Okay, are you both absolutely sure you got everything?" I asked through my headset. It was two in the morning, and I was on a video call with TheBigSix and Yellowshoes.

I drank several glasses of water as soon as I got home. I'd needed to sober up enough to explain the situation to them after running out of the nightclub like I'd left a candle burning next to a set of linen curtains. Neil was clearly furious with me, but he could yell at me and hate me later. Right then, I had a plan to put into motion.

After Annabelle had pulled that USB drive from her bag, I knew it could work. She didn't seem like the kind of woman who kept backups of her backups. More than likely, the USB was the only place she'd saved the screenshots other than her computer and phone.

I'd swiftly destroyed the drive before hurrying home and explaining the situation to my friends. It hadn't taken too much grovelling to convince them to do me this massive (if somewhat illegal) favour.

Okay, so I promised to buy them a bunch of new weapons and ammo in *Greenforest,* and they'd readily agreed to hack Annabelle's computer, phone, and cloud files.

"We got everything," TheBigSix reassured me. "Veritably scrubbed clean. I'm nothing if not thorough."

"Yeah, hon, relax. We got you," Yellowshoes added. "Of note, while rooting through this Annabelle person's files, I noticed a few workout videos where she's blatantly padded her ass to make it look bigger."

"Don't they all do that nowadays?" TheBigSix asked. "I thought it was the norm."

"I guess it's no stranger than putting chicken fillets in your bra," Yellowshoes mused.

"New business idea. We could start manufacturing backside padding. We'd make a fortune in fudge," TheBigSix joked.

"Oh! That could definitely work," Yellowshoes agreed.

I couldn't believe how quickly they'd moved onto other topics. They didn't even seem phased that they'd just committed a cybercrime, even if it was for the greater good. Clearly, I had excellent taste in friends.

And clearly, they'd both done far shadier things online in the past.

Best not to question it.

"Sorry to burst your bubble, but padded underwear is already a thing. You'd be entering a competitive market," I said.

"What if it wasn't underwear but an actual synthetic butt that looks real?" Yellowshoes countered.

"That's a bit weird, love," TheBigSix commented. "Even for my standards."

I shook my head in amusement as the two of them continued discussing their hypothetical arse enhancing business, my thoughts wandering to Neil. The look on his face when he realised I'd told Leanne the truth cut me to the quick. I didn't regret what I'd done, though. In fact, I was relieved that it was finally over. Leanne had reassured me Neil wouldn't be fired. She actually seemed to blame herself a little since she and Callum getting together had contributed to Neil's low self-esteem at the time. That, combined with him having to pretend to be Callum as part of his work duties, well, she clearly understood it was a lot to take on.

Now, I just needed to worry about how badly I'd fucked up Neil's and my tentative … whatever it was. Okay, so I was pretty sure I was in love with him. And now

I had to do whatever was in my power to earn his trust back. But what if I couldn't? What if I'd ruined things forever?

The thought made my heart feel like it had fallen out of my chest and plopped onto the floor where it was about to be sucked up by a diligent Roomba.

Feeling particularly morose, I logged off with TheBigSix and Yellowshoes, then climbed into bed with my mobile phone. I wanted to call Neil and fully explain myself, but I had no idea how I'd be received. Would he even bother to answer?

Taking the plunge, I hit his number and pressed call. It rang out before going to voicemail. Inhaling a deep breath for courage, I decided to leave him a message.

21.
Neil

I felt like someone hit me over the head with a cricket bat. After a hellish night, I'd slept only a handful of hours. I hadn't even had that much to drink, but the after effects of emotional turmoil were wreaking havoc with my cranium.

Callum and Leanne had been far too understanding and not nearly angry enough about what I'd done. I struggled with whether I deserved their forgiveness. We'd gone back to their flat after the club and talked for hours, hashing things out. I hated that they felt guilty for the position I'd been put in because I was the one who'd abused the power I'd been given. They had nothing to feel guilty for.

I was still considering handing in my resignation. They were too fond of me to see my deception clearly. And perhaps they just didn't want to train in a new assistant. I was like a pair of old boots; reliable, comfortable, familiar despite my faults.

And then there was Afric. She'd told Leanne everything without asking my permission. It was a huge violation of trust, and I was fuming mad about it. Don't get me wrong; I still adored her and there was no changing that. I knew she'd only talked to Leanne because she cared about me, but it was still shitty of her not to give me any prior warning.

Grabbing my phone off the nightstand, I saw I had a missed call and a new voicemail. Both were from Afric. The voicemail had been left last night. I lifted the phone to my ear and hit play.

Hi, Neil. It's Afric. Well, obviously, you know it's me. I guess you're probably asleep right now. Or not answering your phone because you hate me, which is understandable.

I'm a drunken arsehole who doesn't deserve your friendship. I'm sorry for what I did, but in a way, I'm also not sorry because it needed to be done. This thing with Annabelle was getting way out of hand, and it was never going to end anywhere good, you know? You're probably wondering why I ran off so suddenly, or, well, Leanne might've already told you, but she supported my idea vis-á-vis ...erm, that thing we discussed in my apartment before we went out last night. Just know that it's all been taken care of. I thought I could do this one thing for you, and then you wouldn't have to grapple with the moral implications. I am obviously far less moral than you since I spilled to Leanne without your permission, and I also have no qualms about the other thing, not when I know what Annabelle planned to do with those screenshots. Honestly, you should be thanking me because that bitch is mad as a box of frogs. Oh, shite. I'm fucking this up, aren't I? I always ramble when I'm nervous. Anyway, I would love it if you could forgive me, but I also totally get it if you're not there yet. Be aware I'm prepared to grovel on my hands and knees. That's literally how much I care about you because Afric O'Connor doesn't grovel for just anybody. I miss you already ... I want to snuggle with you on that pristine sofa in your neat little living room and watch cosy eighties romcoms. I might also remind you that we made a pact never to fight again, so technically, you can't be fighting with me since it goes against the pact. Then again, pacts can always be broken, can't they? The way you looked at me in the club probably confirms that. There was a chimney on top of your head, and it literally exploded. I was covered in soot. Okay, now I really am talking shite. I should get some sleep. Again, I'm sorry. I don't want you to stop being my best friend, but I understand if you never want to look at my stupid face again. It's up to you, and I'm here ready and willing to be yelled at and finger-pointed at until you feel better.*

The message ended, and I put my phone down, leaning back against the headboard. She was adorable and frustrating and ridiculous, and a part of me just wanted to forgive her right now because I wanted to snuggle on my couch and watch romcoms, too, but she'd also broken my trust. I was a wounded deer, and I wasn't ready to let the person who'd shot me come and mend my wounds just yet, no matter how nice it would feel.

I needed a day to be angry at her. After that, I was obviously going to forgive her. That was the extent to which my feelings had grown. What she'd done was bad, but it didn't counteract how I felt for her. Afric was under my skin and deep inside my heart, and at this point, there was very little I wouldn't forgive her for. That didn't mean I wasn't going to make her stew for a day or a few hours at the very least.

Afric

"I'm not normally one to rain on someone's murder parade, but I think you need to take a break," TheBigSix said through my headset.

"I don't need a break. What I need to do is finish killing all these blasted trolls," I shot back grumpily.

It was Sunday afternoon, and I hadn't heard back from Neil. I was too upset to try and call him again, and besides, I'd spilled my guts in the voicemail I left last night, and I knew he'd listened to it.

Seemed like he'd decided to take the stubborn route by going silent on me.

Well, that was fine. Really, it was. I deserved the silent treatment for being such a big, drunken blabbermouth. At least I still had *Greenforest*. Here I could be as morally unscrupulous as I liked, and there was no one to look at me with sad, betrayed, bottomless brown eyes. No one to make me feel like I was the worst best friend in the world.

Every time I had a quiet moment, my mind would fill with Neil's face when he realised I'd told Leanne about Annabelle. And every time the image came, I felt like someone was pouring vinegar into a stab wound in the centre of my gut.

Speaking of stabbing, my gargoyle was acting like an absolute psychopath today, and TheBigSix clearly feared for my sanity. The virtual ground around me was littered with dead troll bodies.

"Committing a needless massacre won't make you feel any better," TheBigSix said. "Why don't you talk to Neil in person? Leaving cowardly voicemails isnae going to win him back."

"You're calling me a coward? Tell me, have you come clean to Yellowshoes about your feelings for her yet?"

He made a disgruntled noise. "I'm working my way up to it."

"Hmm, well, you can leave off lecturing me about my love life until you get yours sorted."

"It's not the same. She lives thousands of miles away, and we've never even met in person."

"No time like the present to book a flight."

"I'm not booking a flight, not until I at least have an inkling of whether my feelings are returned."

"Then you're going to have to tell her."

"I know, and I will, just not today."

My phone buzzed with a message, and I snatched it up, my heart in my throat. To my disappointment, it wasn't Neil. It was only Michaela inviting me over to her house for a late lunch. Apparently, she had big news. I replied, saying I'd be there. If nothing else, it would be good to get out of the flat for a while and away from all the temptation to murder mythical creatures in *Greenforest*.

I logged off from the game and went to take a much-needed shower. I still hadn't washed away my eyeliner from last night, and I was starting to resemble Paudy O'Shea, a neighbour of mine from back home who refused to let go of his rocker youth. Supposedly, he'd been a roadie for Black Sabbath in the eighties.

Once out of the shower, I threw on a hoodie and some leggings, pulled my hair up into a messy bun, and set off for Michaela's house. My friend had landed on her feet moving in with James. He was a few years older than her and owned a house in a leafy, residential part of London. What I wouldn't give to be able to afford a place with a garden. My flat didn't even have a balcony.

I pressed the button for the doorbell, and a few moments later, Michaela appeared.

"You're looking very cheerful. Not working today?" I said as I stepped into the hallway.

"It's my day off. Neil is on duty today," she replied, and even the mention of his name had my metaphorical gut wound reappearing. "Speaking of, how have things been with you two? I haven't seen you together since the night of Isaac's party. You seemed pretty cosy."

I blew out a breath as she led me into her kitchen, where she'd prepared a pot of tea and a selection of sandwiches. "Ooh, Salmon Sensation and cucumber. Someone's feeling fancy," I said as I plucked a dainty sandwich and shoved it in my mouth. When I felt like crap, food was my drug of choice.

"I remembered you liked them the last time you came over for lunch," Michaela replied, eyeing me studiously. "Why are you avoiding the subject? Has something happened with Neil?"

"Yes," I replied, not bothering to lie. This was Michaela. I could tell her anything, and she wouldn't judge. Sarita was a little different. I could tell her anything, but she would judge. I didn't mind, though. It was good to have a balance of friendship types.

"Well," Michaela said. "What is it?"

I swallowed down the lump of masticated sandwich before lifting my eyes to hers. "I'm in love with him."

Michaela stared at me, her brown eyes round as saucers. "Seriously?"

I nodded sombrely.

"What ... I mean ... how did that happen?"

"Slowly and insidiously, like a thief who takes their time slipping their hand inside your chest cavity to rip out a vital organ."

"Okay, now you're just being melodramatic."

"All I'm saying is, he made me fall in love with him by being all cute and awkward and kind and endearing and sexy, and now I've fucked everything up. Typical Afric behaviour."

"Stop referring to yourself in the third person. And whatever you've done, I'm sure it can be rectified."

"It can't. He hates me. Or, well, he doesn't want to talk to me at least. I broke his trust."

"How did you break his trust?"

"I revealed a secret of his to someone I shouldn't have." I wasn't going to tell Michaela all the details because that would just be further disrespecting Neil's trust. It had never been my secret to tell in the first place.

"Do you think he loves you back?"

"I think he lusts me back. I'm not too certain about love. No man has ever loved me before."

"You can't know that. Just because your past boyfriends might not have said it doesn't mean—"

"I know you're trying to be kind, but they didn't love me, Michaela. And even if they did, they obviously fell out of love with me at some point because they all broke up with me in the end. I came to terms with the fact that though I can be charming for a while, at some point, the spell breaks, and men get sick of me. I might be temporarily loveable, but I'm not long-term, forever loveable."

"Yes, you are. I know this for a fact because I love you. I've loved you for the entire ten years that I've known you."

"Oh, crap. It's happening. She's finally coming out of the closet. Sarita's gonna be pissed that she's not the only lesbian in our friendship group anymore."

Michaela reached out to swipe me on the shoulder. "Don't be an arsehole. You know what I mean." She paused to eye me a moment, then asked, "Does it feel different with Neil compared to your past boyfriends?"

Yes. A million times, yes. Neil was the only man I'd ever actually wanted to kiss. He was the only man who could make my entire body feel like it was burning just by looking at me. He was the only man who made my heart feel all twisted up inside, like the ball of tangled wool my sister Helen stored in the top drawer of our shared cabinets after abandoning her attempt to learn how to crochet.

I nodded, and Michaela made a noise of commiseration as she came and wrapped her arms around my shoulders.

"It'll work itself out. Neil will come around. He's a forgiving type."

I hoped she was right. She hugged me for a few moments before drawing away and going to pour us both some tea.

"So, what is this good news you wanted to tell me?"

"Oh, it's not a big deal," she said, looking rather sheepish now.

"Hey, just tell me. I'm in full depression mode. I need some good news to lift my spirits."

"Well," she said, glancing at the table as she lifted her hand. My eyes were drawn to a sparkling diamond ring on her finger.

"Oh, my God! You and James got engaged?"

Her lips began to pull into a smile. She was obviously overjoyed but felt bad telling me of her romantic success while I was wading through the ditch of heartbreak. "He took me to dinner last night and popped the question. I wanted to tell you and Sarita together, but she's at work today, and I was impatient. I'll tell her later tonight when she gets off."

"That's amazing news, Michaela!" I exclaimed. I didn't even have to fake being thrilled for her. She was one of my best friends, and her happiness was my happiness. She and James made a wonderful couple.

"Thank you. We're having a small engagement party next weekend. You're invited, of course. It'll be an intimate affair, just family and close friends."

My stomach tensed. "Will Neil be there?"

She chewed her lip. "Well, yes, he's my friend, and he and James have known each other for years."

"Oh."

"If you think it'll be too awkward, I completely understand if you want to give it a miss."

"No way. I'm not missing your engagement party. I'm sure if Neil's still mad at me by then, he'll just ignore me. He's already demonstrated that he's adept at the silent treatment. And you don't need to worry about me making a scene. I'll be on my best behaviour."

Her eyes turned sympathetic. "I could reach out to him. See if he could be convinced to talk to you."

"No, I don't want to force anything on him. If he wants to see me, he knows where to find me."

Michaela nodded, though she still had that sad look on her face. She shouldn't be feeling sad right now. She should be feeling excited about her engagement. I swiftly changed the subject, and we talked about the party next weekend, which was to be an outdoor, afternoon tea affair in the gardens of a swanky hotel. Then we discussed what type of wedding she envisioned having.

An hour later, Michaela was walking me out when the doorbell rang. Through the colourful stained-glass panes on her front door, I spotted a familiar silhouette.

Neil.

Michaela glanced at me. "I don't know what he's doing here. Do you want to hide while I talk to him?"

I shook my head and inhaled a breath for courage. "No. It's fine. I'll leave. He probably wants to talk to you about work or something."

She nodded and went to open the door. "Michaela, hi," Neil said before his eyes fell on me. Ooof! The eye contact felt like a stomach punch. He frowned. "Oh. Sorry to disturb. I didn't realise you'd have company. I can go."

"It's fine. What did you need?" Michaela asked.

It was on the tip of my tongue to say goodbye to her and leave, but I was frozen in place. I couldn't stop staring at him. He looked tired, and I yearned to take his glasses off, smooth out the stress lines in between his eyebrows, and run my hands through his short brown hair.

Neil dragged his eyes away from me and cleared his throat. "Trevor asked me to visit an archive to find the original architectural drawings of an old building where he wants to shoot a *Running on Air* episode. Supposedly, the archive is run by some cranky old geezer who's difficult to deal with, but he tends to be more accommodating to women, so I was going to ask if you'd come with me."

Again, his eyes flicked briefly to mine before returning to Michaela. "I'm so sorry, Neil. I can't go," she said. "My parents will be arriving for a visit soon, and I have a big dinner planned."

"Right, James mentioned the engagement," Neil replied. "Congratulations."

"Thank you. I haven't told Mum and Dad yet. That's what the dinner's for."

"Well, I'm sure I can manage a curmudgeonly old archivist by myself. I've dealt with worse."

"I can come with you," I offered impulsively, drawing his attention.

Neil's frown returned. "I'm not sure if—"

"Oh, for crying out loud. Just take my help, Neil. And quit acting like you don't know me."

His gaze cut to mine. "I wasn't acting like—"

"What a great idea. Thank you so much for offering to help, Afric," Michaela interjected enthusiastically. "Now, get going, you two. Most archives close at five, so you don't have a lot of time to get there."

She practically shoved me out the door, and then Neil and I were left standing on her front stoop, staring at one another like the most awkward pair that had ever existed.

"You don't have to come," Neil said, averting his gaze.

"I want to come. We need to talk."

"I'm not sure I'm ready to talk."

"Is that why you ignored my voicemail?"

One eyebrow rose. "You mean the one you left me at three in the morning rambling on about how you were sorry but also not sorry?"

"Yes. That one. Though that was only one part of what I said. I was mainly apologising." I paused, inhaling a deep breath and channelling as much sincerity into my voice as I could muster. "You have no idea how sorry I am. I meant what I said about grovelling. Whatever you need from me, I'll do it."

There was a flash of emotion in his eyes as they locked on mine. I nearly fell over from the intensity of his gaze, and I yearned to know what he was thinking. We must've been standing there locked in a stare-down for a while because Michaela opened her living room window and stuck her head out.

"Why are you two still standing out there? Didn't you hear what I said about the archive closing at five?"

My eyes flickered between Neil's. Feeling unsure, I reached out and touched his hand. "Do you want me to come with you?"

His eyes closed for a second, his reply little more than a whisper. "Yes."

Just like that, my spirits lifted. There were a hundred helium balloons beneath my feet, propelling me into the air.

"We're going," I said to Michaela before motioning for Neil to lead the way.

We walked quietly in the direction of the nearest Tube station, and I let Neil lead us onto the appropriate train. There weren't many seats, so we ended up sitting side by side, our backs to the window.

His elbow brushed mine, and he coughed, pulling it back. "Sorry," he muttered.

"You don't need to apologise for brushing my elbow," I said, then leaned close to murmur in his ear, "I've always liked it when you touched me."

His Adam's apple visibly bobbed in his throat as he swallowed. He looked a little embarrassed, so I relented and changed the subject.

"What's the game plan for dealing with the old geezer? Do I need to charm him? I think I have some lipstick in my bag that I could put on."

He cast his gaze to mine, his eyes running over me, and I felt his attention like a physical caress. "That won't be necessary."

I reached up to pull the elastic from my hair. "I can let my hair down," I said as it fell around my shoulders. "Men like it when women wear their hair down, right?"

My hands were in the process of fixing my hair when he caught my wrist. I froze, sucking in a harsh breath as I glanced up at him. There was a storm in his eyes. "Don't do that," he said, voice thick as he let go of my wrist, and my hands fell into my lap.

"Sorry. I forgot for a second that you hate me right now and I'm supposed to be grovelling for forgiveness."

Something I said made him frown. "What makes you think I hate you?"

"Well, you never responded to my voicemail for a start," I reminded him, shoulders hunched. I felt defensive. I couldn't help it. In the grand scheme of things, it had only been half a day, but I was hurt that he hadn't made contact. Hadn't he promised me just last night that he wouldn't abandon me as the others had?

"I'm mad at you, Afric. That doesn't mean I hate you."

"And you have every right to be mad. Yes, a part of me is glad I was drunk enough to tell Leanne about Annabelle, mainly because it means we never have to see that bitch's face ever again, but I'm also so, so sorry for doing it. It was a dickhead move. I am a dickhead."

"I'm the only dickhead in this situation," Neil said, exhaling. "And you're right. A part of me is glad that you told Leanne and the secret is finally out in the open."

"What is it then? Are you mad about the hacking?"

"I would be if it weren't for the fact that Leanne gave you the go-ahead. It's her relationship that would be affected if those screenshots ever saw the light of day."

"So, what then?"

Neil's jaw moved in a weird way, his expression broody. "What you did was fucked up, Afric. I need some time before I'm ready to forgive you for it."

All those helium balloons I mentioned? Someone just stuck a pin in them. Several moments of quiet passed before I spoke tentatively, "Since you're still working, I take it you didn't get fired?"

At this, several emotions flickered behind his eyes, the most notable being guilt. "Yes, Callum and Leanne insisted I stay on."

"That's good news."

He shook his head. "I'm going to resign. I just need to find a suitable replacement, train them up, and then I'll hand in my notice."

"But why? If they want you to stay on, then they've clearly forgiven you."

"It's not as simple as that. From a moral standpoint, it wouldn't be right for me to stay on. And besides, I have other plans, and I've been using my job as a crutch not to pursue them."

"Really? What sort of plans?" I asked, curious.

"The next stop is ours," Neil said in a flat voice before standing and joining the group who were waiting to get off. I followed, a little miffed that he refused to answer my question. I stood next to him, making the mistake of not grabbing hold of a bar as the train came to a stop, which meant I fell right into Neil. His hands came up to my shoulders, steadying me, and I got a waft of his familiar scent. It was so powerful I had to close my eyes for a second.

"Afric, are you okay?" he asked.

I nodded and opened my eyes, glancing up at him. Our gazes locked, and I couldn't look away. We'd been apart for less than a day, and it already felt like a lifetime. I missed him so much. The emotional wall he'd thrown up was the worst part. I wanted my Neil back, the one who tried not to smile too hard when I teased him or said something funny. The one who I'd catch looking at me with worship in his eyes when he didn't know I was paying attention.

"I'm fine," I whispered, and he nodded, eyes running over me.

Then he glanced to the side and swore. The doors had closed, and the train was on the move again.

"We can get out at the next stop and come back this way," he said.

"Sorry. I distracted you," I whispered.

He cast me a soft glance. "You have a habit of doing that."

Tingles skittered down my spine at the husky note in his voice, at the glimpse of warmth. We fell into silence again and stayed by the doors until we arrived at the next stop. We got off then hopped on the train going in the opposite direction. When we finally got back to our intended destination, it was only a short walk to the archive. The building was old and rundown. I took the lead and did all the talking, and the archivist, a cranky old guy in a green jumper, admitted us entrance. He led us down a narrow, musty hallway and into a dank storage room lined with filing cabinets.

"You should be able to find what you're looking for in here. I clock off in an hour, though, so you better be done by then."

"We will be. Thanks for your help," Neil said, and the man shot him an unimpressed look, grunting as he left.

Neil went to the first cabinet and pulled it open, flicking through folders.

"Can I help?" I asked.

"No, thank you. It shouldn't take too long to find the schematics, so long as they've been filed correctly."

I nodded and leaned against one of the cabinets. Neil's back was to me, and I noticed he was wearing jeans. Most days, he wore slacks, especially while he was working. It was a rare and wonderful occasion to see him in jeans; his cute backside encased to perfection in the dark denim.

"I can feel you staring at me. Stop it," he said gruffly.

"Well, what am I supposed to do? There isn't anything else to look at in here."

He heaved a sigh. "Just ... I don't know ... Look at your phone or something."

"I don't want to look at my phone."

"You are so bloody irritating," he huffed.

"And you're so easy to wind up," I shot back, not expecting it when he swiftly turned around. A millisecond later, he was on me, backing me up into the cabinet as his hands cupped my face. "Infuriating woman. Why am I so obsessed with you?" he asked in a gravelly voice that had me clenching my thighs.

I didn't have a chance to respond because his mouth came crashing down on mine, his tongue an invading army I was helpless to defend against. He groaned into the kiss, and I melted, my pulse racing. Neil's knee came between my legs, nudging them apart as his mouth practically drank me in. I felt thoroughly consumed as I brought my hands up to rest on his shoulders. I had to admit; his kiss was an onslaught I wasn't prepared for. It was an angry, passionate, punishing kiss. It was a kiss that said, *I'm not ready to forgive you, but I am ready to take things out on you in a sexual manner.*

I had no problem with that.

He could take things out on me all he wanted. He could be mad at me so long as he didn't stop doing whatever he was doing with his tongue. My fingers reached up, scratching into the base of his skull. He groaned, pressing closer, his erection hard against my belly. My core ached for him. I needed him inside me, filling me up until I forgot everything else that existed except for the two of us.

Almost like he could read my mind, his hand slipped inside my leggings and past my underwear. His mouth left mine, and I inhaled large gulps of air while he planted kisses along my neck, sucked on my earlobe.

"I need you," he rasped as his fingers slid into the folds of my sex. "You're so wet. Is this for me?"

I bit my lip, burying my face in his shoulder. Something about his dirty talk made me shy. And what were we even doing? That old archivist could be hiding somewhere, spying on us through the keyhole. But at that moment, I was too far gone to care.

"Yes. It's for you," I replied breathlessly as Neil found my clit, circling it with two fingers. I gasped when his tongue slid inside the shell of my ear, causing tingles to skitter down my back and culminate at the base of my spine in the most pleasurable way.

His mouth returned to mine, and I didn't think it was possible, but he kissed me even more ferociously than before. I was nothing but sensation as his free hand went under my top, firmly gripping my breast, his thumb flicking over my extremely sensitive nipple. I moaned again, and this seemed to please him.

"Your tits are perfect. I dream about them," he said into the kiss.

"I want your mouth on them," I said past a whimper, and he groaned.

"I want that, too, beautiful."

His fingers moved away from my clit to sink inside me, and my eyes opened. Neil was already watching me, his irises ablaze in the dimly lit room. I couldn't look away as his fingers gently pumped, mimicking the motions of what his cock might do if he were inside me. My head fell back against the cabinet. Neil flicked my nipple, and a fresh shockwave of arousal went through me.

"I love the feel of you," he said, gaze worshipful.

"I love the feel of you loving the feel of me," I answered back, and the look on his face was one of pure devastation. His fingers returned to my clit, and I felt something building in me. It had been a long while since I'd had a non-self-inflicted orgasm. I'd almost forgotten how intense it could be when someone was attuned to you, when they just naturally found the right rhythm to drive you to release.

Neil and I had spent the last few months syncing up, and now, the symphony of us was in perfect harmony.

"I'm going to come," I gasped.

Outside, we both heard footsteps clipping down the hallway. I tensed, staring at Neil in panic, but his eyes held masculine determination. He wasn't stopping, not for anything. Not even for the possibility of someone walking in on us right now.

Thankfully, the footsteps continued past our door, and I was on the precipice of coming. Neil's circles sped up, and a split second later, my orgasm hit. I shook against him, waves of divine pleasure washing over me as his mouth came to my neck, pressing kisses to the sensitive hollow as he drew out the final few tremors.

"Now, we're even," he murmured huskily against my skin.

"If you keep kissing my neck, I'm going to shove my hand down your pants and make us uneven again," I warned. His answering chuckle was low and deep enough to be felt in the pit of my stomach.

Reluctantly, he moved away, his gaze dark and sumptuous. My jaw dropped when he brought his fingers to his lips and sucked them clean, tasting my pleasure. There was something so carnally sinful about it. I felt like I could come again just from watching him.

Neil Durant had a naughty streak. Who would have known?

I swallowed as I fixed my rumpled clothing.

Neil's eyes were apologetic. "I shouldn't have jumped on you like that."

"I liked you jumping on me. And besides, I was the one goading you by staring at your arse."

He chuckled quietly, then raked a hand through his hair. "I suppose we should have that talk."

Nerves flooded me. I'd been dying to talk to him, but now I feared it. What if he said he couldn't forgive me? What if that was merely a parting orgasm? A farewell finger fuck? I would be devastated.

"Shouldn't you find that file you're after first? We don't have much time left."

Neil nodded soberly. "Right, yes, I should find the file, then we'll talk."

With that, he turned and opened a cabinet. Thirty seconds later, he had the file in his hand. We found a photocopier down the hall, and he quietly made a copy before returning the file to its rightful place. Leaving the building, I noticed it had started to rain. Neil motioned to the small coffee shop across the street.

"Want to go over there and grab something to drink?" he asked, and I nodded even though I really just wanted to run away. Anything to avoid the possibility of him saying that though he still lusted me, he couldn't forgive me. I followed him into the coffee shop, and we found a wobbly, cramped table in the back. A woman with dyed black hair served us two frothy cappuccinos, and then we just sat there looking at each other.

"Go on, then," I said. "Feel free to tell me what an awful bitch I am. I can take it."

"You're not an awful bitch. If anything, I'm the awful one." He paused, rubbing his chin. "I've been doing a lot of thinking, and it wasn't fair of me to drag you into my mess with Annabelle, especially not after I started having feelings for you."

"Oh," I said, fiddling with a coaster. "Well, it's not like you could've known that would happen. You didn't fancy me at all in the beginning."

"That's not true. I thought you were pretty," he said, then smirked as he amended. "Pretty, but annoying."

I laughed softly. "Well, if it's any consolation, I thought you were handsome but stuck-up."

He shot me a disbelieving look. "Handsome? Really?"

"Yes, really."

"That's good to know," he said, shooting me a sexy smile. "And you're right. I probably was a little stuck-up."

"I probably was a little annoying."

We both laughed. Our gazes held. Neil emitted a long sigh.

"I miss you so much it hurts right here," he said candidly, tapping the centre of his chest.

I reached across the table to take his hand into mine. "I have a matching hurt in the exact spot."

His eyes flickered back and forth. "I guess we should forgive each other. To make the pain go away if nothing else."

"You're the one who needs to forgive."

He shook his head. "Not true. As I said, it was wrong of me to string you along and involve you in my Annabelle mess. I'll never do anything like that ever again."

Hope bloomed. "Ever again? Does that mean—"

He squeezed my hand. "I want to be with you, Afric. I want you to be mine. The way you make me feel, I'll never have that with anyone else."

My eyes lowered to the table, an unusual feeling of shyness coming over me when I said, "So, you want to be my boyfriend?"

"Yes. I want that. More than anything."

Water filled my eyes. The tenderness of this moment was too much.

"Hey," Neil said, leaning across the table and lifting his other hand to wipe at the tears rolling down my cheeks. "Why are you crying?"

I lifted my gaze to his, sniffling. "I was just so worried that you'd cut me out of your life. It's happened to me before too many times."

"Afric," Neil said. "Please listen to me and believe me when I say this. The way I feel about you is unlike anything I've experienced before. I could never cut you out of my life, not even if I wanted to. You're in here now," he said, touching his chest again. "I need you."

"I need you, too," I whispered. And he had no idea how much I'd needed to hear those words, how much I needed the reassurance.

Amid the chatter of the small café, his fingers weaved through mine as he brought my hand to his mouth and pressed a sultry kiss to my knuckles. I felt it all the way between my legs. He stared at me with such male possession that I had to look away, using my free hand to lift my mug and take a small sip.

"There's just one outstanding matter," I said as I set the mug back down.

Neil arched an eyebrow. "Oh?"

"We're currently even on the giving and receiving of orgasms front," I said and relished the faint hint of red that marked his cheeks as he glanced around to make sure no one was listening. "But where it concerns the revealing of secrets, I'm one up on you. So, this means you have my permission to tell everyone about the time I fashioned an adult nappy for myself before failing to achieve the world record I was trying to break. I think that one is sufficiently humiliating."

At this, Neil gave a low chuckle. "I thought you said Michaela and Sarita already knew about that."

"Oh, feck, you're right. That means it's technically not a secret anymore. Okay, how about this one—"

"Let me stop you there," Neil interrupted. "You can tell me as many secrets as you like, but I won't be revealing them to anyone."

"Why not?"

He gave my hand another squeeze. "Because I don't want to. And also, because the secret you revealed was one I should've revealed myself months ago."

"I still hate that I did that to you. Normally, I'm like a sealed vault when it comes to secrets."

"I know that. It was an unusual circumstance, not to mention alcohol was involved."

I nodded, falling silent as I continued to sip my coffee. I felt Neil's eyes on me as I brought my gaze to his. I shot him a questioning look. "Why are you staring at me like that?"

"I actually wanted to ask you something."

"Oh?"

"How do you like being your own boss?"

"Um, it has its pros and cons, but mostly the pros outweigh the cons. Why?"

"Hmm."

"What does 'hmm' mean?"

"I'm thinking of starting my own business," he said, and my eyes widened.

"You are. That's exciting. What kind of business?"

"Event planning."

"Oh! That's perfect," I said, remembering him once telling me how much he enjoyed that part of his job as an assistant. "You and Michaela seem to be constantly planning birthdays and special occasions and private screenings and whatnot."

"Yes. All the Annabelle drama aside, I thought it was about time I moved on with my career. I don't want to be an assistant forever."

"You seem happy about this decision," I said. "It's a good look for you."

"You're a good look for me," he shot back, and I barked a laugh.

"Oh, my God, I love flirty Neil. He's my favourite. Wait, since we're officially boyfriend and girlfriend, does that mean you're going to start taking me on dates? Will you wear a shirt and tie? Will I get chocolates and flowers?"

"Yes. Yes, to all of that. In fact, we should make Michaela and James's engagement party next weekend our first official date."

I grinned at him. "I'm excited. This is very exciting."

He didn't reply, instead he leaned across the table again and captured my lips in a kiss.

22.
Neil

I sensed the attention of a few of the coffee shop patrons as I gave Afric a less-than-appropriate kiss for a public space. When we finally broke apart for air, I relished the dreamy look in her eyes. I wanted to make her look like that all the time, preferably while lying naked in my bed.

I was still holding her hand as I brushed the inside of her wrist with my thumb and watched a tremble go through her. I could sit gazing at her all day, but I still had to get the photocopies over to Trevor's flat before I clocked off. I also had to talk with Callum and James and tell them I wouldn't be joining them in their sportswear venture. Morally, I couldn't continue working as their assistant, not after what I'd done. But personally, I felt like it was time to move on, go out there and see what I could achieve on my own. I had no interest in sportswear, and it wouldn't be fair to Callum and James to take on a job I didn't feel passionate about, even if it came with a significant pay rise.

Don't get me wrong, working on a TV show like *Running on Air* gave me experiences I'd cherish forever, and the friends I'd made along the way would be friends I kept for life, but I needed a change. I needed to take a risk. I'd been staid for far too long.

"I know we've technically moved onto eighties romcoms," I said, "but I discovered an older adaptation of *Persuasion* that we haven't watched yet. It's supposed to be better than the newer version."

"*Persuasion* was one of my favourites," she said, eyes alight.

I know, that's why I searched for it. I cleared my throat. "Do you want to come over to mine later and watch it? We could order in?"

"I'd love that," she replied, and my immediate impulse was to blurt, *And I love you,* but I managed to reel it in. My chest was filled with so many feelings it was almost impossible to contain them all, but I knew for certain that I loved her. I just feared her reaction. What if she wasn't there yet? What if the intensity of my feelings scared her away?

"I have a few more work things to do, but I can walk you to the Tube if you like," I said, and she nodded. We left the coffee shop, and all the way to the station, my throat felt tight, my tongue heavy. Despite my fears, there was a pent-up need in me to tell her how I truly felt. I was going to burst with it. That was probably why, just as she was stepping onto the train going in the direction of Brixton, I uttered a quiet, "Just in case you don't already know, I'm in love with you."

The doors closed. Afric stood behind them, her eyebrows all the way up in her forehead, her blue eyes round with shock and surprise.

I saw her mouth a stunned, "What?"

And then the train was moving, and she was getting farther and farther away from me until she drifted completely from view.

Well, that was one way to tell her without having to worry about a response.

Great move, Neil. Played a blinder there.

I expected my phone to light up with a call, or maybe a string of messages, but it remained silent. I didn't know whether to be relieved or depressed.

I didn't have time to wallow, though, as I got back to work. It didn't take long to drop the papers off at Trevor's before I went to see Callum and James at the gym. The two of them had just finished a workout. Neither of them was happy with my news, but they also understood my need to go it alone. I'd spent years working in the shadow of their success, and now I had to prove to myself that I could build something on my own. I had some savings, plus a vast accumulation of knowledge and experience. Everything else, well, I could learn it as I went along.

After our chat about the sportswear venture, Callum pulled me aside and filled me in on the Annabelle situation. She hadn't posted anything online, nor had she tried to make contact, but he and Leanne had handed her details over to their security company so that they could keep an eye on her. If she made a move to try to mess with them, then the company would alert them. It was a relief to know they were taking pre-emptive action on that front.

When I got back to my place, I hopped straight into the shower, needing to wash away the stress of the day. I must've sweated buckets during the few moments I declared my love to Afric and the train had taken her away at a steady pace, like she was on one of those travelators at the airport and I was just standing there, awkwardly watching her get farther away. Why did I have to be such a weirdo? Why couldn't I express my love like a normal person?

I still hadn't had any calls or texts from her, and I wondered if she would still come over tonight to watch the movie. Maybe I'd messed everything up. I swallowed down a lump in my throat at the thought.

I'd just gotten out of the shower, dried off, and changed into a T-shirt and some sweatpants when there was a knock at my door. My heart leapt.

She was here.

I stared at my front door a beat too long before I finally forced my legs to move. Opening it, I found Afric standing there, a smile on her face like everything was perfectly normal. She stretched up and kissed my cheek softly in greeting before stepping inside my flat.

"Hey, so what type of food are you in the mood for?" she asked, walking by me and into my living room. "I was thinking Chinese, but if you have your heart set on something different, I'm open to suggestions."

I ran a hand through my damp hair. "Um, there are some menus in the cupboard. Let me grab them," I said, going into the kitchen.

When I returned, she was sitting on my couch. I sat next to her and placed the menus on her lap. She started to peruse them.

"Ah, feck, now I have too many choices. What about Turkish kebabs? I love that garlic sauce they slather all over the kebab meat."

"A kebab sounds good."

"Hmm, but then I always get garlic burps after."

"Right, those aren't pleasant."

"I love you, too, by the way," she said, so casually that I didn't register it at first. Her attention was still fixed on the menus. "Oh, and now I want Italian. I'm actually ridiculous."

"Afric," I said, my pulse pounding.

"Hmm?"

"Can you repeat what you just said?"

"What? That I want Italian? I know, I'm so greedy. Maybe we could order a selection."

I pushed the menus off her lap and grabbed both her hands in mine. "Stop talking about food for a second and look at me. Did you say you loved me?"

She rolled her eyes, a grin tugging at her lips. "Since you decided to blindside me today as I was leaving on the Tube, I thought it was only fair that I return the favour."

"You love me?" I whispered, a happy feeling in the pit of my stomach.

"I think I started falling for you the day you sent me that adorable selfie of you standing in Central Park," she said, and I huffed a laugh.

"I think I started falling for you the day I sent you that selfie and you slagged me endlessly for it."

"I am quite fond of teasing you when you get embarrassed. This is true."

Without warning, I tugged her close, smashing my mouth to hers in a hungry, feral kiss. I felt a puff of air leave her. Then she reached up, her hands sinking into my hair. I groaned at the scrape of her nails on my scalp before she crawled into my lap. A rumble emanated from deep in my chest. I pulled back, my breathing ragged.

"We should order food," I said. *Before I end up fucking you on this couch.*

Afric nodded, looking just as worked up as I felt.

"Right. Good idea. Food. What were we going to order again?"

I smiled and caressed her cheek. "How about we just go with your original plan and get Chinese? I feel like showing you all those menus was a bad idea.

"Okay, Chinese it is. But we're double carbing it. I want noodles *and* fried rice."

I went to grab my phone. "Your wish is my command."

"I like being your girlfriend," she said, a contented smile on her face as she lay back on the couch. I had to resist staring at her lips and how puffy they were from my kisses.

I like being your boyfriend.

Once I'd placed our order, I returned to the couch and lined up the movie. Afric settled in beside me, her head resting on my shoulder. There was something peaceful about just being with her like this. I felt at ease for the first time in who knew how long.

"Wow, I had no idea what a hunk Ciarán Hinds was in his youth," Afric said a little while into the film.

"Please don't start thirsting after actors again. My ego couldn't handle it," I said, placing a kiss on her temple.

She chuckled. "Don't worry. It's just a bit of window shopping. You're the only man I want to defile in real life."

I lifted my arm and threw it around her. She snuggled in close.

"*Defile* is an interesting choice of word."

"You have no idea what's in store for you," she teased. "I've been having some serious thoughts. You may be a little traumatised by the time I'm done, just FYI."

The buzzer sounded, and I reluctantly went to collect our food. I really wanted to stay and have Afric explain these so-called thoughts of hers in greater detail. When I returned, we dug into the food and continued watching the movie. At one point, Afric sat forward and removed the baggy jumper she'd been wearing. I watched with rapt attention, no longer interested in what was happening on screen. She wore a white T-shirt underneath, and it was tight enough for me to appreciate the womanly curve of her hips and the swell of her breasts.

It took all my willpower to finish the meal without dragging her into my bedroom.

Finally, the movie was over, and the end credits rolled down the screen. Afric burrowed her face into my neck. "All that food has made me so sleepy. I don't want to go home."

"Stay over then," I suggested, lazily stroking her arm. She was practically lying on top of me; her breasts pressed flush to my chest.

Her full lips curved into a grin. "I'll stay over on one condition," she said, stretching up so that her mouth was a hair's breadth from mine.

"And what's that?" I asked, my voice raspy.

"That you promise not to behave," she replied right before she dragged her lips across mine, featherlight, and I felt it down in my groin.

I struggled to form a coherent response. My hands went to her hips as I shifted her so that she was fully on top of me. Her tongue dipped out, delicately dancing with mine. We kissed, and things escalated fast. Before I knew it, I was picking her up and carrying her into my bedroom. I threw her down on my bed, and she giggled loudly, looking around.

"Wow, it's tidy in here."

I shot her a dark grin as I climbed between her legs. "It's about to get messy."

She let out a delighted laugh. "Oh, my God, you're so cheesy. I love it."

I pulled at the waistband of her leggings. "These must officially come off."

"Far be it from me to argue with official mandates," she replied, her pupils large as she watched me. I pushed up the hem of her T-shirt and pressed my mouth to her bare stomach. A soft breath escaped her. I made sure to hold her gaze as I did away with her leggings and underwear. At the same time, she reached around and pulled her T-shirt off, swiftly followed by her bra. Now, she was completely naked, and I was ... entranced.

I literally couldn't react. She was beautiful, *magnificent*, her long blonde hair hanging about her bare shoulders. She was the definition of sexiness, and I was ... Well, I was still fully clothed and stiff as a board.

"Neil Durant, are you speechless?" she asked, her voice flirtatious.

"I'm having a moment, so just ... give me a moment."

Her laughter filled my ears, and it was the sweetest sound.

"Take a moment then. I'll just lay here and get things started."

She reached for her breasts, and my moment passed. Milliseconds later, I was on her, pushing her hands away as I caught her nipple in my mouth. I swirled my tongue around it, and she moaned, her head falling back into the pillows.

I palmed her other breast, and her hands went to my shoulders, clawing at my T-shirt. She dragged it up over my head, forcing me to release her nipple, and then she was touching me everywhere. Her soft hands slid across my shoulder blades and down my bare back before fully cupping my backside. A shiver of need tip-toed down my spine.

"Finally, I get what I want," she said triumphantly, and I groaned, lowering my mouth to her neck before returning to her breasts.

"I'll be with you shortly. These need more attention."

"Oh, God," she gasped when I licked one nipple then the other. My hand drifted down over her silky, rounded stomach to the silky, wet heat between her legs. I stroked her there, and her moans increased. I continued moving down her body until my head was between her legs and I was tasting just how much she wanted me.

The moment my tongue met her clit, she cried out, and I watched as her eyes fell shut and a look of sheer pleasure came over her. I ran my hand along the inside of her thigh before sinking a finger inside her, my mouth still on her clit.

"Fuck, Neil. Yes. There. Keep doing that," she urged breathlessly, back arching.

A feeling of deep, possessive satisfaction took over me. I flicked my tongue over her clit then made fast circles that had her hands fisting my sheets. Her body drew taut, her moans quieting, and then, she shuddered against my tongue. The pleasure of making her come was like nothing else in this world. I was certain I'd never tire of it.

Afric reached down to stroke my hair away from my face, her fingers caressing my jaw. "You are really very good at that."

"And you are really very sexy," I shot back, massaging her thighs.

She bit her lip. "Oh crap, this isn't good."

"What isn't good?"

"I'm having an urge to lock us in this bedroom for the next two days so that you can go down on me for hours at a time."

A smirk tugged at my lips. "I don't see anything wrong with that."

Afric

I didn't think Neil could ever look more appealing than he did right then, his hair askew, eyes adoring as he gazed up at me, his head resting between my thighs.

I loved him so much.

I'd never loved a man before. He'd literally stolen my heart.

"Come here," I whispered.

A dark, seductive gleam entered his eyes as he climbed up my body and captured my mouth in a searing kiss. I tasted myself on him, and it sent an erotic shiver through me.

"Neil," I moaned into the kiss. "I need you now."

Together, we tugged down his pants, and then his hot, hard erection was against me, skin to skin. I shuddered. He reached over to his nightstand and quickly found a condom. I watched with rapt attention as he slid it down his length. Overcome with need, I grabbed him and flipped us so that I was straddling him. A grunted breath went out of him as I lifted my hips. I inhaled sharply, our gazes locked as I lowered myself down on his cock. He let out a low expletive as I rocked my hips gently, his hands roaming my stomach before coming up to cup my boobs.

"You're perfect," he breathed.

"And you're mine," I declared.

His eyes lit up at this as he responded, "You're mine, too."

I started to rock against him, and the hot, wet slide of his cock as he filled me had my eyes closing in rapture, my head falling back. Neil's hands were on my hips now.

I opened my eyes and found him looking between our bodies, a dark, erotic gleam in his eyes as he watched his cock go in and out of me. I rocked faster, and he groaned, gazing up at me now like I was a goddess and he was worshipping at my altar.

I soaked up every detail of him, particularly obsessed with how the veins in his throat stood in relief and the masculine cut of his shoulders. I loved our bodies together. We were softness and hard edges.

My inner muscles undulated, and he let out a sound of raw pleasure. I felt him grow even harder, thicker, inside me, and I knew he was close. I wanted to make him come while I rode him. I needed to see his face as he filled me.

"Afric, I'm so close," he grunted, one hand holding my hip as the other came up to massage my breast.

I pumped my hips, holding his gaze as he strained beneath me. Then, just like that, he flipped us, driving into me from above as he came. "Wow," I breathed when he lowered himself next to me and pulled me into his warm arms.

Neil's breathing was ragged as he pressed a kiss to the hollow of my neck.

"We're going to need to do that again as soon as you're ready," I said, a fond note in my voice as Neil continued to try and catch his breath. I felt his teeth graze my shoulder.

"Pretty sure I'll be ready to go again in a minute or two."

"That's impressive."

He reached for my chin, tugging my mouth to his. "When it comes to you, I always aim to impress," he rasped before capturing my lips in a heated, languid kiss.

***

All week, Neil and I grabbed every stolen moment we could to spend together. We were in a sexy lust haze, the two of us lost in our own little bubble. I could barely concentrate enough to work, and I knew I was coming across completely distracted on my livestreams, but there was nothing to be done.

Every time I let my mind drift, it inevitably wandered to images of Neil and me tearing at each other's clothes, desperate to get our hands on one another.

Because of work, I didn't get to see him all day on Saturday. Sunday was Michaela and James' engagement party, and I'd gone all out and purchased a new outfit online for the occasion. I even paid for expedited shipping like the luxurious bitch that I was.

What was the point in life if you couldn't treat yourself from time to time?

I'd certainly treated myself. The dress was from Alexander McQueen, and it cost the equivalent of two months' rent. There wasn't anything baggy or oversized about it, either. It was emerald green, sleeveless and backless, with thin straps and a sweetheart neckline. I'd purchased a studded belt to cinch it in at the waist. The skirt was calf-length and puffed out slightly. I was pairing it with some Louboutin flats I'd purchased second-hand last year.

Sarita appeared in my doorway. "Wait, is it St. Patrick's day, and no one told me?" she asked, eyeing me up and down with a grin.

"Nope, green's just a good colour on me," I shot back, sticking out my tongue.

"Well, are you ready to go? Your man friend's downstairs, and it looks like he parked on double yellow lines."

"He's not my man friend. He's Neil. He's my *soulmate*," I crooned, and Sarita made a gagging noise.

"Oh, man. You've gone all romantic. Is this why you're dressing like a proper lady for once?"

"Partly," I replied, waggling my eyebrows secretively.

I'd been thinking a lot about what Neil said to me after I told him that I dressed in oversized clothes to avoid unwanted sexual attention on the internet. He'd then pointed out that I dressed in oversized clothing all the time, not just while live streaming. It had happened so gradually that I didn't even realise the clothes thing had leaked into my everyday life. Now, I was making a conscious effort not to hide myself under layers of fabric and instead celebrate the shit hot body I'd been blessed with.

"Right, well, we'd better get a move on. The party starts soon, and traffic might be heavy."

I nodded and grabbed my handbag. The gods had been benevolent and decided to bless Michaela with sunshine for her outdoor engagement party. In London, there was always a chance of rain.

Sarita and I headed downstairs, and Neil was standing outside his car, looking shiftily from side to side to make sure there were no clampers lurking in the shadows. He was wearing a suit, and I just about fell over, swooning so hard.

"Pardon me, Mr Bond, but you don't happen to have seen a man hanging around? Brown hair, glasses, about this tall?" I asked teasingly as I approached.

Neil rolled his eyes and grinned as his attention fell appreciatively over my dress. "You look …"

"Like a stalk of broccoli. I know," I finished for him, sticking out my tongue. He reached forward and grabbed my wrist, pulling me to him.

"That's not what I was going to say, and you know it," he murmured, whispering his lips across mine and sending a flurry of dirty thoughts through my head. "You look beautiful."

"Let's go," Sarita said, hopping into the back seat. "We still have to pick up Mabel, and I hate being late."

Neil cast me a searing smile before walking around the car and opening the passenger side door for me. I could certainly get used to this gentlemanly behaviour, I thought as I climbed in and strapped on my seatbelt.

On the drive, my phone buzzed. I sifted through my bag and pulled it out.

Adam: Okay, I did it. I just told Winona that I like her.

My pulse pounded as I read the message. This was so exciting.

Afric: Oh, my God! What did she say?

Adam: She said ... the feeling is mutual.

Afric: Gah! I'm so happy right now!

Adam: And I just booked a flight to Miami to see her. This could end disastrously. I burn like bacon in the sun.

Afric: Pack lots of sunscreen, then. I want all the details. You have to promise to update me in real time.

Adam: Lol. I'll try my best.

I put away my phone, still grinning as Neil pulled up to the hotel. A young guy in a waistcoat took his keys to park the car for him. I slid my arm through his as we took the elevator up to the rooftop garden where the party was being held. The doors opened into a gloriously sunny scene. There were tables topped with pretty flower arrangements while hotel staff handed out glasses of champagne to guests.

Michaela and James appeared, James in a suit and Michaela wearing a pretty red sundress.

"You two managed to work things out then?" she whispered in my ear as we hugged and I handed her the gift I brought.

"Yes, we did," I replied.

Her smile was pleased. "I'm glad."

"Me, too."

Michaela turned her attention to Neil. "James tells me you're starting an event planning business."

Neil dipped his head. "It's still early days, but yes."

"Great," she said, casting her fiancé a little glance. "Because James and I wanted to be your very first clients."

Neil blinked. "Pardon?"

"We want you to plan our wedding," James said, and my chest filled with happiness for Neil. I knew he was nervous about this career change, and getting the chance not just to plan an ordinary wedding, but a wedding where the groom was a celebrity, was a big deal. He could really make a name for himself with this.

"Wow, um, I don't know what to say," he replied, taken aback.

"Say you'll do it," Michaela urged.

"Okay," Neil bobbed his head. "I'll do it."

"Fantastic. I promise not to turn into a Bridezilla," Michaela joked, and we all laughed.

Two hours later, I was veritably stuffed on scones and cakes and tiny, tasty sandwiches, not to mention copious amounts of champagne and tea. Neil warned me the mixture would give me a stomach ache later, but I assured him I was made of stronger stuff.

Neil and I stood by the edge of the roof garden, staring out at the city skyline beyond. His hand came to rest on my lower back, and I felt the heat of him sear into me like a brand. I'd never tire of his touch, of the way he looked at me with such love and affection in his eyes.

I nudged him with my elbow. "So, have you had a nice day?"

"Yes, aside from having to avoid a mountain load of dairy, it's been very pleasant."

"Afternoon tea is quite dairy heavy, isn't it? I never realised before."

"So much clotted cream," Neil groaned, and I chuckled.

"I salute your willpower for resisting. But damn it, now I have to rethink my birthday plans. I was considering making it an afternoon tea."

"No girlfriend of mine plans her own birthday," Neil chided. "And besides, I already have a surprise in mind for you."

"Oh?" I said, curiosity piqued. "What's the surprise? Give me a clue."

Neil's lips twitched as he bent close to murmur. "It might involve me dressing up as a certain actor from a certain episode of *Lip Sync Battle*."

My eyes widened in delight. "Oh my God, seriously? I'm going to die of anticipation. Why does my birthday have to be so far away? The wait will be agony."

"Speaking of agony," he said, lowering his mouth to my bare shoulder and delicately scraping his teeth across my skin, awakening all the tiny nerve endings that lived there. "I'm surprised I've managed to keep my hands off you in this dress."

I arched my back as Neil's hand drifted lower. "Be careful," I whispered. "You'll scandalise the other guests."

"Most of them are drunk on champagne and refined sugar. I doubt they'll notice," he whispered back, nipping my ear and soliciting a quiet moan.

"Can I stay over at yours tonight?" I asked, turning to gaze up into his handsome brown eyes.

"You can stay at mine every night if you want."

I moved closer, pressing my lips to the underside of his jaw. "That's a dangerous invitation, Mr Durant. I might end up leaving a toothbrush in your perfectly ordered bathroom."

His eyes glinted. "Do it. I dare you."

"What if I clear out a drawer for myself and leave all my night things in it? Won't that mess with the neat structure of your personal space?"

He was already shaking his head. "I welcome you to be as messy as you like. In fact, I insist. My life has been way too ordered for way too long. It's about time I let in a little chaos."

I reached up, placing my hand on his neck, and he practically undulated at my touch. "Okay, then," I said close to his mouth. "Dare accepted."

He smiled right before I kissed him, and then his hands were in my hair, and he was backing me up against the railing. We were being incredibly inappropriate for a daytime affair, but I was too lost in him to care. Besides, Neil was right about most of the guests being drunk on champagne. I was pretty sure I spotted Michaela's dad, who was a vicar, cheekily pinching his wife's backside as they danced to Michael Bublé.

Neil groaned into the kiss, and my body melted into his. His hand in my hair gripped firmly, tilting my head so that he could deepen the kiss. I had so much love for him there was excess slipping out and going everywhere like someone left the bath running too long and water and suds were overflowing. I loved him so much I would fight to the death for him. I'd climb mountains for him. I'd do anything to ensure his happiness and health, and I knew the feeling was mutual.

I never imagined I'd find someone like Neil. Someone who didn't get tired of my overzealous personality or my gaming or my need to tease him relentlessly. He loved me for those things instead. He loved me for exactly who I was, and that was a rare feeling, indeed.

Looking back, I couldn't believe I'd considered his friendship merely a sidequest when the whole time he'd been a brand-new adventure, an all-encompassing journey that wouldn't be completed in a few short hours but would instead last an entire lifetime.

END.

Thank you for reading *Sidequest for Love*! Please consider supporting an indie author and leaving a review <3

Six of Hearts Sneak Peek

If you enjoyed *Sidequest for Love* then you might also like L.H. Cosway's highly acclaimed Hearts Series, available now in Kindle Unlimited. Read on for a sneak peek of book #1, *Six of Hearts*.

BLURB:
When Jay Fields, world-renowned illusionist, walks into her dad's law firm Matilda is struck speechless. Not only is he one of the most attractive and charismatic men she's ever met, he's also a mystery to be solved.

Jay wants to sue a newspaper for defamation, but all is not what it seems. Matilda is determined to discover the true story behind Jay, however, when he becomes an unexpected roommate, she is not ready for how he will wheedle his way into her affections and steal her heart.

The man is a mystery wrapped in an enigma, and though she can't yet see the bigger picture, Matilda can't resist following along for the thrilling and heart-stopping ride.

EXCERPT:

Making my way down the narrow staircase that leads out of the building and onto the street, I bump into a tall man with golden-brown hair. I wouldn't normally notice a man's hair so specifically, but this guy has some serious style going on. It's cut tight at the sides and left long on the top, kind of like a sexy villain in a movie set in the 1920s. I stare up at him, wide-eyed. He's wearing a very nice navy suit with a leather satchel bag slung over his shoulder. Even though it was the first thing I noticed, his hair pales in comparison to the wonder that is his face. I don't think I've ever been up close to such a handsome example of the male species in my life.

Why can't men like this write to me online? I ponder dejectedly.

Because men like this don't even know the meaning of the term "socially awkward," my brain answers.

My five-foot-something stares up at his six-foot-whatever, and I think to myself, *what's a prize like you doing in a dive like this?* Actually, now that I'm looking at him, he does seem vaguely familiar, but I can't put my finger on where I've seen him before.

Probably on the pages of a fashion magazine, if his looks are anything to go by.

If it hasn't already been deduced from the fact that I can't even find a date using the romantic connection slut that is the Internet, then I'll spell it out. I'm useless with men, and I'm talking all men. Even the nice approachable fellows. And I'm not looking at a nice approachable fellow right now. I'm looking at a "chew you up and spit you out" tiger.

Rawr.

Since the entrance to the building is so narrow, we have to skirt around each other. I give him a hesitant smile and a shrug. His eyes sparkle with some kind of hidden knowledge as he lets me pass, like beautiful people know the meaning of the universe and are amused by us ordinary folks who have to bumble along in the dark.

I'm just about to step out the door when the tiger starts to speak. "I'm looking for Brandon Solicitors. Do you know if I have the right place?"

I step back inside.

He sounds like Mark Wahlberg when he's letting his Southie roots all hang out. His deep American accent makes me want to close my eyes and savour the sound. But I don't do that – because I'm not a complete psycho.

"Yeah, this is the place. I work here, actually. I'm the secretary slash receptionist slash general dogsbody. It's my dad's firm," I reply. Too much information, Matilda. Too. Much. Information.

The tiger smiles, making him better-looking, if that's even possible. And thankfully, he doesn't comment on my fluster. "I have an appointment with Hugh Brandon at nine. I'm Jay," he says, and takes a step closer to hold his hand out to me. My back hits the wall, his tall frame dwarfing mine. I don't think he realises just how narrow this space is, and now I can smell his cologne. Wow, it's not often that I get close enough to a man to smell him. And Jay Fields smells indecently good.

"Ah, right. Jay Fields. Yeah, I have you pencilled in. You can go on upstairs, and Dad will take care of you," I reply, shaking his hand and letting go quickly so that he doesn't notice my sweatacular palms. "I've got an errand to run."

He stares at me for a long moment, like his eyes are trying to take in my every feature, but that can't be right. When he finally responds, it's a simple, "I won't keep you, then, Matilda."

God. Why does the way he says "keep you" in that deep voice have to make my heart flutter? It's been literally thirty seconds, and I'm already well on my way to developing a crush.

He makes some keen eye contact with me, then turns and continues up the stairs to the office. I'm already on the street when I realise I hadn't offered my name, and yet he knew it. Perhaps he'd been browsing our website. Our offices might be shoddy, but I always make sure to keep our online presence up to scratch. There's a picture of me, Dad, and Will, the other solicitor who works for the practice, on the "About Us" page.

So if he knew who I was already, why did he ask if he had the right place?

Miracle of all miracles, was he actually, like, chatting me up or something? Be still my beating heart. Or is he just the friendly, chatty type? I consider these questions as I walk inside the café three buildings down from our office and order two lattes to go. I briefly think about ordering something for the tiger, aka Jay Fields, but he might be one of those picky coffee drinkers, so I don't.

When I get back, I find Dad's shut himself inside his office with Jay, and the next appointment is already waiting to be seen. She's a middle-aged woman wearing a neck brace. I haven't had the chance to look at her information, but I can imagine what she's here for. Some sort of accident claim.

What I really want to know is what Jay's here for. Yep, I'm already wondering about this man way too much. I remember him calling up last week to make the appointment, and somehow I neglected to ask him what kind of a claim he wanted to make. It's weird, too, because I have my set spiel for appointments, and I never forget to ask for all the information I need. It's almost like my subconscious knew I was speaking with a gorgeous man, thus rendering me double "F-ed": frazzled and forgetful.

Knowing Dad will want his caffeine fix as soon as possible, I knock lightly on the door and wait to be let in. Dad calls for me to enter and I do, opening the door with the paper coffee cup in my hand. Jay's sitting in the seat in front of Dad's desk, his hands clasped together over his head as he lounges back, casual as you please. I can feel his eyes on me as I walk to Dad and give him his beverage. He seems a little out of sorts, so I put a hand on his shoulder and ask, "Everything okay?"

Dad looks lost in his own head for a minute, and I have to repeat the question a second time to get him to answer me.

"What? Oh, yes, everything's fine. Thanks for the coffee, chicken," he mutters.

"It might be me who's the problem," Jays puts in. "I just presented your old man with a case he's not sure he wants to take."

I look at Jay now, my brow furrowing. Who the hell is this guy? What he's said has piqued my curiosity, though, so I close the door and fold my arms. Unless I'm needed to take notes, I don't normally sit in on meetings with clients, but Dad's demeanour has put me on edge, my protective instincts kicking into gear.

Jay grins in a way that makes me think he's pleased with my attention. "Oh, now she's curious."

Okay, this man might be beautiful, but he's also kind of strange.

"Did you want to make a claim against someone?" I ask, because Dad still isn't talking. I suppose he's still considering whatever Jay's case is.

"Nope. I want to sue someone," says Jay, all matter-of-fact.

"For what?"

"Defamation of character," he answers before pulling a newspaper out of his bag. He flips through it, folds it open to the page he's looking for, and hands it to me. I glance down at the tabloid, scanning the bold headline that reads, "Illusionist Jay Fields Causes Death of Volunteer." I let my eyes drift briefly over the article, which features a promotional picture of Jay holding up a six of hearts card. *Oh.* Now I remember where I know him from.

A couple of weeks ago *The Daily Post* broke a story about an Irish-American illusionist with a new show coming to RTÉ. He was filming an upcoming episode when a tragic accident hit. I scan the article before me, recalling the details. A couple of hours after wrapping up the filming of an episode where Jay was paying homage to Houdini by re-creating a version of his "Buried Alive" stunt, the volunteer who'd taken part had died of a heart attack.

What Jay proposed to do was to put the volunteer, David Murphy, into a hypnotic state whereby he would only breathe in very little air, allowing him to be buried for twenty-four hours in an empty grave and not suffocate in the process. An impossible feat, many would say. The volunteer was given a panic button, and if anything went wrong, he could press it, and he'd be immediately dug up. In the end the panic button wasn't needed, and he miraculously managed to survive the entire twenty-four hours underground. However, when he went to bed that night, he suffered a fatal heart attack and died.

Needless to say, the tabloids caught on to the story and began posing questions about whether or not Jay's stunt had somehow caused David Murphy to have his heart attack. After all, being buried alive is quite the traumatic experience.

The piece before me, written by a well-known crime journalist named Una Harris, who was the one to break the initial story about Jay, is certainly extreme. It delves into Jay's background in America, where she claims he spent a year in a juvenile detention facility for assaulting a man on the street. Before that he'd been a runaway, squatting in derelict buildings in Boston.

Harris poses questions about Jay's less than squeaky-clean background. She wonders how a man who spent time in prison, even if it was a young offenders' prison, would be given permission to carry out dangerous stunts as he had been doing in his show. She also wonders why Jay, who had been performing some very successful live shows in Las Vegas, would give all that up to move to such a small pond as Ireland to film a series that would only reach a tiny audience in comparison to the States.

Overall, she basically out and out claims that Jay had shady motives for coming here, and perhaps he even *intended* for David Murphy to die. He did, after all, almost beat a man to death when he was just fifteen. Perhaps he's simply come up with a more elaborate way to feed his need to harm people, Harris muses.

Whoa, this woman really doesn't pull any punches with her insinuations. It's almost like she's begging for a lawsuit. I mean, I've worked with my dad long enough to know that you should always have hard evidence before you publicly make claims about people that could be construed as libellous. And aside from a few hazy pieces of information about Jay's teenage years, Una Harris has zero evidence.

I draw my attention away from the newspaper to find that my dad and Jay had been having a conversation while I was lost in the article.

"Don't get me wrong," says Dad. "The thought of taking on such a case excites me. I haven't worked on anything like this in years, but at the same time I need to be selfless and tell you that there are far better solicitors out there for the job. I can even give you a few names to contact. You do actually want to win this case, I presume?"

Jay uncrosses his legs and folds his arms. "Hell, yeah, I want to win it. And I know you're the man for the job, Hugh, no matter how much you try to convince me otherwise."

I silently hand him back the newspaper and he takes it, his fingertips brushing mine. The contact makes my skin tingle. Stupid handsome bastard.

Dad stares at Jay, and I can tell by the look in his eyes that he wants to say yes — he just doesn't have the confidence to do it. In all honesty, I'm hoping he continues to say no. I know how stressful the kind of case Jay is proposing can be, and I don't want Dad going through all that. He just turned sixty last month. The landmark birthday only functioned to make me more aware of how many years he might have left.

"I'm sorry, Mr Fields, but I'm going to have to stick to my guns on his one," Dad says apologetically. "Taking on a journalist is one thing, but suing a newspaper is going to require a top-notch firm. As you can probably see, we're not that."

Oh. Jay wants to sue the actual newspaper? I'm impressed. That takes some serious balls.

Okay, Matilda, stop thinking about the man's balls.

Jay lets out a long sigh and turns his head to the window. A second later he gets up from his seat and thrusts his hand out at Dad. "Well, if there's no way I can convince you," he replies, and the two men shake hands. "Thanks for your time anyway."

Jay goes to walk out the door but then turns back for a second, an impish gleam in his eye. "Oh, before I go, can you recommend anywhere I might be able to rent a place close to the city? I've had to move out of the apartment I'd been staying in."

I take in a quick breath as Dad's eyes light up. A couple of weeks ago he got it into his head to renovate the spare bedroom in our house so that he could take on a lodger and make a little extra money. I haven't been too keen on the idea, since I don't really want to share my living space with a stranger, but once Dad settled on the idea, there was no deterring him.

I certainly don't want to share my living space with Jay Fields. Not because of his supposed history mapped out by Una Harris, but because I wouldn't be able to relax around him. He has this magnetic energy that makes me feel anxious and excited all at once.

"It's funny you should ask," says Dad. "I've been planning on renting out our spare room — if you're interested, of course. It's got an en-suite, newly refurbished."

I squeeze my fists tight and walk back out to the reception area, taking a seat at my desk and slugging back a gulp of my coffee. I don't like how rapidly my heart beats at the thought of Jay moving into that room, so I leave before I hear his answer. Please, please, please let him say no.

My Dad's raucous laughter streams out from the office; Jay's obviously in there charming the pants off him. I silently curse my father for being such an easily charmed hussy.

No more than a minute later, both Dad and Jay leave his office. I can see Jay looking at me out of the corner of my eye, but I continue typing into the computer in front of me, feeling like if I look directly at him, he'll somehow be able to tell how attractive I find him.

"Matilda, could you do me a huge favour and bring Jay out to the house on your lunch break to see the room? I'd do it myself, only I have a meeting to go to."

Oh, Dad. You have no idea how you're torturing me right now. It takes me several beats to answer. When I finally do, my voice is quiet. "Yeah, okay."

What I really want to say is *hell, no*, but that would make me look like a bitch. And I'm not a bitch. Well, outside my own inner dialogue, I'm not.

"Great," says Dad before turning to the waiting neck-brace woman. "Ah, Mrs Kelly. You can come on in now."

Mrs Kelly follows Dad into his office, leaving me alone with Jay.

"What time do you have lunch?" he asks in a low voice, stepping closer to my desk.

"One o'clock. We'll have to get a taxi, because I need to be back here by two."

"That's okay. I can drive us," says Jay, and I bite my lip, looking up at him now. Wow, his eyes are kind of mesmerising, not quite brown, not quite green. We stare at one another for a long moment, and there's a faint smile on his perfectly sculpted lips.

"All right. See you at one," I tell him breezily, and then my eyes return to the screen in front of me as he leaves. On the outside I'm all business. On the inside I'm a nervous wreck. How in the hell am I going to act like a normal human being while spending at least an hour in his company? He really doesn't know what he's in for.

Meet the Author

Greetings! 'Tis a pleasure to make your acquaintance. My name is L.H. Cosway and I wrote the book you just read. I hail from Dublin, Ireland, where I live with my husband and two tiny dictators of the canine variety. My favourite things in life include daydreaming about fictional characters, eating in fancy restaurants, looking at dresses online that I'll never buy, having entire conversations with my dogs, listening to podcasts and of course, reading books. I happen to believe that imperfect people are the most interesting kind. They tell the best stories.

Here is my website where you can find various and sundry information about me and my books: **www.lhcoswayauthor.com**

Want to chat about my stories with like-minded readers or pick my brain? You can join my reader group by searching for The Blue Queens on Facebook.

You can also keep up with all my latest book news and goings on by subscribing to my newsletter: **www.lhcoswayauthor.com/newsletter/**

Books by L.H. Cosway

Contemporary Romance
Painted Faces
Killer Queen
The Nature of Cruelty
Still Life with Strings
Showmance
Fauxmance
Happy-Go-Lucky
Beyond the Sea

The Cracks Duet
A Crack in Everything (#1)
How the Light Gets In (#2)

The Hearts Series
Six of Hearts (#1)
Hearts of Fire (#2)
King of Hearts (#3)
Hearts of Blue (#4)
Thief of Hearts (#5)
Cross My Heart (5.75)
Hearts on Air (#6)

The Running on Air Series
Air Kiss (#0.5)
Off the Air (#1)
Something in the Air (#2)

The Rugby Series with Penny Reid

The Hooker & the Hermit (#1)
The Player & the Pixie (#2)
The Cad & the Co-ed (#3)
The Varlet & the Voyeur (#4)

The Blood Magic Series
Nightfall (#1)
Moonglow (#2)
Witching Hour (#3)
Sunlight (#4)